THE PERFECT MOTHER

THE PERFECT MOTHER

Sherry Ashworth

MICHAEL JOSEPH
London

MICHAEL JOSEPH LTD
Published by the Penguin Group
Penguin Books Ltd, 27 Wrights Lane, London w8 5tz, England
Penguin Books USA Inc., 375 Hudson Street, New York, New York 10014, USA
Penguin Books Australia Ltd, Ringwood, Victoria, Australia
Penguin Books Canada Ltd, 10 Alcorn Avenue, Toronto, Ontario, Canada m4v 3b2
Penguin Books (NZ) Ltd, 182–190 Wairau Road, Auckland 10, New Zealand

Penguin Books Ltd, Registered Offices: Harmondsworth, Middlesex, England

First published 1994
1 3 5 7 9 10 8 6 4 2

Typeset by Datix International Limited, Bungay, Suffolk
Filmset in Monophoto Plantin
Printed in England by Clays Ltd, St Ives plc

FOR ROBYN AND RACHEL

Remember, you don't have
to be perfect either!

In the Beginning . . .

His weight, and his familiar, excited, shallow breathing. No more tingling from fingers probing secret places. Just the pressure of his body, and then the breaking through, and bouncing and thrusting. Nice to feel full. Hope he likes it. Easier to breathe as he rises and falls. He groans with pleasure; she does too. Not long now, she knows. Oh! he says. And he tightens, and then softens imperceptibly, and she relaxes, and he lies still, on top of her, his hot breath on her shoulder.

'Wow!' she says, although she's not sure what she means by that. 'A cigarette?' she offers, keen for an excuse to shift from under him and clean herself, her mother's fastidiousness being part of her. His Silk Cut are lying by her *Early Middle English Verse and Prose*. She passes them to him, extracting a cigarette for herself, and joins him on her bed, amid rumpled sheets, and leans against him, aware of the fine hair on his legs next to her. Jasmin inhaled greedily. She loved the combination of nicotine hitting the stomach and the dark thrill of having made love.

He spoke of his tutorial that morning and an essay he was considering writing – words that washed post-coitally over her. She glanced slyly at his prick: a sullen red, shrivelled now. She wanted to laugh. She was glad of the privacy of her own body and the secrecy of its reactions. She had directed her anglepoise lamp away from the bed and it illuminated a random corner of her room – an electric socket, his discarded jeans, an empty mug of coffee. Next to it, her wardrobe, with its poster of the Oxford Playhouse

I

production of *Measure for Measure*. Her desk, with its untidy piles of books, pads, coffee mugs and cosmetics, lay in shadow.

She preferred to be here with Tom; better to be with him than to be alone. She encouraged the surge of affection she felt for him; she liked the way his blond curls contrasted with his firm jaw line – that was attractive. She watched him stub out his cigarette and yawn. He kissed her gently on the mouth and pulled the sheet over him. Tom shrouded himself in white sheet. Jasmin cursed herself for feeling so wideawake. But she wouldn't wake Tom; he had finals in a few weeks and needed his sleep. She was only completing her second year at Oxford; she had no pressure.

Jasmin thought she might read; there was just enough light from the anglepoise lamp. Underneath her bed, she knew, was her Chaucer. She had promised her tutor to get through 'The Parson's Tale'. A medieval sermon, she had told her, centred on the Seven Deadly Sins; you decide if it's parodic. She had left off reading several days ago at *Luxuria* – Lechery. She reached down for the book and it fell open easily, as she had placed some sort of bookmark between the pages. What could it be? Her pills, of course. She looked at the flat packet surrounded by a margin of Chaucer's words.

Four days ago. She had last read her Chaucer four days ago. Sunday. Today was Thursday. There were her pills. Calmly, as if in slow motion, she turned over the packet and counted the pills. Four too many. It was true. She had not taken a pill since Sunday. Her heart pounded against her ribs. Tom snuffled in his sleep. Does it make a difference, not taking four pills? Or would her body not notice? She held the packet in her hands, wondering, should she take one now? But what if she was pregnant, she thought, with a dispassionate logic. Would a contraceptive pill harm the baby? She would wait, she thought, until the end of the month, and then see. Wait and see. It was impossible, really. She had never been pregnant before. Things like that didn't happen to her. Four days? It couldn't make a difference. She slipped her pills back between the pages of 'The Parson's Tale', and turned over, and composed herself for sleep.

CHAPTER ONE

The Prime Minister shook her hand warmly.

'I see it all now,' he said. 'Oh yes.' He adjusted his glasses. 'We will start up crèches in every district, run by men who will be trained properly in child care, thus enabling women to be free to go back to work and stimulate the economy. And I do see I've been misled in running down local libraries, and will immediately order an influx of money, staff and books.' He opened the door of 10 Downing Street. 'Susan Turner,' he said, 'I would like you to become my adviser on all matters relating to women's and cultural affairs.'

She nodded her head soberly, in acceptance. He shook her hand warmly again. She turned and smiled at the hordes of reporters and cameramen, and walked into their midst, brushing against bodies, and then she noticed: down in White-hall were hundreds of well-wishers, other mothers like her . . .

Other mothers like her were standing at the school gates and hearing, very faintly, the sound of the school bell. She adjusted her mind to tell her eyes to look for Lizzie and Emma. Children came running across the playground. There were her two: Lizzie with blonde hair awry, skipping, and Emma with her characteristic plod – stump, stump, stump – by her sister's side.

Lizzie took Sue's hand. 'We had to write a poem and mine was read out and I think she might put it on the wall and I played with Kirsty at playtime but then Hazel said she wanted her to be in her game and I said I didn't want to be in that –'

'Listen to me! It's important! You've got to remember to give me a bag of soil and two yoghurt pots with holes in and you haven't asked me what I got for my spellings!'

'Shut up, Emma! I was talking to Mummy first. Anyway, Mummy, there's going to be a book fair and I want some money because –'

'Now I've forgotten what I was going to say!'

One girl pulling at each arm, like two heavy shopping bags. Hands confident and assertive in hers, tugging. Lizzie let go and skipped ahead to the car. Emma, whose coat was buttoned unevenly, stayed with her mother, beginning her usual catechism: what's for dinner? And when am I having it? And will there be chips with the dinner?

Sue wondered if there was time for a quick return to Downing Street, or perhaps she could fit in Jeremy Paxman. But there was her blue Vauxhall Nova parked on the double yellow lines. She shooed the children into the back and squashed herself into the driving seat.

Sue was a tall woman, and still she was faintly embarrassed by her size. She had learned to adopt an apologetic air. Or rather, she had a permanently surprised look, as if she was taken aback to find herself so tall. Her dishevelled hair did not know if it was short or long; the mascara she had hastily applied that morning had now smudged below her eyes; despite faint lines on her face, there was a pleasing attractiveness; it was a face one's eyes could rest on. Sue glanced at herself in the driving mirror and grimaced. My God, she thought, it's one of the living dead.

She edged the car into the flow of traffic leaving the school. None of the other mothers would let her out. She revved her engine with increasing impatience. Then, miraculously, a gap appeared. She was out, and accelerating quickly, past the rows of semi-detached houses, and she was soon on the perimeter of the estate.

6

'Do you think, John Smith, that it's just a coincidence that you and the Prime Minister are both called John?'

'Hardly, Sue. I don't see what that's got to do with –'

'And that you both wear glasses?'

'These questions are quite –'

'Is it not the case that both of you belong to one and the same party, consisting of faceless, colourless male bureaucrats, that you are, in fact, the Stepford Politicians? And I have one more question . . .'

'Mummy, what's a condor?'

Sue swerved to avoid a parked van. 'A condor? It's a big bird, I think.'

'Do you get female condors?' Lizzie continued.

'Of course. Otherwise there wouldn't be any baby condors.'

'I don't get it,' she said. 'Michael said you have condors to stop you having babies.'

Sue bit her lip. How much should she say? Lizzie, at ten, had every right to ask about condoms; Emma, however, was only eight and her innocence needed to be preserved a little longer. Besides which, she was basically untrustworthy. Any information imparted to her would be all over the playground.

Emma piped up. 'You don't mean condors, Lizzie. You mean condoms. Boys put them on their willies. It stops them getting HMV positive.'

The car came to rest in the drive at the end of the cul-de-sac. Sue took the key out of the ignition. Since her hours had been reduced at the library, she had been able to collect the children from school on Tuesdays and Wednesdays, and she knew this was an opportunity for her to spend quality time with them. She had learned that either you're there all the time with your children, in which case it's OK

7

to be bad-tempered and read the paper, or you go out to work but spend quality time. And then there was Cheryl, who gave up her job for Jenny, so that all their time could be quality time.

But as for me, thought Sue, I can't even manage the quality time. It was her guilty secret – one of her guilty secrets. She pushed down the front seat and watched her two daughters climb out of the car with a leisurely indifference. What was quality time anyway? She knew what it wasn't – letting them watch too much television while you sat in the dining room with your feet on the radiator, daydreaming. It wasn't being constitutionally incapable of settling quarrels. It wasn't giving in to demands for a second packet of crisps.

'Out of the way!' she ordered, and the girls moved from the front door and Sue opened it. There was a letter on the mat. Lizzie eagerly scooped it up.

'Can I open it?'

'No, me! You open all the letters!'

'I've got it!' Lizzie smirked triumphantly.

Sue took it from her daughter. Sue Turner, the envelope read. Sue did not recognize the handwriting. Sue Turner, 8 Heaton Close, Boltham. Interesting. The girls, meanwhile, had dropped their coats on the floor and had dashed into the lounge, slamming the door behind them. Between them and the television set, Sue knew, was an intense romantic attachment. Neither the set nor the girls could live without the other.

A moment of delightful anticipation as she held the envelope. This really was a complete mystery. She slotted her finger into a corner and tore it open. There was a handwritten letter and a form.

'Dear Sue,' it opened. 'We are having a reunion of the Wednesfield High girls who left in 1973.' Sue glanced at the bottom of the letter. It was from Michelle! Her eyes scanned the contents. In Leeds, it read; date to be fixed; exact location to be fixed; please fill in enclosed form . . . part of a newsletter to be circulated before the reunion . . . chance for those who cannot attend to catch up on the last twenty years.

Twenty years! Michelle Fielding, marvelled Sue. She can't be married, she thought. But clearly Michelle knew that Sue was, or else the letter would have been addressed to Sue Finch. Children's TV chortled in the background. Michelle Fielding. Would you fancy that!

Still holding the letter, Sue made her way to the dining room – a small, square dining room that looked over the turning circle of the cul-de-sac in which she lived. In it were an old G-plan teak table and four chairs. The dining room was another guilty secret. For a start, they rarely ate in it: at meal-times Mark and the kids kept the television company, and she preferred to read the paper. And so the dining room had become Sue's room, her space. She entered the dining room when she wanted to think. As she did now.

Wednesfield High. Those awful bottle-green skirts. The transistor radio in the common room. Sally. And Jane and Felicity. My God. She looked down Heaton Close with unseeing eyes. Ruth. Bev and Ros and Maggie. A reunion!

Well, I'm not going, she decided. It's bound to be in the summer holidays, and to get to Leeds I'd need the car, which grounds Mark and the kids, and the train's impossible, and means committing myself far in advance, which is always a mistake. No. Out of the question.

Sue felt safe again. She picked up the letter and looked at the form that went with it. Name? Married? Children? Employment? News? Publications? Publications! Here was space to write about the last twenty years.

Sue put the letter and form on the table. The last twenty

years. What did she have to write? She was married (Michelle was not). She had two girls. She was an assistant librarian. She had put on weight.

Well, that was it, really. The girls would laugh if they knew she was a librarian. At school she was impulsive and scatterbrained and always doing essential homework just before lessons. She was impossible to shut up. She chatted in the back row and joined in all the discussions. She was the one the class elected to ask the new biology teacher what an orgasm was. She was Eliza in the school's *Pygmalion*, and Higgins was half her size. She ran the debating society in the sixth form.

'Your problem,' Miss Burns had told her, 'is that you can't get it down on paper. Orally you are impressive, and I'm sure you'll interview well.' Sue got her place at Lancaster. 'But your essays are muddled and often don't make sense. I'm not absolutely sure you're cut out for the academic life.'

'What can I do?' Sue asked.

'You could always try librarianship.'

Sue had decided there and then that librarianship was the last thing she would do. Nothing more dry and dull and boring, and you wouldn't meet any interesting men. When she left university she took a librarian's diploma.

Lizzie and Emma! *I have two little girls*, she said proudly to Michelle. *Aged ten and eight*. All her class would be so surprised that she had children. She was the least motherly of all of them. Wouldn't even babysit. *It's amazing*, she said to Michelle. *I have two children – real children. They just came.* Sue knew dimly that her children were special, and weren't quite like anybody else's children, but everyone else did have children, and she imagined most of her old class might be mothers now.

And I'm married, she said proudly to Michelle. *You won't know Mark. I met him at Lancaster. I've been married for thirteen years.* Michelle would laugh. Sue was the one who brought the copies of *Spare Rib* into the common room, and declared she would have a string of lovers and never, ever marry. But she had Mark. The Sphinx. The Creature from the Black Lagoon. He Who Must Not Be Disturbed. She thought of him with resentment, affection and despair.

But just in case all husbands weren't like Mark, she wouldn't go to the reunion. She preferred to think that all husbands deteriorated like hers had; like the cauliflower that skulked at the back of her vegetable tray in the fridge whose florets had browned and softened.

A dead-end job, she thought, looking out over the cul-de-sac. A half-dead husband. But, she reminded herself, there are the children. She glowed as she called to mind Lizzie's undoubted beauty and Emma's quirky intelligence. She was all the more proud of her children because they had achieved a reasonable standard of social behaviour and academic achievement despite her. Despite her bouts of vicious temper and retreats into the dining room and long telephone calls to her friends, and her inability to control their television watching or eating patterns, or solve their bitter quarrels.

Just in case all the other girls at the reunion did bring up their children properly, she'd better not go. Did they all dream like her? Did they all have long imaginary conversations? Did they also ask themselves, is this all there is?

Probably not, thought Sue. Most of them were cleverer than me anyway. I was only ever good at talking.

She saw a car approach the end of the cul-de-sac – a red Fiesta. It was Arthur's car. It pulled into the drive next to hers. She saw Mark's shape in the passenger seat and, shy of being seen observing them, she left the dining room and made her way to the kitchen, to greet Mark when he came in. She would show Michelle, she thought. She might not have done anything with her life, but she'd be damned if she couldn't be the perfect wife and mother! Tonight she would show them all. It wasn't too late to change. She'd start by making her family sit up and notice her. Sue loved nothing more than a challenge.

Perfect wives and mothers cook, Sue decided. Her plans for fish fingers and microwave chips and frozen peas were laid aside. What, what could she do? Of course, the ideal mother, rather like the *Blue Peter* presenters, would have a meal they had prepared earlier. She rifled through her cookery books. Most of the recipes had exotic ingredients: artichoke hearts, fennel seeds, rocket. Anton Mosimann grinned at her with a schoolboy's charm. Sue picked up a wholefood cookery book. She would prepare a devastatingly healthy meal for her family. The children would clear their plates and, pink with health, go and play a constructive game like Junior Scrabble.

Wheaty Beefburgers. She scanned the ingredients. She had them. *Wholemeal breadcrumbs add fibre and give a lovely texture to minced beef in these easily made burgers, which will please all the family.* This was perfect. There were some burger buns in the freezer, and she could prepare carrots (vitamin A) and a few new potatoes. A perfect family meal. They would eat in the dining room and talk about their day. I *can* do it if I try, Sue thought.

She took the frozen mince from the freezer, a milky film of frost on its cellophane wrapping, and opened the microwave. As she pressed 'defrost', Mark came in. There was the alien presence of man in her kitchen: Working Man – in suit, with briefcase – that outdoors, impersonal, sweaty smell of Working Man. Working Man sighed, sighed audibly. This was, of course, the first move in 'Who's Had the Worse Day?', one of their favourite games. But tonight Sue was not going to be drawn into it. Tonight she was perfect. It was as if she was aware of someone watching her. Michelle? Sally? Bev?

'Had a hard day, dear?' Sue turned and kissed Mark lightly on the cheek. His flesh was cold and his cheek somewhat stubbly. Mark was tall, like her. His hairline had receded, although he had not begun to go grey; his hair retained its dark colour. His was a full, fleshy face now; his brown eyes were no longer dreamy but distant.

'Getting changed,' he murmured, and vanished into the hall and ran upstairs. Sue stopped herself thinking that he did not bother to say hello to the girls, that he needed a shower; tonight she was going to stifle all criticism. If she could behave herself for one night, she might be able to do it for two. And so on.

The microwave pinged. She turned to it and examined the meat. Some had cooked at the edges, but that shouldn't matter. She laid it aside as she took several slices of bread from the bread bin and decided how to make the bread-crumbs. She turned to her food processor, inserted the bread and pressed the 'on' button. No response. Then she remembered. Mark had removed the plug some weeks ago for his printer. She retrieved the bread and picked at it with her fingers, making crumbs.

'*So will you give a hand for Sue Turner! Sue, hello! Since your recent award as Boltham's best mother, I know your phone hasn't stopped ringing. So we're more than delighted to have you on the show tonight. "Her success in combining job, family and house left us astounded," say the judges, Dr Miriam Stoppard, Penelope Leach and Sheila Kitzinger. "She's one in a million," says your husband, Mark. "When we grow up, we want to be like Mummy," say your two daughters, Lizzie, aged ten, and Emma, eight. "She makes us lovely dinners and cuddles us when we're miserable, and helps us with our work and never shouts." So tell us, Sue – and you don't look a day over thirty – tell us, what's your secret?"*

"Well, Michael, I . . ."

Sue felt her eyes dim with tears. The breadcrumbs were rather large, but never mind. *Soak the breadcrumbs in the stock and soy sauce for fifteen minutes.* She took a chicken Oxo cube and crumbled it into her measuring jug. For one glorious moment she felt just like Katie Boyle. She poured in hot water from the kettle, added the aromatic soy sauce and put in soft handfuls of breadcrumbs. She regarded the lovely gooey mixture with pleasure.

'Mummy, I'm starving!' That was Lizzie. She stood at the kitchen door with a pained expression.

'Me too!' said Emma. 'Can I have a biscuit?'

'No, darling. I'd prefer it if you didn't. I'm making something rather special for dinner tonight.'

'What?' they piped in unison.

'Burgers,' she said. The two girls looked at each other and then slowly nodded their approval.

'I'm still hungry now, though,' Emma said warningly.

'We'll be eating in about ten minutes!'

'Ten minutes is a long time,' whinged Lizzie.

'You can help me if you like!' Sue invited brightly.

The girls vanished. She returned to the recipe. She shaped the burgers as suggested. *Lay them on a board or flat plate and refrigerate them for thirty minutes to allow them to hold their shape.* Thirty minutes! The girls couldn't possibly wait thirty minutes. But then, if she was to lay the table and prepare the potatoes and carrots too . . .

She scrubbed potatoes, sliced carrots, bent down for saucepans, wondered where a tablecloth was.

'Mummy! I'm *so* hungry!' Emma stood in the centre of the kitchen. 'I can't *wait*! Please can I have a biscuit.'

'You won't eat your dinner,' Sue reminded her gently.

14

'Yes, I will. Oh, please!'

'Just one Digestive!'

'I'll take two 'cause Lizzie will want one.' Exit Emma, with two Digestives. Sue prepared the grill. Perhaps, she thought, they could open a bottle of wine and, while the girls finished their meal, she and Mark could talk and drink Beaujolais. A lovely, leisurely family meal. She always found Mark more attractive after half a bottle of wine.

'Mummy!' said Lizzie, furious. 'Emma has eaten two Digestives and I haven't had *any*!'

There it all was. Four plates lined up in the kitchen, two burgers on each, some new potatoes and sliced carrots. Sue realized she had forgotten the buns, but then, there were breadcrumbs in the burgers. Four healthy meals. She had already set the table: drinks for the girls and for her and Mark, a bottle of wine with the cork already removed. Knives, forks, all in pristine order.

'Dinner's ready!' she cried from the hall, so both the girls and Mark could hear her. She felt triumphant.

Lizzie and Emma appeared, the television still chattering from the lounge.

'Can we have it in the lounge?' Lizzie wheedled.

'No. I've got a nice surprise tonight. Look!' Sue gestured into the dining room. Lizzie looked baffled.

'Why do we have to eat in *there*?' cried Emma.

'Because you're supposed to. Mark!' she shouted, somewhat louder. 'Dinner!' No response.

The girls slouched into the dining room. They had not turned off the television.

'Mark!' Sue screamed. 'DINNER!'

'I HEARD YOU THE FIRST TIME!' came a male voice. 'I don't see why everybody has to shout in this house,' he muttered, as he came down the stairs.

'Mummy's done a strange thing,' Lizzie informed him, coming out of the dining room again. 'We've got to eat in here.'

'Can I start?' asked Emma.

'Wait for Daddy!' Sue cautioned her.

Mark peered in the dining room and then vanished into the downstairs loo. Sue and the girls took their places. They listened as the toilet was flushed and Sue bit her lip at these assaults on her patience. Mark eventually sat down and raised his eyebrows at the food.

'Mummy?' questioned Emma. 'These aren't burgers.'

'Yes, they are.'

'Not like in McDonald's,' she persisted.

Sue took her knife and fork and cut into her burger. She could certainly taste the sage and thyme. Emma pushed her food around with her fork, looking at it distrustfully, as if it was capable of doing her some unspecified harm. She speared a carrot and eyed it suspiciously. She nibbled some.

'Euch! Mummy, these carrots have a funny taste!'

'No, they haven't!' Sue insisted. Admittedly, she had kept them in the fridge for over a week, but they were only carrots.

Mark ate silently. Lizzie was cutting her potatoes into very small squares.

'Had a nice day?' Sue inquired of her husband. 'Look, you've had no wine. Can I pour you some?'

Mark shook his head. 'No, I'm working tonight. I've got to look at a few projects, and there's a heads of department meeting tomorrow. Might have some later.'

Sue looked at him, eating stolidly, his mind God only knew where. I will not resent him, she said to herself. I will not resent him. Emma had moved all her potatoes and carrots to the perimeter of the plate, where they were in

16

extreme danger of falling off. Her burger sat isolated, as if waiting for an operation. Sue watched as she cut into it. Emma licked the morsel of burger on the fork, and grimaced.

'Euch!' she said. 'It's horrible!'

'I like it,' said Sue. But she tensed, nevertheless.

'I'm not having mine,' Lizzie said loftily, 'because I'm going to be a vegetarian!'

'You can't, Lizzie,' Emma declared, 'because you don't eat venchtables. She doesn't eat venchtables, Mummy!'

'You don't have to eat vegetables if you're a vegetarian,' Lizzie explained.

'Can't you begin tomorrow?' asked Sue. She was fighting a growing sense of disappointment. This wasn't how it was meant to be.

'No. I feel sorry for all the dead animals. I wouldn't want to be killed for somebody's dinner. Emma!' Lizzie said, in sepulchral tones, 'you are eating a dead animal!'

'No, I'm not.'

'I saw you eat a bit!'

'I didn't!'

'You did!'

'You're a snotbrain, Lizzie!'

Lizzie's face froze. Sue watched her squeeze the muscles in her eyes, watched her face crease, steeled herself for the scream to come.

'She called me a snotbrain! I can't eat my dinner!' Lizzie ran from the dining room. Mark raised his eyebrows and carried on eating, as if nothing untoward had happened. The children were not his department. Sue put down her knife and fork and watched him. Once he had finished, he looked round the table.

'Bit of a waste,' he said. 'All that food.'

'You're a snotbrain, Mark!' Sue said, and stormed out of the dining room.

Right, she thought, if Lizzie can throw a tantrum, so can I. She pushed her way past Lizzie, who was playing happily in the hall with some trolls, and thudded up the stairs. Lizzie stopped to watch. The same thoughts beat out a pattern in Sue's mind. All that food. All that effort. What's the bloody point?

She sought refuge in her bedroom, slamming the door behind her, and threw herself on the bed. She despised herself for her childishness but experienced too some unexpected relief. At least she wouldn't have to try to be the perfect mother, not if her best attempts were met with indifference. She would apologize for her tantrum later, but not now.

She heard a tapping at the door.

'Mummy?' That was Lizzie.

'Sue?' came Mark's voice. 'Are you all right?'

'I'm fine,' she said, deliberately sounding as angry as she could.

She heard Mark's voice. 'The best thing to do if Mummy's upset is to leave her alone. That's what I always do.' She heard footsteps returning down the stairs. Well, she thought, at least I've earned myself some space.

Opposite her bed was a desk on which sat Mark's computer, inanimate now. Next to it, an untidy pile of textbooks, boxes of disks, two empty mugs that once contained coffee, a Filofax, a sheaf of papers and, by the desk, boxes and boxes of more paper. Mark's suit was hanging on the back of the chair. Mark's shirts were lying on most available surfaces, on the backs of chairs, over open doors of wardrobes. His shoes were in various places.

It wasn't the mess that got her down; it was more than that. He was playing Space Invaders, and he was winning. It was his room; she happened to sleep there. She wasn't sure whether it was intentional or not. Or whether she was wrong to resent him. She lay now in the middle of the bed, her arms folded behind her head, looking at the alien world of Mark's desk.

Michelle wasn't married and she envied her. But the reunion was a silly idea. The past was best left unexamined. An unpleasant truth dawned on Sue: life got worse. Life was full of promise when you were young, and it all reached a sort of peak around twenty-five, and then it got worse. If you didn't marry, you were lonely. Then the kids came. Then your life is over.

She turned on to her tummy and cupped her chin in her hands. Again she despised herself – for her temper, for her despair. How dare she be so negative when she had the things that every woman wanted – a husband who was generally kind to her, healthy kids, a house, a job. Perhaps she just needed a rest. She turned over on to her side now, so that she was facing the wall. She would rest.

'*Good evening, and welcome to tonight's edition of* Changes. *Tonight we examine the dilemma of the woman in her late thirties who feels that something is missing from her life. So we have as our guest this evening Sue Turner, thirty-eight, married to a lecturer in Information Technology, with two daughters of ten and eight, and who is an assistant librarian in a small northern town. Sue has agreed to come along tonight to be helped by our panel, who will tell her what changes to make in her life.*

'*And let me introduce you to our panel. On our left is Sue Turner, feminist historian and writer of* Malecrime. *Next to her is the editor of* Metropolitan *magazine, the glamorous Sue Turner. Finally, on our right, Businesswoman of the Year and Managing Director of Femtec Enterprises, Sue Turner. Each of you has heard our volunteer's dilemma. She's done every-thing expected of her: she studied, she married, she had children, she has a steady job. She ought to feel fulfilled, but something's missing, she tells me. She feels this can't be all there is. So the question tonight is, what ought Sue to do?*'

19

'She's a victim,' said Sue Turner, feminist historian. 'A victim of men-as-a-caste, who have reduced her social function to that of support system for the rearing of young, but deprived her of the means to rear young effectively – that is, money – and so have ensured her dependency. Sue must leave her family. She must walk out. She must learn to define herself as an autonomous human being, free from societally imposed roles.'

'What do you think of that, Sue? She's shaking her head. I don't think she's impressed with your suggestions! Over to you, Sue Turner, editor of Metropolitan.'

'Hello, Sue! There's so much you can do to improve your life. Try a high-vitality diet! Have a pedicure! Pamper yourself. Use a night cream that penetrates deeply. Lose some weight. Colour your hair. Find your G-spot. Take a holiday. Shave around your bikini line. Try one of our delicious gâteaux! Get rid of cellulite. Buy a vibrator. Step off the fast track. Be assertive. Get a classic chambray shirt with free leggings for only £18.95!'

'I can see that Sue Turner doesn't think much of that. She's put her hands over her ears – enough's enough. Let's hope our final panellist has some worthwhile advice.'

'So many women, Sue, never achieve half of their potential in life because they allow things to happen to them, rather than taking charge of their own life. Life isn't something that happens to you; you must organize and control your life, just like a business. Organize your time; make lists; get targets; make them "SMART" – specific, measurable, appropriate, realistic, with a time constraint; make a rota for your family so they run their own departments within the family unit; create systems for regular jobs. I built up an international business from my living room.'

'Well, Sue, you've heard our panelists. What's your verdict? What changes are you going to make to your life? The clock's ticking. You have sixty seconds to decide. Are you *going to leave your family, buy that night cream or construct that database? Starting from now!'*

Well, I actually don't want to leave the family, thought Sue. Although I think men have a lot to answer for. And I'd love to be more glamorous, but I'm not sure that's what I want. I know I'm not business-like enough, but I don't want to be.

Sue smiled to herself. Thinking it through like this did cheer her up. But she must be realistic. When you have kids, when you have a family, you can only make small changes. But she would change. Surely there were things she could do.

For example, she didn't have to stay in Boltham Central Library. Her job gave her nothing any more. She had been there ever since Emma started at playgroup. What, she wondered, what if she were to look for another job? It might not be easy right now, with the libraries starved of resources, but why not try? One day she might even be a chief librarian!

Sue sat up and hugged her knees, thinking. Yes! This was better than having tantrums. She would get herself another job! That would provide her with challenge, stimulation, variety. Of course, it would have to be in a library. That was all she knew – librarianship – all she could do. Another library was a good idea. Perhaps she could run one of the branches. Adrenalin flowed through her. She would tell Mark and the girls. She would pop in to Cheryl and tell her too.

A new library would give her just the stimulation she needed! Sue smiled at the thought and opened the bedroom door.

CHAPTER TWO

The springs gave on the armchair as Jasmin sank into it. She placed her arms defensively around her tummy and felt its thickness. Clunk. That was Dr Cooper's grandfather clock. Clunk. Clunk. In the distance were muffled sounds of tea-making, an essential prerequisite for a tutorial. Clunk. Clunk.

When Jasmin had first come to Dr Cooper's house for tuition, she had been instantly disappointed. She had walked down the Banbury Road, taken a left turn as instructed, and had knocked on the dark-red door of a perfectly ordinary semi. Dr Cooper – she had contributed more articles to *Modern Philology* than any other lecturer, the author of *Chaucer's Women: A Reconsideration* and *Divine Intimations: Langland and the Malvern Hills* – Dr Grainne Florence Cooper lived in a perfectly ordinary semi-detached house in north Oxford, with an ordinary hallway with nothing more intellectual than a hatstand; held her tutorials in a lounge with an elderly matching three-piece suite with flowery fitted covers; made tea on a tray with the skyline of Florence depicted thereon and ate Bourbon biscuits.

Jasmin watched the fake coal on the gas fire glow orange and observed Cressida, Dr Cooper's cat, slumped in sleep below it. Jasmin was aware too that she had brought no essay, no books. She had come to speak to Dr Cooper in her capacity as moral tutor, as the tutor responsible for her social welfare. She did not know how Dr Cooper would respond to her news, but in a way it didn't matter, as it was too late. Besides, all the last months had had a dream-like quality: Jasmin had been an actress in her own story; someone or something else had been pulling the strings.

Her period had been two weeks late before she had thought it necessary to carry out a pregnancy test. She had hidden the kit in her hand luggage, and sat in the Ladies at Heathrow, holding a little paddle under her stream of urine, and then she had waited in the cubicle, watching the white turn blue, listening to a nervous traveller throwing up in the toilet next to her. As she had sat, strapped in at her window seat and felt that familiar terrified excitement of take-off, she had held her breath and thought, I'm pregnant, I'm actually pregnant. Her breasts tingled; the nose of the plane pointed upwards. She remembered clinging to the arm of the seat.

Her mother had claimed her at the airport and driven her back to the ostentatious apartment that Jasmin had never fully recognized as home. Joyce had complained about the heat, and Jasmin had thought, I'm pregnant.

Her mother had put her sickness down to the change of diet and the hot, humid Turkish weather. They had sat, one evening, while her father was still at the Embassy, on the veranda, looking out over the Bosporus, sipping gins and tonic, and Jasmin had hugged the knowledge of her pregnancy to herself. She had watched her mother's brow furrow, and her fingers stroke her glass repeatedly. No, I can't tell her. Besides, she thought, I may miscarry, and then, rising up in her, there was that alien, metallic, bitter taste and she breathed deeply and tried not to grimace. She had gone to the Grand Bazaar and bought several large T-shirts reading 'Hard Rock Café – Istanbul'. These hid her thickening waistline.

When she had left the Ataturk airport, embracing both her parents and promising to write soon, they had suspected nothing. That was her plan.

23

The jingling of teaspoons and clatter of crockery brought Jasmin back to her present surroundings. Dr Cooper edged in with the tray and Jasmin sat up, agreed to the milk, shook her head at the sugar, and then held in her hand a flowered teacup with a scalloped saucer.

The cat shifted in her sleep and raised her head to glance blearily at her owner before collapsing again.

Dr Cooper was a barrel of a woman, dressed in a grey pleated skirt and an Arran sweater. Her hair had been severely cropped and, as a result, her eyes seemed to protrude and her lips seemed full and fleshy.

'Well, Jasmin. Have you enjoyed your vacation?'

'Oh, yes. I was in Turkey with my parents.'

'Good, good.' Dr Cooper was silent. She disliked small talk. She was not all that comfortable as a moral tutor, but accepted that the system had to exist. She simply hoped that her students would be sufficiently amoral not to need her. Jasmin Carpenter was a good student: essays revealed insight, an eye for detail, a number of pleasing stylistic flourishes; there was a distinct possibility she would make a first. Her work on Pandarus as 'makere' was quite impressive. She had responded to Jasmin's request to see her, trusting that her problem was academic. Perhaps she had changed her mind about her set poets; more likely she wished to discuss the subject of her dissertation. She brought the teacup to her lips and slurped as she drank.

'Dr Cooper,' Jasmin began. 'I have a problem.'

Dr Cooper inclined her head in a scholarly fashion. Jasmin saw the slack skin on her neck wobble and noticed the mole on her chin, and wondered if Dr Cooper had ever made love. Then once again some dim, impersonal force took Jasmin over. She was a puppet; she was acting from a script.

'I'm pregnant.'

24

'Excuse me, Jasmin dear. I thought you said you were pregnant.'

'I am.' Jasmin felt herself blush hotly. The cat rose, stretched and coughed, flattening her body and pointing her head at Jasmin as she did so.

What does one say, thought Grainne Cooper? 'Are you glad?' she asked.

Jasmin had finished her tea. Her fingers were now cupped round her stomach again and she addressed herself to it.

'Well, yes and no. I mean, I didn't mean to get pregnant. It was an accident. But now I am – well, I don't mind. That's odd, isn't it?'

Thank God, thought the don, that she isn't crying. She warmed to Jasmin's academic detachment.

'It is somewhat unusual, I think. Why have you reacted in that way?'

'I'm not sure. When I realized I was pregnant, I thought about an abortion, but in the first place I would have had to go to my parents' doctor, and he's a good friend of theirs – they play bridge and have dinner parties. I didn't have enough Turkish to go anywhere else. But then, in a funny way, the abortion scared me more than having the baby – and I would have had to have the abortion immediately, and I suppose having the baby seemed a long way off. Then I thought – it might be nice to have a baby.'

Dr Cooper was listening intently. She had always wanted to visit Istanbul; a close friend of hers had written a monograph on the harem. She wondered if one needed inoculations. Poor Jasmin, she remembered.

'Do your parents know about your pregnancy?'

'I've written a letter this morning. I'll post it tonight – It should get there in about two weeks. The post to Turkey is abysmal.'

Dr Cooper cogitated. Jasmin's parents did not know, but

they were about to know. That put her, she realized, *in loco parentis*, as it were. She shifted uneasily on her chair.

'And the father?'

'My father's been seconded to the British Embassy.'

'No, no. The father of your baby.'

'Oh, Tom. Yes, he knows.'

'And to what extent does he intend to involve himself? Will you marry?'

'Oh, God, no! I don't want to get married. Not at my age. Actually, I'm not sure. I'm meeting him this evening for a drink. He seemed rather shocked. He's just started his new job. He wants to be a management consultant eventually.'

Dr Cooper could not imagine anyone wanting to get married. For that matter, she couldn't imagine anyone wanting to have a baby, but she knew from her study of English literature that these things were ineluctable for a certain sort of woman.

'So you want the baby, and you're undecided as to whether you want a husband,' she summed up. 'I see. There doesn't seem to me to be a particular problem, Jasmin. The days are long since past when the college would have cast you out upon the waters; no moral opprobrium will attach itself to you.'

'Yes, but there's my degree.'

'Yes?' Dr Cooper inquired.

'The baby is due in February. That's the middle of the Hilary term. Then all through Trinity I'll have a little baby to look after, and I should be taking my finals.'

'Could you not arrange a place at the university crèche? I'm sure together we could discover how these things work.' Dr Cooper felt quite proud of herself for offering some help.

'Yes, but I've heard that babies cry a lot and keep you awake at night.'

26

Dr Cooper ran her tongue along the edge of her teeth and thought hard. If it was true, if babies did wake in the night, then Jasmin would be handicapped during this, her most important year. Moreover, she remembered that Jasmin was to move back into college for her third year and her whole staircase might be disrupted.

'Won't your parents have the baby?' she asked, flailing.

'No,' Jasmin said quickly. 'My father has one more year to go in Istanbul. Anyway,' she said, 'it's *my* baby.'

Dr Cooper considered what she knew about babies. Her second cousin in Taunton had had one several years ago: it went to school now and had presumably stopped crying at night. She affectionately recalled curled black and white photographs of herself in a little bonnet in a pram waving a rattle, and decided that babies might be quite nice. But if only Jasmin had waited until next year. Her mind ranged over the Chaucerian canon, its familiar territory. There was a baby in 'The Reeve's Tale' and it needed feeding in the night, thus nudging the whole tale to its climax. In fact, she realized, this was probably the only baby in the whole of Chaucer. How very interesting. She would corroborate this with her concordance later that evening, and mull over the significance. Would the same be true of Langland, and the minor medieval poets? If so, and if –

'Actually, Dr Cooper, what I think I'd like to do is have a year off.'

'Sorry, Jasmin?'

'A year off. I know there might be trouble with my grant and everything, but if that side of it could be arranged . . . Then I could have the baby and settle it, and then my parents would be back from Turkey, so they could help. Then I could do my final year.'

'Oh, oh, I see.' It was an interesting idea. 'So you will have the baby in Turkey?'

'No,' Jasmin said. 'I'll go and live at home. In Boltham.'

'Boltham!' interjected Dr Cooper. 'I never realized you were from the North too. I come from Heckmondwike, you know.' Jasmin did know; Dr Cooper's affinity with the North was legendary. 'I suppose Boltham is a tightly knit community.'

'I've lost touch with lots of the people in Boltham, with Mum and Dad being abroad. But I don't think there really is a sense of community as such; it's quite a big town. We live just north of it.'

'Out in the country?'

'No. Just behind a cul-de-sac actually. Mum couldn't get the council to refuse planning permission. Our house was a Victorian rectory.'

'How interesting, Jasmin. Just like the Brontës!'

'Yes, I often used to imagine I was Charlotte. But can I? Have a year off?'

The feeling of discomfort returned to assault Dr Cooper. 'Will you be alone in your house?'

'No. I rang my old schoolfriend Vicki. She's got two babies. She said I could stay with her.'

'Aah!' Dr Cooper thought hard. It really did seem a very sensible suggestion. Jasmin would be off the college's hands, and staying with someone who actually knew about babies. Then, reasonably uncluttered, she could return and complete her studies. She fingered the mole on her chin. Allowing Jasmin a break to have the baby was sympathetic, progressive. The Principal would be impressed. Jasmin might name the baby after her too. Jasmin would also have so much more time to read.

'Shall I see what I can do?' Dr Cooper offered. 'I think your proposal is very practical. I shall telephone the Principal this morning. A year off – you'll miss this academic year

28

and complete your degree the next year. Yes. I'm sure that would work.'

Jasmin was filled with relief. This was what she wanted. A breathing space. A whole year off with nothing to do except have the baby. First, there had been nursery at three, and a private kindergarten, then the Preparatory Department of Boltham Grammar School, then Boltham Grammar itself, then straight into St Luke's. One exam after another. All that fussing and checking. Now she'd go and stay with Vicki, and, if it didn't work out, there was always her own house. The most recent tenants had left in the summer; it was presently standing empty. She visualized its lich-gate and stern double-fronted exterior. Home.

'I shall miss our tutorials,' Dr Cooper said.

'Me too,' added Jasmin, eager to please her amenable tutor.

'So what are you reading at the moment?'

'I've just started on Penelope Leach.'

Dr Cooper frowned in thought. She had not heard of Penelope Leach. Perhaps one of those modern feminist novelists, or a social realist.

'Penelope Leach's *Baby and Child*. It's quite good.'

'For your dissertation?'

'No. It explains the different stages of pregnancy. My baby's about twenty centimetres long and all its limbs are fully formed and it's even got tiny fingernails and toenails!'

Dr Cooper regarded Jasmin's tummy. How odd to think there was a living being in there.

'How do you feel?' Dr Cooper inquired.

'I feel great now. I was dreadfully sick in Turkey. Sometimes now I feel I'm not really pregnant at all. The doctor said soon I'll be able to feel the baby kick. In a way, I can't believe it – I can't believe that there's another person inside me and I don't know it. I don't even know whether it's a boy or a girl.' Jasmin looked again at her tummy.

Fleetingly Dr Cooper was struck by a sense of the miraculous. This young student, slender, with her boyish short, dark hair, the long pale-blue sweatshirt with holes in the arms, her denimed legs crossed at the ankles; Jasmin, with her eager, bright expression and intelligent hazel eyes, who had written so fascinatingly about Pandarus; she contained within her the one impenetrable mystery. Madonna and child. For all conceptions were immaculate, all incomprehensible. The mechanics of sex, she imagined, were not enough to explain it all. There were three of them in that room; four, if you counted the cat.

Jasmin considered her tutor's reaction. Never again would she laugh at Dr Cooper's idiosyncrasies – the way she spat when she lectured, the fact she never wore a bra. Dr Cooper had been brilliant – non-judgemental, helpful, so wonderfully free from emotion. Jasmin felt sure that years of studying literature gave one this detached wisdom. She saw herself in time to come advising undergraduates like herself, her own daughter, or son, playing at her feet.

'I've got to go now,' she said. 'I have to meet Tom – the father.'

For a moment Dr Cooper was jealous; yes, that pang, that contraction, was jealousy. It was akin to the feeling she had when Cressida sat on a visitor's lap. Jasmin had come to her *in loco parentis*. Jasmin's baby was her first baby; other tutors had counselled pregnant students, but not she. Grainne Florence Cooper wondered if she might teach herself to knit. What did one knit for babies? Matinée jackets? Bootees?

'You must keep in touch, Jasmin. Do see me before you leave. I wouldn't wish you to sever your connection with the college.'

Jasmin insisted she would never do that and rose, aware of a strange fluttering in her stomach. She thought it was

30

wind and clenched the muscles in her bottom, just in case. She took her coat, bade Dr Cooper farewell and walked into the street, shivering slightly; it was an unusually cool September.

Now, she thought, for Tom. Her soul flinched at the forthcoming meeting, the purpose of which, he had decided, was to 'discuss it'. He made it seem like some item on an agenda. The funny thing was, she couldn't even remember properly what he looked like any more. She made herself catalogue his charms: his curly strawberry-blond hair, the cleft in his chin, a pale poetic beauty. In fact when they had first met, Jasmin had thought he was gay. But, she reflected, he was not.

She turned into the Banbury Road and, just as she did so, a bus appeared and, within a few moments, she was on it. She took a window seat and watched familiar buildings move past her, one changing into another. There weren't many students back yet. Oxford had a half-empty feel, paused and waiting.

Tom, of course, was no longer part of it. He had taken his finals this June, only a week or two, Jasmin had worked out, after she had conceived. Then shortly after finals he had gone to the States and bought a Greyhound ticket. That was his family's treat; his reward for three years' hard work. They had agreed that they could see other people during that time, but they would meet again at the end of the summer to see how they felt about each other. Jasmin could not write to him as he was on the move. So she had rung his home in Reigate a week ago and told him then.

The bus had reached St Giles; she rose to disembark. There was the Lamb and Child; that was where they had planned to meet – all familiar territory to Jasmin. Often she had stood in the passageway by the entrance with her friends, watching people they knew go in and out. She was

31

early, but she went straight inside, keen to get a seat. She ordered a Perrier for herself, found a table along the wall and sat there expectantly, like a good, small child.

Tom had been incredulous at first. Are you sure? Are you going to have an abortion? What shall we do? She had heard the panic at the back of his voice. The meeting here in the Lamb and Child was his idea. He had started work in London, as a trainee accountant in a well-known firm. This despite his English degree – Tom had decided that he was going to have fun as a student, but then settle down. There was money in management consultancy. He was sharing a small flat in Battersea with a friend called Alastair. He had told her all this on the phone with some evident pride. She had been on the payphone in the hall of her old rented house, her trunk in the hall, awaiting its new destination.

She was looking forward to seeing him. They had been together for three months and he had treated her well. He was amusing company, especially after a drink or two, and gratifyingly appreciative of her body. They had avoided the word 'love'; one does. It would be nice to see him again. But Jasmin's growing uneasiness had another cause: it was simple, and it was this. She didn't know what she wanted from him. He might propose marriage, and then she could go and live with him in his flat, and transfer her degree to London, and – no, she wouldn't give Oxford up. Or he would continue to see her, to be with her – but then what?

Someone put money in the jukebox and the pub throbbed to techno-pop. Jasmin watched some men at the bar – postgraduates, she assumed; one with John Lennon specs and an emerald-green sweater too short for him, another hirsute and Tennysonian. She absorbed their interested glance and wondered, if they knew she was pregnant, whether they would be repelled, or intrigued. A considerably older man came in and joined them, dressed in an obviously expensive suit – not the usual Lamb and Child clientele. He was with someone – a younger boy, with strawberry-blond hair – Tom!

Jasmin found herself rising in her seat – 'Tom!' – and smiling involuntarily, and Tom noticed her, and the smile that crossed his face was one of pleasure, followed swiftly by embarrassment. He came over to her and kissed her on the cheek; soft lips, Christian Dior aftershave. There was a light blush in his complexion, but then Tom always blushed easily. He sat on a stool opposite her, scraping it on the stone floor. Then the man at the bar arrived too, and took the other stool next to him, and placed two halves of bitter on the table, carefully, square on to the curled beer mats.

'This is my father,' Tom said. 'He drove me here.'

Tom's father looked about the same age as her father. He was a tall, substantial man, well dressed, his white shirt with a pale stripe in it, a sober coloured tie. He wore glasses, quite thick ones, that obscured the expression of his eyes. He exuded authority. He sat upright and then put his hand across the table to shake Jasmin's.

'I've heard a lot about you,' he said.

She glanced at Tom. He looked shifty. Jasmin felt very, very ill at ease, out of her depth. She wished she'd had someone with her too. Dr Cooper perhaps, or her mother. Well, maybe not her mother.

'Funny to be back,' Tom said.

'Tom's started at Mitchell Metcalf,' Tom's father said. 'Two weeks ago.' It was a threat, and Jasmin was aware of it.

'How are you?' asked Tom. He ventured a slight smile. He could not help but look down at her stomach, and Jasmin felt his look. She moved nearer the table to hide her stomach; it was hers.

'I'm fine,' she said. 'Very well.'

'Are you getting lots of rest?' Tom said.

'Not really. I've been packing the stuff from Walton Street. But at least now I know where I'm going. I'm taking a year out. Cooper said it would be all right. I'm going home for a year to have the baby.'

'Where's home?' Tom's father cut in heavily.

'Boltham. Just north of Manchester.'

Tom's father nodded in satisfaction.

Then there was a silence. Jasmin could not think of a thing to say. She was conscious of the almost rude stare of Tom's father and the awkward way he perched on the stool, ungainly and out of place in her favourite pub. She looked at Tom. Do I still fancy him? she thought. No, she decided. There's nothing special about him at all. But still she was tense, as if expecting a blow.

'Yes, Tom's been at Mitchell Metcalf for two weeks. It's an excellent opening. The salary is minimal at the moment, of course, but it's one of the best outfits in the City. They're giving him a mere pittance at present. We're supplementing his income, of course. He's our only son.'

Jasmin knew all that was a warning. She could sense a kind of complicity between father and son, and it made her wary.

'Well, it's a fine business altogether,' Tom's father began. 'Somebody was careless.'

Tom smiled sheepishly at Jasmin, accepting this hectoring.

'Tom tells me you're too far gone to have an abortion. Well, there's no point beating about the bush. Tom won't marry you. He can't. There isn't the money, and his mother and I won't let him. He doesn't know his own mind yet. If in five years' time he still wants to, we'd reconsider. But we've invested too much of our life in Tom to sacrifice it all for a silly mistake.' Tom's father was red-faced and breathing heavily. Jasmin watched him in horror and repulsion. But worst was Tom. He sat there, his head hanging, not daring to look up, as his father slung this dirty water over her.

Jasmin put her arm over her stomach. She couldn't decide what to say.

Panting, Tom's father continued.

'Now, we're not saying that we won't help out. Tom's been well brought up; he'll do the decent thing. But maintenance is out of the question. He can't make the long-term commitment. Besides which, I'm retiring in two years. What we're proposing is a lump-sum payment – something to tide you over the expense of the next few months. Two and a half thousand, we thought.'

From inside his jacket he brought out a stiff white envelope and passed it to Jasmin. She took it.

'There's a cheque in there for you,' he said. 'Tom, you can have a few words with her, but only a few. We have to be getting back to London. I'm flying to Edinburgh in the morning.'

He rose, straightened his suit and left the pub. Tom reached out and took her hand. 'Is that all right?' he said.

'I didn't want to marry you anyway,' Jasmin said.

'I know.'

'I don't think I want this money.'

'Take it!' Tom ordered guiltily. 'I really want you to take it. Look, it's not for you – it's for the baby.'

She heard him – 'the baby', he had said. Not 'our baby'. But the point was, she was glad. He was going to leave her alone. He was horrible, she decided, seeing his freckled skin for the first time, and that weak chin and effete smile. What did she ever see in him? He shrank, became insignificant as she looked at him. She felt contempt and hatred for his father and, by extension, for Tom. My baby's not going to be anything like him, she decided. She did not want to touch their money.

35

And yet, she thought, just in case, just in case things don't work out with Vicki – and besides, she would need to help Vicki with the housekeeping ... She allowed the cheque to stay on the table. She took her hand from Tom's grasp. His hand was cold and clammy.

'You can go now,' she said to him. 'Coward.'

He knew what she meant. He blushed. 'He wanted to come,' Tom said.

'And you didn't want to stop him.'

She saw Tom swallow hard. The Adam's apple in his neck bobbed up and down.

'You can go now,' she said again. 'Go to Daddy. Daddy's waiting.' She knew she was being cruel, but she felt she had a right to be. It was better than crying anyway. He pushed back his stool, stood up and bent over to kiss her. She turned her head away. She knew that would hurt him.

'Bye, Jasmin,' he said, inadequately. She didn't watch him go.

Then Jasmin felt very, very lonely, as if she had experienced a little death. There were tears to be shed, she knew, but she wasn't going to shed them here. She would ring up Juliet shortly and spend the night with her. Then she would return to Boltham. She was drowning in loneliness.

Again she felt that wind and clenched her bottom. But nothing happened. It was a strange feeling. Jasmin paused in her thoughts; then she knew. It was her baby. Her baby had moved. She wasn't alone. A heady excitement dispersed her loneliness.

Hello, baby, she said. *I'm your Mum. I'm afraid you've only got me, but your Dad's a bastard. You don't want anything to do with him. I'm Jasmin Carpenter, and I'm twenty years old. I'm going to be twenty-one on New Year's Day. I'm very young to be a mother, but that's nicer for you, baby, because I won't be stuffy and old-fashioned. I expect I'll make lots of mistakes, but you'll like that because we can learn together. Honest, you won't regret a thing!*

Now, baby, let me tell you what we're going to do. We're going to go home to Boltham and stay with my friend Vicki Merchant. And I'll show you Heaton Rectory, which is where I was born. And when you're born, we'll go for walks and I'll push you in the pram and . . .

Me with a baby, thought Jasmin. I'll never cope.

CHAPTER THREE

Sue had to get off the bus at the bottom of the hill. Boltham Central Library stood at its top. She fumbled with her umbrella and managed eventually to provide some sort of protection for herself against the driving rain. Mark had the car today, as Arthur was on a course. So Sue, seeing nothing but red umbrella, climbed the high street, past the newsagent's, Unichem, the lingerie shop, aware of the roar of car engines and the splashing of tyres on the wet roads.

Sue rose and addressed the Boltham Council. 'Do you realize what your short-sighted policies are doing to our children? Today, when TV soaps and ingeniously marketed computer games fight for their attention, when they need books, and the promotion of books, more than ever, what are you doing? Cutting the library budget, reducing staff, slashing the schools' library service.'

Sue strode with vigour up the hill, overtaking two small old ladies.

'Your children – our children – will grow up illiterate, blind to the beauties of literature, unpractised in the use of imagination, ignorant of the powers of the written word.'

There was a muttering in the council chamber. The Lord Mayor, red-faced, seething but defeated, left the chamber. It was a signal. The councillors stood and gave Sue Turner a rapturous ovation.

'You're right,' the clerk said. 'We're convinced. We shall transfer funds from the refurbishment of the council offices immediately, and appoint two new members to the Children's Team. And we'd like you to reconsider your decision to leave us. Boltham Central Library needs women of your calibre!'

Sue's resolve was momentarily shaken. 'I'm sorry,' she said, 'but there's a time for everything. It's time for me to move on.'

The town hall clock chimed the quarter; Sue was late. That was Mark's fault for needing the car. As she climbed the stone steps to the main entrance of the library, she shook the rain off her umbrella and pushed open one of the double doors. She didn't notice the smell of floor polish and disinfectant as it was so familiar.

She walked briskly through the main lending library, nodding at Barbara on the counter, and climbed another flight of linoleum-covered steps to the library office, unbuttoning her mac as she did so.

Pinned up on the noticeboard outside the office was the counter cover list. She searched for her name but was relieved to see it wasn't there. She entered the office. Betty was deep in paperwork, Chris was on the phone and Glenys was talking to Mick.

'Morning!' Sue said, hung her coat on the coatstand and made for her desk. Usually when she faced the teetering piles of books and avalanche of paper, her heart was heavy. But this morning, despite her late arrival, she felt cheered.

She was getting out! Yes, her time as Assistant Librarian, Children's Team, was actually finite. She would get another job and she could leave all this mess behind her. She surveyed what she had to do today. There were the week's approvals, a pile of invoices to process and some mail needing her attention. By the side of her desk were boxes of books to be opened and checked.

'Oh, Sue, there you are!' said Betty, taking off her glasses. 'I'm ever so glad. I wonder if you'd let me share your keys today. I've left mine at home. The annoying thing is, I know where they are. Just by the weighing scales in the kitchen. Bert and I have a system, you see, and always put

39

the keys there – his house keys and my house keys, and the library keys, and Bert's garage keys, as he needs a set as well as the manager for his late nights – so we always know where the keys are. Except Bert sometimes forgets and leaves them in his trouser pockets. And I said to Bert this morning, don't let me leave without my keys, but then the post came and there was a letter from my sister – I've told you about Frances and the kiddies – well, I couldn't decide whether to read it there and then, or . . .'

Sue coped with Betty's wittering by not listening, just nodding occasionally. Betty was well meaning, but entirely incapable of gauging her audience's reaction. That was just as well, as no one ever listened to her. Chris was on the phone again. Chris had spearheaded Boltham's Playsafe Campaign, promoting safer playgrounds for children. She was always on the phone, talking to local journalists and council members. She was the only other woman on the Children's Team who had young children; Sue often wondered how she had time for them. Glenys, who lived alone, treated her colleagues to blow-by-blow accounts of her physical and emotional well-being, and poor Mick, nursing yet another hangover, was listening to her.

There were times, Sue considered, when they all had fun – in fact she liked them all. But confined in the small library office, everyone's faults seemed magnified. She had an accurate idea of what her colleagues thought of her: she knew that she talked too much, kept going on about her kids, was absent-minded. But she hoped they thought she had a sense of fun too. She wondered how they would react when she told them she was leaving.

'Yes, Betty. Here, take them now. I'll be at my desk all morning. I must read my approvals.'

In front of Sue was a pile of children's books; they looked appealing. It was her job to decide how many of each to buy. She was happier reading the books than trying to bring some order to the swathes of computer printouts and coffee-stained letters that littered her desk. Before she left, however, she would have to go through them all. She picked up the first book.

Monica lived in a tiny fishing village near the seaside. I'll need to find a job with the right hours; it's vital that I can still take the children to school. *She sat on the quayside with her little fishing net and plastic bucket.* I couldn't manage with anywhere that was more than thirty minutes' drive, and I'll have to think what to do if I can't get the car. *Along came a large crab with beady eyes and cruel claws, and gave Monica a fright.* If I go for promotion, they might expect longer hours, and what if I don't quite make it? I don't mind a sideways move. *Claude was a friendly crab and told Monica to jump on his back and he would take her to visit her friends. Monica laughed when she discovered that he moved sideways.* Yes. A sideways move. That means I can pick my library.

Sue shut the book. It hadn't caught her interest. She saw that Mick was making coffee and decided to join him. He took a dirty mug and shakily filled it with coffee granules and hot water.

'Good night last night?' she asked him.

'Got any Solpadeine?' he muttered.

Glenys joined her.

'I *did* go to the doctor last night,' she said. Sue desperately tried to remember what it had been this time. 'Stress,' Glenys said. 'He put the sleeplessness down to stress.'

'But it can't be the job,' Sue reminded her. 'Librarians have one of the most stress-free jobs there is.'

'For you it might be stress-free,' Glenys said darkly. 'I'm on counter cover again this afternoon, and I know whose idea that was. He's got it in for me. If ever he becomes

41

District Manager, I'm leaving. Except that's what he wants me to do. It's all right for you, Sue, you have a family. But I brood about these things.'

For a moment Sue imagined how lovely it would be to leave work and come home to an empty house. A tidy house. A silent house. But she nodded in sympathy. She watched the Coffee-Mate whiten and disperse into her coffee.

'Look!' said Chris, thrusting the *Boltham Times* under her nose. 'They've covered our survey of Greenfield Recreation Ground.' Sue focused on a mugshot of Chris.

'Here, have a look at it with your coffee.'

Sue welcomed the excuse not to get back to her approvals. She shoved the books and papers to one side, made room for her mug of coffee and scanned the paper. She read Chris's article and made some approving comments. She leafed through the other pages idly, sipping at her coffee. There was a boxed ad for Boltham Grammar School for Girls. That was where her next-door neighbour Cheryl used to teach. Boltham Grammar. They were advertising for a librarian. A librarian. Adrenalin coursed round Sue's body. This was it. This was the one. Boltham Grammar. She would be a school librarian. Nothing could be better. It was near home; there would be no more trekking from branch to branch on counter cover; her experience on the Children's Team would be relevant; the holidays, just think of the holidays; she would have a whole library to herself; she would be the boss. Sue could contain herself no longer.

'Have you seen this? Boltham Grammar – the girls' school – they're advertising for a school librarian!'

'Are they?' said Betty. 'Are you going to apply?'

'Well, I might,' said Sue.

'Why don't you?' said Chris, who enjoyed being a Ms Fixit. 'It would suit you enormously. Your school readings always go down so well. It's a good school, Boltham Grammar. Have a shot, Sue.'

Sue's hand trembled as she held the newspaper. She read the ad again. 'A full-time librarian, initially to help supervise a computerization programme, then to run the extensive school library in the new audio-visual wing. Interest in children's fiction an advantage; willingness to support junior library lessons essential.' I could do all that, Sue thought. Suddenly she felt full of energy, full of optimism.

'Shall I?' she asked Chris.

'Go for it!' she said. 'I would, if I was you. It'd be a sideways move, though, wouldn't it?'

'Yes, but I'm not bothered. Until the girls are older, I wouldn't want to go for a promotion.'

'You'd interview well,' said Chris thoughtfully.

Sue blushed with pleasure. 'Heavens!' she said. 'I haven't had an interview for I don't know how long. Since I first came to Boltham. I was interviewed for this job, but when I came back after the children, they took me on again without an interview. It'll be a challenge.'

'I'll miss you,' said Chris.

Sue was glad. 'Hold on,' she said. 'I haven't got the job yet. I bet there'll be thousands of applicants. It's the best school round here. I'll have to find out everything I can about it. But the thing is, Chris, I'm really in an excellent position to find things out. You know my friend Cheryl – the one who lives next door?'

'Cheryl who makes the earrings?'

'Yes, her. She used to teach at Boltham Grammar. Art. Until Jenny was born. Then she threw it in.'

'Why?' asked Chris.

'Well, because she had Jenny.'

'Oh.' Chris raised her eyebrows. Her children were three and ten months. She had returned to the library directly

43

after a short maternity leave, and threw herself into her work.

'Cheryl will give me the low-down. Chris, I'm so excited. I need this. I need a challenge. Although I like it here – I like all of you – I've just been bored lately. No, not bored, just . . . No. It was that letter last week about my school reunion. It just made me feel dissatisfied somehow. But getting a new job, now that would be different. I reckon with a new job I could –'

Chris's phone rang again. She apologized and went to answer it. Sue looked at the ad again, even though it was now utterly familiar to her. She would draft out a letter tonight and get Mark to print out her CV for her on his computer. She'd call in on Cheryl and ask her for advice. Thank God, she thought, something was happening.

The nice thing too about the job change was that it wouldn't put anyone out in her family. She wouldn't need the car; she would be able to be with the children for all of the holidays; she would be at home *more*. The girls would like that. Her own parents would approve. She glowed when she thought of that. It was definitely, definitely the right move. You see, working in a school, with school hours, not only would she have the stimulation of a new job but she would be a better mother too. She would be in a school, like her children. Everything would improve. And if she was happier, she suspected that she might be more tolerant towards Mark. How could he not see the advantages of this move? He would be bound to be pleased! So would Lizzie and Emma. So would her parents. Chris approved! Cheryl would too.

Glenys came over, cradling a mug of pungent fruit tea.

'Tell me exactly what the doctor said,' Sue asked her. It was going to be a good day.

*

44

'Listen, girls! Mummy's got some exciting news!'

Lizzie and Emma were playing with Jenny in Cheryl's front garden, their coats buttoned up tightly. They came up to Sue to hug her. Jenny stood watching, rubbing her running nose.

Lizzie and Emma let go and looked up at Sue expectantly.

'I'm going to apply for a new job!'

The girls looked baffled.

'In a school,' Sue added.

'Our school?' questioned Lizzie.

'No,' Sue said.

'Mummy, just before Emma said I couldn't play with her and Jenny because it was her game.'

Sue let that wash over her. She left her children playing and pushed open Cheryl's front door. Cheryl was in the kitchen, stirring something on the stove. She turned round with pleasure as she saw Sue. Cheryl was a petite woman, hair tied back in a ponytail, and always doing something: she was either baking, or sewing, or making earrings, or crocheting; she was stencilling the walls of the spare bedroom, or embroidering Jenny's T-shirts, or preserving fruit. No one made Sue feel as guilty as Cheryl did.

'The girls have got on wonderfully today,' Cheryl said.

'Thanks for picking them up,' Sue said.

'I like to,' Cheryl said simply. 'Jenny loves their company. It's difficult being an only child.'

Sue knew she meant it.

'Guess what!' Sue said, pulling a stool out from under the breakfast bar. 'I'm going after a new job.'

'Oh, where?' Cheryl asked, turning from her cooking.

'Boltham Grammar!' Sue had been looking forward to saying that.

'Boltham! Sue – of all places. But what as? You're not a teacher.'

'No. They want a school librarian!'

'You must apply. I know *you'll* be so happy there. You'll love it!'

Cheryl turned the gas down, put a lid on the pan and, wiping her hands on a tea-towel, came to sit opposite Sue. Her large eyes were alight with excitement. Sue enumerated the advantages of the job, as she had been rehearsing them to herself all day long. Cheryl listened eagerly and agreed with all Sue said. Sue was delighted by her reaction.

'It's a wonderful place to work,' Cheryl said. 'The girls are so friendly. The view from the art block is superb; you can see all over Boltham. It's a very academic school. Last year they had the best A-level results in the area. They get places at Oxford and Cambridge. And the wonderful thing is, even though the girls are so clever, they're so unassuming and so pleasant.'

'It must have been hard for you to leave,' Sue prompted her.

Cheryl shook her head and smiled. 'I didn't want to be away from Jenny.'

From the front garden came the whoops and shouts of children playing.

Sue accepted that Cheryl was different from her. It didn't stop her feeling guilty. Cheryl had given up work completely when she fell pregnant with Jenny. That was something she had had little choice about. She had experienced two late miscarriages when she was already thirty-four. But Jenny, although a breech Caesarean, was a normal, healthy child, and Cheryl had been thrilled. She and Arthur had worked out they could survive on his income from the university, supplemented by selling Cheryl's jewellery at the occasional craft fair.

So Cheryl stayed at home. She was, Sue supposed, the perfect mother, and it was Sue's bad luck to live next door to her. Sue did wonder frequently about Cheryl, though. Why didn't she feel the need to get away from Jenny? Sue knew there were times when her own children drove her mad; it was distressing to think that other mothers didn't get like that. She felt mischeivous.

'Have you ever thought of going back to work? If Boltham Grammar ever needed a part-timer?'

Cheryl returned to her pot and stirred the contents. 'Not yet,' she said. 'Jenny is still very young. But all being well, when she's eleven . . . What I'd like,' she continued, stirring slowly, knocking potatoes and vegetables, 'is for Jenny to get into Boltham when she's eleven. Arthur and I are saving up now. She would have to pass the entrance exam. Then, if Jenny was there, I might see if there were any openings. I'd love that,' she said with certitude. 'And you would be librarian and we could all go to work together.'

The aroma of Cheryl's cooking filled Sue's nostrils. She wanted some fresh air. She explained to Cheryl that she was writing her letter of application that night, that Cheryl was to give her a ring if she thought of anything that could be put in, and that Mark was able to pick the children up tomorrow. She took Lizzie and Emma's school bags from Cheryl's hall and rounded up her children.

Cheryl replaced the lid on her casserole and followed Sue to the front garden to call in Jenny. Jenny came, in her red coat with its black velour collar. Cheryl put out her arms and Jenny flung herself against her mother, throwing her arms around her legs. The sense of her preciousness, her uniqueness, had never left Cheryl. Jenny was her baby. She was her beloved responsibility. There was nothing that she wouldn't do for her.

Cheryl lifted Jenny up and sat her on her hip. She took her into the house. She assumed Sue felt the same way about her daughters; all mothers must. Perhaps if you had two the preciousness dimmed a little, she supposed. She would never go out to work while Jenny was young. There was plenty to do as it was: jam-making, running up dresses, shopping, cleaning, ironing, decorating, a hundred and one things to remember, and there was even her own jewellery. She couldn't find time to go to work.

She kissed Jenny's damp, cold, salty cheek and nuzzled her soft curls. When she was at Boltham Grammar, she had had those miscarriages. She did not wish for that time again. She was not jealous of Sue. Besides, Sue was cleverer than she was. Sue would fit in better than she had at Boltham. At prizegiving Cheryl, because she was not a graduate, had no gown to wear. She had thought that some of the girls looked down on her. That was why she preferred the non-academic girls.

She unbuttoned Jenny's coat and hung it in the cupboard, scooped her child up again, and took her into the lounge, where she sat her astride her lap.

'How did you get on at school today, darling?'

'Teacher said "Good!"' Jenny crowed.

Cheryl's heart leapt. 'Why? What did you do?' Maths? Spelling?

'I helped the teacher. I putted away the pens.'

'How did you get on with your sums?'

'They were silly sums.'

Cheryl felt the weight of the child on her knees.

'But teacher helped me and she putted in the right answers.'

Still no progress. A sharp anxiety gripped Cheryl and controlled her.

'Don't you want to be one of those big girls that go to Boltham? Because you will have to try hard. Very hard. Much, much harder than you do now.'

She heard Arthur's key in the door. The spell was broken. The child left her lap and both ran to the front door.

★

Sue was on the phone to her mother, enumerating the advantages of the new job.

'. . . school hours, and just think of the holidays! And a new set of people, and . . .'

Emma came into the bedroom and looked at herself in the dressing-table mirror.

'. . . yes, I think I stand a chance. I'm a chartered librarian, and I've given readings in local schools, and I have my own children . . .'

Emma removed her sweater and looked down at her belly button. She took off her jeans and stood there in her vest and knickers.

'. . . applying tonight and I just think I need the change . . .'

Emma leapt on to the bed, where Sue was sitting, and began to jump rhythmically up and down, up and down. The bedsprings creaked.

'. . . it's an independent school.' Creak. 'The salary might not be much different, but I will ask for more.' Creak. Sue rose up and down on the bed. '. . . sorry, Emma's jumping up and down. Yes, I will have more time for the kids . . .' Creak. Bounce. 'Stop it, Emma! Look, Mum, I'd better go.' Sue replaced the receiver and fell back deliberately on the bed. Her mother approved. It was definitely the right thing to do. Emma fell on top of her and pushed her face into her neck. Lizzie burst in and, not to be outdone, fell on top of both of them. Three wriggling bodies on the bed. Sue tried to tickle her daughters, who shrieked and giggled with delight.

Then Lizzie left them and sat on the end of the bed.

'Mummy, I don't want you to get another job.'

'Why not?' Sue asked her. Lizzie's eyes were half hidden under her fringe.

'I just don't.'

Sue felt a twinge of guilt. 'But I'll be able to be with you

49

more, and all through the holidays.' Lizzie was silent for a moment. Then she grinned.

'All right, Mummy. I give you my permission.'

'Tonight?' Mark had said. 'I'm rather busy.'

He had stood at the door leading to the lounge, holding a plate of spaghetti bolognaise, the bottom button of his shirt open, revealing the hair on his stomach.

'The closing date is Friday,' Sue had said evenly. She wasn't going to let him spoil her good mood.

'All right. Give me an hour or two.'

Sue's watch told her it was ten o'clock. The children were asleep. So she opened her bedroom door, and there was Mark, hunched at the desk, framed by turquoise curtains, the computer screen incandescent with figures.

'Mark?' she said softly.

He turned, running his fingers through his hair in a distracted manner.

'Five minutes?' he asked.

She said nothing, but sat on her side of the bed and read through the letter she had written again. It was brief, but informative. She was pleased with it.

'*An impressive letter of application, Mrs Turner. Now, can you tell us how you would encourage more girls to use the library?*'

Sue looked the headmistress straight in the eyes. 'Buying good, relevant, modern stock is essential, of course. But I would also publish a library bulletin for every class, so they knew what was available, and I would appoint a class librarian too. I would try to get children's writers to visit the school to promote interest in fiction, and arrange displays of non-fiction to tie in with school projects.'

'*To be honest, Mrs Turner – may I call you Sue? – that last question was unnecessary. We had already decided to offer you the job, based purely on your letter, your glowing references and your CV . . .'*

'Mark, my CV!'

Mark turned round again. Sue saw the faint stubble on his chin and noticed bags under his eyes. She turned away from him.

'OK,' he said. 'We'll do it now. It won't take long, as I've got it on disk. It's only a matter of updating it. Bring me a drink of something and we'll press on.'

'What? Something alcoholic?'

Mark nodded, absorbed again. Sue returned downstairs and poured two glasses of wine from a bottle in the fridge. Perhaps she was wrong to expect him to drop everything to do her CV. He had said he thought the move was a good idea. But still . . .

She mounted the stairs with the wine. Mark did not turn as she re-entered the bedroom. She placed a glass next to him.

'Damn!' he said. Sue stiffened. She tensed against Mark's temper. 'Damn, damn, damn!' he repeated.

Sue forced herself to ask what was wrong. She looked for comfort into her wine glass, as she sat on the end of the bed.

'I can't find the bloody thing!'

'What thing?'

'Your damned CV!'

'What on earth do you mean?'

'I don't think I could have transferred that data on to the new system. It's definitely not here.'

'You've lost my CV!' Sue wailed.

A memory flashed across Mark's mind. There was a file called 'Sue'. He had erased it. He had thought it was nothing important.

'Never mind,' he said patiently. 'We'll do it now. Just dictate to me the details and I'll bang it in.'

She removed Mark's socks from the bed and lay down on it. He didn't turn to look at her. She commenced.

'Education. Wednesfield High. Lancaster University 1973–6.' She thought, that was when I met him. At a party. His long black hair and leather jacket ... 'Preston Library, 1976–7.' I visited him as he was finishing off his Ph.D. All that sex. Strange, she thought. 'Then Leeds Library School – when you started at the Poly.'

'When was that?' Mark asked.

'The year before we got married.'

'When was that?'

'We married in November 1979,' she said dully. 'Then you'd better make a section for employment. Perhaps you should have put Preston in that. Put down the year I spent in the university library, and then I transferred to Boltham in ... When was it?'

'*I* don't know!'

'1981, I think. Mark,' Sue said, staring at the ceiling. 'You don't remember anything about me.'

He did not hear her. He was concentrating on the page layout.

The Alien, she thought. *My ways are not your ways*, the creature said. *I need to work; work is all. I am programmed to delete extraneous data. The machine functions less efficiently when it is forced to remember personal history, birthdays, the getting of provisions. I cannot be expected to remember to wash up. I am Man. I work. I do not need to talk. I am programmed to filter out all trivial conversation. Admire me*, the Alien said. *What a wonderful piece of work is Man!*

But, thought Sue, I don't admire him. It was another of her guilty secrets. Feeling guilty, she sat up.

'Let's have a look,' she said. 'There isn't much more to put on now.'

She moved over to Mark and stood by him, looking at

the screen. Glancing down at his head, she noticed his hair was thinning. He had not mentioned that to her. He smelt musty; he needed a bath. She thought she ought to put a hand on his shoulder, but she didn't. He did not turn to look at her.

'That should do,' she said. 'I'll list the courses I've been on as well, as that should impress them.'

'Mmm,' he said.

Later Sue was reading in bed, with her pillow doubled and supporting her back. She heard the sounds of splashing from the bathroom and Mark spitting into the basin as he cleaned his teeth. He entered the bedroom, wearing only pyjama bottoms. Sue looked at him and imagined that the hair he had lost from his head had fallen and settled on his chest. He sat on his side of the bed and began to cut his toenails.

'Do you think I'll get the job?' Sue asked. Today had seemed like a dream.

'Could do,' Mark said. She heard the snip of toenails.

'Chris said she thought I'd interview well. Do you think she's right?'

'You've always got something to say,' he said, with just a trace of criticism, which Sue chose to ignore.

'I'll have to tell the District Manager tomorrow, as they might ask for references.'

Mark offered no comment.

'What do you think they'll ask me at the interview?'

Mark heaved himself into bed. 'Let's talk about it tomorrow,' he said. 'I'm tired.' He patted her bottom dismissively and turned over, his back towards her.

Sue turned out her bedside lamp and pulled the covers over her, tugging them away from Mark. She turned on her side, her back towards Mark's back.

'*How do you feel about working in an all-girls school?*'

'*I should love it,*' Sue said. '*Are you absolutely sure there isn't a man on the premises?*' she asked.

'*None whatsoever.*'

'*Excellent,*' Sue said. '*I'll take the job!*'

CHAPTER FOUR

The taxi turned right and ascended a steep, rutted track. Jasmin's swelling womb bounced on her bladder and she grimaced. The driver swerved to avoid a pothole. The taxi suddenly arrived in front of two expansive houses sharing a patch of wasteland at the front. One bore a notice reading 'Sunnybank Kennels and Cattery, Boltham'; the other remained anonymous. Jasmin slid out of the front seat of the taxi and regarded Vicki's house. It was large, much larger than she had imagined. The taxi driver heaved open the boot of his car and deposited a suitcase and a capacious sports bag on the ground.

Jasmin's black leather purse was in her coat pocket. She passed the driver several pound coins and instructed him to keep the change. He was surprised and pleased, and visibly softened in his manner towards her. But she declined further help with her luggage and he climbed back into his shabby Cortina.

Jasmin waited until she heard the car thump down the hill. Then she went to the old chimney pot that stood by a white door and lifted a brick, revealing some dank soil and a single key. She looked up once more at Vicki's house. It was possibly an old farmhouse, she thought, or some converted outbuildings that once belonged to the kennels. Vicki and John must be wealthy, she supposed. John Merchant, his name was. So Vicki was now Vicki Merchant.

She inserted the key in the lock and the door opened easily, giving access to a roomy, square kitchen. It was not tidy. The wooden table in the centre held a jumble of used breakfast things: mugs, plates, plastic bowls, plastic spoons, a plastic bib with a lip containing congealed food, half-full glass jars of baby yoghurt, half-chewed fingers of toast, a rubber Garfield, a rattle and some assorted Duplo bricks. A high chair stood empty; attached to another chair was a red plastic booster seat. A washing machine gurgled and stopped, gurgled and stopped. The floor was littered with children's books and bricks that had overflowed from a trolley. There was a plastic yellow car with 'Noddy' emblazoned on the side and a boy's shorts and pants discarded in a wet heap.

Next to some Thomas the Tank Engine slippers and some bright-blue wellington boots she placed her two bags – neatly, side by side. She looked again at the table. Under a plastic bowl still containing cold porridge (I'm like Goldilocks, Jasmin thought) was a note in Vicki's bold handwriting. 'Hi Jaz! Sorry about the awful mess – we all overslept. Bad night with Seb. Back from playgroup at 11.45. Make yourself compleatly at home and have coffee and stuff. Can't wait to see ya!!!! Vicki.' And there was a big heart too, with an arrow through it. Jasmin smiled to herself. Vicki still couldn't spell. She put the note back on the table. Ought she to wash up for Vicki? Perhaps. But maybe, thought Jasmin, there's a special way of washing up for babies, and in that case she'd better leave it.

What was that sweet, rich smell that made Jasmin want to retch? It seemed to be coming from a white bin liner, tied with a knot, lying on the floor by the sink. Jasmin tried to ignore it but could not. She found herself becoming more and more aware of the cloying aroma. Yet she was involuntarily taking larger and larger sniffs of the infected air. She knew she had to leave the kitchen.

To her left was a flight of stairs barred by a metal safety gate. Instead Jasmin moved into a modern lounge with low

56

armchairs and settees, and a television with a remarkably wide screen. The video below it flashed the time with its characteristic nervous tic. Scattered around it were video tapes: *Winnie the Pooh's Blustery Day*, *Disney Singalong Songs*, *Dumbo*, *The Dinosaurs*, *Postman Pat*, *Thomas the Tank Engine*. There were more children's books on the floor, and magazines too: *Practical Parenting*, *You and Your Child*. Close to the settee was a red plastic box – more plastic – bursting with a profusion of toys: engines, cars, Duplo bricks, Sticklebricks, cloth dolls, teddies with plastic eyes. Jasmin was attracted to the box. She took from it a hand puppet with tawny fur and staring eyes. She inserted her hand in it, aware of the obscenity of the gesture. She felt something between her finger and thumb that she could squeeze. She squeezed it. She was startled by the harsh squeak the puppet emitted. But she squeaked it again anyway.

Beyond her was a conservatory, leading out on to an extensive garden where there was a baby swing and a blue and orange plastic slide, and in the conservatory itself was a playhouse, again of sturdy plastic.

Jasmin could not settle. The house felt distinctly alien to her. So much plastic. Did she have so many toys when she was a child? She thought not. She remembered some wooden bricks that she had endowed with particular identities, but she supposed her mother must have used toys to play with her. Uncomfortable, she left the lounge and decided to look upstairs. She unlocked the stairgate and ascended the carpeted stairs, feeling for all the world like an intruder.

Vicki's bedroom had its door open. One wall was all mirror, and Jasmin saw, reflected in it, a bed with its covers and its sheets bundled on the floor, and just a bare mattress exposed to her sight. Clothes lay askew across chairs and on the dressing table. Jasmin flinched; she felt she could not live like that.

This little bedroom was evidently the baby's room. Jasmin peeked inside. It was lovely. All round the wall was a frieze depicting characters from Beatrix Potter, and the curtains too – they had drawings of Peter Rabbit and Tom Kitten and Mrs Tiggywinkle. The cot quilt and cot bumper – they were Beatrix Potter. And the changing mat too! A mobile hung from the ceiling and an activity quilt was spread out on the floor.

My baby shall have a room like this, Jasmin decided. Except she shall have a little crib I can rock, with a lacy white cover. Jasmin inhaled the distinctive fragrance of Johnson's Baby Powder and the sharper note of antiseptic Wet Wipes. She moved to the next room, but her way was hindered by another safety gate. Evidently Sebastian's room. The Teenage Mutant Hero Turtle duvet was flung to the ground. She could see little else.

She decided she would use the bathroom. It was a large, square bathroom, with an oval bath set into one corner. The toilet was in the same room and she sat on it, feeling exposed and absurd relieving herself in these palatial surroundings – mirrors everywhere, turquoise deep-pile carpet. And yet, here too . . . plastic toys in the bath, water pistols, ducks, buckets and a baby bath in the bath itself. To get to the sink to wash her hands, she needed to kick away a plastic step. A tiny blue toothbrush lay blocking the plughole.

So the last bedroom, Jasmin guessed, must be hers. She pushed open the door. Here was a low single bed with a pink duvet and a pale grey sheet. An empty wardrobe with its door swinging open. Two full boxes of disposable nappies. A chair. Some shelving. A single electric bulb.

Jasmin walked into the room to take ownership. The

window looked out over the kennels and she could hear the faint yapping of dogs. She sat gingerly on the bed; the mattress felt firm and new. There, opposite her, on the shelf, was an old photograph of Vicki in her school uniform, just as Jasmin remembered her. Royal-blue jumper, the knot of her blue-and-white-striped tie just showing; a cascade of dark, shaggy hair, eyes blackened with mascara and her characteristic pout, half defiance, half a come-on.

The teachers had hated Vicki – that was, except for the art teacher, Mrs Davidson. Vicki was bright, but she was lazy, and why bother to try at school when you were already signed up to the Charles Mason Modelling Agency? Vicki was effusive and outrageous with her friends; obstinate and rebellious in lessons. Jasmin loved her because she flouted authority. She thrilled to Vicki's lurid accounts of her sex life, although some people said it was all lies. Jasmin knew it wasn't.

But Vicki never became a model. She enrolled in a course for beauty therapists and met John Merchant. Unpractised in saying no to men, she said yes when he proposed to her. He was twenty-eight and owned two health clubs. So Vicki was a child bride (Jasmin was a guest at the wedding) and was already the mother of two – both accidents, she told Jasmin, but better to get kids over and done with while you're young! Jasmin started. She heard the sound of movement below – Vicki was home.

'Jaz?' screamed a voice.

'Yes, it's me!'

Jasmin ran down the stairs to Vicki and hugged her tight. The girls clung to each other for a moment, feeling young and excited. Then Vicki pulled back from Jasmin and looked at her figure.

'Yeah! I can see it!' She placed her hand on Jasmin's bulge.

Jasmin looked at Vicki. She was as slender and shapely as she had ever been. She wore a fetchingly short navy skirt and a tailored navy jacket over a pink camisole. Jasmin wondered how appropriate this was for playgroup, but then, it was comforting to think that Vicki was evidently still Vicki. At that moment a toddler in an all-in-one anorak came lumbering into the hall and stopped in his tracks, staring at Jasmin.

'This is Sebastian,' Vicki explained proudly. 'Chloe is asleep in the baby seat.'

Sebastian sidled up to his mother and put his arms around her leg, as if Jasmin were an unknown assailant who was planning some harm to his mother's left knee.

'Sebastian, say hello to Jasmin. He can speak a bit, Jasmin.'

Sebastian remained silent.

'Hello, Sebastian,' Jasmin began.

Sebastian turned from her and looked at Vicki's stiletto.

'Never mind,' said Vicki. 'How long have you been here?' And Jasmin told her, and they exchanged gobbets of information hungrily, as Vicki led Jasmin back to the kitchen.

'Pooh!' she said. 'I forgot to take that nappy out. 'Scuse me!' She disappeared out into the front, holding the offending bin liner. Jasmin looked at the plump baby suspended in a timeless sleep, cocooned in a baby seat which had evidently been taken straight from the car. It's so big, thought Jasmin.

'She's big,' Jasmin said, as Vicki returned.

'Not bad, eh?'

'Are they all as big as that when . . . I mean, when she was born . . .'

'Heavens, no! Eight nine, Chloe was eight nine.'

The baby wriggled in her sleep. Her fists were tightly clenched.

'Are you drinking coffee?' Vicki asked Jasmin.

60

'I am now,' she replied, 'though I couldn't for the first three months. I've given up smoking, more or less.'

'Yeah, I did. Do you drink?'

'Sometimes.'

'Great! Then we must open a bottle tonight. I'm dying for you to meet John; he's heard so much about you. We're going to adore having you here!'

Jasmin had held the baby, who was very heavy and pulled away from her, and Sebastian had kissed her in the end, but had spent most of the evening screaming and banging his toys on the floor whenever Vicki had tried to talk to her. Vicki had said you could never talk properly when children were around and they would wait until the kids were in bed. Chloe had sat in the bath like a little Buddha – she was a human being who was a doll, or not a human being at all. Babies were like another species, thought Jasmin. But not her baby. Her baby was like her, Jasmin. Sebastian had padded in, wearing a furry grey sleep suit like a tame bear, and that was when he had kissed her.

But what she had not been prepared for was the absolute domination of the household by these two babies. No, not domination. It was worse than that. They'd turned Vicki and John's domestic life upside-down, like marauding Goths and Visigoths, Vandals and Huns of the Dark Ages. The Dark Ages, she reflected.

John came in, his shirt sleeves rolled up, looking happy and victorious.

'They're down!' he said, and walked over to the drinks' cabinet and asked Jasmin what she wanted. She said nothing alcoholic yet. She took her feet off the footstool and said she would get herself some water, but John insisted she stay there, and said she must put her feet back on the stool – very important for pregnant women!

But Jasmin felt a fraud. She was not ill. Recently she had been feeling more richly, more vividly alive than ever. She liked John, she decided. He was boyish and good-natured; indulgent to his wife and children, but not at all like the students she had known. He was more assertive and more real. Tom – and Nigel and Martin – had adopted a pose; never for a moment did they lose consciousness of the impression they were creating. John was different from that.

John returned with a glass of mineral water for Jasmin and, as she began to sip it, Vicki entered the lounge.

'Right!' she said, her enthusiasm for life undimmed. John passed her a large gin and tonic, and she gave him a kiss, then looked guiltily at Jasmin. Jasmin nodded her approval, like a liberal maiden aunt. But she was aware of a pain some-where.

'Let's hope we don't have a repeat of last night,' John said.

'What happened last night?' asked Jasmin.

'He started screaming at two, was it, Vick? And we told him to shut it, but he carried on, and Vick said, go on, let him in our bed, didn't you, Vick –'

'Yeah, so I took him into our bed and he falls asleep and that, and then about twenty past four there's this wet feeling –'

'He's peed in the bed again, so Vick's off changing all the sheets and he's sitting there playing, the little ratbag.'

'He doesn't do that every night?' Jasmin asked, aghast.

'More often than not,' John said, enjoying being the martyr. 'If I've something important on at the club, I sleep in the spare room. We have to –'

'– put the stairgate on his door,' Vicki continued. 'Other-wise he gets out and roams.'

'He's a right bugger,' said John, with evident pride.

My baby won't be like that, Jasmin decided. I'll teach her not to wet the bed and she can sleep with me anyway. For Jasmin was feeling lonely. Perhaps it was due to the way that Vicki and John finished off each other's sentences. They had an intimacy which excluded her. But then John rose.

'Right, well, I'm leaving you two to it. Girls' night in, OK? I'm off to the Three Arrows, Vick. Said I'd see Dave and Richard down there.' He winked at her. And shortly he was gone.

'Do you like him, Jaz?' Vicki asked.

'Oh, yes.'

Vicki giggled. She was sitting on the settee, her legs tucked under her, sipping her gin and tonic.

'He's all right, isn't he? You know he's thirty-two!'

Jasmin nodded.

'He's a wonderful dad. He's bought the kids nearly all those toys, you know. He's got Seb a Fisher-Price Action Workshop for Christmas and for Chloe a Matchbox Activity Bear Play Centre.'

'It's only October,' Jasmin said.

'I know,' said Vicki. 'But you've got to buy in early in case the shops run out.'

'Vicki!' Jasmin spoke impulsively. 'I'll never be able to do all this! It's different for you – I mean, you're different from me. I only know about Chaucer and the Great Vowel Shift. How do you learn how to look after babies? How do you know if you're doing it right?'

Vicki shrugged. 'Now, don't get worried,' she said. 'It's easy. Honest it is. Look, you're clever anyway. It *is* easy,' she repeated, with conviction.

'Do you mean you have an instinct when the baby is born?' asked Jasmin.

Vicki drew a deep breath as she thought. 'No, it's not that. But ... but ...' She was struggling for a thought.

63

Jasmin always made her think deeply. 'You just get a lot of information!' No, that wasn't it either, but Jasmin's face seemed to clear.

'Books, you mean. Right. I've bought myself a few books.'

'And I'll help you, Jaz. Who would have thought it? Me and you the first two to have kids. Well, me they would have expected, but you, Jasmin! But look, we'll go shopping together. There's stuff you'll need. You'll have to decide if you're going Silver Cross or McLaren – or there's the Mothercare range. I'll help you get some Babygros – there are lovely ones with Winnie the Pooh. Look, Jaz, it'll be fun!'

'Thanks,' Jasmin said. Her suspicions were correct. There was so much she didn't know.

Vicki's eyes dropped now. She fingered a lock of her hair.

'You haven't said much about your bloke, Jaz,' she asked. 'Tom, wasn't it?'

Jasmin knew Vicki was fishing but she didn't mind.

'He wanted to disentangle himself as soon as he heard about the baby. No, that's not fair. I think even if it wasn't for the baby we'd have split. He's working in London now. I liked him at the time, and we had fun, but I always knew it wasn't going to last.'

Vicki nodded. She was wildly curious about Jasmin's sex life. First, Jasmin had been so quiet and respectable at school. She had kept the boys at arm's length. Besides, Vicki had suspected that students' lives were full of sex and drugs and rock and roll . . .

'How long were you with him?' she prodded.

'About three months.'

'Was he your first . . . boyfriend?' Really Vicki wanted to ask something more intimate, and Jasmin knew it.

64

'He wasn't the first bloke I had sex with. I lost my virginity in the first term with a boy in my college . . .' Jasmin laughed to herself. It had been the first time for both of them. There was a lot of fumbling and laughing, and, oh, the embarrassment. But she was glad she had done it, very glad indeed. A spell was broken, she knew it. Then she told Vicki about Nigel and Martin, and relived it all, forgetting for a time her new position.

'Hold it right there!' Vicki demanded. 'Must have a pee!'

And Jasmin was left suspended with memories of her old life.

Vicki ran up to the bathroom. Jasmin's accounts of her relationships had interested her but were reasonably tame compared with those of her own misspent youth. That made her feel good, in a way. Strange that Jasmin should ask her for advice about babies; Vicki remembered copying maths homework from Jasmin. She looked around her bathroom as she washed her hands. There were the Johnson's Baby Bath, Baby Oil, Baby Shampoo, Baby Powder; there were the Sudocrem and the Milton disinfectant; there was the Mothercare toilet seat lock that John was fitting this weekend.

It was then that she knew the answer to Jasmin's question. It's easy being a mother; it's just a question of buying the right things. And the shops make it so easy for you. She didn't worry about getting it right. She shopped at Mothercare and Boots; she bought Fisher-Price and Tommee Tippee; Sebastian watched Disney and pulled a Kiddicraft caterpillar behind him. He was bound to turn out all right. She must explain that to Jasmin.

She returned to the lounge. Jasmin was lying back in the armchair, her hands on her distended stomach.

'She's moving!' Jasmin announced.

Vicki came over and knelt by her, put her hands on Jasmin's tummy and held them there.

'How's your mum taken it?' Vicki asked her.

'Don't know yet,' Jasmin whispered, waiting for her baby to move again. 'She won't get the letter for a week or so. She won't be pleased. I told her I was staying here. Promise me if she rings you'll stop her coming here.'

'Yes. Yes! I felt it!' Vicki removed her hands and knelt by Jasmin.

'Why don't you want your mum?' she asked her.

This was the question Jasmin found most difficult. She equivocated.

'I'm scared she'll make me go back with her to Turkey, and I don't want to have the baby there.' Vicki nodded. That made sense. 'I can't see her wanting to leave Dad there. And . . . this is my baby,' she concluded lamely.

'But my mum was dead good,' Vicki said. 'It's nice to have your mum there when you're having a baby.'

'No!' Jasmin said, suddenly angry. 'I don't want her. I won't change my mind.'

'OK. Whatever you want.' The strength of Jasmin's reaction surprised Vicki. She didn't want to upset Jasmin. It might be bad for the baby. She would change the subject. She would tell her what she had been thinking earlier.

'I felt a bit like you, Jaz – you know, when I was pregnant. About not knowing what to do. But these days it's a lot easier. If you just stick to the right names.'

'Names?'

'Milupa, Heinz, Cow and Gate – for baby food. And Mothercare – all of their stuff is good. McLaren for prams. Boots have a baby section, and Fisher-Price and Matchbox and the Early Learning Centre – that'll suit your baby. There isn't anything you can't buy for them these days. I mean, it helps, John's business doing so well. But you're not too badly off, are you?'

Jasmin shook her head hurriedly. So that was how you

66

did it. It was a matter of knowing how to shop. The perfect mother bought her baby clothes in the right places. Did all mothers do that? Spend their time shopping?

'Vicki, I've been thinking quite a lot about having this baby too. I asked my doctor at Oxford if it hurt, but she wouldn't give me a straight answer. Nor do the books. These contractions, are they painful? What happened to you?' Jasmin held her breath, waiting for the answer. She had wanted to ask Vicki this.

'I'm the worst person to ask!' Vicki grinned at her. 'Soon as I began to feel anything, I panicked. I begged for an epidural and I was lucky – the anaesthetist was available. I didn't feel a thing. Then with Chloe I booked an epidural weeks in advance. Some people say you get headaches afterwards but I didn't.'

'An epidural is a spinal anaesthetic, isn't it?'

Vicki nodded.

'I've read about those. I think –'

Vicki yawned. She was obviously very tired. Jasmin caught her yawn and yawned back. It had been a long day. Each agreed quickly it was time for bed and soon Jasmin found herself once more in her new bedroom. The unshaded electric bulb cast a harsh glow and Jasmin made a mental note to ask Vicki for a lamp.

She undressed, loving the opportunity to gaze at her bulge. She did not feel ugly. Her roundness pleased her. Her long nightie fell to the floor from the bump. Jasmin pulled back the duvet and sat on the bed. She didn't want to read; she decided to listen to the radio. Her Walkman, she believed, was in her sports bag, which she had not yet unpacked. At least she thought so, for Jasmin was somewhat absent-minded.

It was not in the main compartment of her sports bag. There was only an assortment of underwear, T-shirts, cosmetics and pregnancy books. She unzipped the side compartment. There it was, along with some tapes, a hairbrush, some hair gel and an airmail letter. Jasmin raised her hand to her lips. The glaring light bore down on the letter. It was the letter to her mother. She had meant to post it after the interview with Dr Cooper, but she had been anxious about Tom ... And then she had been in such a turmoil ... So here it was, the letter to her mother. The Annunciation.

No doubt, when her mother got it, she would ring Vicki, or Dr Cooper, or even the Principal. Or she would fly over and take Jasmin back to Turkey. She would be a prisoner. She would be locked in her parents' fairy-tale villa on the Bosporus like an enchanted princess, growing bigger and bigger. These first few steps of freedom she had taken would be over. It would all be over.

It was then that Jasmin became possessed by the absolute certainty that she would not tell her mother – at least, not yet. All she needed to do was to destroy the letter. Then – Jasmin thought rapidly – then, she would ring Juliet in Oxford and tell her to forward all letters, and she would get Juliet to post her letters from Oxford too, so her mother would never know. And she would write to Dr Cooper to ask her just to delay contacting her parents, or she could tell college that her parents were back in Boltham and to write to her home address. Yes! She would do that. Then there was Christmas. But that was not for three months. She would think of something for Christmas. This way her baby really would be her baby. And it wasn't lying, was it? It wasn't even being economical with the truth. It was just delaying the truth. That's not wrong, is it? Is it, baby?

Jasmin rubbed her stomach in a circular motion. She was no longer sleepy. In fact, she felt full of life.

'Dear Mrs Turner,' the letter read. 'I should be delighted if you would attend the school to be interviewed for the position of School Librarian . . .' On the top of the paper was the Boltham Grammar School crest. She had done it! She was on the shortlist! Although she knew there was no reason why they shouldn't interview her, and she had allowed herself to hope, the reality still came as a wonderful surprise. She had an interview! In eight days' time!

'Lizzie?' she shouted, compelled to share the news with someone.

'I'm on the toilet!' came the response.

'Lizzie! I've got an interview for my new job!'

'Wait a minute. I'm wiping my bottom,' Lizzie shouted. Emma was not at home – she was playing with a friend – and Mark would be home late.

An interview! What should she wear? A suit, most definitely a suit. Or perhaps that would be too formal and a skirt and blouse would be more suitable? Would they expect her to know anything about teaching? Should she have her hair done? What about the National Curriculum? She had to talk to someone. Cheryl. Cheryl was at home, she knew. She would tell her about the interview.

Lizzie came downstairs and found herself bundled out of the house and pushed through the gap in the hedge that Arthur had cut especially for Cheryl and Sue. Within a moment Sue was rapping on Cheryl's glass door, the Boltham Grammar letter still in her left hand.

Cheryl, wearing a flowery apron, opened the door.

'Cheryl, look! I've got an interview.'

Cheryl looked bemused for a moment, then her face brightened as she remembered.

'At Boltham Grammar! That's wonderful. Come in.' Sue and Lizzie entered. 'Come into the kitchen and tell me all about it. I can't stop as it's Wednesday, Arthur's mother's day.'

'Sorry, I'd forgotten. Shall I come back later?' Sue asked.

'No, please don't. They won't be here for half an hour yet and I'm almost done.'

Sue made her way to Cheryl's kitchen, where there were plates of cling-filmed sandwiches, a tiered cakestand displaying slices of Battenburg and Madeira and some fruited fairy cakes. Cheryl opened her oven and a delicious aroma of hot scones assailed Sue's nostrils. Cheryl put the scones carefully on a rack to cool and went to the fridge to get some butter to put into the butter dish.

'Is it a special occasion?' Sue asked, impressed by the lavish preparations.

'No. Arthur's mother has a delicate appetite, so I'm trying to tempt her.'

Sue called to her mind a picture of Cheryl's mother-in-law – a frail, bird-like lady, never without a hat, whose formal manners had rebuffed Sue's attempts to get to know her better.

'Eight days!' Sue said. 'What shall I do to prepare for it? What will they ask me? Do you know?'

Cheryl smoothed the butter with the flat side of the knife.

'I don't know. About your experience as a librarian, I guess. And why you want to work in a school.' Cheryl went to the pantry to get a jar of her home-made jam.

'If only I knew the library. I just feel I'm disadvantaged because I only know about public libraries. What if the other people being interviewed are already school librarians?'

'I'm sure you'll do just as well as they will. You know so much about children's fiction.'

'You must tell me all about the Head, so I know what to expect. Is she –'

Both women started as they heard the front door open.

Then there was the skittering of small feet, and a cry of Grandma!, and Lizzie came into the kitchen to rejoin her mother.

All of a sudden, it seemed, Cheryl's small hall was full of people: Sue making apologies, and saying hello, and saying goodbye, first to Arthur – a short, rather dishevelled man, his habitual expression concerned and deferential – and then to Arthur's mother, in her powder-blue hat and navy coat, her skin wrinkled and leathery. She seemed embarrassed by Sue's heartiness, and this made Sue uncomfortable. Cheryl came out to the hall too, wiping her hands on her apron, and kissed the slack, soft skin on her mother-in- law's cheek.

'Sue's got an interview at Boltham Grammar – as a school librarian!' she explained. Arthur congratulated her. Arthur's mother smiled graciously.

'That's a coincidence,' she said.

More polite words were spoken. Then Sue said she really had to go, and Lizzie pulled at her arm, and the door was opened again, and out they went into the darkening street.

Arthur helped his mother take off her coat, in the way she had trained him. He folded it carefully and put it over the banister. She was wearing a simple maroon dress with pearl buttons at the neck. The dress hung loosely over her insufficient figure. Arthur took her into the lounge, where Jenny had things to show her.

Cheryl began to take the cups and plates into the dining room. She knew she was tense. It wasn't that Arthur's mother often refused her food; it wasn't that Arthur's mother didn't like her. No, it wasn't that. What worried her was that she felt Arthur's mother's approval was conditional; it was dependent upon her getting things right. Arthur's mother exerted an indefinable pressure, and Cheryl believed

71

that she had a right to do so. She was a widow now and lived alone. What else did she have in her life but her family?

'Would you like something else, Grandma?' Cheryl said. 'Another scone, perhaps, or some Battenburg?'

'No, I've enough here,' she replied, glancing at her plate. One quarter of a scone lay there, with a scraping of butter. On the corner of the plate were the raisins that she had removed from the scones, as Cheryl had forgotten that she did not like raisins. Arthur looked at Cheryl. Cheryl knew he was neurotic about his mother's health; she knew it was her duty to push her into eating more.

'Take a Digestive for later,' Cheryl wheedled.

'I'll have a little more tea,' she said.

Jenny had separated the different colours of Battenburg and was deciding which to eat first. She would certainly save the pink till last.

Arthur's mother coughed. It was a deliberate cough, a warning cough. Cheryl and Arthur looked up.

'I want you to know,' Arthur's mother said, 'that I've made a decision.' Cheryl and Arthur stopped eating. 'I'm an old woman now and I'll be gone soon. As you know, I've made equal provision in my will for you and Margaret, Arthur.' Arthur shook his head furiously. He hated it when his mother reminded him of her own mortality. 'But there's a lot of money sitting doing nothing and I've decided what I'm going to do with it. Now, I don't want you saying no, Cheryl!'

Cheryl held her breath. There had been gifts of money before. She always felt an unbearable, painful gratitude and a guilty reluctance to accept it. Grandma had bought a pram for Jenny and paid for her bedroom to be decorated. But to refuse Grandma's money would amount to a denial of her, she knew. She was trapped.

72

'I've decided it's time we sent Jenny to Boltham Grammar!'

'Oh, that's all right,' Cheryl cut in quickly. 'We're saving for her fees already. Remember you gave us some money for that three years ago.'

'Yes, I know. But I'd like her to start before she's eleven. The Preparatory Department takes them at seven. I'd like Jenny to start next year. I will pay the fees.'

'You can't do that, Mum,' Arthur cut in.

His mother reached over and ruffled Jenny's curls. 'She's my granddaughter,' she said affectionately. 'This isn't money for you, Arthur. It's money for Jenny. Come here, Jenny.'

Jenny climbed off her chair, having finished her cake, and scrambled on to her grandmother's knee.

'Would you like to go to school with your cousin Francine?' she was asked.

Jenny decided that 'yes' was the right answer, so she agreed.

'Good girl,' Grandma said. 'It's not too late to enter her for the test. I rang the school yesterday. It's a very easy test, Margaret tells me. Francine had no problems. Once Jenny is in, she can stay at Boltham Grammar until she's eighteen.'

Jenny at Boltham Grammar Prep. The idea fixed itself as a picture in Cheryl's mind. Jenny, now, in the royal-blue Boltham uniform – that little pinafore dress the preparatory girls wear. It was too seductive. Jenny waving bye-bye to her as she skipped into Boltham Grammar School. No more anxieties about her progress, for everyone knew that Boltham Prep was the best junior school in the area. Jenny would be bound to flourish there. She would do so much better. Jenny *needed* pushing; that was why she hadn't done so well up to now. What an opportunity for

Jenny! Cheryl knew her silence was being interpreted as assent.

'Well, Arthur?' Grandma said.

'Cheryl?'

There was a momentous silence. Jenny's academic future hung in the balance. Cheryl suddenly had an irrational impulse to refuse, but then, just in time, she heard herself saying, 'Grandma, thank you so much. How can we say no?'

Enormous pleasure all round. Hugs for Jenny, who wasn't sure what she'd done to deserve it. Cheryl experienced a strange sort of breathlessness. Was it excitement? Fear?

'I'm so glad you see it my way,' Arthur's mother said. 'It's never seemed fair to me that one of my granddaughters should go to Boltham Grammar and not the other. Francine is so happy there. Have a word with Margaret about the test. You can coach her, Cheryl; you're a teacher. When you pass the test, Jenny, I shall buy you a special present.'

Cheryl took the plates back into the kitchen. Jenny at Boltham. That was what Grandma had meant, when she remarked on Sue's interview as a coincidence. Imagine it! Next year, she would go to Boltham Grammar every day again, but this time to take Jenny, and she would give Sue a lift too!

She scraped the crumbs into the bin with a febrile excitement. Jenny would do it. She would pass the test. She would be clever after all. Her daughter would be clever, would go to university (not like her). Jenny would be clever like the Davidsons. Jenny would get the degree that Cheryl had coveted and never achieved.

Was it wrong to be ambitious for your daughter, she asked herself? How could it be? Everyone knew that educa-

74

tion was the one thing that mattered. Jenny would never, never suffer the humiliation she had felt when she came last in maths three years running.

Cheryl began to wash up automatically. She wasn't quite ready to rejoin her family. She was too excited. I never had a choice, thought Cheryl. I was only ever good at art, so I ended up making earrings. But Jenny will be good at everything. She will have the freedom to make a choice. I will do everything I can to make sure that she gets into Boltham. Learning, she thought, like everything else, begins at home.

The spurt of envy that Sue had engendered had dissolved. *She* would not go back to work in Boltham Grammar. She would do something better than that: She would send her daughter there.

CHAPTER FIVE

'No, they're my knickers, Emma. Look, they've got a tear in them. Emma, give them back! Mummy! She's got my knickers! Stop it, Emma!'

'Mummy! Lizzie hit me!'

Like the morning birdsong, the familiar rhythms of the children quarrelling washed over Sue.

'I know you hate me, Emma. You think I'm the worst sister anyone could have!'

'Give me back my knickers!'

It was a pity, thought Sue, that the girls were so close in size when it came to underwear, but Mark would have to sort it all out. He was already up, shaving in the bathroom. She was still officially in bed, because today was her interview at Boltham Grammar School. She had taken the day off work and did not have to be at the school till ten. The girls both began crying together and Sue marvelled at how their sobs hit the same note. Did Emma copy Lizzie's cry, or was it genetic? She heard the bathroom door open and Mark sprinting down the stairs.

Sue's bedroom door burst open.

'Emma's stole my knickers!'

It really didn't take a minute to look in the drawer and work out whose knickers were whose – Emma's were, after all, rather smaller – but it was something Mark could not manage. Everything to do with clothes was her department. And food. And all domestic arrangements. One day she would change all that, when Mark finished preparing for the new course, and had more time. But she was not going to spoil today with her usual resentments. She watched Emma sitting on the floor, pulling on her socks.

'Mummy, can I sit on your lap?' Sue put her mug of coffee back on the table and Emma pulled herself on to Sue's knees. She undid the buttons of her dressing gown and then did them up again. 'What does "figure" mean?'

'Figure?'

Sue saw Lizzie pause while eating her Weetabix to listen to the reply.

'Well, it depends what sort of figure. It could be the shape of somebody's body, or it could mean to guess – that's how the Americans use it –'

'My teacher says, "Write the figures in your book . . ."'

'She means numbers. Write the numbers in your book.'

'Oh,' Emma said, as if she had lost interest.

Any minute now, she knew, Mark would take the girls off to school, and then she would be free to get ready for her interview. She hurried Lizzie up with her breakfast – Emma would never eat in the morning – and thought guiltily how much she was looking forward to having an hour in the house by herself. She willed Mark to hurry.

Five minutes to go. Sue fetched the girls' coats from the cupboard, found their bags, checked their biscuits for play-time, the money Lizzie needed, reading books – yes, all there – and Mark came thudding down the stairs again, looking rushed and harassed. She presented him with the girls, looking faintly bemused – Daddy didn't take them to school usually – and pushed them out of the door, and then silence. *Her* day was about to begin.

The Headmistress of Boltham Grammar School ascended the stage, and the masses of parents and girls examining the many bookstalls ceased their various conversations.

'If I can have your attention for a few moments,' she began. *'Thank you. Today's book fair, as we all know, has been the most tremendous success. I want to express my appreciation to all the publishers who have supported us, to the many authors who have come along for the writing workshops – too many to mention – but there is one person in particular – one person without whom none of this would have taken place . . .'*

Sue squirted some shower gel on to her hands and rubbed it vigorously on to her arms.

'. . . taken place. Little did I know, the day when I appointed our new school librarian, that our school was about to become the cultural centre of Boltham. Her enthusiasm, her innovations, her enterprise . . .'

Sue balanced her foot on the edge of the bath to wash in between her toes.

'. . . her enterprise is legendary. Our day is only darkened by the fact that Sue Turner will be leaving us shortly –' mutterings of surprise and discontent – *'to become Senior Cultural Coordinator for Boltham Council, although she will still help us in a consultative capacity . . .'*

Sue stepped out of the shower to dry herself. She wondered why she wasn't nervous, for the surprising fact was, she felt as excited as a child waking up on her birthday. I know, she thought. Someone will be listening to me! I shall have the opportunity to answer questions and be heard. She imagined the nodding, wise face of the Headmistress. She would be taken seriously; she would be noticed. It was an intoxicating thought. And what if she got the job and was able to say to Mark, I've got it? And then to go into the library in the morning, smiling, so that people knew that someone had chosen her . . .

Back in the bedroom she pulled on her skirt, twisting it round to reach the zip. She would get this job, this would be her new beginning. New responsibilities, a new working environment, new colleagues – and then she could begin to make other changes too. She would get the children to tidy their room. And she would speak to Mark, and tell him how she felt. If she got the job.

Sue drove slowly along the Boltham Road, looking for the gap in the hedgerow that was the main entrance to the Grammar School. She had driven along this road many times, and had known the school was there, but had paid scant attention to it, and, besides, it was scarcely visible from the road. But now she turned the car right and drove towards an imposing red-brick building.

As she skirted its exterior, she heard a bell ring, and by the time she pushed the glass door that gave way to the entrance hall, the corridors seemed full of girls of all shapes and sizes in royal-blue pullovers. Everyone ignored Sue. She felt swamped. Seeing the office, she moved towards it and gave her name. She was reassured by the secretary's welcoming smile and was led, rather dazzled by the newness of it all, to a small room with 'Deputy Head' on the door. She was ushered in.

There, on chairs square against the wall, were two more women. They greeted her as she came in, then fell silent. The secretary left her and Sue stood awkwardly, looking at them.

'Are you for the library job?' the small woman with glasses asked her.

Sue nodded.

'So are we,' she said gloomily.

Sue had not imagined other applicants, which, she realized now, was silly. There were bound to be other interviewees. She took a chair next to the other woman, a large, blonde lady, about her age, whose flowery skirt hung unevenly at mid-calf. There was a silence so tangible that Sue felt it as an oppressive weight.

She was dimly aware of the furniture in the office: there were a computer, timetables on the walls, cardboard boxes with files, paper everywhere, shelves of ring binders. She was also uncomfortably conscious of the two other interviewees appraising her, and she saw herself as if from outside – a tall woman in a light jacket, probably creased, over a striped blouse and beige skirt. The silence became unbearable. Sue broke it.

'Is there anyone else, do you think?'

The blonde lady next to her answered. 'No, just us three. I asked at the office.' She cleared her throat with a little cough. 'I'm Marian Garnett,' she said. 'Do you know the school?' she asked Sue.

'No,' Sue admitted, easier now there was some conversation. 'Do you?' she asked, widening the inquiry to include the other woman.

'My daughter comes here,' the lady called Marian said. She coughed again. 'It's a lovely school. What do you think they'll ask us?'

Sue replied that she didn't know.

'Because I hate interviews,' Marian continued. 'I go to pieces. I shouldn't be saying that, I know, because it's a self-fulfilling prophecy, isn't it? That's what my therapist says.' She cleared her throat again. 'She told me I must be positive.' Marian stopped talking, and Sue noticed that she began to breathe deeply, placing her hands on her stomach. Sue addressed the other lady.

'I'm Sue Turner,' she said. 'Who are you?'

'Joan Hogg.'

'Are you a school librarian?'

'Yes.'

'Where?'

'Riverside.'

'Do you like it there?' Sue persisted.

80

'No,' she said, and folded her arms over her chest. Sue swallowed nervously. She had not meant to interrogate her.

'What you have to do,' continued Marian, 'is to relax your shoulders before the interview, which takes away your tension, and I must open the door confidently, and –'

At that moment Sue heard footsteps in the corridor and into the room came a trim woman in her thirties, in an attractive green woollen dress, which set off her auburn hair.

'I'm Jane Travis,' she explained. 'I'm the Deputy Head.' She looked with interest at the three women and once again Sue was aware of being on show. 'Before your interview proper, we thought you'd like to see the library, and I can show you the school on the way there.' The Deputy Head stood holding the door open and Sue felt slightly overawed by her brisk manner. They all filed submissively into the corridor.

'Along here are the junior formrooms, used generally for arts subjects, and here, to your left, is the physics block – no, this way – and here are the chemistry laboratories.' Something powerfully familiar assailed Sue's nostrils, that characteristic smell of chemistry laboratories – dilute hydrochloric acid? That was a name she remembered. She rose on her toes to look in through the window. There were clusters of girls in white coats.

'Biology opposite,' announced the Deputy Head. Sue knew what would be in there – luxuriant plants and cages with small animals and dissection sets. She had forgotten none of this.

'Now, the audio-visual department is in its new wing, near the library, and we do envisage a close liaison between the two. You'll also be meeting the head of IT before he goes to the PDC to discuss the SATs.'

Sue glanced at her two companions to see what they had

made of that, but they seemed impassive. The strange rumbling, she guessed, was not from her stomach but from Marian's.

'The Head of IT will be present at the interview, as will Mary Austin, the teacher who is currently i/c library, the Head and a school governor.' Then the Deputy Head stopped by a turn in a corridor and dropped her voice. 'I ought to tell you, in fairness,' she said, her eyes sparkling, 'that Mary Austin is very reluctant to give up her position. You may encounter some resentment. I say this purely because her questions may be off-putting. Oh, and we also thought, as part of your interview, you would like the opportunity to meet the girls. We've arranged for each of you to take part of a library lesson. Ah, here we are!'

They had arrived at the library. Sue's first impression was that it was small – small, that is, compared with her own library. But for a school library it was generous, she assumed. It was a modern, airy building separated into two halves – a square, larger section containing the bulk of the stock and a number of large tables, and a smaller, slightly raised section where bookshelves at right angles formed booths in which girls were working. The Deputy Head explained that the sixth form studied here, and that the lower library was the junior library. Sue noticed a small office – a partition – which she guessed was the library office. It was a mess. That would be her office. It was a cubbyhole, really.

The Deputy Head continued to explain about the computerization programme. Sue stole glances at the sixth-formers bent over books. They looked so old to her – not as she imagined schoolgirls to look. Had she looked like that once? Again she was swamped by a feeling of familiarity, and something more disturbing too: yes, it was envy – a pure, refined envy – and a sense of loss. The uncomfortable memory of her reunion letter nudged at her.

'. . . so is that all right?' the Deputy Head concluded, questioningly.

'I didn't come here prepared to teach!' Joan Hogg said.

'Oh, dear. Oh, well. Yes, if I don't have to go first!' Marian said. Sue realized she had not been listening and prayed she would be able to work out what had been said. The Deputy Head continued.

'So the first-year class is coming in now, and if you wouldn't mind, Mrs Turner. Mary Austin's idea was that you should introduce yourself and talk about some aspect of the library, and give the girls a task to perform. We'll just wait in the library office.'

'But I don't know what . . .' Sue began lamely.

'Ask them to look something up,' the Deputy Head said brusquely. 'Ancient Egyptians or something.' With that, she took the other candidates into the library office. Meanwhile, through the main door came, in twos and threes, small girls, not much bigger than her own, in royal-blue pullovers with blue-and-white-striped ties, carrying piles of books. They settled at tables and looked with curiosity and expectation at her. Sue's knees felt weak; the muscles in her throat tightened. The girls looked alien to her: small girls with hair in ponytails; large ungainly girls with boyish faces; girls with glasses; girls without glasses – all of them looking inquisitively at her. In the school visits she had made as Children's Librarian, she had been accompanied by teachers, and as a guest she had been accorded some respect. But now she was alone and unprotected. She thought quickly.

'Do you know how to use the library?' Sue asked.

'Yes,' some girls chorused. 'No,' came from others.

The girl who was sitting nearest Sue put up her hand. She was scholarly-looking, with thick horn-rimmed glasses and a black hairband that framed her face.

'Miss Austin taught us where to find things. In this lesson we get on with our projects or read.'

Sue blessed her. 'Well, you do that, and I'll come round and see what you're doing.' There was a buzz of activity and girls moved towards the shelves. She watched them, feeling rather cut adrift. Then, gaining confidence, she walked towards a table and bent over to see the girls' work. It was something about ancient Greece.

A rather pimply child looked up at her. 'Miss,' she enunciated. 'What's a republic?'

'Well,' said Sue. 'It's a sort of state where there's a president, rather than a king or queen, I think.'

'Was there a president in Greece?'

'No, I don't think so.' Sue felt helpless. She continued her walk among the girls. Then she was accosted by a small girl with spiky hair.

'Is this all right?' she asked, proffering a book with a diagram of something or other. The child stood close to her. Sue could feel her body pressing against her own and was taken aback at this familiarity. Sue admired the girl's work, but was relieved when she sat down.

'Miss! Karen's nicked my encyclopedia!' said an outraged voice behind her.

'Karen had it first,' came another voice.

A cold sweat broke out on Sue's brow. She was to play Solomon too? Just then, to her immense relief, the Deputy Head appeared.

'I think you get the idea now,' she said. Sue wondered if she detected something malicious in the Deputy Head's attitude. But there wasn't time to consider that, for once again she was being whisked off, along more corridors – impossible to find one's way around – and then to a door marked 'Headmistress'. The Deputy Head knocked deferentially and popped her head round the door. Then she

84

opened the door fully and Sue was ushered in.

Still flustered from her experience with the first years, Sue found it difficult to orientate herself. The Head's study was a spacious room with a wall of books and facing her was a large desk. Behind it a pleasant woman rose to greet her – a woman as tall as herself with a refined but affable smile. Sue shook her hand and let the names of the other three people seated behind the desk wash over her, but there they all were, as the Deputy Head had explained: two men and a woman – the woman's face locked in steely resentment, a frail, sparrow-like man with hooded eyes and a lanky man with a crew cut.

'. . . Mr Granger, Head of Information Technology,' the Head concluded. 'Do take a seat,' she said to Sue.

Sue sat down carefully, crossing her legs at her ankles. Here she was, about to be interviewed. Now was her opportunity to use all those wonderful speeches she had stored.

'Let me tell you a little about the history and development of our library,' the Head began again. 'The library was started in 1897 by the wife of our founder, and then it consisted purely of dusty reference books which the Headmistress then, Miss Wentworth, catalogued and . . .'

Sue looked around her. From the Head's window it was possible to see girls playing hockey. That brought back memories too. The school governor – the man with the hooded eyes – seemed to be nodding in time to the Head's words. The Head had a beautiful speaking voice.

'. . . in 1949 the splendid gift from Miss Pendlebury's estate enabled us to open a new section in the old library, where the school's archives were also kept . . .'

The woman who was Mary Austin raised her eyes to the ceiling. Somewhere outside the room a bell rang.

'. . . the new building was opened five years ago and we have been delighted with it, but books have a habit of

85

walking – no reflection on you, Mary – and so we feel it's high time we computerized our stock –'

'Can I ask a question?' Mary Austin rapped out. A gap was made for her. She glared at Sue. 'Do you have any teaching experience?'

Sue thought quickly. 'Not as such,' she said. 'But I do have two daughters of my own – they're eight and ten – and obviously I have to help them.'

Mary Austin sniffed audibly. The governor continued to nod, his hooded eyes lowered. Sue felt more confident now that she had mentioned Lizzie and Emma. They were her talismen.

'And,' Sue added, 'as part of my job in the Children's Team, I go into schools to give readings – primary schools, mainly.'

'What a splendid idea!' announced the Head. 'Being an independent school, we rarely get to hear of the services offered by the authority. I know the English department occasionally organizes talks by writers and travelling theatre companies, but I don't think we've used the borough library . . .'

Mary Austin snorted. The Head of IT cracked his knuckles audibly.

'. . . stimulating for the girls. But I'm sure you know all this, Mrs Turner. Tell me which areas of this job interest you?'

At last, thought Sue. A real question. She gathered herself together.

'I'm particularly interested in children's fiction – there are so many excellent books being written for children these days – and I'm keen, too, on finding ways of getting children to read. Having children of my own, I'm only too aware of how difficult that can be. And I'm eager to have the challenge of starting up a new borrowing system using the computer –' She glanced at the governor. His eyes were fully closed now. Surely he hadn't fallen asleep? 'I feel it's time for me to –' yes, that noise coming from him was a snore – 'to . . . work in a new, er working environment.' Sue felt herself flailing. But the Head nodded reassuringly.

'How will you know what stock to get if you've only worked in children's fiction?' barked out Mary Austin.

Sue felt riled. 'I'll ask,' she said. 'I'll keep in close contact with the teachers and find out what they need.'

Mary Austin snorted again. 'Geography would spend all of my allowance if it could,' she muttered.

The Head smiled benignly at Sue. 'Did you know,' she said, 'that our geography results at advanced level were the best achieved by any independent school in the North-West? We are particularly strong in geography. We regularly take a field trip –'

At that moment there was a sharp rapping at the door. At the appearance of the Deputy Head's face, the Head drew smoothly to a conclusion.

'Due largely, I believe, to the excellent resources both in the department and in the school library. So lovely meeting you, Mrs Turner. I shall contact you as soon as possible. Good morning!'

As the Deputy Head escorted her back to the main entrance, Sue asked when she would be likely to hear.

'The Head should reach a decision by lunchtime,' she was told. 'It's not as if it's an important post. She usually rings successful applicants at home. Good luck!' The Deputy Head held open the door, and Sue exited into the chill but bright October morning.

Well, that was it. It was over. To Sue, as she made her way back to the car, it seemed as if the whole experience had taken no longer than five minutes. Yet her fate was decided. She unlocked the car door automatically, sat in the front seat, clicked her seatbelt into place. It's over. And how did I do?

For that was the burning question. How did she do? Did they like her? She turned out of the school grounds. She tried to remember what she had managed to say. She had mentioned Lizzie and Emma. Was that a mistake? The van in front of her stopped and Sue had to jam her foot down on the brake. She bounced forward in the driver's seat. She had taken a lesson – part of a lesson – an exquisite terror. She would tell Cheryl, Mark, Chris. What did the Deputy Head think of her performance, for she was watching from the office? Did the children like her? Would they be asked, she wondered? The road in front of Sue was empty and she began to think she might just have gone through a red light. She was certain she had gone through some traffic lights, quite certain. But had they been green? She knew she was in no fit state to drive.

Sensibly, she turned left, along the road that led to Springfield Park. She had taken the precaution of having the whole day off work and felt that a brisk walk might clear her head, and help her to prepare an edited version of the interview for her family and friends. So she parked the car and within a few moments was striding along the broad path that led into the heart of the park.

The movement was doing her good. She struck off towards the boating lake, passing women with dogs and elderly couples proceeding slowly arm in arm. They loved me. (I answered my questions well. I mentioned my school experience.) They loved me not. (That man fell asleep. The Head did all the talking.) They loved me. (The other candidates were odd. I said nothing silly.) They loved me not. (That English teacher was a cow.) They loved me. (I coped with those little girls, didn't I?)

It was impossible to know. Sue reached the boating lake,

its brownish waters still now, the small island in the middle flat and deserted. The shack from which boats could be paid for in the summer was boarded up and desolate. Sue, energized, walked on, over a hill, towards the children's play area.

At least, she thought, it was over. (There was a slight feeling of anticlimax.) All she would have to do was wait for the result. That felt comforting, that felt familiar. That delicious abandonment when one waited to see what the fates had in store, knowing one didn't have to do anything about it. Sue remembered waiting for her degree results, waiting for Mark to propose to her, waiting for the results of her pregnancy tests, in the same frame of mind. She remembered herself as a schoolgirl when she had that crush on Leon Dixon. He said he would ring her during the week, and she had waited, and asked her mother if she should ring him, and her mother had said, No! You wait. It doesn't do to be too forward. What would the boy think?

True, Sue had decided. And found in fact it was easier to let other people make the decisions. So now this period of waiting for the job that would change her life felt right, somehow. The park smelt of wet grass and dog turds. A small boy cycled past her with a mother some way behind.

She would get the job. She would walk into Boltham Grammar School every day. (The office was too small – she would have to alter that.) She would acquaint herself with the stock, and she would have to win the confidence of the English teacher. She would be subservient to begin with. She would take library lessons. In her mind, little girls clung to her, asking questions, presenting her with their quarrels. It was all so familiar. It felt *right* somehow, this job – home from home.

Please God, she prayed, let me get the job. Let the Head ring me at home this afternoon and offer it to me. Let me be able to tell Mark that somebody liked me. Let me give my notice in at work. Let me . . .

Sue had reached the children's playground. She realized it was some years since she had been here. There was a period when she had come to the park almost every day with the girls. They were toddlers then, and it was something to do. She had pushed them in swings and stood at the bottom of slides and applauded their efforts on the climbing frame. It was with immense relief that she realized she was free of all that now. It was like emerging from some tunnel.

In fact the playground was more or less deserted. There was a man zipping up the anorak of a small boy, preparing to leave. And apart from him, only a young mother sitting on a bench with a baby in a buggy and a toddler. Sue looked at them and for a moment saw herself. Her path crossed the play area and she drew closer to the mother. Yes, it could have been her, all right. The baby was grizzling and crying; the toddler was shouting. But then the mother did a most astonishing thing . . .

CHAPTER SIX

The baby, when it was born, was entirely composed of woollen matinée jackets; it had been crocheted. The nurse in the hospital fed it with porridge from a rusty teaspoon. Then Jasmin had another baby – it was twins. The other baby told her its name was Alistair. Then the crocheted baby began to cry and Alistair knocked it on the head – bang, bang, bang.

Bang. What was happening? Bang. Jasmin emerged from her dream, heavy in all her limbs, her need for sleep clutching at her with tendril-like fingers, seducing her to come back.

'Jasmin? It's me, Vick! It's half-past eight!'

Jasmin's eyes opened, saw the single light-bulb dependent from the ceiling. She was exquisitely tired. Her limbs ached with tiredness. She could not get up. She lay there, remembering. All night long, that noise. The baby had a cold and coughed and cried and spluttered in the bedroom next door, and then she had been sick and Vicki and John were busy changing the bedding. And just when they had got her off, Sebastian had woken and there had been the usual battle. And all through the night the dogs in the kennel barked and howled. Little dots of tensions pressed on Jasmin's temple as she recalled it all. She was so tired. Why was Vicki waking her?

Because, her rational mind informed her, she had promised to look after the children while Vicki spent the day helping John at the health club. John's receptionist had a day's leave and Vicki badly wanted to step in – it would be a break for her as much as help for John. So Jasmin had volunteered to stay at home with Sebastian and Chloe; it was the least she could do after all Vicki and John had done for her.

'Can I come in, Jaz?'

Jasmin made a noise of assent. Her eyes took in Vicki's tailored pin-striped jacket and her matching skirt, calf-length, but split to the thigh. She wore a low, white camisole; she had brought her hair back and her face was immaculately made up.

'Aren't you tired?' Jasmin asked her.

'Desperately,' Vicki said, 'but I'm on overdrive right now. John's downstairs feeding the kids. We'll be going in about ten minutes.'

Vicki closed the door gently and Jasmin heard her footsteps retreating down the landing. Ten minutes. Jasmin heaved herself out of bed and, as was her habit, patted her growing stomach. She was still dizzy with tiredness. The bathroom first. As she crossed the landing, dressed only in an extra-large T-shirt that served as a nightdress, John bounded up the stairs and grinned at her self-consciously. She felt naked, clumsy, exposed and distinctly unattractive. When she had finished brushing her teeth she examined her pale face in the mirror. There were shadows below her eyes; her expression was bleary. Back to her room, where she pulled on yesterday's jeans and sweater. Still barefoot, she padded downstairs.

The door to the kitchen was open and Jasmin could hear Chloe crowing: 'A – ga! A – ga!' Then she paused. Vicki and John were standing by the sink, locked in an embrace. John's hand slid up Vicki's thigh. Jasmin stood paralysed at the door. 'A – ga! A – ga!'

Vicki finally sensed Jasmin's presence and disentangled herself from her husband, blushing and apologetic.

'Look – we're just about ready to go. Seb's nearly finished his Coco-Pops. Don't bother washing up or anything if you don't want to. Just let them play – and there's the video and stuff. If they get ratty it means they're tired, so just plonk them in their beds.'

'Thanks, Jasmin,' John said, straightening his tie.

And they were gone.

Jasmin moved to the kettle to make herself some coffee. Vicki had not wiped the work-surface; rings of blackcurrant juice stained it. The kettle was splattered with coffee stains. Jasmin washed herself a mug and teaspoon – her dream recurred to her – and found a half-full milk bottle on the table. She glanced at Sebastian, who was stirring his bowl of Coco-Pops. She was apprehensive: she had only had sole charge of the children for a couple of hours; this was her first full day with them. Vicki had taught her how to change a Pampers; Jasmin prayed both children would be constipated for the day. Vicki had left instructions about lunch; that bit sounded all right. Yet the children seemed to her like time-bombs, just waiting to go off. And she was so, so tired.

She looked again at Sebastian. From both nostrils ran a thick, yellow stream of mucus. She retched. Bravely, she took some kitchen towel and wiped him, taking care that her fingers did not come into contact with anything wet. Chloe was emitting a high-pitched squeal of which she was particularly proud. Jasmin assumed that meant she had finished her breakfast, so she let her down from her baby seat and put her on the kitchen floor. Like an animal, she took off on all fours and crawled to the toy box, and pulled herself up on it. Sebastian, seeing this, climbed down from his seat to join her. He was dribbling now, Jasmin noticed. As Chloe reached into the toy box, her brother began to throw out all the toys on to the kitchen floor. The baby screamed.

'No!' shouted Jasmin. Sebastian stopped to look at her, and decided to pretend he hadn't heard. He carried on. So, leaving her coffee, she dragged him by his arm through to the lounge. Ought she to bring the baby? she wondered. Was it safe to leave her by herself in the kitchen? She would, just for a while. She had to separate them.

Jasmin surveyed the lounge. Vicki and John had not cleared up from the previous evening. There were glasses on the coffee table and an empty bowl. John's socks lay discarded by the settee. The surface of the coffee table was sticky, Jasmin noticed. She put a Postman Pat tape in the video slot and switched on the TV set. Sebastian stood rigid with attention in front of it.

'Postman Pat, Postman Pat,
Postman Pat and his black and white cat . . .'

The baby! What was she up to? Jasmin returned to the kitchen, but Chloe was still standing clutching the side of the toy box. Her face was red and she gave a soft grunt, and a strained smile. Then there was an unmistakable smell. Jasmin fought her nausea. She would have to change Chloe's nappy.

Jasmin, she addressed herself sternly. You must get used to changing nappies. There are times when it doesn't do to be squeamish! Her inner voice was authoritative and severely practical. She recognized it; it was her mother's voice. Yet her profound distaste, her horror, as she applied a series of Wet Wipes to Chloe's brown-encrusted bottom was her mother's too, she knew it. Jasmin tried not to breathe, as the baby raised both her chubby legs in the air and brought them down hard on to the changing mat.

Jasmin had changed Chloe's nappy. She had cleared a space for herself in the lounge. She had read Sebastian *Spot the*

Dog three times. She had taken him to the bathroom, but he had refused to pee into his teddy bear potty. Chloe had chewed half of Vicki's copy of *TV Quick* and was grizzling and giggling on the floor, in a landscape of toys. Sebastian was building a teetering tower of Duplo. Jasmin watched them. That, she supposed, constituted looking after children.

It was a bitter thought. Her tiredness had not entirely lifted, and she was feeling irritable and slightly hysterical. She didn't think Vicki was a very good mother. For one thing, the house was such a mess. You can't bring children up in a mess! And for most of the day she ignored them. She surrounded them with toys and painted her nails in the kitchen, or took them to playgroup and chatted with the other mothers. Jasmin had never seen her sitting down and teaching Sebastian anything, and she never corrected his baby language; he said 'num-num' for food, and so both Vicki and John called dinner 'num-num'. Surely this was wrong? Yes, both Vicki and John played with the babies, but only for short bursts. How can a baby thrive, unless you give it undivided attention?

And yet, Jasmin reflected, as she sat there watching the children play with a dispassionate detachment, *she* wasn't doing anything with them. But then, they weren't her children. Her baby would be different. She would be different – she would be the perfect mother.

Jasmin bit her nails. 'Ma – ma – ma,' said Chloe. There was an uncomfortable thought trying to emerge in Jasmin's mind. Her tiredness, her atrophy, pushed it down; it would not go away. 'Fixit! Fixit!' said Sebastian, clutching his plastic spanner. She didn't like Sebastian and Chloe. There – it was out! Or rather, it wasn't them, as people – if they were people – it was babies she didn't like.

It was true. She had been with Vicki and John for two

weeks now, and she had learned a lot. But the awful – the true – thing she had learned was that she just wasn't cut out for motherhood. She had no maternal instincts whatsoever. With rising hysteria, she said to herself that she would never be the perfect mother, that it was all a mistake, that she should never have let herself get pregnant. She shouldn't be having this baby. She didn't want it. Her skin pricked in panic. She was trapped. Trapped in a welter of Pampers and potties and internal examinations and tons of brightly coloured plastic and sleepless nights and Postman Pat and Coco-Pops and activity centres!

Quick! she commanded herself. Think of something else, something nice. *The Battle of Maldon* – her favourite Anglo-Saxon poem. She thought of *The Battle of Maldon* and tried to remember the shapes and patterns of the words. But they would not come. Some Chaucer, then – anything!

> 'The double sorwe of Troilus to tellen,
> That was the kyng Priamus sone of Troye . . .'

> 'Postman Pat, Postman Pat,
> Postman Pat and his black and white cat . . .'

No, she would not cry, Jasmin thought. She would get out instead. She would take the children out somewhere. It was a bright day. She would take Sebastian and Chloe to Springfield Park. It was only five minutes away. Her desire for fresh air, for activity, for movement, became a fever that consumed her. She laced up her Doc Marten's, dashed into the kitchen, found Sebastian's anorak and Chloe's all-in-one – keep busy, don't think – she wiped noses, switched off the TV, switched on the burglar alarm, bade farewell to the appalling debris of plates and cups and toys, took her long black coat and thank God, she was out – Chloe

96

strapped up in the buggy and Sebastian hanging on to the metal sides, his Teenage Mutant Hero Turtle baseball cap backwards on his head.

Jasmin, to allay her hysteria, began to talk to the children.

'I'm taking you to Springfield Park,' she said. 'You can go on the swings. It's a nice day today, isn't it?'

I wish I wasn't pregnant, she thought.

'Can you hear the dogs barking? They go woof, woof, don't they? Woof, woof, woof. What noise do cats make, Sebastian? No, cows say "moo". And ducks? How do ducks go?'

Please, somebody, help me.

'Good boy, Sebastian, hold on to the side of Chloe's buggy. Now hold on very tight as we cross the road.'

Traffic roared by them as they reached the end of the track that led from Vicki's house. There is no escape.

'I'll tell you a story, Sebastian. Yes, all right, with animals in it.' What animal stories did she know? There was the story of Chaunticleer from Chaucer's *Nun's Priest's Tale*. That would do.

'Once upon a time,' she began, 'there was a poor widow who lived alone and owned a little farmyard. In this farmyard . . .'

She entered the park, pushing the buggy at breakneck speed, drowning her panic with words and movement. Then Sebastian saw the playground. He let go of the buggy and ran eagerly towards the slide, and clambered up it. Jasmin watched him go.

She felt hot with her exertion and unbuttoned her coat. She noticed that the baby had fallen asleep, her head slewed drunkenly to one side in the buggy. Her cheeks were hectic. What if she's getting a fever? thought Jasmin. Then she may get a convulsion, and I wouldn't know what

97

to do. She looked wildly around the park. It seemed deserted, except for a man pushing a small child on the baby swings. Sebastian slid down the slide and then climbed it again; slid and climbed.

Jasmin knew there was still a lump in her throat. She would not cry. But what could she do? She had to have this baby, she knew. And she had to keep it. But she felt as if her body was being taken over by some alien being; it looked different, reacted differently. There was Sebastian's head bobbing up over the top of the slide again. In the distance she heard the engine of a lawnmower groan, and birds kept up a ragged twitter. Sebastian paused at the top of the slide. Jasmin wondered why. Then he slid down, but this time ran to her.

'Wee-wee,' he said, rather proudly. Vicki had recently succeeded in potty-training him.

Panic rose in Jasmin. Where could she take him? Then she looked at him again. 'Wee-wee,' he said, pointing at his jeans. His jeans were sopping wet. So were his socks. And shoes.

'Wee-wee,' said Sebastian.

What should she do now? He can't go home like that, she thought. But she had no spare clothes. Oh, God, what should she do? Her brain, fuddled with sleep and hysteria, was not functioning. He needs dry clothes, Jasmin decided. I will take off Chloe's outdoor suit and put it on Sebastian, and cover the baby with my coat. So she took her own coat off and laid it on the bench where she had been sitting. Then she knelt down and pulled off Sebastian's shoes, socks, trousers and shorts. He began to cry.

'Mummy! I want Mummy!'

'Sssh, Sebastian! Mummy's at work!'

'Mummy, Mummy, Mummy!'

Ignoring him, Jasmin picked up the heavy Chloe and

98

unzipped her suit. The baby began to cry. From both children, insistent, echoing sobs that met in an appalling harmony.

'I need your suit!' Jasmin explained to the baby.

Sebastian collapsed on to the gravel path, screaming.

'Oh, no,' Jasmin shouted. 'You can't do that! You've got a bare bottom.' She got Chloe back in the buggy and threw her coat over her. The baby's screams were apoplectic with rage. All of Jasmin's world was noise and heat and horror.

'Help!' she screamed.

'What do you want me to do?' said Sue.

CHAPTER SEVEN

Jasmin turned. She looked up into a friendly female face.

'He's wet himself,' she said. 'I've no spare clothes.'

Sue looked at the girl. She seemed pregnant, and in charge of this baby and toddler. Surely she wasn't old enough to have all three? Her voice was rounded and articulate; the dowdy sweater and jeans she was wearing were the badge of the privileged middle class. Was the girl an au pair? Or an elder sister? But why was she pregnant?

'Not yours surely?' said Sue, pointing at Sebastian and Chloe.

'No,' said Jasmin above the squalling of the children. 'They're my friend's, Vicki's. I'm staying with her, and I said I'd look after them, but I'm not very good at it.'

Sue looked again at the children. She picked up the little boy and brushed the specks of gravel from his bare bottom. The child quietened as he looked at her.

'Pick the baby up,' said Sue, 'and put her suit back on.'

Jasmin did as she was told, happy to receive orders. Being handled, the baby calmed.

'Have you got something to wrap the boy in?' Sue asked.

'Shall we use my coat?' Jasmin said.

'How far have you got to go?' Sue asked. She sized up the situation. The girl could not put the wet clothes back on the toddler, nor could she carry him with her coat wrapped round him if she had to push the buggy.

'Mill Lane,' she said. 'Off Greencliffe Road.'

Her car was nearer than that. She made a decision.

'Come with me back to the Boltham Road exit and I'll drive you home. I've got the car.'

'Oh, no,' said Jasmin, meaning yes.

'Come on,' said Sue, 'it's no trouble.'

She took Jasmin's coat and wrapped it round the boy, and Jasmin walked by her side, pushing Chloe in the buggy.

'Thank you ever so much,' Jasmin said. 'I'm sorry I panicked. It's just that I'm not used to babies and I didn't know what to do.'

'I know the feeling,' said Sue. 'I've had two myself.'

'*I'm* pregnant,' said Jasmin. She paused, waiting to see how her statement would be taken.

'I thought you were,' said Sue. 'How many months?'

'Five,' Jasmin said.

Sue took a quick glance at the girl as they both walked quickly along the path leading out of the park. She looked so young. Nineteen? Twenty? She was a very attractive girl – short, dark hair, an aristocratic lift to her chin, proud eyes – yet there was something intensely vulnerable about her. And she was pregnant. Sue's interview at Boltham Grammar, her everyday life, all this had slipped away out of her consciousness. The girl beside her absorbed all her attention.

Jasmin was a shrewd judge of character. She knew her instinctive liking for the woman next to her was not only due to the fact she had helped her. There wasn't a trace of criticism or unhealthy curiosity in the way she had sized up the situation and sorted out the children. Jasmin wondered how old she was. Not as old as her parents. But old – old like her tutors at college. Jasmin knew she would be easy to talk to, and now, moving quickly through the park, locked accidentally into this intimacy, Jasmin was overwhelmed with the need to talk.

'I'm sorry about this, and I'm very grateful for your help,' she said.

'It's all right,' Sue replied. 'I could do with the distraction. No, that sounded sarcastic, and I didn't mean it to be. I really don't mind – in fact I've got the day off work.'

'What do you do?'

'I'm a librarian. At Boltham Central Library.'

'A librarian!' Jasmin repeated, expressing pleasure. This was something from her world. 'I'm a student – except I'm having a year out, to have the baby.'

Ah, thought Sue. An accidental pregnancy. Poor kid.

'I'm really at St Luke's, Oxford,' the girl added. 'I'm in the third year of my English degree.'

'I did English too,' added Sue.

Jasmin grew excited. 'Did you? That's a coincidence. Well, during the summer, I discovered I was pregnant, and so I asked my tutor – have you heard of Grainne Cooper, she's a medievalist – I asked her if I could have a year out, and so I came home to Boltham. I live here, but my parents are abroad. That's why I'm staying with Vicki.'

'So it's Vicki who lives in Mill Lane?' Sue asked.

'Yes. I live in Heaton Rectory.'

Now it was Sue's turn to be surprised. 'Heaton Rectory? Behind Heaton Close?'

'Yes.'

'I live there – in Heaton Close.'

Sue and Jasmin looked at each other closely. But they did not recognize each other. Their lives – up to this point – had followed very different paths. Sue tried to call to mind what she knew about the people at the Rectory. For the past two years an Indian couple had lived there; they had recently moved out. Before that there was a family, she remembered, that kept itself to itself. She had only ever seen a man in a BMW and a woman in a Volvo. Was there a girl too?

'I don't know you,' Jasmin said. 'But then, I never walked through the Close. Mum drove me to school.'

They had reached the park gates. Sue arranged Jasmin in the back seat with Sebastian and Chloe, and got the buggy into the boot. Jasmin continued talking.

'Can you imagine it?' she said. 'I was never allowed to get the bus. Although my school was an awkward journey. Boltham Grammar School – do you know it?'

Sue did not turn the key in the ignition. She looked over her shoulder. 'I've been there this morning,' she said. 'For an interview for school librarian.'

'No!' Jasmin cried. 'This is amazing. You've been at my old school. Did you like it?'

'Yes, but I –'

'Imagine, me meeting the librarian from school!'

'No.' Sue stopped her. 'I haven't got the job yet. I was on my way home to wait for a phone call.'

'Oh, then you must go home,' said Jasmin. 'You mustn't be out when Mrs Hamilton rings. You haven't got time to take us home.'

Sue paused. What Jasmin said was partly true. She didn't want to miss the phone call. What if they rang her at home to offer her the job, and she wasn't there? Would they offer it to someone else instead? But this girl needed to be seen to first. The phone call, the job, had to wait.

'When did they say they'd ring?' Jasmin persisted.

'Lunchtime,' Sue said.

'I know!' Jasmin said. 'Let's go to your place and you can drop me off at the Rectory. I need to see if there are any letters. And then – oh no! – I'd forgotten the children.' Sebastian, who was reasonably quiet now, was still bare from the waist down.

Sue started the car. 'Come into my house first,' she said. 'I've some old things from Emma that he can put on. You pick up your letters and then I can drive you home after lunch. You can have lunch with me, if you like. It would be nice to have some company.' What am I doing? thought Sue. I don't know this girl. But she wanted the company, that was true. The experience of her interview had left her feeling jittery; she needed someone with whom to talk.

'I'd love to,' Jasmin said. 'I'm Jasmin Carpenter,' she added.

'Sue Turner,' said Sue, as she moved into the traffic.

Jasmin felt as if she had been rescued, rather like someone who had thought she was drowning and then had discovered herself prostrate and panting on a beach, safe but exhausted. Safe but exhausted. Sue Turner had improvised lunch for the babies and had actually got them to eat something. She had presented her too with a plate of cheese on toast and steaming coffee. Now Jasmin was sitting with her feet up on Sue's settee, watching the children play quietly with Emma's old toys, Sebastian dressed in some old red trousers of Emma's and a pair of girls' knickers underneath. Fortunately, he was still too young to care.

Jasmin was in an ordinary suburban lounge, but, a trained observer of people and places, she looked around the room for what was extraordinary, those things which would tell her more about Sue. There was a sizeable number of novels on the wall unit: Alice Walker, Barbara Pym, P. D. James, she noticed. In a pile by the settee were women's magazines, the *Beano* and computer monthlies. There was the detritus of children too: discarded trolls, some felt-tips rolled into a corner, a small effigy of Ronald McDonald and a hair clip. Jasmin noticed that the curtains, dark green, did not match the three-piece suite exactly, and that the bean bag in the corner had been sewn clumsily a number of times.

Sue returned. She grinned conspiratorially at Jasmin. This was the most unusual day she had ever had – the interview, and then meeting this girl in the park and playing the Good Samaritan. And bringing her back here, without telling anyone, without consulting Mark, or Cheryl, or mentioning it at work, just doing it – it felt most unlike her. But there was something about Jasmin's acceptance of the situation that made it seem the most natural thing in the world. Sue sat down on the armchair facing Jasmin, tucking her legs under her, as was her habit.

'Well,' she said, 'no one's rung.'

Jasmin looked at her watch. 'The lunch-hour at school will have only just begun.' And both of them looked at the phone that sat innocuously on the window-ledge. It was buff-coloured and modern.

Apart from the children playing quietly in the corner, Jasmin could have imagined she was in a tutorial. This situation, facing an older woman in a private room, felt comfortable. It restored her sense of normality. It cleared her mind. It made her ready to think it all through. She was simply waiting for a question from Sue.

'Feeling better now?' Sue said.

'Yes, thank you. It's as if this morning was a nightmare. It's so nice to be here,' Jasmin exclaimed, looking round her.

'Here?' said Sue, surprised.

'Yes. I suppose I mean away from Vicki's. It's not Vicki,' Jasmin said slowly, feeling her way around her thoughts, 'and it's not John either, although I think it is both of them together. They're nice to me, but . . . I feel excluded – no, I feel jealous!'

'But you told me over lunch,' Sue reminded her, 'that you never wanted to see your boyfriend again.'

'I don't,' Jasmin said quickly. 'But just being with a couple who do want each other –'

'Oh,' remarked Sue. 'That'll wear off!'

Jasmin didn't hear her. 'I utterly reject the view that a woman needs a man to feel complete, but I think it must be the contrast, between Vicki and John together and me alone, with –' and she gestured at her stomach.

Sue felt very sorry for her and ached to find something reassuring to say. 'You're only twenty, Jasmin. And very pretty. It won't be long before you'll find someone, baby and all.'

Jasmin considered Sue's words. They helped her see that she did not want another boyfriend, or Tom. It was the baby that was meant to give her the love she craved. Men were fine for sex, and there were plenty of men around.

'No,' Jasmin explained. 'I really don't want a boyfriend. I'm just beginning to feel that I'll be better living on my own. It's not only Vicki and John's claustrophobic relationship,' she said, 'but . . . there's something else too.'

Jasmin had changed her mind about making her next statement, or at least she didn't want to shock Sue. It was evident from the brief conversation they had had at lunch that Sue's daughters meant a lot to her – she mentioned them frequently – and, more than anything, she wanted Sue's good opinion. She looked at Sue and saw her eyes stray involuntarily to the telephone.

'What else?' said Sue, bringing her concentration back. 'What else are you unhappy about?'

'I don't like being with children,' Jasmin said. There, it was out. 'I thought it would be different somehow. But –' she bit her lip anxiously – 'but the children are messy and noisy and demanding and not like human beings, and Vicki doesn't do anything about it. The house is always a tip, and Vicki and John just leave things for days, and just buy the kids more stuff and more plastic and – no wonder the children don't talk to them!'

Sue looked at the baby and toddler in front of her, surrounded by Duplo. 'They're too young to start conversations,' she said gently.

'Oh, I don't mean proper adult conversations. But Vicki and her babies seem to ignore each other. I thought, when you had a baby, it would be a companion.'

'I think it's a long time before that's true. A lot of what babies do is very boring. Even now I think my kids are often happier without me, and I have to admit I'm quite happy without them.'

'Really?' said Jasmin, with horror.

'Well, I feel guilty about it, of course. But that's the way it is. And don't blame your friend for not looking after the house,' Sue said. 'Having two children so close in age, it must be difficult for her. I remember living in chaos when Lizzie and Emma were that young. I think we even had a cleaner in for a while. A happy mother, I think, is one who can train herself not to see the mess.'

Jasmin was quiet. She felt the rebuke, and liked Sue for it.

'When you have your baby,' Sue continued, 'you'll only be too grateful to the toy manufacturers. I could have canonized Mr Fisher-Price, whoever he is! When a child learns to play independently, it's a boon. Anyway,' Sue said, feeling herself on less firm ground, 'children need stimulation.'

'Stimulation,' said Jasmin. 'Doesn't that mean telling them stories and playing with them? Not shoving them in a corner with heaps of plastic things.'

Sue felt guilty again. Jasmin's idealism, like a sharp arrow, pierced the Achilles' heel of her inadequacy. She wasn't a good mother, she knew it. But she would try to defend herself, nevertheless. She was experienced; Jasmin was not. She eased her legs from under her, planted them on the floor and sat forward on her chair.

'Perhaps the perfect mother gives her child undivided attention,' Sue said. 'But the rest of us play with our kids sometimes and ignore them for the rest of the time.'

107

'My mother played with me all the time,' Jasmin said.

At last, Sue thought. She's going to talk about her mother. For the one thing that Sue could not understand, when, over their frugal lunch, Jasmin had explained her situation, was why Jasmin's mother had been left in the dark. How would she feel if Lizzie had done that to her? Sue remained silent, encouraging more confidence. The harsh ringing of the telephone cut across her thoughts. Sue and Jasmin jumped. Sue leapt off the armchair, stood by the phone, paused to collect herself and picked up the receiver.

'Hello,' she said.

'Hi,' said the voice at the other end. 'It's Tracey from Warmrite Double Glazing! We're in your area right now –'

'Sorry,' said Sue. 'I'm not interested.' And she replaced the receiver. 'Double glazing,' she explained to Jasmin.

Jasmin nodded, waving aside the interruption. 'There are two problems really,' she said, continuing her train of thought with a youthful selfishness. 'One, I don't want to stay with Vicki any more. Two, I . . .' Jasmin couldn't articulate whatever it was she wanted to say.

Sue was silent, as a sort of prompt.

'I don't want to bring up my baby like Vicki brings up hers! But I know you're right and think all mothers probably mean to be perfect and they all fail! And that's dreadful! Because it means I might fail. And there's another thing too. I'm scared of giving birth. I've been reading all the books I possibly can about pregnancy and labour, and there's so many things that can go wrong, and there's so much you have to get right, and . . . I should never have got pregnant in the first place!' Her hysteria was returning. Jasmin breathed so she could carry on. 'I don't know what you're thinking of me. I suppose you must despise me. But please don't. If I don't say what I've been thinking to *someone* I'll go mad. But I feel so trapped. No, not trapped – it's as if I'm on some juggernaut and I can't get off.'

Sue pitied her. 'I felt like that too sometimes,' she said. 'It's quite natural. I don't suppose you know many women who've had babies.'

'None,' said Jasmin. 'Except for Vicki. I don't have any family, you see. I've no brothers and sisters, and no cousins either. Having a baby seems very alien to me.'

'Why didn't you have an abortion?' Sue asked her.

Jasmin shrugged, looking mulish. 'I'm not a Catholic,' she said, 'but I think it's wrong to have an abortion. Wrong for me,' she said, remembering her feminism.

Sue sensed a mystery here, but delicately refrained from pushing further. Instead she thought she would help where she could. 'Must you live with Vicki?' she asked. 'Can't you go to Turkey to your parents?'

'No,' Jasmin said.

Here was the mystery, Sue thought.

'Can you go back to Oxford?'

'No. Everything's been arranged for me to have the year off. Besides, I'd feel worse there, in a way. But I know what I really want to do.' She paused. 'I want to go back home and live in the Rectory. It's empty now. And it is my house.'

'Alone?'

'I'm used to living alone. And I could still see Vicki every day. And you,' Jasmin said shyly. Sue was touched. That was when the phone rang. This time she moved more slowly to the window. She saw her towels blowing softly in the wind on the washing line. She picked up the phone.

'It's Cheryl,' Cheryl said. 'I'm ringing from my mother-in-law's. Would you like me to pick the girls up from school? How did it go?' Sue explained, said she had a friend with her, someone Cheryl knew. They had a brief conversation, Jasmin watching, Sue running her fingers through her hair. She replaced the receiver.

'We've spoken enough about me,' said Jasmin. 'If we're going to be friends, you must tell me about you, now.'

Sue was startled. Jasmin was an odd girl, hopelessly immature about some things, but direct, rather bossy too. Young. But clever. Sue had never met anyone quite like her.

'Me?' she said. 'There's nothing to say about me.'

'Nothing?'

'Married, two kids. Librarian.'

Jasmin saw Sue's eyes stray to the phone again.

'You really want this job, don't you?' she asked her.

'It would be nice.'

'Why?' Jasmin asked.

'Oh, because it would be a change, and I'd like to be the one they chose, and the holidays are good, and I could be with the children more.'

'Is it a promotion?'

'No, no. Actually it's a little less money, but that's because of the holidays.'

'Did you have a good interview?'

Sue laughed. 'It was certainly an ordeal. One of the interviewers fell asleep; the Head wouldn't let me get a word in edgeways; I had to take a class in the library, and they were demanding and squabbling just like Lizzie and Emma; the English teacher who used to be in charge of the library was looking daggers at me –'

'Not Miss Austin?'

'Yes, that was her name. But I think I did all right, on the whole.'

'It sounds awful.'

'Well, we'll have to wait and see.'

Jasmin reflected. 'Looking after the school library would

be quite a good job for someone who liked working on her own. Do you? I'm surprised old Austin's letting anyone else take over; it used to be her kingdom. Do they still have that tiny library office?'

'Yes. It was minute.'

'Don't you like your job at the Central Library?'

'Yes,' Sue said. 'But it's time for a change.'

'Why?'

The school reunion letter flashed into Sue's mind. She had not thrown it away. It was in a drawer with her discarded make-up. That was her youth in there.

'I want to make more of myself,' she said, half truthfully.

'What? By going back to school?'

Back to school. A wave of claustrophobia engulfed Sue. The tiny library office, the smell of bunsen burners, children tugging at her, teachers and their frosty disapproval. Her head throbbed. The day had been too exciting.

'If I was you,' Jasmin said, 'I wouldn't go back to school. If my children were growing up and I was free to get a new job, I'd go for something really exciting and different.'

She's hopelessly naïve, thought Sue, but then she's only twenty.

'What will you say if they offer you the job?' Jasmin asked her.

'Yes, of course,' Sue replied.

'So you really liked it then,' Jasmin asserted.

'Well, no,' admitted Sue. 'I can see there would be problems, but it would be lovely to get it. But I shan't get it anyway. I'll let the fates decide.'

'That's why Criseyde never went back to Troilus,' Jasmin said. '"Tendre-herted, slydynge of corage." She just waited to see what would happen. She didn't have the courage to leave the Greek camp and just do it.'

'What do you mean?' said Sue.

III

'Do you want the job at Boltham Grammar School, Sue? *You* decide.'

'I want to get it,' she said, thinking carefully.

'But do you want the job?'

'You know, Jasmin, when I was fifteen I went out with a boy, Dennis – what a silly name! – because he asked me. And then, after three weeks, he finished with me. And I thought I would be devastated. But actually I was very relieved. I never liked him anyway.'

'Ring the school up and say you've changed your mind,' Jasmin said, enjoying herself.

'I can't do that!'

'You can,' Jasmin said. 'I can't change my mind, but you can.'

There was a silence, apart from the thumping of toys on the carpet. Sue tried to imagine what it would be like, to turn down a job one had been offered. Telling someone to stuff their job. Intoxicating. Her eyes were caught by Jasmin's boots, lying tidily side by side next to the settee. They were large, rather clumsy Doc Marten's, both threatening and rather battered too. Imagine wearing boots like that, she thought. When she was Jasmin's age, the fashion was quite different. What shoes did she wear when she was twenty? She couldn't remember. But when the phone rang this time, Sue knew it was the school. And prayed it wasn't.

'Hello? Yes, it's me. Hello, Mrs Hamilton. Yes, yes, of course. Of course I understand. Yes . . . No . . . I quite see . . . No, I enjoyed it. Thank you very much . . . Thank you . . . Bye-bye.'

She turned to Jasmin. 'I didn't get it,' she said. 'They decided not to appoint. That English teacher's keeping it.'

Sebastian ran to Jasmin and the baby began to grizzle.

Sue breathed deeply to regain her composure. It was all over. She had not got it. She would have to tell everyone.

But worst of all, she felt she had been cheated. Because, in that infinitesimal moment before lifting the receiver, she had decided. She was going to turn the job down. At least, she thought she was going to. And now she would never know.

'Back to square one,' she said, with more cheerfulness than she felt.

'Never mind!' said Jasmin. 'You've got me instead.' She laughed. It was Jasmin's first laugh for some time, and Sue laughed with her. 'I've made a decision,' said Jasmin. 'I'm going to move out of Vicki's. I'm going home. I've got money and I know I'll feel so much happier. And then we can be neighbours. And you're right – I need to meet other mothers. A student environment is no preparation for motherhood.'

Sue picked the baby up and cuddled her.

'It's funny,' continued Jasmin. 'Here I am, about to be a mother, and here you are, having nearly done your time, and we're both terrified!'

Sue wasn't listening. She was practising accepting the fact that she did not have the job. Then she realized that the baby was wet through.

'Jasmin! I'll have to run you home now. The baby needs changing and I don't have any nappies.'

Jasmin swung her legs off the settee and bent down to put on her boots. It was awkward lacing them up over her growing stomach. She would have to go back to Vicki's now and maybe she would never see Sue again. Once her boots were on, she stood up.

'Sue,' she said. 'Please can I see you again? If it's not too much trouble. I like you very much. Can I?'

Sue did not understand why Jasmin's words healed the wound of her disappointment, but they did.

'Yes, of course,' she said. 'Give me your phone number

at Vicki's, and I'll give you mine, and you let me know when you're moving, and I'll give you a hand. I daresay Lizzie and Emma will too.'

'Thanks!' Jasmin said. 'You're much too good for Boltham Grammar. I'll think of something else you can try. It'll be something for me to do.'

'Want Mummy, want Mummy!' demanded Sebastian.

'Come on,' said Sue. 'We'd better get these two home!'

CHAPTER EIGHT

The knife rasped on the toast as Cheryl scraped on the Marmite. Then one, two, three deft strokes of the knife and there were four fingers of Marmite toast for Jenny's afternoon snack. Marmite contains vitamin B, thought Cheryl. What is that for? Is there a vitamin that helps develop your brain? Should she put Jenny on Multivitamins?

'Jenny!' called Cheryl.

Jenny arrived, expectant, looked round the kitchen and saw her Marmite on the stripy plate on her pussycat mat. She climbed on to the kitchen chair and picked up one finger of toast, nibbling at it with her front teeth. A pretty child, with a round face framed by wisps of curly hair.

Cheryl felt energized. The task facing her she saw as a challenge whose rewards were infinite. Jenny at Boltham Grammar Prep. Jenny at Boltham Grammar. 3 A-levels, grade A. University. Jenny in a mortar board and black gown. Jenny at the helm of industry. No! She would be a professor. Professor of Logic. At Harvard.

Jenny continued to nibble at her Marmite.

Cheryl had three months, give or take the odd week, to transform her daughter from a child who was bright – certainly bright, yards of potential – but who hadn't quite shown that potential at school yet – clearly the school's fault – to a child who would pass the Boltham Grammar Preparatory entrance examination with ease and assurance.

For that afternoon, after returning from Arthur's mother's, she had sat by the telephone, flexing her fingers with nerves, and dialled the Boltham Grammar School number, had requested an entry form and had been assured that Jenny stood as good a chance as the earlier entries. And at her request she had been put through to the Head of the Preparatory Department, who had told her what level candidates were supposed to have reached. Her words buzzed in Cheryl's mind, weaving in and out of her everyday thoughts. She washed the knife, placed it in the rack. Addition and subtraction up to twenty. She scrubbed the new potatoes. Simple sentence construction. She listened to Jenny's tuneless hum. Telling the time, independent reading, giving change.

'Jenny, love,' said Cheryl, suddenly possessed by an idea. 'Would you like to play a game?'

'A game!'

'I'll just wash my hands,' Cheryl said, 'and you go into the lounge.'

Cheryl followed her, bringing her purse and a tray of earrings she had been sorting that afternoon. Once in the lounge, she poured the earrings out on to the glass coffee table in a soft profusion of colour and glitter. Jenny advanced. She did not know why, but she supposed she had been a good girl, as Mummy did not often let her play with the earrings. She feasted her eyes on the tiny beads and glittering crystals and twists of metal, her fingers itching to gather them all up. She risked a poke at the one like a gold leaf.

'We're going to play shops!' announced Cheryl brightly. 'Who do you want to be?'

'A shopping lady!' Jenny said.

'I'll be the shopkeeper. Here's some money for you –' Cheryl pushed over a handful of coins – 'and here's some for me. Lovely. Now you can come to my shop!'

'I have these,' Jenny said, taking the pair of gold leaves.

'That's seven pence,' said Cheryl.

Jenny took the earrings and held them up to her ears.

'Seven pence, please!'

From her store of money Jenny counted out seven coins and pushed them over.

'No,' said Cheryl. 'That's too much. You've given me forty-one pence.'

'I want to buy the red ones now!'

'No, no. You must give me seven pence.'

Jenny pushed over all her money.

'No,' Cheryl said. 'Look. Two and two and two and one are seven!'

'Mummy, I be a lady who's going to a party and I put the earrings on. Thank you, Mrs Shopkeeper. You got a very nice shop here. I come back next week. Bye-bye.'

'No, look at the money. I want you to count the money. Come back with those earrings, Jenny! They're expensive and you could break them. Jenny!'

'Sue! It's Sue. Mummy, it's Sue.'

Cheryl scrambled off the floor, flustered and frustrated. But next time, perhaps, next time she would capture Jenny's attention. She would get those Multivitamins after all.

At the front door, as Jenny had indicated, stood Sue. Cheryl eagerly let her in, remembering her interview and searching in Sue's face for signs of her success or failure.

'It's me!' Sue said redundantly. 'When you were at Boltham did you know a girl called Jasmin Carpenter?'

'Jasmin Carpenter? The name sounds familiar. Come in.'

Sue threw herself on to the settee and Jenny sidled up to the earrings and began to sort through them.

'Jasmin Carpenter,' repeated Cheryl. 'She was a very clever girl, wasn't she? She used to win prizes.'

'What did she look like?'

Cheryl shrugged. 'I never really knew her. Medium height, quite slim. I think she had hair tied back in a pony tail, very quiet.'

'I met her today!'

'What? At the school?' said Cheryl, confused.

'No. And by the way, I didn't get the job. But I didn't want it anyway. No, in the park.' And Sue related to Cheryl the story of her encounter.

'So will you see Jasmin again?' Cheryl asked.

'I must. There's no one responsible to look after her. Her parents are in Turkey.'

'Fancy getting a place at Oxford and then getting pregnant. Poor thing!'

Sue nodded, but she knew her nod was automatic, and somewhat deceitful. Jasmin was not an object for pity. She had sensed that much. Jasmin, despite her predicament, had a self-possession that Sue envied. Her afternoon with the girl had left her excited, fizzing. She *liked* Jasmin, coveted her poise and wished to see her again for her own pleasure, not out of a sense of duty. But she would not say that to Cheryl.

And she was glad. Sitting there in Cheryl's lounge, with Jenny paddling her fingers in Cheryl's earrings and the familiar disposition of Cheryl's furniture – Cheryl's lounge was back to front to Sue's lounge – made Sue realize that Jasmin was different; different from her, different from Cheryl, different from all the women she knew. Jasmin was her adventure, her quest, her maiden in distress. She felt suddenly possessive, and changed the subject.

'No, the school wasn't for me,' Sue said. 'I would have been lonely working there. I'd miss the company at the Central Library. I'm not sure I'd want to work with children all the time.'

'But it's a lovely school, isn't it? Sue's been to Boltham Grammar School today, Jenny! You can go there if you try very hard to do the things Mummy tells you to do! Sue, is there anything in the library about teaching your children at home? I'd be so grateful. The exam is in January.'

118

'I'll see what I can come up with,' Sue said. 'But I must go now. I've left the girls with Mark and that means pandemonium. See you later! Bye, Jenny.' And she got up to go.

'Are you sure you don't mind me going out?' Sue asked Mark, as he sat, with his back to her, contemplating the sports pages of the Saturday newspaper. Mark lifted and dropped his shoulders in an expressive shrug. It said, of course I mind but I'm far too easy-going to object and, anyway, why should I care? Sue knew it was the best she could expect. Now she would attempt to say goodbye to the girls, and quickly, or else she would be late in collecting Jasmin. Sue heard sounds of giggling and thumping from their bedroom, ran upstairs and opened the door.

'Bye, girls. I'm just off out.'

'Where are you going, Mummy?' asked Lizzie, flushed from some energetic bouncing game.

'To help someone move house,' she said. 'I did tell you. She's a girl called Jasmin who's going to have a baby.'

'Can I come?' Lizzie asked.

'And me!' That was Emma.

'No. I'll be carrying lots of things and I don't want you in the way. I think you'd find it boring. Daddy will look after you.' Their faces dropped and then lightened again at some thought, and Sue caught a look they exchanged, a knowing look, a look that spelt mischief. Well, she thought, that's Mark's problem, not mine. I'm going out. The girls came and hugged her, Emma pushing her face into her mother's stomach.

'Remember to go to bed reasonably early and brush your teeth properly and don't make too much noise!' Sue said in parting. She was eager to go. She shut her daughters into their bedroom, ran back down the stairs, shouting a general

'Bye' – no reaction – and was out into the darkening evening street.

First she was to drive to Jasmin's friend who lived at Mill Lane to collect Jasmin and her belongings, then she had promised Jasmin she would help her settle in the Rectory. New scenes, thought Sue, as she pushed down the back seats of the car to maximize space. The thought pleased her. She felt nervous and excited, as a young girl. For Jasmin had that effect on her. It was as if her youth was catching. And besides, she had not made a new friend for some time.

And what, she thought, as she drove down the cul-de-sac, shall I think about tonight? Quite conscious what she was doing, she tried to select a fantasy from her repertoire. Being offered promotion. What she would say to the Education Secretary about the state of Lizzie's school building. Going to the reunion, and seeing Michelle and everyone turn and look at her with admiration. No. None of them appealed tonight. She was living in the present. She was going to help Jasmin move.

'Thank God!' breathed Jasmin, as she shut the car door. 'I've escaped.'

'Come on!' said Sue. 'I thought they both seemed very nice, and very fond of you.' She had come away with an impression of a very pretty girl and her doting husband, living in a friendly chaos. Each treated Jasmin with genuine concern.

'Yes, and I like them too,' Jasmin said. 'But not to live with. I want to live at home. Home,' she said, her voice resonating.

Sue kept her eyes on the road as she drove back to Heaton Close but was superaware of Jasmin's presence. She noticed when Jasmin lifted a finger to rub the side of her nose, and then gazed straight ahead of her, lost in thought. She answered Sue's inquiries about her general health very fully and promised she had caught up with her sleep, but there was a desultory quality in her answers, and Sue suffered a momentary sense of dislocation – what was she doing, driving along the high street, past the launderette, the Traditional English Chippy and the darkened doorways of tobacconists, with a girl she hardly knew? For Jasmin was only ten years older than Lizzie! Bags of books, boxes, suitcases bumped and banged in the back as Sue drove along. This was the contents of Jasmin's trunk that had arrived last week at Vicki's.

Driving around the perimeter of the Heaton estate, Sue found the lane that led to the Rectory. In fact the Rectory was only a few minutes' walk from her house, but of course on this occasion it was necessary to approach it by car. A tall shadowy hedge hid most of the house. Sue slowed the car down and drew to a halt, feeling like an intruder.

'No,' said Jasmin. 'You don't need to leave the car here. You can drive round the back and park by the kitchen door. It'll be easier for carrying things.'

She indicated to Sue the presence of a driveway that led around the side of the house. Headlights illuminated dark brick walls, two rusty dustbins and a car-port. They got out into darkness, and silence too. Sue watched Jasmin as she extracted from the deep pockets of her coat a set of keys, which she had picked up from the agent earlier. She inserted one into the kitchen door, and the door opened. More darkness. Jasmin disappeared, and all of a sudden there was a blaze of light and a real kitchen appeared – a large, square kitchen, complete with Aga, oak table in the centre and Laura Ashley wallpaper. It was a bare kitchen: the dresser was bereft of china, the hooks for the saucepans were empty; there was a dank, damp aroma.

121

'I haven't been here for over two years,' Jasmin whispered, looking around her with something rather like awe. She whispered, because she believed the house was asleep. This was her home, this was not her home; the room was the same, the room lacked something. Jasmin felt the need to tiptoe round the house, to watch it sleep and to wake it up only very, very gently.

'Come with me, Sue,' she said.

Together they left the kitchen and Jasmin illuminated next a large front room, with polished floorboards and a fading Indian carpet. There was a *chaise-longue* under the window; there was another empty display cabinet; there was a mahogany dining table with upholstered chairs. Jasmin then led Sue into the hall – a square hall, with panelled walls and a painting of the Rectory in a late Victorian style. Opposite was the entrance to another front room and this, like its partner, had a wooden floor and antique furniture, but also rows of empty bookshelves. Here was a piano. Jasmin lifted its lid and played a few notes. They reverberated and thumped their way around the room. Beyond an archway Sue thought she could make out a study.

Then, upstairs. Past more panelling and framed prints. A narrow landing, squeaking floorboards. One double bedroom – 'my parents' room' – another, apparently a spare room, a bathroom with a free-standing white porcelain bath and then – 'My room!' said Jasmin at last.

First Jasmin noticed that there were neither sheets nor duvet on her bed; her mattress lay bare. Her shelves were empty too. But there, from her window, was the darkness of the trees that had been so familiar to her.

'Once I bring all my own things back into here,' Jasmin said, 'it will look like it's mine again. I think there's some bedding at the top of my wardrobe.'

Sue watched Jasmin move over to her bed and sit on it, very, very slowly, and look round her room. She placed a hand on either side of her on the mattress and pressed down.

'I'm having a baby,' she said, to the room, to the house, to herself. She looked down at her thick waist. Then she looked up at Sue, framed in the doorway, anxious, concerned.

'I feel like some girl out of a kitchen-sink drama,' she said, wonderingly. 'Comes back home pregnant. Lost childhood.' She was silent. Sue ached for her. Then Jasmin grinned suddenly. 'An empty room; a brimming womb!' Jasmin flung her arms out and fell back on her mattress, letting herself bounce gently, and once again Sue was struck by her resemblance to Lizzie.

'I'm home! I'm home! I'm home!' Jasmin spoke as she moved up and down on the bed. A fleeting memory of Tom on her, of men and sex, made her sit up, and then she became more fully aware of Sue.

'You must think I'm mad,' she said. 'I suppose I am, a bit. But I'm glad to be home, and such a lot has happened. Thanks for bringing me here.'

'That's fine,' Sue said. 'Let me empty the car now. Come down with me and tell me what goes where. I don't want you to do any lifting at all.'

'That's the last one,' Jasmin said, as Sue staggered upstairs with another box of books. 'Leave it with the others and tomorrow I'll put them all away. Then it's just the suitcase and that goes upstairs too. I'll sort out the pots and pans and stuff I bought and put them in the kitchen.'

Sue felt hot and knew that she was sweating slightly. That always made her hair go lank. Panting, she reached the top of the stairs and took the box into Jasmin's bedroom, and laid it next to several other similar ones. Just the suitcase now. She pressed on, back down the stairs, out through the kitchen, where Jasmin was sorting things, and then out to the car. She took the suitcase and locked the boot. Leaning to one side to compensate for its weight, she took the stairs more slowly this time and soon was back in Jasmin's bedroom. Then, on a sudden impulse, she took the chair from the desk and stood it against the wardrobe. She climbed up and, sure enough, there were sheets, and even a duvet. She threw them all down on the floor and proceeded to make up a bed for Jasmin, tucking in the pale-blue sheet, pulling the duvet cover over the white duvet, finding a pillow and a pillowcase – and there – a made-up bed! Sue was pleased with herself and wiped the sweat from her forehead.

Now, she thought, she would return to help Jasmin in the kitchen. She opened the door, and Jasmin was no longer bent over a box. She was sitting at the kitchen table smiling, a bottle of champagne in front of her and two fluted champagne glasses.

'This is for you, Sue!' she announced, with obvious pleasure. 'Thank you for all your help, and please will you come to my housewarming party!'

'Oh, Jasmin, you shouldn't!' Sue immediately regretted the platitude. The truth was, she knew, that nothing was more appealing to her right now than a glass of champagne and a chance to talk with Jasmin.

'It's not very cold, I'm afraid. It's been in the fridge at Vicki's, and she did lend me a Cool Bag, but I don't think it's been very effective.'

Sue placed her hand on the side of the bottle. 'It's fine!' she said. 'But if it's travelled all the way from Vicki's, it's going to be a very lively bottle of champagne.' At Jasmin's insistence, Sue took the bottle, opened the kitchen door, removed the metal fastening around the cork and gently, gently eased the cork out of the bottle. She tensed for the explosion. Then, a very satisfying 'pop' and a gush of champagne, spraying all over the kitchen doorstep. Jasmin ran to her with the glasses and they filled both, mostly with bubbles, and drank.

'A toast!' cried Jasmin. 'To my homecoming, to my baby, to Sue Turner – and to both of us!' They drank again. Sue loved the clear, sharp taste of champagne; she did not often buy it. She enjoyed the tingle of bubbles in her mouth as she drank. Both Sue and Jasmin now sat down, each pleasantly aware of the intimacy of the setting; each, for their own reasons, excited.

'I shall only have one glass of champagne,' Jasmin said decisively. 'The rest is for you. You can walk home from here and collect your car in the morning. I read in a book that expectant mothers should only have one drink at a time, and, anyway, it makes me feel hot and heavy.'

'You can't sit there and watch me getting drunk!'

'Don't worry about me,' Jasmin replied. 'I have something else too.' From the embroidered bag lying on the table, she took a small cosmetic purse of the sort that Sue herself used to be discreet about her tampons. From it she watched Jasmin extract a brown envelope and, from that, a small package containing a dark-brown block. Sue knew immediately what it was. Jasmin continued to fish around in her bag for a packet of cigarettes and some papers; then, with the skill born of practice, she constructed an elegant joint.

Sue felt uneasy. Cannabis was illegal. Once or twice as a student she had tried a little but, not being a smoker, she had never dabbled further. Now her perception of drugs had changed. Drugs, like Sex and Strangers and Unemployment, were shadowy entities waiting to threaten Lizzie and

Emma. Jasmin inhaled with pleasure and a lack of concern for Sue's silence.

'Do you?' she said, offering Sue the joint.

Sue shook her head hurriedly. 'No,' she replied. 'I don't smoke.' She could not help but inhale the pungent smoke, smelling, she thought, like some sort of scented tea, or burning leaves in the autumn. 'It won't harm the baby, will it?' she asked. It was a way of voicing her discomfort.

'It'll harm her less than half a bottle of champagne, and far less than regular smoking. I only do it on special occasions, and tonight is a special occasion for me. There, look,' she said, placing her hand on her stomach. 'She's kicking. Cool!'

Sue laughed. 'So it's a girl?'

'Mmm. Alison Grainne Carpenter. No – Alison Susan Grainne Carpenter. Nearly all of Chaucer's heroines are called Alison. Grainne is my tutor, and it's a beautiful name. And Susan is for you.'

'Me?' said Sue, incredulous and flattered.

'Yes. Because you're helping me, and all my other friends belong to my other life, and I'm taking a year off my other life.'

'Who are your friends?' Sue asked, enjoying listening to Jasmin's clear articulation, and studying her fine, mobile features.

'Juliet – she does English too. She's in my year at St Luke's. She's very bubbly and lots of fun. Sarah and Laura. We all walk to lectures together, when we bother to go. There was Isabel too, but she was older than me. She's working in Manchester on some pirate radio station. She's hoping they'll get a proper licence soon. I must ring her and find out.'

'That must be fun, working in radio,' Sue mused longingly. 'Is that what you want to do?'

'No,' said Jasmin, with decision. 'I want to go on and do a Ph.D. Then teach. Or write. Criticism or biography. Or poetry.'

'Poetry!' said Sue. 'You write poetry?'

'Yes,' Jasmin replied. 'Not very often. It's sort of experimental poetry. I don't think poetry always has to make sense. Sometimes it's sense not to make sense. I like the sound of words.' Her face lit up. 'Do you know, Sue, some of the best words I've ever met are in the pregnancy books I've been reading. I've collected them and I'm building up a poem. Listen. I'll read it to you!'

Excited, Jasmin once again scrabbled in her bag and this time brought out a small notebook with Winnie the Pooh on the cover. Lizzie had one just like it. Jasmin flicked through its pages, then smiled, as she found what she was looking for. Resting her joint in the ashtray, she stood up and cleared her throat in mock seriousness.

'Trimester,' she declaimed.

'Trimester
Vernix trimester.
Vernix lanugo trimester.

'Prostaglandin meconium
Prostaglandin meconium
Braxton Hicks.

'Primagravida
Perineum
Braxton Hicks.

'Braxton Hicks
Episiotomy
Human
Chorionic
Gonadotrophin.

Vernix lanugo trimester
Braxton Hicks
Braxton Hicks!'

Jasmin exploded with infectious laughter. 'Braxton Hicks!' she repeated. 'Who on earth was he? Imagine being remembered in perpetuity as a contraction! Braxton Hicks. Good chap, worked in reinsurance; caught the 8.06 from Purley every morning. And lanugo. Isn't that wonderful? It sounds like an imaginary island. I'm a primagravida: that sounds like a dowager duchess. The honourable primagravida is entering now, on the arm of the Right Honourable Lord Vernix.'

'Jasmin,' warned Sue. 'Have you had too much of that cigarette?'

Obligingly, Jasmin stubbed the joint out. 'Yes, I probably have. I feel quite light-headed, but that could be the tobacco, as I've not smoked for a bit. Well, I think it's a good poem!'

'So do I,' said Sue. She realized she was feeling a little light-headed too, and she enjoyed it. 'So you've been reading pregnancy books!'

'Yes. Aren't they sexist? One said, "Now it's time to relinquish a few of your chores to your husband!" I understand pregnancy and labour now, and I could probably write an excellent essay on them.'

'No,' said Sue. 'You're not expected to write an essay. You just *do* it.'

'I know,' Jasmin exclaimed. 'And the books don't prepare you for that. No one prepares you for that. But I want to be prepared. I'm going to the hospital next week, you know. For my first scan.'

'Isn't that a little bit late?'

'Yes. It's because I transferred from Oxford to Boltham,

128

and it took ages for all the records to come through. So I'm off to Boltham General on Friday. I'm looking forward to it.'

'Friday? I'm working. Otherwise I'd have taken you.'

'Thanks, Sue. Another time would be lovely. I'll take a taxi both ways. I have the money.' Jasmin thought of her cheque. 'Look,' she said. 'I must go to the loo. I won't be a moment.' She rose from her chair and left the room.

Sue traced the flutes on her glass with her finger. Jasmin was extraordinary, she decided. She wondered what sort of mother she would make. Original, certainly. A better mother than she was, more than certainly. Imagine giving up Oxford for a baby. It was an incomprehensible act of self-sacrifice. Sue pictured Jasmin's other life. Jasmin and Juliet and Sarah at parties; sophisticated young men, shadowy cloisters, anticipation and excitement, and that sense of having a future. She ached with envy.

'Oh, God,' said Jasmin, stumbling at the doorway. 'It's the way you're sitting at the table. For one minute I thought you were my mother!'

Sue felt hurt by that. 'No, I'm not,' she said. 'But now you've mentioned it, what does your mother think of you living here? Will she come and join you?'

Jasmin's face closed. She shook her head as she resumed her place at the table. Sue, emboldened by alcohol, decided to press on. There were certain questions she had to ask: things she had to know to regularize her relationship with Jasmin; things she had to know – just because she was curious.

'Jasmin, why haven't you told your mother that you're pregnant?'

A silence.

'Jasmin?'

Jasmin looked down. Sue watched her expression change. First she looked sombre, then her mouth twisted and she was smiling. A ripple of laughter escaped her.

'It's worked beautifully,' she said. 'Mum writes to me at Oxford and Juliet forwards my letters. I don't want her to know because it's a surprise!'

'Some surprise!'

Jasmin swallowed her laughter. 'Sue, you must think I'm awful. Look, come with me.' She rose, and Sue followed her into the dining room, to the display cabinet, and watched Jasmin open a small drawer. She took out a framed photograph. 'This is my mother,' she said.

Sue took it greedily. She saw a woman in her early fifties, grey hair impeccably styled in soft, regular waves. Jasmin's fine bone structure and aquiline nose. The eyes assured. No, not assured. The eyes absolutely certain, highly intelligent, penetrating, proud – very proud. A flattering silk blouse, fastened at the neck with a cameo brooch. But those eyes. Sue quailed before them.

'That,' Jasmin said, 'is the perfect mother.'

Jasmin's mother smiled back at Sue with ineffable wisdom. She held the photograph, spellbound. Jasmin sat on the *chaise-longue*, swung her legs up and lay back. When she spoke, it was to herself, but Sue knew she was privileged to listen. All the time she held the portrait in her hands.

'When she finds out about my baby, I bet she won't be shocked. She will arrange the delivery, the baby's welfare and decide precisely what the best thing is to do next. She'll plan my baby's future like she planned mine. That's why I won't let her near my baby.

'I've never spoken about this before. But it's coming clear now. Maybe it's the dope. But my mother really was the perfect mother. She told me she was only going to have one child, so that she could bring it up properly. That was me.

She gave up her job – she's a child psychologist – and cared for me. All my food was homemade, and she read to me every night, and played with me. She never lost her temper, never. When I was naughty, she would sit down and explain to me why my behaviour was antisocial, and its possible negative consequences. Once I deliberately threw a slice of wholemeal bread and butter on the carpet and trod on it. I knew she was watching. She just explained that I did that because of my unconscious desire for rebellion and assertion.

'But I didn't have an unhappy childhood. Far from it. I was constantly occupied and I learned to read when I was three. I was – I am – very intelligent, I know, and I think my mother's constant company made me even more preco-cious. I was teased at school – that was the worst of it – but I soon learned to act like the others, so I would be left alone. Even when I wasn't at school, my life was timetabled. Piano lessons, and the clarinet. The Brownies. French les-sons at eight. Swimming. All that sort of thing. My parents never left me with a babysitter; I went with them when they went out. At twenty-three months, my mother told me, I could recognize three different types of cheese.

'When I was a child I was very proud of my mother, and I boasted at school that we were best friends and that I could tell her everything. When I started at Boltham Gram-mar, she became a parent-governor, and helped with fund-raising. She drove me to school and collected me, and took me to the library for project work. I knew some of my friends were jealous of my mother. Often it was just us. Dad's always had to travel. He's very sweet but he's ruled by her.

'I was allowed out when I was a teenager. She never stopped me meeting boys. She wasn't a restrictive mother; she was the perfect mother. She drove me to parties, and discussed contraception and relationships and peer group pressure. She offered her services should I need to talk things through with her. The awful thing was, I did. I would regale her with accounts of my boyfriends' speeches and behaviour. She made useful comments.

'In the sixth form, we were alone all the time. Dad had his posting to Istanbul, and she decided that she would stay in Boltham with me, and then, when I went to university, she would go out and live with him. Then I would fly out there for vacations. When I was in the sixth form, I read and read and read. I read about mothers in fiction and I began to understand that my mother was stifling me. It was terrifying, that thought. I wrote a story which I've never shown anyone about a girl who was born by parthenogenesis and her mother turned her into a clone of herself so she could have eternal life. But reading all those novels provided me with the solution to my dilemma. I learned that there was one way that worked, to throw off your mother's influence, and that was having sex.

'So when I went to Oxford I decided to lose my virginity as soon as possible. I did it in my third week. And all the time I thought I saw my mother watching me, advising me on technique. And I thought I hadn't shocked her quite enough. So I had other men. And I felt better, but still haunted. Every vacation I went back to her, and nothing had changed. She was utter perfection. It froze me.

'Now I can see why I got myself pregnant, Sue. I've never been able to shock my mother. And it's not only that. If I become a mother, then I stop being a daughter, in a way. And I'm free. The spell is broken, and I can't start all over again.'

Jasmin closed her eyes. She felt suddenly very sleepy, very relaxed, very calm and clear. Sue regarded the woman in the photograph again.

'Sue,' said Jasmin sleepily. 'What's your mother like?'

132

Sue sat by Jasmin on a straight-backed chair. 'Not like yours. She worked very hard, as my dad was unemployed for some time. She worked and looked after us, and often got in terrible tempers or sulks. She always told me and my sister we were to get ourselves an education, so as not to be like her. I watched her cook and clean for us while Dad took long walks to cheer up. I knew she didn't have a fair deal. So I got an education. But I've ended up rather like her anyway. It's frightening, isn't it?' There was no reply. 'Isn't it?'

Jasmin was breathing deeply and regularly. She had fallen asleep. For a few moments Sue watched the rise and fall of her body. Then, rather sleepy herself, she whispered Jasmin's name, to wake her. She helped her off the *chaise-longue*, and then up the stairs, and took her to her bedroom. Jasmin did not notice that the bed was made. Unaffected by Sue's presence, she pulled off her leggings and sweatshirt, revealing her swollen womb and her young body. Sue turned away, to tidy some boxes. When she turned again, Jasmin was tucked up in bed.

'Goodnight,' Sue said. 'I've enjoyed myself very much.'

'Come and see me tomorrow,' Jasmin murmured. 'Thank you, Sue.'

'Thank *you*,' Sue replied.

All the lights were out at 8 Heaton Close. Sue turned her key in the lock and stepped into her hall. Mark must have gone to bed. She looked into the lounge: the floor was scattered with colouring books and crayons and socks and leggings and T-shirts and trolls and torn sheets of paper; Mark had evidently not bothered to tell them to tidy. There were empty glasses by the gas fire and newspaper littered the armchair.

She shut the door firmly. She would sit in the kitchen for a while. She could not possibly go to bed. The champagne had made her mind race. She wondered about a coffee, or perhaps another drink. The work-surfaces in the kitchen were un-wiped; dirty knives littered them; the wrapping from a packet of Abbey Crunch biscuits was waiting to be thrown away.

In disgust, Sue left the kitchen and went to sit in the dining room. It was late – nearly twelve o'clock. The street was quiet. Jasmin was lying asleep in her large house. Sue pictured her there, and absorbed what she had learned tonight. Ought she to persuade Jasmin to inform her mother? Was she wrong not to? But Jasmin was twenty and had therefore reached the age of majority.

Jasmin's mother was the perfect mother, then. So perfect that her daughter hated her. It appealed to Sue that her daughter should reject her so utterly. It shed a kind light on her own imperfections. The perfect mother has imperfec-tions, then, she thought, her head spinning.

And are we all like our mothers? I shout like my mother, and sulk like her, and, even though I know I ought to share the children fully with Mark, I don't. Because the perfect mother does it all herself. My mother did it. Which is why she shouted and sulked. As I do. And what about Jasmin? She's trying not to be like her mother. Sue wondered how Jasmin would bring up her child. Would she smoke canna-bis too? And recite poetry?

Jasmin lying on the *chaise-longue* . . . Jasmin reclining at the table with her joint . . . Jasmin's eyes alight with mis-chief as she read her poem . . . Jasmin at Oxford, walking and laughing with her friends in a college quad . . .

I wish I was Jasmin, she thought.

Sue rose to go to bed. She turned off the light in the dining room and walked into the hall. There she was, in the hall mirror. When she saw herself she was shocked. She was a nondescript woman approaching forty. There were

134

shadows under her eyes. Compared to Jasmin, she was old; Jasmin had mistaken her for her own mother. Not surprising. Sue looked again at the woman in the mirror. She saw her ageing skin and shapeless features.

She turned from the mirror. She couldn't remember what she looked like when she was Jasmin's age. Yes, she could. She wore eyeliner – black cake eyeliner that you spat in, with a little brush. Mascara on wands like Christmas trees. Mary Quant green eyeshadow. She was a delicious confection – a feast for the opposite sex. Jasmin wore no make-up; girls didn't so much nowadays.

Sue breathed in deeply and made herself look in the mirror once more. Now, at her age, she really did need make-up. What if, she thought, what if I had my hair cut? Short. And what if I began to wear make-up again? She smiled at herself alluringly. What if I bought something new to wear?

Several women stood in a close group, holding glasses of wine, talking, laughing. Their heads turned as a newcomer walked into the room.

She was a tall, powerfully attractive woman, with a gamine hair cut, translucent skin and deep, liquid eyes, thrown into relief by the skilful application of cosmetics. No one recognized her; no one could suppress a spurt of envy. She had kept her figure too.

'Sue!' cried a voice. Michelle ran to her and held both her hands, looking at her with flattering astonishment. 'You look better than you ever did!'

If I go to the reunion, thought Sue, ascending the stairs, I shall need a new outfit, of course. And perhaps a new look too. As a sort of consolation present for not getting the job. When I was a younger mother, she thought excitedly, brushing furiously at her teeth, I couldn't take care of my appearance. I let my standards slip. But now, I'll make up

135

for lost time. Already, she thought, as she smiled at herself in the bathroom mirror, her mouth flecked with white foam, I'm looking better.

The landing light revealed the humped form of Mark in the centre of the bed. If I look good, Sue thought, he'll notice me again. It might be what we both need. She undressed quickly. I shall make a day of it, she decided. I shall have my hair done, and I shall have my face done too.

Jasmin would approve, she thought, as she tugged the duvet from Mark. She'll see that I'm actually doing something. I never got the chance to turn down that job, but I'll show her I can change something.

CHAPTER NINE

The Hair and Face Place, it was called. Sue remembered a time when all hairdressing salons and beauty parlours had French names at the very least, but Boltham's was characteristically chummy and down to earth. The Hair and Face Place. The hairdressers worked downstairs and the beauticians upstairs, and it was the hairdressers Sue could see now as she approached the shop.

She was just a little early. She had managed to get the appointment in an extended lunch-hour at work. Yesterday she had stayed late at the library, so she would be free for the two or three hours it would take to reconstruct her. She had gone to work that morning with hair unwashed and without even the slightest touch of make-up. Everyone had inquired whether she was feeling ill. She had explained to Chris and Betty and Glenys what she was about to do, and their interest had been aroused. They had persuaded her to leave early and she had munched a sandwich as she walked along.

Now she was excited. It was true, she thought, peering into the interior of the glass-fronted salon, seeing young, intent hair stylists at work, responding to the throb of rock music. Here she could be transformed into something quite new – someone quite new. There was a familiar line of poetry in her head. Yeats, was it? 'A terrible beauty is born.' She stepped inside.

To her left was a reception desk and she approached it, taking in at once the extreme youth of the girl at the desk, and her unkempt appearance – she wore a wide-necked pullover which revealed black bra straps; her hair seemed to be deliberately knotted. This must be grunge, Sue realized. She explained her double appointment to the girl, who announced breezily, 'Take a seat!'

But Sue did not want to sit down. Nervous, she wanted to stand, to pace around, but ordered in this way she felt it impossible not to comply. So she lowered herself on to a black plastic settee opposite the reception desk and proceeded to wait. Over the insistent pulsing of the music, she heard a crackling Boltham voice announce 'Karen!' That was her hairdresser being summoned. She reached out for a magazine on the glass table by her side as a camouflage. She did not want to read; she wanted to study the other clients. The hairdresser who had given Sue her perm a year ago was a local woman who was mobile and had come to Sue at home. It was some time since she had been in a fashionable salon. It interested her that there were men being coiffeured, as well as women, both staring with a fixed, abstract concentration into the large mirrors in front of them. Sue regarded the hairdressers and wondered who Karen could be. When she had booked several days ago, the receptionist had said that Karen was very good, very experienced, and she could personally recommend her. Sue guessed she was probably the tall woman dressed in a short, uneven black frock, with sleek black hair in a short bob.

She turned her attention to the magazine, scanning the shout lines on the front cover. The Thinking Woman's Guide to Finance. Bianca Jagger. Cellulite. I was a Sex Addict – one woman's story, page 73. Sue turned to page 73: 'Nina (not her real name) slammed her front door shut, turned, and threw herself into the arms of the man she had just brought home from her local nightclub. His name, his identity, were immaterial. She clawed at his shirt . . .'

'Mrs Turner?'

Sue put down the magazine reluctantly and looked up into the face of another very young girl, with a mane of rich brown hair, the fringe neatly styled into a kiss-curl, held in place with some brittle-looking hair preparation.

'I'm Karen,' she said.

Sue rose, flustered. She followed Karen over to a black plastic seat like a dentist's chair and, when invited, sat down and looked straight ahead of her, at a pale, rather jowly woman, with straggly, mousy hair. Karen grinned at this apparition conspiratorially.

'And what are we doing for you?'

Jasmin slammed the door of the taxi shut and paused at the main entrance of Boltham General Hospital. The taxi driver had explained that the maternity department was in the main building and she would have to walk through it to reach the antenatal clinic.

Jasmin could not remember the last time she had been in a hospital. There was the time, a few years ago, when her father's sister had broken a leg, but she was in a small private hospital which had oozed discretion and affluence. The main entrance of Boltham General Hospital was vast, with a bewildering array of direction signs. Jasmin stood to read them. Antenatal clinic, straight ahead. She set off along the wide corridor, occasionally glancing down corridors labelled 'Neurology', 'Pain-Relief Clinic', 'Radiography'.

She had dressed in subfusc. She wore her black skirt, a baggy white blouse and black woollen tights. She had thought it advisable, fearing that the doctor might question her single-mother status – she wanted to appear old and responsible. There were bound to be questions, she knew, about why she had left this first hospital appointment so late. But it was not entirely her fault. She had not visited her GP in Oxford until she had returned from Istanbul.

She was already fifteen weeks pregnant. Jasmin had informed her that she wanted to have the baby in Boltham, and so the GP had written to Jasmin's home doctor, and there was delay in forwarding some notes. Then she had waited again to receive an appointment letter from the hospital, and that was why she had reached her twenty-fourth week today and was only now booking in.

Over her shoulder, in the same embroidered bag that had lain on the kitchen table last Saturday night with Sue, was a small mustard jar containing her specimen, her appointment card and the text of *The Revelations of Divine Love*. Here it was. The antenatal clinic. Down a short corridor, to the right.

Jasmin walked into a large, busy reception area. Women were sitting around coffee tables, some talking, some reading magazines. To her left was an area only accessible through a little wooden gate, and here were a jumble of plastic toys that made her think of Vicki. That was the crèche. Two toddlers rummaged among the tops and shape-sorters and pull-along telephones. Jasmin looked around her again. So many pregnant women! She felt quite diminished. Partly aware of eyes following her, she made her way to the reception desk and gave her name, in round, ringing tones.

'Take a seat!' announced the receptionist cheerily. 'We'll call you in a moment.'

Jasmin turned back to the waiting area. All the small tables had chairs around them, and every group was occupied by two or three women. Jasmin did not particularly want to talk, and would have stood, reading her book, but she was aware of the possibility of swelling ankles and did not fancy that. So she sat when the opportunity was there, and made her way to a table where an elegant, self-contained woman sat reading a magazine and another woman, more obviously pregnant, sat doing a crossword. She looked up and smiled as Jasmin joined them.

'Your first, is it?' the woman inquired.

Jasmin nodded.

'My second. My mother's looking after Gemma today. How many weeks are you?'

'Twenty-four,' Jasmin said.

'First appointment?'

Jasmin nodded again.

'You'll be going for your scan, then. I hope they don't make us wait as long as they did last week. It's absolute hell. I had to go, and then they made me have drink after drink until I was ready, so I didn't get home till way past five.'

These remarks confused Jasmin, and her interlocutor picked up that fleeting look of incomprehension.

'Have they told you that you need a full bladder for the scan?'

'Oh, yes!' Jasmin agreed. But in fact she had forgotten. She focused on her bladder to see if it was full. Yes, it was quite. If she had to wait an hour or so, she should be fine.

'They think my baby's small for dates,' the woman continued. 'So I'm coming in every week for a scan, and they take blood, and I'm doing this kick chart too. But I told the midwife, we have them small in our family. Gemma was six one when she was born and there wasn't a fuss about her. Forceps, she was. It seemed like hours I was pushing. It's always worst with your first. I always told Melvin I never wanted to have another, but then this one came along.'

Jasmin tensed. Other women's labour stories frightened her. Well, she thought, I shall insist on an epidural like Vicki. And then if it hurts I shall have a Caesarean. She noticed a television set in another corner of the room, showing a poor-quality video of a woman breast-feeding, the voice-over crackling. No one was watching.

141

'They're very nice here,' Jasmin's companion continued. 'When I had Gemma –'

'Jasmin Carpenter!' announced a woman in a pale-blue housecoat. Jasmin stood up and made her way to the woman, who proceeded to walk briskly down a corridor beyond the waiting area. She ushered Jasmin into a small office that had a vacant/engaged sign on it, like a lavatory. Once Jasmin was inside, the midwife locked the door. She indicated that Jasmin should sit by the desk and then she took her place at it.

'I'm Mary Whelan. I'm your midwife.'

'And what are we doing for you?'

'Well,' said Sue, rather lamely, 'something different.'

Unasked, Karen picked up a stray lock of Sue's hair and examined it. 'Do you want all this off?'

'I think so, don't you?' Sue was floundering. She realized she did not know precisely what she wanted. The image in her mind, the image of this new Sue, young again, attractive again, successful, the head-turning Sue, was an outline only. She had vaguely thought it was the job of the hairdresser to say, what *you* need is . . .

'Are you going for something shorter?'

'Yes,' Sue said. An image of Jasmin came into her mind. Jasmin's hair was cut like a boy's, with a side parting. But then, she had that heart-shaped face and fresh complexion.

'What we could do,' Karen continued cheerfully, 'is take off the sides, and leave some straggly bits at the back to give it a softer outline, and we can brush the fringe to one side. That'll do. Tracey! Back-wash, please.'

An even younger girl arrived and mumbled to Sue that she was to follow her to the basins, where two other women were already having their hair washed. Sue did so, and sat up as the girl fastened a black smock around her, obligingly

142

stretched her head back and rested her neck on a porcelain ridge, waiting for the rush of water on her head.

Sue loved having her hair washed. The gentle, hesitant massage of the girl's fingers on her scalp was soothing, sensuous and utterly undemanding. Sue felt herself relax.

'Is it too hot for you?'

'No, no. It's fine.'

Sue opened her eyes. The ceiling was made up of mirrors. There it was, that reddened, jowly face of indeterminate age, with its uncertain eyes. There were faces on either side of her. One woman with well-defined cheekbones and deep-set eyes; the other with plump, pretty cheeks. Each, she thought, looked more real than she did. She closed her eyes again to enjoy the second shampoo.

Within a few moments she was sitting up, a towel wrapped round her head, and allowing Tracey to lead her to another seat, facing another huge mirror.

'Karen,' she called.

Sue could not resist sticking out her tongue at herself. She certainly was an apparition, towel-turbaned, the antithesis of glamour. Laughter came to rescue her from her self-consciousness. She felt delightfully silly.

Karen returned, removed the towel and began to snip away with cheerful assurance. Sue watched familiar locks of hair fall discarded to the floor.

'Going anywhere special tonight, then?' Karen asked.

'No, no,' Sue said.

More hair fell to the floor. Sue watched with a detached fascination.

'Just time for a change, is it?'

'Yes,' she said.

'Nice, isn't it, to have a change? Do you live local?'

'Yes, in Heaton.'

'It's nice up there. Near the park. Married, are you?'

'Yes, I've two little girls, eight and ten.'

'Lovely. I'd like a little girl myself, one day.'

Sue watched herself talking, watched how her wet, darker hair began to outline her face in a new way. Did she look younger? Better? It was too early to say.

'Going anywhere nice for Christmas?'

'No, just staying at home.'

'Me and my boyfriend are off to Marbella,' Karen said.

Sue watched her snip more off. Was it getting too short? Ought she to say something? Surely this Karen knew what she was doing?

'He's in timeshare. We get a free week as part of his commission.'

My God! thought Sue. She's cutting it too short.

'Lovely apartment. All mod cons. There. I'll just run some mousse through and give you a quick blow-dry.'

The woman staring at Sue in the mirror looked alarmed. Hot air buzzed around her as Karen wielded her hairdryer and styling brush. Sue watched herself take shape.

Karen switched off the dryer. 'There!' she said. 'What do you think?' She turned to fetch a mirror to show Sue the back.

It was as Karen had said. There was a soft outline at the back, where tendrils of hair framed her neck. Her fringe was full, but swept to one side. She saw how her hair was shaped above her ear. She certainly looked tidier . . . and different . . .

'It's lovely' said Sue. 'I really like it!'

Karen grinned.

Different . . . and more sophisticated, possibly. But not really younger. Sue pouted at herself. Yes, she did like it. No, it revealed too much of her face. Yes, it was an improvement. No, it . . .

Karen removed Sue's smock and led her back to reception. Sue glanced at herself surreptitiously in the mirror behind the receptionist. It wasn't too bad.

'Julie!' shouted the receptionist. 'Your appointment!'

Julie, Sue remembered, was her beautician for the afternoon. She looked impatiently at the far end of the salon, from which she expected the beautician to emerge.

'I'm Mary Whelan. I'm your midwife.'

'Hello,' said Jasmin. She took in all of her appearance at once, her rough, short, curly ginger hair, small, scrubbed, reddened face and cheerful, brisk manner. She gave an explanation to Jasmin of the hospital procedures, about records and blood tests and scans, but Jasmin wasn't really listening. She noticed the patterned wallpaper in the room, the rack containing leaflets on benefits and healthy eating in pregnancy, the fact the room had no windows.

'Now, I just have to go through some routine questions with you, which shouldn't take too long. Name?'

Jasmin answered.

'Address? . . . Date of Birth? . . . Married?'

'No,' Jasmin said.

'Any previous pregnancies? . . . And details about your medical history . . . Diabetes? Heart disease? Asthma?'

No, no, no. Jasmin felt her series of negatives was almost unintentionally abrupt. But really she had had hardly any contact with hospitals or ill-health. Her mother's sound nutrition had seen to that. But she felt unreasonably proud too of the illnesses she had not had, and the speed with which the midwife was able to complete the forms.

'So you're twenty,' the midwife commented thoughtfully, when she had finished completing the registration forms.

'Twenty-one on 1 January.'

'Are you living with the father?'

Jasmin shook her head.

'With your parents?'

'No,' said Jasmin. Taking a deep breath, she explained her situation. The midwife's face was impassive. 'And so my parents are in Turkey and can't possibly come over, but, as Sue is an old family friend, they're only too happy for me to live at home and for her to keep an eye on me,' Jasmin concluded brightly. She watched the midwife's eyes narrow as she absorbed all this. She crossed her fingers tightly on each hand and feared for her deception, because there was something in the midwife's face, an astuteness bred of having dealt with life perhaps, or at least the beginning of life.

'Are you happy about this pregnancy?' she asked Jasmin. Yes, there was a trace of an Irish accent.

'Oh, yes!' Jasmin said eagerly. 'I want the baby. It was an accident, but now I feel glad it's happened, in a way.'

Then, tactfully, the midwife probed Jasmin's financial situation, seeming satisfied, finally, with Jasmin's explanation.

'Have you thought about the type of maternity care you want?' she asked Jasmin. 'We offer the full range at Boltham, from home delivery with a community midwife, or the domino system, shared antenatal care, to total hospital care.'

'Yes,' said Jasmin. (She was in a tutorial again.) 'I've read about this. I have a number of books on pregnancy at home. Since I'm a first-time mother, and rather young, I suppose I really ought to have a hospital delivery, but as I'm very healthy and really will look after myself, I think I'd like shared antenatal care.'

The midwife observed Jasmin's self-possession with interest. 'That's fine. A wise choice. Now, as time is pressing, I'll take you to the examination room, where we'll just do the routine checks, and the doctor will take a look at you.'

146

She rose, and Jasmin rose, noticing now that she was an inch or two taller than the midwife. The locked door was opened and Jasmin followed Mary Whelan out along another corridor and into another small room, where there was a high, narrow bed, covered with a wide strip of perforated paper like a giant-sized kitchen towel. Jasmin tensed. It was silly, she knew, as her own GP had a similar one. But the bed spelt 'hospital'.

The midwife instructed her to remove the bottom half of her clothing and then left the cubicle. So Jasmin stepped out of her shoes, pulled down her tights, took off her knickers and, rolling up her skirt, got on to the high bed and took a cotton sheet that was provided to cover herself. She lay supine, and then she thought, no, she would like to sit up. When the midwife came back, Jasmin was sitting cross-legged on the bed, with the sheet swathed around her.

Jasmin held out her arm for her blood pressure to be taken, felt her arm tighten as the midwife inflated the tube wrapped around her. She reached down for her bag, passed the midwife her specimen and watched as the midwife quickly inserted a slip of card into it, like the litmus paper she used at school, and then discarded everything. Meanwhile, they chatted. Jasmin talked a little about her course at St Luke's, and about Boltham. But all the time she thought, how odd it is, to have a conversation with someone about medieval literature and the new shopping precinct while wearing no knickers.

'Everything seems to be fine,' the midwife said, smiling at Jasmin. 'I'll just go and see if Dr Rogers is ready.'

She looked impatiently at the far end of the salon, from which she expected the beautician to emerge. And she was not disappointed. The woman coming towards her was not

147

dressed in black and white, like the hair stylists, but wore a pale-blue housecoat; she looked brisk, efficient, clinical, inspiring confidence. She wore a name badge, inscribed 'Julie'.

'Are you my one o'clock?' she asked.

Sue nodded and rose to follow her, up a flight of metal stairs, like those on a ship. On the top floor were several cubicles, two with doors closed and two with doors open. Julie led her into one of these and closed the door.

Sue was surprised. The room was tiny, and in the middle was a high, narrow bed, covered by a long strip of perforated paper like a giant-sized kitchen towel. She had not imagined this. She had thought she would be sitting up in front of a mirror, and the beautician, like an eighteenth-century personal maid, would fuss around her, applying puffs, powders and patches. So Sue stood hesitantly by the side of the bed, fearing there had been a mistake. At the head of the bed was an array of equipment, and at the end of the bed something terrifyingly electrical, black straps hanging down by the side of it. Now she was reminded of the tale of Frankenstein.

'What's that?' she asked.

'Our Slendertone equipment,' Julie explained. 'I thought I had you down for a tint and make-up.'

'Yes, that's right,' said Sue, still puzzled about the bed.

'Hop on here, then,' said Julie, 'and we'll do the tint first. No, lie down on it,' she instructed Sue. 'No, you can keep your shoes on.'

Sue lay supine on the bed, feeling naughty for keeping her shoes on. When she had booked the appointment, and talked with the receptionist about ways of approaching a makeover, the receptionist had strongly recommended an eyelash tint, as she said it did away with the need for daily applications of mascara. That aspect of it appealed to Sue. Besides, Chris had hers done regularly.

148

'Is this for anything special?' the beautician asked, busying herself at Sue's head with certain preparations that Sue could not see, as she could see only the ceiling.

'No, no,' said Sue. 'I just want a change of image. To look more modern.'

The beautician laid what felt like strips of cotton wool just below Sue's bottom eyelashes and instructed her to close her eyes, which she did, immediately, and then the beautician applied something heavy and sticky – Vaseline? – to her eyelids. Then she felt a brush pass to and fro across her closed lashes, bringing something cold and wet with them. The dye, Sue supposed. It was peculiar and very interesting.

'Going away for Christmas?' asked the beautician.

'No', said Sue.

'Right. That's that done. I'll just leave you for a few moments while the dye takes. Don't open your eyes!' Sue heard the door open and close. She was alone.

'I'll just go and see if Dr Rogers is ready.'

Jasmin watched her go. Thinking that the doctor would come in any moment, she lay back on the bed and pulled the sheet over her tummy. There was no pillow, but the head of the bed was tilted up, although not enough for Jasmin's comfort. The blood rushed to her head. Soon she became acclimatized to this position.

Yes, her bladder was full. She was acutely conscious of it now, lying down. In fact, she was at that stage when, were she at home, she would have got up and gone to the loo. The feeling was like a sort of pressure, an itch, an urge to go. She imagined her bladder as a small balloon, filling with water. That made the feeling worse. She shifted slightly, hoping to get more comfortable.

She would think of something else. Of Sue. Sue was

having her hair and face done today, she knew. Perhaps it was a good thing. Sue needed some sort of boost. Jasmin was certain that life didn't end for a woman once her children were growing. And – ow! – yes, she really did need to go. There were little jabbing pains now. What if she couldn't control her bladder and she wet the bed? Unthinkable! She consciously tightened her bladder muscles. That made the desire to go even more unbearable.

Surely, she thought, the doctor would not be long? Surely they had a routine? Ought she to get up now and just find a toilet? But then, she would not be able to have the scan, and that was the main reason for coming here. Oh, no – the baby was moving. It shoved against her full bladder. Jasmin tensed. Exquisite agony. Her bladder pulsed with pain. Where was the bloody doctor?

Footsteps in the corridor. They passed her by. To go to find a toilet she would have to dress again. She could not possibly walk through the hospital corridor without any knickers. She looked at her watch. How long had she been on the bed? She did not know. All she was was a bladder, swollen and throbbing and agonizing. Where was the doctor? She would have to go. She would have to –

The door of the cubicle opened. In came the midwife with a young, white male in doctor's garb. He said nothing. He picked up her card and examined it, then lifted the sheet covering her. He is a doctor, Jasmin reminded herself consciously. He Is Not Interested In Me As A Woman. His cool hands felt her stomach, pressed lightly around her baby. She felt as if she were being moulded. He nodded in silence. Distracted, Jasmin felt the pain in her bladder recede.

'How many weeks are you?' he asked.

'Twenty-four,' she said awkwardly, for she was still on her back. He towered above her, it seemed.

150

'Are you sure of your dates?' he asked.

'Yes,' Jasmin said.

'Hmm,' he said.

Jasmin had never felt at such a disadvantage in her life. Here she was, bare from the waist, lying flat on a high table, her bladder full, an impassive male above her. The humiliation of it angered her. It felt like some strange pagan ritual, not like having a baby at all. So she sat up. The doctor looked faintly surprised.

'If you don't mind lying down again,' he said. 'There's a routine internal examination.'

'Why do I have to have an internal examination?' she asked.

'Routine. It's hospital policy,' he said.

'I don't want an internal,' Jasmin said. She looked at the midwife, who had her eyes directed to the floor.

'It doesn't hurt,' he said, as if he were talking to a child.

'I know it doesn't hurt,' Jasmin said. 'I've had them before. But I don't want one now.'

For a start, she was terrified that were she to submit to one, she would not be able to control her bladder. But there was something about the whole situation that made her rebel.

The doctor spoke with barely concealed irritation. 'I can't force you to have an internal examination, but I must warn you that we will not have the full complement of test results and this will prevent us from detecting a range of future complications.'

'OK,' said Jasmin. You wanker, she thought. He left the cubicle brusquely. The midwife remained. She winked at Jasmin.

'Can I go to the toilet?' Jasmin asked.

'Can you wait ten minutes?' she pleaded. 'There's only the blood tests, which I can do immediately, and then the scan.'

Her tone was kind, humorous and conspiratorial. Jasmin liked her. She dressed quickly, remembering her encounter with the doctor. Difficulties in labour, he had said. She might have difficulties in labour. What were they? Would she be all right? Would the baby be all right? Surely women didn't still die in childbirth? Difficulties? She thought of the books she had been reading. Breech delivery. Caesareans. Toxaemia. Foetal distress. All these things might happen. Feeling slightly nervous now, she followed the midwife down the corridor once more.

Sue heard the door open and close. She was alone. Don't open your eyes, the beautician had said. Don't open your eyes. Well, that was easy enough. She could have a rest, just relax. No. She desperately wanted to open her eyes. She must open them. The cotton wool the beautician had laid over her eyelids gently reminded her not to.

Sue tried to tense the muscles in her eyes to ensure that she wouldn't open them. If she opened them, she imagined, the tinting would not work. Or whatever was in the dye might make her eyes sting. She had better not open her eyes. Her eyes watered with the effort of keeping them closed.

She crossed, uncrossed her ankles. She was alone and felt claustrophobic, panicky. She would think of something else. Jasmin. Who had gone to Boltham General today. Jasmin, who would also be lying on a table like her, a sacrificial victim. Don't open your eyes. Sue remembered having Emma at Boltham General; she had liked it there. She had to remember to buy some extra potatoes for tonight. Don't open your eyes. She squeezed her eyelids together.

Something was stinging. Or was it her imagination? No, something *was* stinging. She would not think about it. She would count a whole minute. One, two, three, four, five, six, seven. Her eyes were watering in response to the irritation. But she knew nothing was seriously wrong as three days ago the salon had tested her for any allergic reaction to the dye. Ow! What a wimp she was! Keep your eyes closed, she instructed herself. Don't open your eyes. Six, seven, eight, nine, ten, eleven.

Surely the beautician hadn't forgotten about her? What if she had? Ought she to go and find her? Or shout? Because she wasn't allowed to open her eyes. Even her nose was throbbing with the stinging. She wanted to sneeze. She must remember to get the potatoes. Nine, ten, eleven, twelve. Two red-hot lines across her eyes. Twelve, thirteen, fourteen.

Sue heard the door opening. 'Right,' said the beautician. 'Let's see how we're getting on.' She lifted the cotton wool. 'Fine. Just a few more minutes.' Sue winced in agony. But this time the beautician stayed in the room, and this calmed Sue. I'll be brave, she thought. No pain, no gain. She concentrated on the movements of the beautician as she busied herself by Sue's head. Potatoes. You say potahtoes, she sang to herself, and I say potaytoes. Or is it tomatoes?

'OK!' said the beautician. 'You'll be done by now.' She lifted the cotton-wool pads again and wiped the excess dye from Sue's lashes, then dabbed them with something cooling. Oh, exquisite relief! Sue's eyes throbbed with gratitude.

'Right! You can sit up now.'

Sue did so, and looked into the mirror facing her. There was a jowly woman with short hair, white skin and two small, red eyes.

'That's great!' Sue said. 'Now what's next?'

Feeling slightly nervous now, Jasmin followed the midwife

down the corridor once more. They entered yet another small room, this one with a window looking out over a small courtyard littered with building material. Jasmin sat, while Mary Whelan busied herself preparing needle and syringe.

'A routine blood test,' she explained. 'For your blood group, and various other screening procedures. Does the needle worry you?'

The midwife noticed that Jasmin did not seem so much at ease now. She was scanning the poster on the wall that listed the tests her blood was to undergo. Some of them she had read about. Alphafoetoprotein, for example. The wrong level could indicate an abnormality. And HIV. That did not worry her so much. Up until her relationship with Tom, she had been scrupulous about using a condom, and although she had not always used one with Tom, she had good reason to know he was a virgin before he met her. What she was thinking about was something quite different. She did not know Tom's medical history. What if there were abnormalities in his family? A history of mental illness? Congenital defects? What if her baby, Alison Susan Grainne Carpenter, was not normal? Then what? She watched her blood fill the syringe. Could the midwife tell from the appearance whether it was all right or not?

'There, I've finished now. I'm sure you're glad that's over.'

'Yes,' said Jasmin.

'The next bit's the best bit,' Mary said, sensing Jasmin's alteration in mood. 'Have you had a scan before?'

'No,' Jasmin replied, as they left the room and proceeded yet again down a corridor. It's like an assembly line, Jasmin thought. A production line for babies.

'The radiographer will explain what you see, and you'll find it doesn't hurt a bit.'

154

The room they entered was bigger now, and the array of machinery intimidated Jasmin. She knew that childbirth was a natural process and yet, since coming into Boltham General, she had begun to feel that she was ill in some way – her urine, her blood tested, dire warnings of difficulties in labour, complex machinery trained to pick up any abnormality. She knew with her intellect that all this was for her benefit, but she was scared. She had not expected it, but she was. She would talk to Sue about it. At least she had Sue.

Once again Jasmin ascended a high, narrow bed. Once again she removed the bottom half of her clothing. Her bladder ached dully. Someone smeared Vaseline all over her tummy, cold and sticky. Then a roller moved across it back and forward, up and down. The screen by her side flickered. I want to go home, she thought.

She turned her head to look at the blurred TV screen, where swirls of darker and lighter shapes defied her interpretation.

'There we are!' said the radiographer, 'Look!'

Jasmin could see nothing. There was a sort of pulsation evident on the screen, and these darker and lighter shapes.

'Look,' repeated the radiographer, one hand on the scanning machine, the other pointing to the screen. 'There's its head, look – can you see that tiny ear? And you can just make out the chin there, and the mouth. Look! Your baby's kicking!' Jasmin felt the movement in her womb, looked on the screen and there was movement, like a sort of waving, from what was apparently the baby's leg. 'There's the baby's backbone,' the radiographer continued, 'and you can see the site of the placenta over there.'

But Jasmin was no longer listening. There was her baby. There was its head and body – she could see it now – it had a chin and it had an ear and it was moving. She really had a baby. A real baby, cradled in her womb. A baby with a face. She loved it passionately. Because that feeling of overpowering excitement and that desire to cry and shout and tell everyone that she had a real baby, that had to be love – and she lay there, mesmerized by the screen, not wanting to break the spell by speaking to the lovely, wonderful radiographer, but she just wanted to say to her baby, hello, baby! And there and then she made a pledge that everything would be perfect for that tiny baby; a baby as precious and mysterious and wonderful as her baby deserved the best, deserved perfection. Jasmin thrilled within herself. She had a baby; she had a mission.

She forgot what she said to the radiographer; she had a memory of the radiographer smiling indulgently at her. She dressed, went straight to the Ladies, relieved herself for what seemed like ages, checked she had her card and left the hospital. Everything was transformed. She kept one hand on her womb. She had forgotten to ring for a taxi. So she went back inside and found a payphone, dialled for a cab and waited outside again.

When she got home, she would ring Sue. She would try to describe the scan to her and the feelings that she had. She would tell her what she had decided. No more occasional dope; a careful, balanced diet; she would learn labour techniques, child care, breathing, relaxation, everything. This was even better than medieval literature. She was aiming for a first in motherhood!

'That's great,' said Sue. 'Now what's next?'

'Your foundation,' the beautician replied. 'If you don't mind lying back on the table.'

Sue did so, surprised again. It seemed odd to have someone apply make-up to you lying down. Several times the beautician applied creams and lotions to her skin and then rubbed them off gently with cotton wool. Sue listened to her running commentary.

'You've got some dry patches here,' she said, 'just by the side of your nose. You'll need a good moisturizer. Just a few broken veins on your cheeks – quite normal for older women. I'll apply a green corrective cream to those ... Don't worry about the jowls – only lack of good muscle tone; I'll put on a slightly darker foundation – use darker shades to conceal, and lighter shades to highlight, that's the rule. Oh, look! That must be a chicken-pox scar from your childhood.'

Sue lay back as the beautician took a small sponge and applied foundation cream to her face. But she was pessimistic. Nothing, absolutely nothing, could conceal those dry patches, those broken veins, those jowls. She was feeling worse by the minute. When the beautician told her to sit up and adjusted the bed, which was in fact nothing but a reclining chair, and she looked again in the mirror, she was a wraith. Black hairband, porcelain skin now, red eyes.

The beautician opened a palette of eyeshadows. 'We have warm shades and cool shades,' she explained. 'I generally recommend warmer shades for the older woman.' From the warm side she selected something olive and dabbed at Sue's eyes. Sue tried not to blink. Her eyes still felt sticky from the Vaseline. Now they seemed slightly smoky at the corners. Sue watched how the beautician applied darker shadow to the outside of her eyes and a paler colour to the inside. A few strokes of eye pencil and then the mascara. Sue sat preternaturally still as the mascara brush hovered and pounced around her eyelashes.

'Good!' said the beautician. 'You're beautifully still. I ask nervous women to apply the mascara themselves.' Sue felt proud of herself. Then the beautician painted on Sue's lips some apricot lipstick, removed the hairband that held her

157

hair back, rearranged it and then stood back. 'What do you think?' she asked. Sue looked long and hard in the mirror.

For a moment she did not recognize herself. She saw a woman with short, attractive fair hair, swept slightly to one side, heavy-lidded, smoky eyes, a flawless complexion, shimmering lips. But it was her. There was her startled expression.

'Well, what do you think?'

Sue tested her smile in the mirror. 'I look very sophisticated,' she said. 'That takes some getting used to!'

'I think you look lovely,' said the beautician.

Sue continued getting to know this new person. She was, in fact, quite attractive. She turned her head slightly, lifted her chin. She blinked to try to clear the Vaseline from her eyes.

'I like it,' she said.

This time, she meant it.

CHAPTER TEN

Sue found that she walked differently. Her posture seemed more upright; she felt more aware of herself somehow. When she stopped to check her reflection in the window of Dixons, she saw that she was hanging her head slightly to one side, like Princess Diana. This was fun. She checked the time on her watch. Time to get back to the library. She walked down the high street with eager anticipation.

She knew she was enjoying this concentration on herself, this wondering what people would think of her. It was like . . . it was like being young again! She remembered going to parties and knowing that one's appearance mattered. But when you are bringing up children, she thought wryly, appearance doesn't matter. When Lizzie and Emma were babies, simply having something clean to wear was an achievement. Even now, what she wore, how she looked, was an afterthought, a luxury.

Today was different, she thought. Today she was pretending to be a glamorous older woman. *Susan Turner, financial director, stepped towards the entrance lobby of the merchant bank* . . . No. Not a merchant bank. *Susan Turner, star of Adrian Lyne's latest thriller, is seen leaving her limousine and walking through the excited crowd* . . . No. She'd never really want to be a film star. *Susan Turner, whose breakfast-time radio programme now had a cult following, walked into Broadcasting House and smiled at the receptionist.* Yes, that was good. Like Jasmin's friend. She'd work in radio. *Susan Turner ascended in the lift on the way to her studio, rapidly running through in her mind the list of her guests for today. It was a children's fiction special. There was . . .*

She climbed the steps of the library and the brief glimpse she had of her unfamiliar reflection in the glass door broke her reverie. Her first public appearance as the new Sue Turner was to be in the children's section and her audience today, only Chris and Glenys and Betty.

'Let's have a look,' Chris said. 'Yes, I like it. The lipstick's a bit heavy, but it makes you look more sophisticated.'

'You mean older,' Sue corrected her.

'But not old,' Chris said. 'Definitely more sexy.'

'No, I think she looks younger,' Betty said. 'It's the lovely way they've done your skin. You look like a china doll. They've done wonders with you! I never would have believed you could look so good.'

'You're lucky,' said Glenys. 'I tried a beauty treatment once, but they couldn't do a thing with my dark rings. It's worry, you know. Worry and stress. It's the sleepless nights. No cream can hide that. You see, you don't have that, Sue.'

Chris winked at Sue and rolled her eyes. Everything Glenys said had as its subtext 'I work harder than you'. It was her *raison d'être*. Glenys returned to her reading and Chris picked up the phone. Even Betty moved over to the kettle to make some tea. That was it, then, thought Sue. Back to work. Back to reality.

She sat down at her desk. There was her pile of invoices to process. But she could not settle. The back of her neck felt bare and her lips were sticky with lipstick. In among the invoices was the list of staff coming to the Christmas do and it was Sue's job to collect the money. Last year they had all gone for an early Christmas dinner at the Dog and Partridge, but everyone had said, nice as it was, it was just one more Christmas dinner and took the edge off the real thing. So this year there was to be a traditional Christmas booze-up and permission had been granted for the library itself to be used. A good way of killing time, Sue thought, would be to go round and collect some money.

Betty found her handbag under her desk, opened it, found her purse, opened that, made a show of counting and finally handed Sue a note. Chris passed over some money with the phone tucked under her chin. Glenys didn't really know if it was her sort of thing, so she would like some time to think about it. So Sue went to find Mick, who, she knew, was sorting through some spoken-word cassettes with Alan in audio-visual.

She made her way to the audio-visual store. Alan Thomas had his back to her, as he was unpacking some computer games. Mick was nowhere to be seen.

'Alan?' she said softly, so as not to startle him.

He turned, and looked at her, and smiled. Now, that smile was not an ordinary smile. His eyes were fixed on hers just a fraction too long. For a moment Sue wondered if he was about to say something and had forgotten what. No, she did know what it was. It was a smile of appreciation. Appreciation of her as a woman. She could not remember the last time that had happened. And Alan Thomas too! The colour came to her cheeks. She could not smile back.

'The library do,' she said. 'I'm collecting. Just a fiver a head.'

He shook his head in amusement at what seemed to be some private joke. He had a lopsided smile, Sue noticed. She watched him put a hand into the back pocket of his jeans and feel for his money. (A man had found her attractive!)

'A fiver, you say. We'll see what we can do.'

He wore a fawn jumper which was slightly small and Sue noticed that he hadn't spread in the middle. He held out a

161

fiver. (She really was attractive!) His hand and the bottom of his arm were covered in a fine blond hair. She took the note, taking care not to touch his fingers.

'Had your hair done?' he said.

'Yes. Just this lunch-time.'

'Suits you.'

'Thanks,' Sue said. 'I must get on with my invoices.' And she went, but before she returned to her office she stopped, just opposite a poster of a Raymond Briggs book, *The Man*. She was breathing quickly. Alan Thomas! she thought.

Alan had been in charge of audio-visual for the last eighteen months or so. Sue didn't know him well. He joked, like all the men, and belonged to that freemasonry that discussed football and athletics. Someone had told her that he was separated or divorced, and she had a vague impression that there were children. She didn't know how old he was and was fairly certain that he lived near the centre of Boltham. Alan Thomas. He had smiled at her. Well, she was grateful. It was the nicest compliment she had had.

Cheryl was more specific.

'I think the olive on your eyes is too dusky. I would have chosen something lighter for you, to lift your eyes. Just a little more mascara too. You're dressed too casually for the look, and I think that spoils it. But really I think on the whole it suits you. Will you carry on doing your face like that?'

Sue wrinkled her nose in distaste. 'I don't think so,' she said. 'Only for a special occasion.' She watched Cheryl's lounge door. Lizzie and Emma were inside and she was curious to see their response to her change. Just then the door swung open and Lizzie appeared.

'Mummy! What *have* you done to your face?'

'Do you like it?'

'Emma! Look! Mummy's gone all strange!'

Her two daughters looked at her and giggled, and assured her that she looked very beautiful, and Sue laughed and hugged them.

'Do you think Mark will like it?' Cheryl said.

'I hope so!' Sue replied.

'I want to show you something,' Cheryl said. She turned to the telephone table in the hall and picked up a child's red exercise book. She handed it to Sue.

'It's Jenny's English book. I asked if I could bring it home. How do you think she's getting on? How does it compare with Emma's?'

Sue opened it. Jenny's handwriting was sometimes large and sprawling, sometimes square and neat. She often wrote 'a' for 'I'. Most of the sentences were marked with a cross, and the teacher's comments were euphemistic. 'Well tried,' adorned one page. 'Oh, dear, Jenny!' read another. On the next was a page of spelling corrections. Wednesday; Wednesday; Wedesday; Wedsay; Wedsay; Wedsay.

'Well?' said Cheryl. 'What do you think? Is that about average for the class?'

Sue remembered Emma's book as being more accurate; she was aware too of Cheryl's desperate hopes for her daughter.

'Perhaps the carelessness happens when she's tired,' Sue said tactfully.

'I'm sure you're right,' Cheryl said. 'But practice will help, won't it? Jenny and I are going to do a little bit of writing every night, aren't we, Jenny?'

Jenny was lying on her back in the lounge, kicking her feet in the air.

'I'm going to get her to write the Christmas cards too, to help her practise her handwriting.'

Sue felt uneasy listening to Cheryl. Either Cheryl was pushing her daughter too hard or, what was more likely,

Sue was actively ignoring Lizzie and Emma's education. She encouraged them to read, true, but she also bought them the *Beano*, *Dandy* and *Beezer*, which they currently enjoyed more than books. So did Mark.

Mark. He would be in soon. She made her excuses to Cheryl, collected together the girls and their belongings and went next door.

Once settled in the house, she glanced again at herself in the hall mirror. Yes, she liked this new look. Perhaps tonight she and Mark would have a drink when the girls had gone to sleep. And have a proper talk, and that might lead to other, more intimate, conversations. She swallowed nervously.

She put some water in a pan for the pasta; there was a ready-prepared sauce from Sainsbury's in the freezer. The girls, she knew, were catching up with events in Ramsay Street. She knelt at the pantry to reach the wholewheat spaghetti from the back. Just then the kitchen door opened, bringing with it a blast of cold air, and Mark. She stood up hastily, presenting herself for inspection.

'What a bloody awful day!' he said. 'Dave Robinson told the Principal he had to have a new office and they're bloody going to give him mine! I've got to share with Steve Enfield! He smokes like a chimney. Then I collected the car from the garage and it failed its MOT and I was lucky they let me drive it home. What's for dinner?' he said, as he left the kitchen and ran up the stairs to get changed.

Lizzie ran in. 'What did Daddy say about your face?' she asked.

As Sue opened her mouth to reply, she realized she was perilously close to tears. Lizzie must not see her cry.

'He liked it,' she said. 'He thought I looked very pretty.'

Jasmin looked again at her watch. Sue did say she would be

164

over once the children were in bed, and it was hard to wait. She had to share with someone what she had seen today. She sat at the kitchen table, the main light off and a table lamp illuminating the books she was reading: *The Experience of Childbirth, Breast is Best*. It was possible, she had discovered, to take control of this whole process of labour and childbirth. It was possible to turn that moment of giving birth into something supremely transfiguring. Today she had seen her baby; today she had learned that you can give your baby the best; Alison Susan Grainne Carpenter would glide beautifully into the world and they would bond instantly. These books tell you how to do it.

She knew it was seeing her baby there on the screen that had done it. Before, she realized now, she was simply pregnant. Now she was carrying her baby within her. When she had got back from Boltham General she had lain on her bed with her hands on her tummy, thinking thoughts to share with her baby. She realized – as the books, as the experts had said – that being a mother does not begin with the birth. Being a mother begins earlier than that; her baby was already almost perfectly formed. Being a mother begins . . . it begins at conception, before conception, the nutritionists say. Well, there was little she could do about that now. She would not think about the alcohol she had drunk in the early stages of her pregnancy. But it was not too late to start from now. From now, she would do everything properly.

She wanted to tell Sue that and to ask for her help. How does one find out about natural childbirth, active birth, birthing pools and the like? But most she wanted to share with Sue that moment when she saw her baby. So intense was this desire that she had almost contemplated writing to her mother. For there, on the table, her mug of herbal tea just resting on it, was a letter from her mother, forwarded by Juliet. The letter asked her to ring to confirm her flight

165

details for Christmas. Even that had been insufficient to dent Jasmin's euphoria.

Seeing the envelope now, she began to think again. Going to Istanbul was out of the question. Think, think, Jasmin. She would say that she had been invited to spend Christmas with Juliet. But, no. There were Juliet's parents to consider, and her mother would insist on ringing on Christmas Day. She needed an ally. There was a rapping on the window of the kitchen door. Jasmin sprang to her feet and saw with pleasure Sue's outline through the glass. She eagerly opened the door.

'I saw her!' Jasmin exclaimed. 'On the scan today. Her head, her body – she has a tiny little ear, and – Sue? Are you all right?'

Sue took off her mackintosh and hung it over the back of the chair. Jasmin sensed a lifelessness in her, which contrasted with her own mood.

'I'm OK,' said Sue.

'No, you're not. Turn around. You've had your hair and face done! I'd forgotten. Oh, yes, it suits you! Very, very sexy. I know what you look like – like one of those newsreaders, or a late-night arts-show presenter. You just need some big specs . . . Sue? Has something else happened? You don't look happy.'

Jasmin's euphoria melted into concern for Sue. There was something defeated in the way she sat in the chair. Jasmin, feeling newly maternal, wanted to comfort her.

'It's nothing, really. I came to see how you are.'

'I'm fine. I had a wonderful time at the hospital, seeing the baby and everything, as I said. But you. Come on – I want to know!'

Sue glanced at Jasmin. She was acutely aware of her youth. How could she explain about Mark, and the lead weight she had carried in her all evening? Jasmin was only twenty. What would she know? What right had an older woman to tell a younger that there was no such thing as a happy marriage?

'Right!' said Jasmin. 'We'll play "Twenty Questions"! All you have to do is answer "yes" or "no". Was it work?'

'No.'

'Your appearance?'

'No.'

'Christmas preparations?'

'No. Oh, this is silly. Mark didn't notice my hair. It's trivial, and it's babyish of me to let it get me down.'

'He didn't notice?'

'He'd had a rotten day at work. I couldn't really expect him to.'

Jasmin was silent. For the first time she let herself think about Sue's husband. She'd seen him once or twice: dark, receding hair, an intelligent face, an abstract expression. Potentially attractive, she thought. But Sue had never spoken about him.

'Are you happily married?' Jasmin said. She wanted to know.

Sue winced. 'As happy as most people,' she said. 'Happier, I suppose.'

'Have you ever been unfaithful to him? Has he ever been unfaithful to you?'

'Heavens, no!' Sue was embarrassed at this direct questioning. She felt herself flushing.

'I want to know all about him!' Jasmin demanded. She swung back on her chair, rocking to and fro. I'm rocking my baby, she thought.

Sue felt as if she was walking the plank. She had not analysed her relationship with Mark. She suspected it would not bear examination. But where she was sitting, she was in the shadow. The lampshade illuminated some pregnancy books on the table, that was all.

'He works very hard,' she said. 'He lectures in IT, and there's lots of preparation for him to do. There's rivalry at work too, and you've got to be seen to be busy. We don't get the chance to talk. He's working, and when he's not he's tired. We watch TV. We talk about the children,' Sue said quickly. 'When we talk. We've just got very used to each other, that's all. Very used to each other.'

'D'you still fancy him?' Jasmin asked.

Sue thought – thought of his receding hair, his stubbly chin, the grime on the soap; thought of his sagging pyjama bottoms.

'Yes,' she said.

'Does he fancy you?'

'Apparently not.'

'I think you need a flirtation,' Jasmin said. 'If you feel attractive, you'll project that, and Mark will see you as attractive. And he might sense you're interested in someone else, so he'll try harder too.'

'Jasmin!'

'Only a flirtation, mind! Go on – what other men do you know?'

'None,' Sue said, quick as a flash. There was Alan Thomas, of course.

'Find someone at the bus stop to smile at,' Jasmin said, enjoying herself.

'Ah!' said Sue. 'You can do that; you're still young. Any man I smiled at would think I was desperate.'

'I think older women are more attractive than young girls,' Jasmin said. 'Men think so too. A woman's libido increases as she gets older and men's diminishes. Women in their late thirties ought to all have toy boys.'

Sue laughed, feeling more comfortable now that Jasmin was deliberately being absurd. Changing the subject, she asked her about her hospital visit, and leant forward on the chair to listen to Jasmin's description.

★

'Did you feel like that? When you first saw Lizzie and Emma?'

'No,' Sue said. 'I had Lizzie over in Halifax. There mothers weren't allowed to look at their scans – all the consultants in the hospital were male. I did see Emma, though. But by that time I'd already had one baby. I didn't feel the same excitement as you. There is a point, though,' Sue ruminated, 'when you begin to realize that they're real and that they're here to stay.'

'That's how I feel. Now, Sue, you must tell me where I ought to go to get the best advice about labour. I have been reading these books, and I know I can talk to you, but if there were classes I could go to ... Oh, and not the National Childbirth Trust.'

'Why not?'

'My mother was an instructor.'

'In that case, apart from the hospital classes, I don't know. Look in the *Yellow Pages*.' Sue thought for a moment. 'Don't let your mother put you off the NCT. They're good.'

'Yes, but I want to do things better than her.'

That was a feeling Sue understood. She remembered deliberately trying to do things differently from her mother. Then she saw the blue airmail letter.

'Has she written to you again?'

'Yes. Asking me if I've booked my flight for Christmas.'

'Are you going?'

Jasmin shook her head.

'You've got to tell her, Jasmin.'

'Soon. After Christmas. I promise.'

'Will you be here for Christmas?' A small nod from Jasmin. Her head was bowed. She was suddenly a pitiful figure. Sue acted on a sudden impulse. 'Would you like to spend Christmas with us?' Jasmin looked up now, her face shining with pleasure.

★

169

Cheryl discovered she could walk more quickly without Jenny. That was an exhilarating feeling. It was a pity to go into Manchester without her, however, as Jenny was missing the Christmas displays in the shops, and the carol singers, and later, as dusk fell, the illuminations that spangled the dark sky. But Christmas presents had to be a surprise. Arthur's mother had Jenny for the afternoon, as well as her cousin Francine. Cheryl and Arthur were therefore alone, shopping for Jenny.

Cheryl went up the stairs at Waterstone's, Arthur a pace or two behind her. She turned the corner to face the children's books and glowed with anticipation. She would fill Jenny's stockings with books. Near the counter were displays of Christmas books: musical Santa books, pop-up books, picture books of the Twelve Days of Christmas. Cheryl walked past these. Fiction was divided into 5–7 and 8–11. She hesitated.

'Arthur? What do you think? I know Jenny is six, but I wonder if books are a bit like clothes sizes. I mean that you buy things for them to grow into.' She picked up an Early Lone Reader. 'Do you see what I mean? These are simple. They won't stretch her.' Arthur, in her wake, picked up the book, with its six lines or so of writing on each page. Cheryl must know what she was talking about, he decided. She had devoted so much time to Jenny's education in recent weeks. She was a wonderful mother.

'Look. This is better. I've heard of some of these.' Cheryl was leafing through a paperback edition of *Swallows and Amazons*. 'It's difficult in places, I know, but I can help her.' Arthur stood by doubtfully. 'You see, we've also got to think, Arthur, that she'll be interviewed, and she's bound to be asked what she reads. They judge a child on that. I know. All children read things like Roald Dahl. If Jenny could just be a little in advance of that. Look! There's *The Secret Garden*.'

Arthur, feeling superfluous, strayed. He had never realized, he thought, as he picked up a book with pads that you pressed, that books could actually speak to you. 'Merry Christmas!' this one said. He'd pressed a picture of Donald Duck dressed as Santa. Jenny would love it. He pressed the panel again. 'Merry Christmas!' He smiled to himself. 'Merry Christmas!'

'Arthur!' Cheryl called to him. 'Come and see what I've found.'

Cheryl had moved now and she was standing in a less crowded part of the children's area. Arthur joined her.

'These are books that help you improve your English!' Cheryl said excitedly. 'See! This one goes up to Key Stage One, which is Jenny's stage, although I think she ought to be a little in advance of that. But here's a spelling book, with little lists in. And a workbook about writing in sentences. Now, I should have got these weeks ago.'

Arthur was still holding the musical book. He pressed it inadvertently. 'Merry Christmas!' it chortled.

Cheryl saw it and took it from him. 'Put it back, Arthur,' she said.

They stood at the queue by the till.

'I wish I had that list, Arthur. You know, the one that the Government prescribe for the National Curriculum. It would be nice for Jenny to read approved authors. That would go down well at Boltham.'

Under her arm Cheryl had a pile of books: *Treasure Island*, *Little Women*, *Swallows and Amazons*, *English to Key Stage Two*, *Spelling Matters* and *Stories from Shakespeare*.

'I do know she can't read these on her own yet. But she has us,' Cheryl said.

She watched the assistant, a scrawny-looking girl with short purple hair, slide the books into the maroon Waterstone's bag. She felt proud of her choice and smiled happily at the assistant.

They crossed the road to look at the display in Kendals. Models were frozen in elegant attitudes in red and green – Christmas colours. Cheryl and Arthur were on their way to the music shop, as Arthur was learning the piano and wanted some sheet music. They passed a window advertising Santa's grotto, where small models of elves were programmed to hack repeatedly at a rock containing rubies and emeralds. Arthur slowed to look. There too was a profusion of toys, spilling from a sack: dolls, teddies, cars, Post Office sets, computer games, jigsaws.

'We ought to get Jenny some toys,' he said mildly.

'We are,' Cheryl said, increasing her pace. 'At the Early Learning Centre.'

After buying the music, they retraced their steps to the Early Learning Centre. The plain, no-nonsense lettering of its logo reassured Cheryl, as she approached, that everything here was useful, was worthwhile and – best of all – was educational. It really was the only place to buy toys. She was a frequent shopper here; in fact most of the mothers she knew bought toys at the Early Learning Centre. They were better for the children, obviously.

In the shop window small children were playing with a Swedish train set and an assortment of Duplo (hand–eye coordination). The centre of the store was set up with a slide, also being used by little ones, and this, of course, was to improve physical confidence. But Cheryl reminded herself that Jenny would not be tested on her physical confidence, yet. She walked to the back of the store, followed by Arthur. She stopped at the videos.

'Just what I was looking for!' she exclaimed. 'A Times Table video. I want a tape too, of course, for the car, but Jenny will enjoy the video. We can all watch it.' Cheryl picked it up eagerly. 'Then I want lots of paper and exercise books and pencils, because the more she is surrounded by writing implements, the more it will encourage writing. And look! They sell globes too. We really ought to get a globe, and possibly a children's atlas. They're bound to have a children's atlas.'

Arthur tapped her on the shoulder. 'Do you mind,' he said, 'if I have some fresh air?'

Cheryl understood his smile. He wanted to go and buy something for her. She pretended not to understand and said, of course, it was so hot and crowded.

Arthur pushed his way out of the shop. He walked rapidly along the street back to Kendals. Pushing shoppers aside, he entered the busy store and took the stairs two at a time to the toy department. There were stacks of soft toys and battery-operated cars and Thunderbirds models. But over there! There was an enormous soft grey elephant, with large appealing eyes and a trunk. Arthur inhaled deeply. Dare he? Jenny would love it. Feeling criminal, feeling positively traitorous, he lifted it. It was expensive, but . . . Jenny loved stuffed animals.

Quickly, he told himself. Before he thought about it and changed his mind. He went to the till, holding the elephant under his arm like a hostage. He handed over his Visa card to the assistant, with orders to wrap the elephant well. He looked over his shoulder. What if Cheryl found him here?

'Don't worry,' said the assistant. 'I know it's difficult Christmas shopping with the children in tow. I'll be quick.'

A few minutes later, Arthur appeared breathless in the doorway of the Early Learning Centre. Cheryl was at the till, a pile of purchases by her side.

'There are counting games,' she told him happily. 'And pretend money just like the real thing. And a teaching clock to help her tell the time. It'll be a wonderful Christmas.'

173

'It will that,' said Arthur.

'Thank you so much, Grandma, for having her,' Cheryl said, as Jenny hugged her leg. 'It's made a great difference.'

'It was a pleasure,' said Arthur's mother. 'Both girls have been very good.'

'What have you been doing with Grandma?' Cheryl asked her daughter.

'Nuffink!'

'Come on now, Jenny,' her grandmother said. 'We've been drawing pictures, haven't we? Francine is still finishing hers.'

Cheryl moved over to Arthur's mother's table, which was covered with an old tablecloth. Here Francine, a squat little child with thick spectacles, was sitting hunched over a drawing. It was of a house with Santa and his reindeer on top. The reindeer looked like reindeer. At the bottom it read, in preternaturally neat writing, 'This is my house on Christmas Night. Father Christmas is bringing my computer.'

By Francine's picture was another. Francine had not done it. It was a scrawl, whirls of colour over the page, with glitter unevenly applied in the middle. 'Jenny', it said, in big letters at the bottom.

'Mummy, Mummy, do you like my pitcher?'

Cheryl held it up. She was both surprised and betrayed. 'But, Jenny! You can do lovely drawings at home. You weren't trying! Why didn't you do one of your best drawings for Grandma?'

'Didn't feel like it. I'm hungry.'

She ran to her grandmother and asked for another biscuit. Cheryl looked at her and bristled with anger. Drawing was the only thing Jenny could do, and she had let her down in front of Arthur's mother, of all people. Her eyes rested on the studious Francine and Cheryl read the words on her picture again. Ought she and Arthur to have bought Jenny a computer?

'Has she been good?' Cheryl asked her mother-in-law.

'Yes,' Arthur's mother replied, red-cheeked, dressed neatly in her apron. 'I love having the girls. Jenny is very affectionate, though she's not as bright as Francine, is she?'

The comment lacerated Cheryl.

'She hasn't had that extra time at Boltham,' she rejoindered.

'True,' said Arthur's mother. 'That's why I think it's important she goes there. Francine is an angel in the Nativity,' she added proudly.

'That's nice,' said Cheryl. Jenny was in the chorus at the back in her school's production.

Arthur was in the hall, getting Jenny's coat. He did not know why he was feeling quietly mutinous, although he had spent much of his childhood that way. He had swung from feeling responsible for his mother at times to a gentle resentment of her subtle control.

'Goodbye, Jenny,' she said, as Cheryl buttoned her coat. 'Now make sure you work hard over the Christmas holidays so you can go to school with Francine.'

Francine did not turn to look at them. She was humming a tune to herself.

'Now, before you go, Jenny,' said her grandmother, 'Can you tell me what five and eight are?'

'No,' said Jenny.

Arthur's mother raised her eyebrows at Arthur, and Cheryl saw her expression. She was cut to the quick. But she would not be defeated. By the next time Grandma saw Jenny, she would be perfect in her number bonds. Or number bombs, as she persisted in calling them.

'Good night, Grandma,' she said.

'Good night, Jenny and Arthur, and Cheryl.'

CHAPTER ELEVEN

Was it the approach of Christmas? Was that why Sue was driving to the library with a frisson of excitement, with a tingling somewhere in the pit of her stomach? Because it *was* fun, planning surprises for the children, and looking forward to the adult bacchanalia. No, it wasn't Christmas; Sue was looking forward to going to work. She was about to lick her lips, but realized she was wearing a generous layer of the new Apricot Mist lipstick she had bought. The windscreen wipers cut a clear quadrant through the slush that materialized on her windscreen. Damp, grey, December Boltham – it was exciting!

Within thirty minutes, Sue was seated at her desk, the first coffee of the morning steaming in front of her. She wasn't ready to work yet. Luckily, nor were Chris and Betty.

'I don't see,' Betty said, 'why sex has to come into everything!'

'But that was the whole point of the play,' Chris said. 'It was about a powerful affair that haunted both of them all of their lives. It explained the rest of the events. They had to show it all, especially the steamy bits. Did you see it, Sue?' Chris asked. '*Shadows in Our Life*?'

'No,' Sue said. 'I was out visiting Jasmin last night. But I gather there was quite a lot to see.'

'Quite right,' Chris continued. 'But what really gets me is that we got to see all of *her*, but all we got to see of him was a bare torso. Male director,' Chris added acidly.

'Do you like naked men?' Sue asked her.

'Frankly, no. I think there's nothing aesthetically pleasing in the male form. The penis is one of God's better jokes.'

Sue laughed. She loved these sexually explicit women-only conversations that they sometimes indulged in in the library office. She deliberately provoked Chris.

'So why are you complaining about the lack of male flesh? *Touché*!'

'It's the principle of the thing,' Chris said uncomfortably.

'I know, but if we treat men as sexual objects, aren't we coming down to their level?' Sue continued, enjoying herself. 'Mind you, it's fun to do that sometimes. Did you ever get a copy of the magazine that had a photo-feature of different-sized penises? I'd have loved to have seen it!'

Sue was aware of someone standing beside her. She turned her head and looked up. It was Alan Thomas. When had he arrived? Had he heard her last comment? She felt a hot blush spread from her neck and suffuse her face. Her heart pounded against her chest.

'Here are the spoken-word cassettes you ordered,' Alan said. He placed some tapes on her desk. He had a husky voice with a strong Boltham accent.

'Thanks,' Sue said, drowning in a sea of embarrassment. She dared to glance up at him only for a moment. But in that short time, their eyes met. He did not indicate whether he had heard her remark. Chris's phone rang, and then Sue and Alan were isolated in the library, despite the everyday background noises, despite the buzz of computers. Alan did not leave her desk.

'Do you know the system for processing those?' he said, indicating the cassettes.

'No, not really,' Sue replied. He was wearing aftershave. Quite a powerful aftershave: it reminded her of a commercial fly-spray. He wore denims today and a hooded top with two white cords hanging loose at the neck.

177

'Come over to the computer and I'll show you.'

She obeyed his instruction and rose from her chair, under a spell. She sat in front of the computer screen and he stood behind her. She could feel the heat from his body. As he explained the procedures, he pressed the keys for her, his arm coming round her back. She saw his fingernail, cut straight across, jabbing at the keys. She was cocooned in aftershave and male heat.

'There,' Alan said. 'I've done that one for you.'

'Thanks,' Sue said, and dared another look at him. Yes, he was younger than her. His blond hair was parted at the side and a fringe flopped over his forehead. His eyes, those were unusual; heavy eyebrows, overhanging eyelids; a square, masculine face. But when he swallowed a muscle jumped in his throat. She noticed his lips were slightly chapped; full lips, but slightly chapped. She saw all this in just a short glance. It was as if she had never seen him before.

'Good weekend?' he asked her.

'Yes, thanks,' Sue said noncommittally.

Then there was a long pause. She felt her toes curl. She was sure, absolutely sure, that he was interested in her. Else why come to her desk to explain about the processing? And she supposed her vivid awareness of him indicated that she liked him too. Jasmin had told her to flirt a bit, but she was out of practice. How did she used to flirt? How was it done? Eye contact, that was it. It was done with the eyes. So once again she looked up at him, and held his eyes with hers, widened them slightly, and smiled, and then looked down. I'm a tart, she thought. She remembered her earlier remark that she felt sure he had overheard. Still Alan did not move. What was it he wanted to say to her?

'See you later, then, Sue.'

'See you,' she said.

178

He left the office. Once he had gone, Sue was able to breathe again. She knew then his visit was what she had been waiting for. She had known that Alan was going to come and find her; that look of his on Friday was a promise. Sue was electrified. Here was a man who was interested in her; an interesting man too. She hoped Chris and Betty had not noticed, for she was feeling wicked – deliciously wicked. Of course, she told herself hastily, she had done nothing – said nothing, nothing at all. She had smiled – it's friendly to smile – and besides, there is no rule against a married woman finding another man attractive, is there? This was fun.

She worked that morning with vigour. She wrote more quickly, offered to make coffee for everyone, joked, hung up some streamers, and always had an eye on the office entrance, just in case . . .

She removed the packaging material from the box by her desk, popping the bubbles in the cellophane with her fingers. She piled the new books on her desk. She looked up quickly as someone entered the office – Glenys, who had taken time off for shopping. Everything seemed more vivid; the scarlet of Glenys's umbrella shouted at her.

It was later the same afternoon when they spoke again. Sue had relieved Barbara on the counter and was returning to her office. She naturally glanced into the audio-visual store on her way. He was there, half-way up a ladder, his back to her. His body was lithe and well shaped. Her eyes travelled down the dip that was the small of his back, and lower. She was surprised at her own lasciviousness. Sensing a presence behind him, Alan turned and saw her. His face lit up.

'Come to visit me?'

'Just passing,' Sue said. 'I've come from the counter.'

'Yes, I noticed you were on.'

He stepped down from the ladder and sat astride a plastic chair, looking levelly at her. Sue knew she ought to go; knew too she could not.

'The trouble with audio-visual,' Alan said, 'is that there's no company. Just one of me. You've got all of the Children's Team.'

'True.' Sue nodded. 'We have quite a laugh at times.'

'Where I am,' Alan said, 'it's lonely.'

'Don't you get to chat with the other men?' she asked. 'I've seen you go down to the Waterloo with Mick and Dave.'

'Yes,' he said, with a trace of a smile. 'I was referring to female company,' he said.

Once again Sue felt as if she could hardly breathe. But she would have to reply to him. 'I thought it didn't bother you men,' she said. She was thinking of Mark. 'I thought it didn't bother you, not having anyone to talk to.'

'That's where you're wrong,' Alan said. 'That's the worst part of living alone. I miss the chance to talk over things. Tell you what,' he said. 'You can be an honorary member of A-V. Stop whenever you're passing and we'll have a chat.' Then he winked at her. And then the Assistant District Manager came up behind her and she went back to her office.

Sue was in an excellent mood. When Emma came up to her pouting and saying that she had maths corrections, Sue sat her on her lap and did them for her. When Emma, later that evening, knocked over a glass of Ribena, and Sue saw a damp purple patch expand on her cream skirt, she laughed, and removed her skirt and soaked it in the sink in amusement. She stood at the sink, holding her skirt under a stream of warm water, rubbing at the stain. There had not been one moment since she came home when she had not been aware of Alan Thomas. His name was pleasant to her ears. Alan. Alan Thomas.

She was cordial to Mark, and was happy when he went upstairs to complete a report. She rang her mother for a chat, hugging her delicious secret to herself. As she prepared the children's clothes for the next day, she replayed the day's events in her mind.

'Mummy,' Lizzie said. 'I need to talk.'

Sue sat on Lizzie's bed. Lizzie was already tucked under the duvet, her head resting on an enormous teddy bear, some books by her side.

'And what do you need to talk about?' Sue said.

'I don't want to be Kirsty's best friend any more.'

'And why is that?'

Lizzie's expression was pained. 'I want to be her *friend* – I still like her – but Rosy said I could be her best friend and I like Rosy because she plays good games and Kirsty plays silly games like Mummies and Daddies and . . .' Lizzie paused. 'I don't want to hurt Kirsty's feelings.' That was Lizzie's current favourite phrase: 'I don't want to hurt her feelings.'

'You don't have to tell her you're not best friends,' Sue said. 'I don't see why you can't play an interesting game with both of them.'

'Kirsty doesn't like Rosy.'

Sue couldn't resist brushing Lizzie's soft blonde hair back from her forehead as she lay down, her small face looking up at her mother. Lizzie accepted the caress comfortably.

'Just be nice to both of them,' Sue said. 'I think you're a good girl not to want to hurt anyone's feelings.'

Lizzie smiled, her eyelids drooping. Sue kissed her forehead lightly. Emma was already asleep, her hands making little fists. Sue turned off their bedroom light, but left the door ajar. She was about to go into her own bedroom to fetch some dirty washing, but stopped at the door. Mark was in there working. It was at that moment, standing on the threshold of her own bedroom, that she first felt a twinge of guilt. Perhaps it was the way Mark's head was hung over his notes.

But a calm, rational voice informed her that she was doing nothing wrong. She had spoken to a man; she had smiled at a man. These things were entirely innocent. As Jasmin had said, a flirtation might inject some life into her marriage. And her friendship with Alan was hardly a flirtation. Was it? She would not disturb Mark. She would go downstairs. And she would think.

Jasmin lifted the *Yellow Pages* and flicked through it. 'Crane Manufacturers', 'Gas Installers', 'Language Schools'. She found a page with the subheading 'Health'. 'Health Clubs', 'Health Authorities'. Nothing there. She turned to 'Counselling and Advice'. She moved her finger down the column, past marriage guidance counselling and victim support schemes. There was the East Boltham Well Women's Centre. Perhaps they might know of a natural childbirth centre. FAM, she read next, and stopped. In brackets, next to it, were the words 'Foetal Awareness Movement'. And an address. And telephone number. Jasmin was intrigued. Foetal awareness. What could that be?

Jasmin dialled the number with anticipation. There was a ringing tone. She prayed she would not be greeted by the impersonal words of an answering machine. She was lucky. The voice that answered was natural, and it was a man's. That surprised her.

'Grant here,' he said.

'I'm sorry,' said Jasmin. 'I think I must have the wrong number. I was dialling the Foetal Awareness Movement.'

'We are the Foetal Awareness Movement,' he said. 'Can I help you?'

Sue could not sleep. She had woken at 3.06. The curse of the modern digital alarm was that one knew exactly when one had woken. The red figures glared reproachfully at her. Mark's face was turned from her in sleep. Sue lay back in bed, the still night sharpening her awareness of her beating heart.

First, then, a quick fix of her drug. She called Alan's face to mind – there it was, those masculine overhanging eyelids, that laughter behind his hazel eyes. Now some of his words: *You're a good friend, Sue – more than a friend*, that was one. *Why don't you come out with me and Mick next Friday?* Mick, she knew, was a sort of chaperon. Now, she would think of when he came up behind her in the office and ruffled her hair. Stop! That was enough. That was her ration. But it was too much. Without even indulging in one of her more lurid fantasies concerning herself and him, she knew she would never get back to sleep.

She commanded herself to think of something else. She remembered Jasmin's excited conversation about the group she had found. She had spoken to a man on the phone who believed it was possible to establish a relationship with a foetus, and that was, apparently, the vital ingredient in a successful labour – a partnership between the mother and baby. Jasmin was sold on it and was shortly going to her first meeting. The group tutor apparently taught natural childbirth techniques and meditation, and, Jasmin informed her, as breathless as a young girl, other innovative techniques too.

She had not told Jasmin about Alan. She had not told anyone about Alan.

3.23 turned into 3.24. Why shouldn't a married woman have a flirtation? Well, why shouldn't she?

*Good evening. I'm Sue Turner and this is Talking Point.
Tonight in the studio we have the eminent psychiatrist Professor Susan S. Turner and Sue Turner, sculptress, artist and
poet, talking on woman's freedom. The particular question I
have for you tonight is, why shouldn't a married woman have
a flirtation? Well, why shouldn't she?*

'Why shouldn't she?' said Sue Turner, concrete poet, inhal-
ing at a long cigarette. 'A flirtation is fun, it's life-enhancing,
it promotes happiness, it's an adventure, it's educational. Most
flirtations are innocent, based purely on the fleeting attractions
that add colour and meaning to our lives. It's part of the
drama of human existence. I cannot count the number of
flirtations I've had – they are art, movement, life itself.'

'Professor?'

'True, but a flirtation is only a prelude to a dangerous act.
These things may easily get out of hand. Where the marital
relationship is already smouldering with unspoken resentment,
the flirtation can ignite the flames. There is no such thing as a
safe flirtation.' The professor settled her glasses on her nose.
'Let me give you a case history. For our purposes, we shall call
the woman Sue Turner. She married some time after leaving
university, as all her friends were marrying. It was the thing
expected of her by her family, by herself. For several years the
marriage prospered, both partners supporting each other in
establishing themselves and their household, each with time to
pursue their own interests. Then, the children. The age-old
pattern recurs: the children become the mother's; the father
retreats, feeling incompetent, out of place, inferior compared to
the Matriarch – the Madonna and child, that most powerful
symbol. He retreats into his work, and in our society, the
workplace is the only place, apart from the battlefield and
sports field, where a man can achieve status. She resents his
lack of interest, his psychic disappearance; he resents her
emotional fluency and position at the centre of things. They

don't speak; they rarely make love; each feels unloved. And into this comes the innocent flirtation. Sue Turner is made to feel as if she is a woman again – the clock is turned back. This isn't fun; this is serious.'

'*Serious fun,' said Sue Turner, surrealist painter. 'Here is a woman whose life has been spent pleasing others: first a husband, whose ego she has cosseted and protected, then her children, who do need all of her love and protection, but, as they grow up, forget they don't need it any more and still demand, demand, demand – make me a drink, where's my jumper? Then a job, with even more expectations of her, and then, here is a man – we shall call him Alan Thomas – who is interested in her purely because she is a woman. Can't she respond? Can't she enjoy herself? Why should a woman's life be over at forty? Why should a woman's life be defined by her duties to others? What about her duties to herself?'*

'*This married woman,' said the professor, 'has two lovely daughters called Lizzie and Emma.'*

'*It's not as if she's being unfaithful to them! It's not as if she's having secret assignations with another eight-year-old, surreptitiously, in a McDonald's in another town.'*

'*As I said, this married woman has two lovely daughters called Lizzie and Emma.'*

3.47. Sue's head tingled with pain. She would need, shortly, to get some Paracetamol. Mark slept peacefully by her side. She felt empty. It was true: she ought to think of the children in everything she did. Ought she? She heard the pattering of raindrops in the guttering on the roof. She felt sad and lonely. She would have a quick fix.

Alan. The fine blond hair on his arms. His direct, teasing, wicked look. His distinctive aftershave. Herself, as he sees her, intelligent, interesting, desirable. She would see him tomorrow, thank God.

★

Jasmin lay on Sue's settee, her feet, in thick black socks, on the armrest. Lizzie and Emma had their hands on her tummy, waiting. The television set paid no attention to this and continued to address an inattentive room. That was how Sue found them.

'They're waiting to feel the baby,' Jasmin explained. 'Now!' she said. 'Did you feel that?'

'I think so,' said Lizzie.

'No, you didn't,' said Emma.

'Did I tell you, Sue, I've learned how to breathe?'

Sue perched on an armchair. She had to return to the kitchen shortly to turn down the rice.

Emma stood up. '*I* know how to breathe. Look.' She drew in deep audible gasps of air and puffed them out. Sue and Jasmin smiled at her. She ended in a fit of coughing.

'Have you started that group of yours?' Sue asked Jasmin.

'The Foetal Awareness Movement? No, not yet. They run proper courses. I have to wait two weeks until a new one begins. But I have a book that teaches relaxation, and I'm mastering deep-breathing. Watch.' Jasmin displayed her new-found skills, breathing in through her nose and then, with a little puff, exhaling through her mouth. Lizzie and Emma, losing interest, went back to the television. Jasmin got up and followed Sue back to the kitchen. Sue was glad. She needed to talk to someone. Perhaps Jasmin was the right person after all.

Sue stirred the bolognaise sauce, disturbing the skin that had thickened on the top. Jasmin repeated the details of her antenatal check at the surgery that morning. Her blood pressure, her weight, the height of her fundus. Really, Sue thought, Jasmin was getting quite obsessive about it all. Alan Thomas's face brooded over the scene. He watched her stir the meat sauce.

186

'The midwife said my blood pressure was very good and she was pleased. She still thinks my weight gain is fine, although I'd have thought I'd have put more on, as I am beginning to stick out in front, but she said that was healthy. The vitamin tablets are making a difference too.'

Sue let the rice simmer. The girls would only eat spaghetti bolognaise with rice.

'It's a lot easier, you know, if I sit up straight. I really can feel the top of my womb pressing against my ribs. And I can't eat green pepper any more. It repeats. I think I'll be all right with the bolognaise.'

Today, she had gone out for lunch at the Waterloo with Mick and Alan. She had asked Chris, but Chris had been busy shopping. She couldn't eat, and the wine had gone to her head. The pub was full of other office parties eating Christmas dinner. Towards the end of the lunch-break, Mick had gone to the Gents. She was sitting opposite Alan.

The intimacy of their eyes was enough. Yes, it was all done with eyes. Their conversation had been quite desultory. 'Happy?' he had said to her. She had nodded. 'Your husband's a lucky man,' he had said.

His foot had found her foot, and really, just touching shoes – that wasn't very wicked – and ankles too, she remembered. But the eyes had it. They looked at each other for far too long. They had exchanged something then, some understanding. And Sue was thrilled. Thrilled and scared. And next week was the library party. Husbands and wives were never invited. All of this – her thoughts of Alan, her constant recall of the things he had said, the way he had looked, what she had felt – all this knowledge was growing inside her like . . . like a baby, wriggling and kicking and wanting to be born.

'Sue! You're not listening to me! I asked you whether

187

you'd drive me to my first FAM meeting. They meet just behind the Waterloo.'

'The Waterloo!' she said, aghast.

'Sue, something is bothering you. Come on. Out with it!'

Sue turned guiltily from the rice. It was a matter of finding the right words to begin. She would have to explain so that Jasmin would not condemn her. That was very important. 'Do you remember,' she said, 'that evening when I came round to you, after my haircut, and –'

The kitchen door opened. Lizzie announced, 'Daddy's home! He's come in the front way.'

Mark, still in his overcoat, stood at the entrance to the kitchen. He was in a good mood, smiling to himself.

'Hello, Jasmin,' he said. 'Joining us for dinner?'

'Yes, Sue said I could.'

'OK, Sue?' he said. Sue nodded, her back to him. She willed him to leave.

'Daddy, Daddy, I felt Jasmin's baby move!' cried Lizzie.

'No, you didn't!' shouted Emma. 'She didn't, Daddy!'

It was better, Sue decided, as she rubbed the shampoo into Emma's hair, that she hadn't spoken to Jasmin. There was something obscene, she decided, about discussing her personal, sexual life, with a twenty-year-old pregnant girl, no matter how intelligent, no matter how original.

'Ow! Mummy! You're hurting me!'

'Sorry,' Sue said automatically.

Besides, nothing at all had happened. Bored housewife, empty life, imagining things. No, came a voice. This is real. This is the most real thing in your life. It was eight o'clock and it was Friday. She had to wait the whole weekend until she went to work again. The pictures in her mind, of her and Alan in the pub, had become tattered and soiled from use. She needed some more. A whole weekend was almost too long to wait.

'Head back!' she instructed Emma, as she poured warm water through her hair.

'I'll help you wash up,' Jasmin said, as she watched Mark collect the dirty plates from the dining room.

'No, you're our guest,' he said.

'I don't want to be your guest. I want to be your friend. You can shout at friends and *tell* them to do the washing up. You wash and I'll dry.'

And so it was that Mark stood at the sink, rubbing and rinsing plates and bowls, and Jasmin stood by his side, leaning slightly against the work surface, drying each plate with meticulous care. Jasmin felt in need of entertainment.

'Mark. Sue has never told me how you met. Go on. Tell me now.'

'At university,' he said. 'We were at university together.'

'No, but how did you meet? Exactly?'

Mark stopped washing up to think. 'It was a party in someone's room. There wasn't a lot of space, and we ended up jammed on the corner of a bed, and I took it from there.' He laughed to himself.

'Did you fancy her straight away?'

Mark had stopped washing up completely. 'Actually,' he said, 'I knew who she was before then. I'd seen her in the campus shop and at some fund-raising disco. Yes. I did fancy her. But I didn't think she'd be interested in me. She was going with someone else at the time, I thought. But she turned up at the party alone and she was friendly . . . It seems like ages ago.'

'Then what?'

'She was much more interesting than all the other girls

I'd been with. For a start, she always had something to say and was so full of questions – a bit like you. We had fun. And then finally we both got jobs here and married.'

'You're lucky,' Jasmin said, with decision. 'You're lucky to have Sue, and you're lucky to be in a family.'

'I know,' he said.

'My baby's not going to have a father,' she said. 'Look. You've stopped washing up. Get a move on!' she went on, with mock severity. 'As I said, my baby's not going to have a father, and sometimes I worry about that. What do you think, Mark? Should I have married Tom, insisted on it, for the baby's sake?'

'No,' Mark said. 'You've got to love someone to marry them. Sue and I were in love.' He scrubbed at the white scum on the saucepan. 'And I'm sure you'll manage with your baby. When Sue had Lizzie, I was in the middle of a busy term and she did it all. She was great.'

'Didn't you help her?'

'As much as I could,' he said. 'But she was better with Lizzie than me. When I had to take over, things went haywire.'

'Why?'

'Women have more patience.'

'That's a generalization!' she said. 'We're not allowed to make those in essays.'

Mark stopped washing up again. Jasmin wondered why he couldn't talk and work as she could. He wore an old navy sweater, and she looked at him, looked at him properly, as Sue's husband. His dark hair, his small nose and mouth were quite attractive and in his movement, in his voice, there was a pleasing, hesitant quality. She tried to imagine him as Sue's lover. She could see it would be possible.

'You said before that you and Sue *were* in love. Aren't you still?'

190

He laughed at her directness. 'Yes,' he said. 'Of course we love each other.'

Jasmin sat down; her ankles might be swelling. 'Why did you say women have more patience? Sue hasn't got any more patience than you. She finds the kids hard work. She shouts at them. You work really long hours. Do you have to?'

'Yes,' Mark said. 'We all do in the department. If you don't, the boss thinks you're not serious about the job.'

'I was thinking, even if I had married Tom, he would never have seen the baby, because he would have been out at work all the time anyway! Do you know what makes me angry, Mark? All the fuss that is made about mothers going out to work and leaving their children, when the average father who's got a job only ever sees his kids at bedtimes and weekends! I only ever saw my Dad from month to month as he travelled, but he was a good father because he made a lot of money. But he wasn't a good father, not really. I never saw him. My mother just took over. And he let her, because his job was foreign trade and hers was me.'

Both Jasmin and Mark were silent. Both were thinking their own thoughts. Jasmin was the first to break the silence.

'I know what I'll do. I'll give my baby undivided attention until she's old enough to have a relationship with a father, and then I'll find myself a new man, so she can have one. But not Tom. Someone else who works from home, like a gardener. Yes, that's what I'll do.'

CHAPTER TWELVE

Once he'd put on his Y-fronts he realized there was a big tear down one side. He considered for a moment. If he could be sure he was taking them off in the dark, or together with his trousers, it wouldn't matter. Or ought he to put on his old Y-fronts, which at least were hole-free? He picked up the old Y-fronts and held them to his nose. They would do. He took off the clean ones and stepped into yesterday's.

Alan Thomas looked at himself in the mirror, pulling in his stomach, flexing his muscles. Yes, he looked good. The weight-training at the gym had paid off. And it had given him something to do in the evenings, since Bev had gone. But tonight he wasn't going to think about Bev. He stepped into his jeans, and lost his balance slightly as he stood on one foot. Tonight he felt certain he was going to strike lucky. Christ, she'd been begging for it all week. And office parties were notorious for that sort of thing. He slipped the packet of condoms inside his jeans pocket, just in case things happened earlier than he'd anticipated. He burrowed his head into his striped sweatshirt and looked at himself again. He looked better than he had for ages.

As he tied his shoelaces, he thought of Sue. He found the fact that she was older than him attractive. She would be good in bed, no doubt of that. He had thought it all out. He hadn't wanted to risk rejection again from a younger woman – Bev's furious face sprang unbidden into his mind – his ego had suffered. Sue would appreciate him, he was sure.

It had been tricky, the past few weeks. He hadn't been

sure quite how fast to play it. But instinct had told him that Sue Turner wasn't used to this sort of thing, and that she would play hard to get. But the way she had looked at him! Those eyes! Of course, he'd keep the whole thing quiet. Reasonably quiet. And now for his aftershave. And plenty of it. Tonight was the night.

It didn't look quite as the beautician had done it. Sue could not remember just how to apply the blusher. But on the whole she looked good. She sat in front of the dressing-table mirror in a peach slip, fully made-up. It seemed strange to her to feel so full of anticipation and dread – like a teenager again, she thought.

But she was not going to dress like a teenager. She was going to wear a simple black dress, black stockings and her black stilettos. This, she hoped, would make her seem sober and yet sexy too. She had planned the evening care-fully. She would take the bus to the library, so that she could drink. Then she could always take a taxi for the return journey. And if it was hard to get a taxi, she was sure *someone* would give her a lift.

She zipped up her dress at the back. It was not fashion-able, but she felt comfortable in it. She considered her figure. There were some bulges where bulges weren't sup-posed to be, but these had not put Alan off yet. He was only thirty-two. Thirty-two! He had told her that this morning. This morning he had stopped at her desk and spoken for some time about the A-V budget problems, and the proposed plans, never taking his eyes from her and touching her hand. Then in the afternoon he had visited a branch library. She had not seen him and his absence was a hole.

She was ready. Sue wished she could vanish and remateri-alize in the library. But she knew she had to say goodbye to

193

Mark and the girls. She swallowed. Her throat was dry. When she got to the party, she would have a drink. She made her way downstairs, taking her coat from the cupboard.

The lounge door was open. The television was on, of course, but none of her family was watching it. Mark was on the floor with the girls and Emma was introducing her trolls to him. Mark, Emma and Lizzie looked up as they sensed her presence by the door.

Mark smiled at her appreciatively. 'You look nice,' he said. Sue did not respond.

'Where are you going, Mummy?' Lizzie asked. And, not waiting for a reply, 'Can I come?'

'It's the office party,' she said. 'It's a grown-up party and it won't be very interesting. I'll see you in the morning.'

'D'you want a lift?' Mark asked her. 'We could all drive you there. Save you taking the bus.'

'No,' said Sue quickly. 'No, it's all right. You all look so comfortable there. I'll see you later. I don't know what time I'll be back.' And she left.

I'm being silly, she told herself. Nothing will happen. We'll talk, flirt a bit more. Everyone does at Christmas. And that will be it. She walked quickly along Heaton Close. Just innocent fun, she thought. She saw Mark again, on the floor with Emma and Lizzie and the trolls. She increased her pace even more, leaving them all behind her.

The library office hardly looked any different. Sue had become used to the Christmas decorations. The only change was that the table in the corner, instead of supporting piles of books, held assorted bottles of wine and cans of beer and lager. She scanned the room. Chris was sitting on a desk by the window, laughing with Mick and Vince from the adult section. Betty and Barbara were arranging some food on plates. The counter staff were in a huddle together. She assumed the people she didn't recognize were from the branch libraries. But he wasn't there. It was already nine o'clock and he wasn't there. Chris waved and she went to join her, pouring herself a glass of wine on the way.

'You look good,' Chris said. 'Escaped the children?'

Sue nodded. Then Chris continued explaining to Mick and Vince, as they sipped at their beer, about the crèche campaign and the fund-raising activities in the New Year. Sue pretended to listen, but she found her concentration was splintered by Alan's absence. She was sure he was coming. But what if he wasn't? As newcomers arrived she turned round to study them. No Alan.

'It's going to get pretty crowded in here,' Mick said. 'Counting the branch library staff, there'll be well over sixty of us.'

'The boss said we could spill out into the library itself,' Vince explained. 'Which we'll have to, if they turn up the music again.' He looked over to where some of the younger branch counter staff, who had brought a tape deck, had congregated. Music with a heavy beat began to throb through their conversation. Sue looked down and realized she had finished her wine. She did not remember drinking it. She excused herself and went to get another.

She picked up empty bottles in her search for some more white wine. Successful, she began to pour her drink, and then looked at the door once more. There – in the striped sweatshirt and jeans. There he was. Her heart raced, thumped against her chest. Her hand shook and wine spotted the paper tablecloth that had been laid on the table. Sue prayed no one noticed. Quickly, she returned to Chris.

She pretended to listen to the conversation, which was now on the death of pop music. Why, she wondered, had Alan not come over to join them? A quick glance told her why. He had been absorbed by the group of branch librarians over at the entrance to the main library. They were all laughing. Sue was filled with a leaden disappointment. What had she been thinking? That he was interested in her? Thank God she had told no one. She would forget all about him. She finished her glass of wine. Vince took her empty glass from her as he went to get more beer.

It was during her fourth glass of wine, and in the middle of Vince's monologue about the new Star Trek series, that Alan came over to them, slapping an arm round Mick's shoulder and a matey arm round hers.

'Good do, isn't it?' he said.

Sue inhaled his aftershave. It caught at her throat. She listened as Alan spoke easily to Mick and Vince.

'Come on, Sue!' Chris ordered her. 'Glenys has arrived and you can help me talk to her.'

Perhaps, thought Sue, it was just as well. He could hardly declare himself to her in front of all her friends at the library. She continued dancing with Chris to some modern pop tune that she did not recognize. He was sitting now by a table, deep in conversation with some man Sue did not know. She felt hot and rather unsteady on her feet. At the end of the record she excused herself to Chris and went to the Ladies.

The Sue she looked at in the spotted mirror was flushed and messy and tired, and she could see too, in the expression of her eyes, a bitter disappointment. She would go home soon, she thought. She could always plead a headache. She left the Ladies. Alan was outside, waiting for her. She was startled.

'Hello, gorgeous,' he said.

He took her hand. Sue looked round nervously, but no one was in the narrow corridor.

'Can we talk?' he said.

196

'Shall we go back to the party?'

'We'll go into the main library,' Alan said. 'It's quieter.'

She followed him past the main desk and into the body of the library. Alan stood in front of Adult Fiction, F–K. Sue came and joined him. They sat on the reading table in the booth. As Alan moved towards her, Sue moved away. This intimacy was almost too sudden.

'It's OK,' he said reassuringly. 'I only want to talk.' Sue stared at the spine of a Dick Francis. Alan placed his finger on her dress and traced a circle with it. The sensation burned Sue's thigh.

'We're friends, aren't we?' he said. 'I really enjoy your company, you know that?'

'I like yours,' she said in a small voice.

He sensed her discomfort. 'Look,' he said. 'We're just having a talk. I'm not going to force you to do anything you don't want to. It's a long time since I had a talk with an intelligent, beautiful woman.'

'Aren't you married?' Sue asked him, curious.

'No. I lived with someone. We agreed to part. I've been on my own a bit too long now.'

He was rubbing her thigh with his whole hand. She took his hand and placed it by his side.

'Someone might see,' she said. She dared now to glance at his face. He grinned at her, and stuck out his tongue, and wiggled it. What an odd thing to do, she thought.

He rubbed her shoulder. 'Relax!' he said. 'You're uptight tonight. We're doing nothing wrong, you know.'

'I know,' said Sue. She needed another drink. There were Graham Greene and William Golding in front of her. *Lord of the Flies*. It seemed appropriate now, somehow.

'Are you happy, Sue?' he said.

'Look, I think someone will see us here. Can we go back to the party?'

197

Alan slid off the table. 'Sure,' he said.

Sue stumbled ahead of him, eager to rejoin the main party. There was Chris. But she was putting her coat on.

'I've got to go early, Sue,' she explained. 'The baby was running a temperature and it's been preying on my mind. Enjoy yourself,' she said.

'Don't go,' Sue said.

'I must. I'll see you tomorrow.'

Once again Alan was laughing with the branch librarians. Sue gratefully found some mineral water and filled a glass with it. Still she was compelled to watch him. He was a distinctive, attractive man and he fancied her. She had promised herself tonight. She had promised herself, wordlessly, that something exciting would happen. But she had given him the brush-off. She knew that, despite her numbing fear, despite her sense of everything being topsy-turvy (the drink), she would have to go through with it. Because she had promised herself. And the part of her mind that was sober was watching all this with clinical detachment, like the viewer of a film, wondering, what happens next?

What happened next was that he approached her again, with a leather jacket slung over his arm.

'Come and say goodbye to me,' he said.

She followed him automatically along the corridor. So he was going. So it was all over after all. He stopped outside the A-V room.

'I must just get my wallet,' he said. He went in and searched on the desk. Sue realized she was about to lose him. It was all to be an anticlimax. That was something she had to prevent. The corridor was empty. So she stepped inside and stood behind him. She noticed that he suddenly became very still. He closed the door gently. They were face to face. He smiled at her knowingly. Then again, he stuck his tongue out and wiggled it. It was a repulsive gesture, she thought.

Sue knew what would happen next. He approached her (she knew she had tacitly given him permission, by entering the room) and he embraced her, pushing her head back awkwardly, squashing her nose so that she could not breathe, and there was that repulsive little tongue worming its way into her mouth. She would not open her mouth. One hand was on her bottom and squeezed it. The other came from round her back and cupped her breast. She could not breathe. Her eyes were wide open. She saw cassettes and videos and computer games. She was absolutely sober. Her mind was terrifyingly clear and she knew, knew for certain, that she had made an appalling mistake. She pulled herself away.

His hair was tousled and he was flushed.

'I've got to go,' Sue said.

'I'll drive you back,' he said thickly. 'My flat's only five minutes away. We can sober up.'

'No,' Sue said. She looked at him. He was repulsive to her. He had held her in an unfamiliar way. He had not kissed her in the way that Mark would do. He had imposed and intruded. But being a man, he reminded her of Mark. With absolute clarity of mind she saw that all men were fundamentally the same: the excitement of the chase ended eventually; Alan – if she did desire him, which she did not – would be far, far worse to live with than Mark. She realized all that. She was crippled with guilt too. But looking at him now, she knew it was not guilt alone. She saw him differently, his stubbly chin, his choking aftershave, the calm assumption in his teasing eyes that she was his for the asking. Why had she not seen this before?

Now Sue felt something quite different. It was a new feeling and one she couldn't immediately give a name to. It was hard and knotted and started in her stomach and spread all through her, and made her want to shout. Anger, was it?

'I am sober,' she said clearly. 'I don't want to go home with you. I've made a bad mistake. I'm sorry. Now go away.'

He winked at her. 'You'll feel different when you get to my place.'

'I just said "no".' Sue found herself rubbing her mouth violently, to clean herself. She was about to open the door of the room, to leave, then hesitated. She did not want anyone outside to see her with him.

'Sue,' he said, approaching her again, touching her arm.

'Stop it!' she ordered. She had to escape. She opened the door and, luckily, no one was there. She stepped into the corridor and slammed the door, leaving Alan in the A-V room. Hurriedly, she found her coat and then stopped still. She remembered she would have to ring for a taxi.

She slipped into the District Manager's office, where she knew it would be quieter. She dialled Orange Cars. Fifty minutes, they told her. They were busy. She looked at her watch. Ten forty-five. She had to get home. If only Mark could come and get her. But there were the children. If only there was someone to look after the children. Then she thought of Jasmin. Jasmin, she knew, did not go to sleep until twelve, and slept in late to compensate. She would ring her.

It took only a few moments. Jasmin agreed happily to relieve Mark and Sue replaced the receiver, sat back on the District Manager's padded seat and tried to relax.

The District Manager was not at the party. Sue was not often in his office and had never sat in his chair before. It was a swivel chair; it was well upholstered; it was a position of power. As she leant back, it leant back with her.

Horrible, repulsive, slimy, revolting! She sat up again with a start. Sue's stomach heaved as she remembered Alan (she could hardly bear to think his name). She thought of that hand on her bottom, and on her breast, those cracked, rough lips, and that tongue, waving at her, like some pink, demented sea-creature. He was awful. But why had she not seen this? Why had she been so obsessed with him for weeks? How could she have let herself become just another conquest? She clasped her head in her hands. It was like some form of temporary insanity. She prayed that Chris had not noticed, that no one had noticed. She thanked God that she had not told Jasmin. What would Jasmin have thought of her?

Actually, she realized, Jasmin would have been pleased with her. Not for almost being duped by that loathsome man, no. But she had rejected him. All by herself. She had said 'no'. Sue knew it wasn't through guilt, strong as her guilt had been. But something had stirred within her, some new decisiveness, some self-respect. She hadn't had an opportunity to turn the job down, but she had turned Alan down. She was getting there. She thought of Jasmin's Doc Marten's. She would ask her if she could try them on.

How could I ever have fancied him, she thought? Sue tried to recall those early scenes with Alan, and all she saw now was a woman acting without decorum, foolishly, like a young girl, a girl without Jasmin's sense and self-possession. What had been wrong with her? What part of her was responsible for it all?

It had started the day he had looked at her appreciatively, when she had been to the beautician. No. It started before that; it started with her envy of Jasmin. No. It lay deeper than that. It was painful for Sue to think, but something compelled her to keep on digging. Was it Mark's fault?

Once, he was everything to her. Those early days, each absorbed the other completely. She knew she did too much for him, but it was fun. Then the children came along. The children. It had been a watershed in their marriage. The children had to come first. Then there was the sense that he had failed her, watching incompetently as she struggled with nappies and screaming toddlers. And his job spread into their marriage – books, papers, computer software everywhere. He retreated. She knew she saw him through a mist of resentment; she retreated too into her daydreams. She had hoped that her barbed comments, that her withdrawal, would have made him notice that she was hurt, that he would change. But they had not. And still there were Lizzie and Emma centre-stage, and she and Mark had become their audience, cajoling them and applauding their progress. Their relationship was now just a shadow, a ghost that haunted her. Was it all over? Did she want him still? And whose fault was it? His, for his blindness? Or hers? That was when Sue realized she had been too passive to do anything about it all.

Jasmin would have done something. Jasmin would have told him that she was resentful, that she wanted him to stop working every night and be there, for God's sake! Jasmin, because she was young, and because she was a product of a different generation, would have taken what she wanted.

Sue remembered how she had rejected Alan. Well, she had stood up for herself once. Now she would stand up for herself again. She would decide tonight if she still wanted Mark. There was a way to find out. She would take it.

She stood at the front entrance, at the top of the stairs. It was a clear night and the wind disturbed the festoons of Christmas illuminations hanging across the high street, so that they swung unevenly. The occasional car raced by her. Any moment now, one of those cars would contain Mark. She took a deep breath. This wasn't going to be easy, but she would do it.

There he was. There was the Vauxhall Nova. It drew up in front of the library. She came down the steps, opened the unlocked door and slipped into the front seat beside him.

'Have a good time?' he asked her.

She observed the soft vulnerability of his features. There was something in his face that roused her.

'Yes,' she said. 'I'm not actually ready to go yet.'

'So why did you ring?'

'I wanted to see you. I just don't want to go home yet.'

'It's past eleven o'clock,' he said, feeling slightly puzzled, 'and Jasmin looked tired.'

'Jasmin would understand,' she said.

'Are we just going to sit here?'

'No,' she said. 'Can't you take me for a drive? Please. We can go up to Fieldhead.' Fieldhead was a small village, just north of Boltham. There were a few farms there; it was surprisingly rural for a spot so near to town. 'Please!' said Sue with urgency.

Mark shrugged. He was not in the mood to argue and wondered if Sue had a reason for her odd demand. Intrigued, he put the car in gear and they drove off.

It didn't take them long to reach the Fieldhead Road. Mark put his foot down until the car reached a steady forty. Sue was silent. He said nothing either; he supposed her silence meant he was not to talk. He slowed and took the minor road left, up to the village. The street-lights gave out here and he turned the car headlights on to full beam. There was a hand on his leg. It was Sue's. Did she want to say something? But, no. She was looking straight ahead.

That hand was moving between his legs. Mark pushed the brake with his foot and looked again at Sue. She was still not looking at him, but her hand was very definitely stroking and squeezing him. He felt himself go hard.

'Over there,' Sue said. 'There's a small lane. Go on, turn up it.'

Mark did as he was instructed. The lane was deeply rutted and the car shook as he drove. There was a gate which gave access to a field. He pulled up there. There were no lights visible. Then Sue pulled him to her and kissed him, long and hard. Excited, he responded eagerly, moulding his mouth to hers and pushing his fingers through her hair. He realized they had not made love since she had had her hair cut. Perhaps it was the haircut that had made her behave like this. He felt her hand fumbling with his belt and he helped her. Her hand squeezed him tightly. Everything else slid from his mind – those final assessments, the late hour, the unusual spot. Sue wanted him now, in the car, in this deserted lane. Well, she could have him. He found the zip on her dress and pulled it down easily.

Sue adjusted the seat so that it reclined. Mark's hands lifted her bra, and she felt that wonderful freedom as her breasts fell loose. Her eyes were closed now and she sighed with pleasure as she felt Mark's head between her breasts. His hand was now stroking her thighs, now his fingers probed between her legs. She was melting, dissolving, all liquid heat. Her body was on its favourite journey. When he entered her, he fitted so perfectly – it was a miracle. And there they were in the car, Mark on top of her, her dress around her waist, like two teenagers, but worse, and better. She wanted to laugh with the silliness of it all. She clung to him. He clung to her. He knew just what to do for her, better than anyone. She let herself scream with pleasure. 'Sue!' he said, in wonder. And then she turned, twisting him and her round, so that she was on top. They made love for a few moments more. Mark breathed out deeply, with a little sigh. Sue relaxed too and softly brought her body down on his.

What was there to say, she thought, as she lay there, her face resting against Mark's, unbothered about the time, the situation? She had said it all. And she had received her answer.

They disentangled themselves, and laughed as they

cleaned themselves, and dressed. When she sat up again, she realized the windows were steamed up. Mark wiped them with his hand. Sue was still vibrating with pleasure.

'That was a surprise,' Mark said, before he started the engine. 'Thank you!'

'No,' Sue said. 'I did that for me. Now it's your turn to surprise me.'

Mark smiled to himself. He turned the key in the ignition. He felt much, much better, and put it down to the sex. Sue felt better too. She had made a good beginning. Yes, she thought. She would certainly get herself some Doc Marten's. She deserved them.

CHAPTER THIRTEEN

'I think we'll only be fifteen minutes late, Jasmin.'

Jasmin didn't answer. Instead she consulted her watch with a nervous gesture. That was meant to be a rebuke to Sue. She had been waiting for almost half an hour for Sue to arrive to take her to the FAM meeting; Sue knew how important this meeting was to her; consequently Jasmin was feeling just a little hurt. But there was not much traffic on the way into Boltham and they made good progress.

'I still think you should have tried the NCT,' Sue said evenly, aware of the frostiness in the atmosphere.

'Everyone goes there,' Jasmin said. 'Besides, when I spoke to this man, he said that it was all very well to focus on the giving birth itself – FAM do that, all of that – but what about the baby? Planning a birth without consulting the baby is like planning a wedding without consulting the bridegroom. That was what he said.'

'Consulting the baby? How do you consult the baby? Damn! Just turned red!'

'That's why I wanted to be early, Sue. I think I need to find out.'

Another silence. 'Look, I'm sorry I was late. I fell asleep. I . . . I didn't get that much sleep last night.' Sue remembered why; Mark had been surprising, very surprising. Then she was filled with contrition. Jasmin didn't have a man, and no wonder she was anxious, going alone to meet a group of pregnant women who, in all probability, would have husbands with them. She had been selfish.

'If you like, Jasmin, I'll come in with you. I'd find it very interesting.'

'No, it's all right.'

'Please don't be upset with me. I know I was wrong.'

Jasmin could not help but think to herself that her own mother would not have let her down. But thinking of her own mother, she was glad Sue was different.

'No, I'm sorry,' she said. 'I think the pregnancy makes me over-emotional. I didn't mean to be so upset. I'm sure the meeting won't start on time.'

In Boltham town centre itself, running behind the main street, stood four large blocks of flats. Although only thirty years old, they had become a familiar part of the Boltham skyline. At night, they displayed a patchwork of lights in the dark sky. This was where Jasmin had been instructed to go. Sue parked in a bay outside the flats and asked again if Jasmin was sure that she wanted to go in alone.

'Yes, I do. I'm sure I'll be fine, really. And yes, I promise to ring when it's over, so you can pick me up.'

Jasmin slid carefully out of the car and Sue watched her walk, still with feline grace, to the entrance of the first block of flats. Then she paused. Sue saw her press some buttons and speak into an entryphone. A moment later, Jasmin pushed the door, it gave way and the building swallowed her up. Sue turned the key in the ignition.

Jasmin wrinkled her nose in response to the disinfectant in the lift, as she was jolted and jerked to the ninth floor. There the door opened, to reveal yet another lobby, and, as instructed, Jasmin turned left and made her way to number 94. In this flat, she knew, would be the people who would help her get everything right, who would teach her what to do. Her mind was cleansed of all expectations. She wanted the best for her baby and she would get the best, even if it meant visiting a rather sordid flat in the heart of Boltham.

The person who opened the door was a man. She assumed this was Grant. He was tall and bear-like, with a full curly brown beard, with bushy sideburns and glasses too. His eyes, magnified by the glasses, seemed unnaturally large. He blinked at Jasmin.

'Are you Jasmin Carpenter?'

'Yes,' she said.

'Good, good. Come in, come in.'

She did so. She felt his paternal arm on her shoulder, guiding her into the narrow hallway. He was considerably taller than she was and was dressed in a multicoloured hand-knitted sweater and baggy black track-suit bottoms.

'You're a little late,' he said. 'But it doesn't matter. It doesn't matter. I agreed with Sylvie that I'd talk to you first, before you joined the others. Explain our approach to you.' He guided her into a small room that had been converted into some sort of study. The desk under the window held a computer and box files. There were shelves of books too, many of which Jasmin had either read or seen in her attempts to master pregnancy.

'Take a seat. Take a seat,' he said.

The only seat was by the computer itself and so Jasmin sat there, first taking off her coat. Grant sat on a large leather bean bag against the wall. Now he was lower than she was.

'You're seven months now, you told me on the telephone.'

'Yes, that's right.'

'Good, good.' Grant rubbed his beard, as if it was itching him. 'I know I told you a little about us on the phone, when I explained about the unexpected vacancy. Sylvie and I call ourselves the Foetal Awareness Movement – to say

208

we're a movement is optimistic, but we hope to become one. We hope to become one. I'm writing a book – *Foetal Awareness*. It's based partly on Sylvie's experiences having Vida and partly on my own research. The group has sprung up around it.'

His mention of a book reassured Jasmin. If he was writing a book, he must be some sort of expert.

'When we were pregnant with Vida, of course we wanted the very best for her.' Jasmin found herself nodding. 'The very best. Sylvie spent some time studying nutrition and we had spent the whole pre-conception period on the correct mineral supplements. Of course.'

'Of course,' murmured Jasmin.

'And, of course, as soon as we knew we were pregnant, Sylvie prepared for an active birth, through sensible nutrition, exercise, relaxation and a study of the choices available. But I was feeling increasingly uneasy. And it was about that time –'

The study door opened. In came a large, fair woman in a kaftan. She had a freckled, English complexion and watery blue eyes. Jasmin stood up and the woman shook her hand.

'Jasmin? I'm Sylvie Findlay. Hello.'

'Remember to say hello to Jasmin's baby, dear,' Grant said.

Sylvie placed a hand on Jasmin's bulge and held it there firmly. 'Hello!' she said. Then she sat down behind the closed door.

'The others are having their usual conversation now. I felt rather sleepy, so I thought I'd have a rest. I thought I'd meet Jasmin.' She yawned.

Grant continued. 'Have you heard about Penny? It was Penny who dropped out earlier this week.' He shook his head. 'It was dreadful. Gas and air, pethidine *and* an epidural. That poor baby. Can you imagine emerging into a numb birth canal to the arms of a mother befuddled with drugs? My book explains the birth trauma in detail. Have you sterilized the nappies, Sylvie? You see, Jasmin, we don't believe in disposables. It's not just an environmental issue; or rather, we're concerned about the baby's immediate environment. Nappies must feel real. Real. But I digress. I was about to tell her your dream, Sylvie.'

Sylvie's eyes were closed. Jasmin noticed that her face was drawn. Grant continued. 'Sylvie saw and heard Vida. You see, we had reached a stage where the choices we had were baffling. There was the birthing chair, or the birthing pool, or a squatting delivery, or all fours, and we discussed all the options for hours, and we said in the end, didn't we, dear, that if only the baby could decide . . .

'Have you noticed, Jasmin, how the dreams you have when you are pregnant seem so vivid? In Sylvie's dream, she heard the baby's voice, pleading for a water birth. She heard the rushing of water too. And she woke and told me.

'It crystallized what I had been thinking. Sylvie had been so careful with nutrition and exercise, and we were caring for our baby's body, but Sylvie's experience with Vida showed us that there was a whole person there and, just as we had the responsibility to care for the body, we had to nurture the mind and the spirit.

'So the Foetal Awareness Movement is the only group that brings together all aspects of foetal development and birthing. We want you to communicate with your baby – childbirth must be a partnership – and we promote awareness of the foetal environment and the role the parents have to play in this.'

'What role?' asked Jasmin.

'You've read *The Secret Life of the Unborn Child*?'

Jasmin shook her head.

'It's a central text. It shows how much the foetus is able

to understand. It can hear music, you know, and can detect the mother's mood – her stress, tension, her anger and resentment. Sylvie's experience proved to us it can understand her thoughts too. Being a mother doesn't start at birth. It starts much, much earlier than that.'

'Yes,' said Jasmin eagerly. 'I've thought that too.'

'The parentcraft classes you take at the hospital only teach you about practical details, such as bathing and nappies. NCT classes teach you about the physical processes of pregnancy and labour. We aim to do much, much more than that.'

Jasmin was impressed by Grant's intensity and interest in the subject. She suspected it must be unusual for a man. She imagined he was some sort of authority. Sylvie seemed to be meditating, or was she asleep? Jasmin noticed that her shoulders were stained with something that looked like a whitish milky mess.

Yet all he was saying made sense to her, for Jasmin had seen her own baby. Her baby existed and, yes, it would have a mind too, and a spirit. And she ought to nurture these. How could any woman, she thought, not do the best for her baby?

Grant placed his hands firmly round Sylvie's waist. 'We'd better return to the class,' he reminded her. She jerked into wakefulness.

'Come with us, Jasmin,' Grant said. 'Did you remember to bring a book?'

'Oh, yes!' said Jasmin. 'It was hard to know which one to choose. Particularly because I don't have any children's books yet. So I brought something *I* like.'

'That's good, that's good,' Grant said approvingly. 'Sharing something you love with your baby.'

Sylvie guided Jasmin into what was the lounge of the flat. It was a small, rectangular room and olive velvet

211

curtains shrouded the windows. The curtains were a back-drop to a remarkable scene. On the floor were three heavily pregnant women and kneeling over two of them were two men, whose hands rested on the women's bulging midriffs. Soft music played in the background. As Sylvie entered, the women opened their eyes and slowly sat up, their partners assisting them.

'Have I missed an exercise?' Jasmin asked. 'I thought you said your class was just talking.'

Grant explained. 'They *were* talking. Each session begins with conversation. We create an atmosphere in which mother can communicate with baby, and father too.'

Jasmin was surprised to hear a thin wail. Confused, she at first thought there must be a cat somewhere. No, it was definitely a baby. There was a thin, broken, distant sobbing. No one else seemed to notice it.

Sylvie sat down cross-legged and Grant stood behind her, his hand close to her shoulders.

'Does anyone want to share their news?' Grant asked.

'My baby felt angry,' one woman said. She was slight, with a noticeably protuberant bulge.

'Have *you* been angry recently, Anna?' Grant broke in.

The woman bit her lip and thought. 'No. Not since our session last week. Kevin and I have made an extra effort not to argue and I don't think I've lost my temper. But it's been a busy week. I've been completing our annual report.'

'Have you been thinking about your baby?'

'Not while I was working,' Anna said doubtfully.

'Aah. That's it. Your baby is lacking attention. That's why he's angry. Babies need our conscious love and our constant thought,' Grant reminded her. 'Your work is clearly distracting you.'

Jasmin thought that the choking, staccato sobbing was getting louder. Sylvie pushed a stray lock of hair behind her ear and turned and looked at her husband questioningly. He did not seem to see her.

'This is Jasmin,' he said, 'who's taking Penny's place.' There was a muttering and a shaking of heads at Penny's name. 'I've told Jasmin a little about us and, if you all don't mind, I thought, as Jasmin is new, we might let her read to her baby first.'

There was general approval at the suggestion and Jasmin was glad. Everyone seemed to accept her quite happily. She was aware of Grant in one corner of the room fumbling with the hi-fi. From it he brought over to Jasmin a microphone. She waited for instructions.

'I'm sure you've read,' he began, 'of the foetal ability to appreciate music. There are well-documented cases of new-born babies recognizing television theme tunes and certainly new-borns are calmed by the sound of their mothers' heartbeats. So it follows that the foetus, who can most certainly hear, can hear the mother's voice, if it is loud enough. We aim to help the foetus to hear and recognize the mother's voice *before* leaving the womb. Then, you see, you can talk to him as he's being born and reassure him.'

Jasmin flinched at the word 'him', but was distracted, for the crying now was furious.

'Our system, which I explain fully in my book, helps mother–baby bonding and also increases foetal IQ. You can read to your baby and tell him the things he needs to know. We recommend a good half-hour's reading aloud a day. You must try now.'

Grant placed the microphone in Jasmin's hand.

'Read into the microphone,' he instructed her. 'We've hooked it up to our amplifiers so that the sound of your voice is loud enough to penetrate the womb. You can easily do this yourself at home. Now, what have you brought to read?'

'It's the *Ancrene Wisse*. It's medieval devotional prose.'

On the word 'prose', the microphone screeched its feedback to the room. Sylvie grimaced and gestured to Jasmin that she should start to read.

'Agein alle temptatiuns, ant nomeliche agein fleschliche, saluen beoth ant bote under Godes grace. . . .'

Jasmin's loud, amplified voice bounced around the room. She did not look at the other parents-to-be; she was having to concentrate on the pronunciation of the Middle English. Grant took the microphone from her and arranged it in a stand. Sylvie took her free hand and placed it on her tummy (for the vibrations, she whispered).

'Hali meditatiuns beoth bicluppet in a uers . .'

Was her baby hearing this? Jasmin was sure she was. She had seen her baby's ear; she could hear and the first words she heard were her mother reading the *Ancrene Wisse*. She saw her baby then as an anchoress, voluntarily secreted away; the cell, her womb. Her voice boomed and ricocheted.

'Euchan of theose word walde a long hwile forte beo wel i-openet . . .'

She was still aware of distant, furious crying. Perhaps, she thought, it came from an adjoining flat.

It was with some reluctance that she nodded to Grant, who had indicated that her time was up.

'That was beautiful,' Grant told her. 'I'm sure your baby understood it, just as it was meant. Now, someone else must have a turn. Glenda, you promised to bring a vegetarian cookbook.' He turned to Jasmin. 'Glenda cooks in a vegetarian restaurant and we felt this would help her communicate best with her baby.'

Jasmin did not really listen to the recipe for butter bean and onion flan. She was entranced by the fact that her baby had listened to the first part of the *Ancrene Wisse*. Dr

Cooper would be thrilled. She would write and tell her. She would certainly, certainly read to her baby every day. There was *Piers Plowman* too.

This was so much better, she thought, than the hospital. There she had felt as if she was a patient, and all the time she and her baby were seen as medical liabilities. So much, it was hinted, could go wrong. Here, the perfection that she craved was within reach. If she read to her baby, thought about her baby, ate correctly, relaxed – if she did all these things, and she would do them (what was to stop her?) – then she could be the perfect mother, giving birth to the perfect baby.

That maniacal sobbing was even louder now. A grimace flickered across Sylvie's face. Jasmin noticed her look at Grant with a strange expression that she would have thought murderous had she not seen what an advanced and thoughtful father Grant was. She rose and left the room. Jasmin listened as she opened a door, and the screaming increased in volume and then seemed to be stifled. Yes, like the Madonna and child, whose image was everywhere just now, she would let the birth transform her. She patted her stomach contentedly.

'While Sylvie's gone,' Grant said, rising from his cross-legged position on the floor, 'I'm sure she won't mind me playing you the tape of Vida's birth. Sylvie spoke to Vida throughout. I have the tape here!'

Jasmin watched him turn a cassette holder, extract a tape and place it in his tape deck. Grant explained.

'I had a small microphone attached to my sweater,' he said. 'For most of this tape I was supporting Sylvie in the birthing pool. I started recording when she got in.'

There was a click from the machine. Then came sounds of a large object entering the water. Cries of 'Oh, that's better! Can you feel it, baby?', and more sloshing and

215

slurping and squelching. Then there was a grunt; Jasmin guessed this came from Grant, as he got Sylvie in position. Then someone breathed in an exaggerated fashion. Jasmin heard Sylvie's voice.

'Aah! It's coming. Aah!' Her panting breaths filled the room. 'I'm with you, baby! I know it's uncomfortable for you. I don't mean to send you from my body. I love you very, very much. I want you for ever. But Daddy wants to meet you too. We're waiting for you at the other end. Aah. Again!'

There were more watery noises, and grunts from Grant. Jasmin listened entranced. She had never heard a baby being born. She imagined the background distortion was the midwife moving around.

'Don't be frightened, baby. I'm not frightened. We're looking forward to seeing you and feeling you and holding you. Oh, Grant! The head. The head is coming!'

Grant switched the tape off. When he spoke he addressed Jasmin.

'I wrote this script for Sylvie. Notice how she was careful to explain to the baby that the birth was not a rejection. This is important, as for a foetus the womb contractions must feel just like a physical rejection. And Sylvie addresses directly the issue of fear, thus ensuring a calm, happy baby.'

Jasmin spoke. 'How can the baby understand her words?'

'The tone and the vibrations come across,' Grant explained. 'Just like when you are in a foreign country, you understand the gist of what is said to you. I believe,' he continued, 'I believe in the absolute centrality of the foetus. A calm, fear-free mother who is able to communicate with her baby during the birthing process delivers a baby who is loved and who knows his own worth. That's the message of FAM.'

Jasmin looked at the other prospective parents. They

216

nodded seriously. Jasmin felt privileged to be here in such an exciting group. If she practised reading to her baby, if she practised antenatal exercises and breathing, if she freed herself from fear, then she too could have a perfect baby.

Sylvie returned, and Jasmin saw that she carried in her arms a small baby, red-faced and tear-stained. It was a scrawny little thing. She took a low stool and proceeded to nurse the baby. Jasmin was entranced. She watched her as she listened to Grant.

'That's the message of FAM. That's the message of my book. I concentrate on the birth itself, but as the small baby grows we advocate constant contact with the mother to ensure environmental continuity for the baby. Separation must be a gradual process. FAM asks a lot. However, we can give the mother the ultimate satisfaction of the entirely satisfied baby.'

Sylvie's baby made a sort of strangulated sound and Jasmin watched Sylvie try to fix it back on the nipple again. But now Grant was asking the mothers to lie on the floor for breathing exercises and Jasmin, in her new position, was unable to watch Sylvie any longer.

Preparing herself to breathe comfortably, she reflected with some surprise how much there was to learn about having a baby. It was lucky, she decided, that she had all the time and space she needed to put FAM's principles into practice. She would have a very busy Christmas.

CHAPTER FOURTEEN

Go on. Tell me. What is the point of Christmas? It's certainly not religious for most families, and anyway the real Nativity took place some time in March. And it's certainly not to have a rest. Sue continued to swipe savagely at a potato with her dented peeler. *And don't tell me it's to restore family harmony. It's the best way I know to reduce even the happiest family to high court litigation.* She thought about how Lizzie and Emma had already fallen out because Emma ate her Cadbury's Christmas selection *in the wrong order*! Sue was furious with Mark too. He had been studiously avoiding the kitchen. Not, for that matter, that she wanted his help. He'd only get in her way. *And Christmas dinner! Who actually enjoys Christmas dinner? Undercooked turkey and the same old vegetables! And you can't try anything different because the children insist on turkey. And why can't we have Christmas after the sales so that everything would be cheaper? Tell me that.*

The small man in the studio quailed at Sue Turner's questioning. Sue Turner, investigative reporter, knew she had him on the run. She winked at her producer behind the glass screen. Christmas would never be the same again.

Christmas was always the same. Same dinner, same arguments, same recycled films on television. The potatoes were ready now. Sue put them in the pan of water. Come on, now, she berated herself. This year was slightly different. She and Mark were getting on better, no doubt of that. And it was also a relief to be away from work. Alan had avoided her, true, but she could not be absolutely sure he had not spoken to Mick. And what had he said? Work seemed more incestuous than ever.

She tumbled out the Brussels sprouts from their green mesh bag. Her school reunion had been delayed and was now at the end of February. She would have to decide whether to go. But what could she say that would astonish them? What could she say to show them she hadn't wasted herself? I have a happy marriage, two lovely children and . . . and . . . I have a friend called Jasmin Carpenter who's coming for Christmas dinner. An unmarried mother-to-be. For Jasmin was coming to dinner, and Sue was glad. That was why Christmas this year *was* going to be different. Perhaps, having a guest at the table, there wouldn't be an argument. Sue was cheered, and turned her attention to the Brussels.

She enjoyed chopping off their bottoms and slicing through the bigger ones. Then there was a sudden hissing. Sue swivelled round to discover the potatoes had boiled over. She cursed. She left the pan standing on an unlit gas ring as she tried to mop up the spilt water, burning her fingers in the process. It was always like this. Food never behaved for her. Ever. Especially the Christmas dinner. She had warned Jasmin. She had told her she was only too happy to have her over for the day, provided she enjoyed substandard cooking.

The turkey! Did it need basting? Taking a tea-cloth to cover her hands, Sue opened the oven door and saw that it had hardly begun cooking. She noticed something else too. It was a large turkey, a very large turkey. She had bought extra for Jasmin. It was so large, in fact, that there was absolutely no room for the potatoes. She could put them in separately, of course, but they wouldn't brown on the oven bottom. Or later. But then dinner would be hopelessly delayed.

Sue had an inspiration. She would depart from tradition. She would rescue the potatoes from the saucepan and make a potato salad. She had bought far too many eggs and so she could make her own mayonnaise. And then, she could use the mayonnaise for the prawn cocktail she planned as a starter. She cheered up. Should she do that now, or carry on with the Brussels? She could make a salad too, so they could have turkey salad in the evening. Sue's brain buzzed with choices. Then she thought she heard the doorbell.

'Mummy! It's Jasmin! Jasmin, me and Emma have bought you presents and Mummy has bought you a present too. I've got a personal stereo – look!'

Lizzie dragged Jasmin into the lounge as Sue emerged from the kitchen. She watched as Lizzie ordered Jasmin to sit and gave her the presents the girls had prepared; she had taken Lizzie and Emma to the Body Shop to choose things for Jasmin. Poised as ever, but pale too, Sue thought, Jasmin opened the badly wrapped parcels and thanked the girls. They stood in front of her expectantly, smiling. It crossed Sue's mind that Jasmin might have forgotten to get something for them. She had seemed preoccupied lately. But no. From her coat pocket Jasmin fished out two very small packets. Both girls opened them eagerly. They were delicate pendants, one with an 'L' and one with an 'E'. The girls were thrilled.

'I've got a special present for you, Sue,' Jasmin said, 'but I don't want to give it to you yet. I didn't know what to get Mark, so –' again she fished in her coat pocket – 'I got him a book token. Where is he?'

'Getting dressed,' Sue said.

Jasmin took off her coat and handed it to Sue. She was wearing a dark-grey smock with a plain lace collar and looked, Sue thought, like a nun. When she sat back on the armchair, she folded her hands over her bulge. She seemed abstracted. The children were squabbling about which presents to show Jasmin first.

'Are you all right, Jasmin?' Sue asked.

Jasmin nodded slowly. 'Sshh,' she said. There was a silence. 'Yes, I'm fine.'

'Is there anything worrying you?'

Jasmin shook her head and gave an inward smile.

'The Brussels!' Sue announced, and fled back to the kitchen. Jasmin had seemed strange lately. Sue had put it down to the cow-like state that expectant mothers often experience; she had with Lizzie. She wondered too about the group that Jasmin had joined recently; she dated her preoccupation from then. Or perhaps Jasmin was fretting about her own mother. Was she missing her, despite the fact that she was adamant in not telling her until after Christmas? The carrots now. Jasmin's alibi was brilliant, Sue had to admit. Jasmin had written to her mother explaining that Juliet had to spend Christmas in Scotland, in a large farmhouse just south of Aviemore; she had invited Jasmin to come too, as she feared her parents would argue again. Unfortunately, there was no telephone. Jasmin had spoken to her mother a few days ago and, yes, Sue was certain this must be responsible for Jasmin's distracted mood. She would be extra considerate to her today, she decided. Sue began to crack open the eggs for the mayonnaise and wondered idly what Jasmin had got her? She too was saving Jasmin's present for later. She smiled to herself in anticipation.

Surely, Sue thought, that damn bird must be done by now. Again, she opened the oven door and contemplated the turkey. It was brown, but was it brown enough? Sue wished she had an oven thermometer, but she considered, if she did, she wouldn't know how to use it. She studied the

221

turkey again. If they only ate the cooked bits, they would be all right. It wouldn't matter tremendously if the very middle was still slightly pink. So Sue turned off the oven and shouted to Mark for help.

The next fifteen minutes were a flurry of activity. Mark entered the kitchen, in his red sweater and dark green shirt, and began to lay the table and shout commands to Lizzie and Emma, and bread sauce was stirred, and gravy concocted, and plates warmed and an extra chair found for Jasmin, and Sue regretted the sherry she had just imbibed as her brain was incapable of focusing properly on the tasks in hand. But miraculously, and quite soon, she found herself taking off her apron, smoothing her hair and entering her dining room, where Lizzie and Emma were sitting in state, Mark was carving the turkey and Jasmin was sitting demurely, taking her red paper serviette, unfolding it and placing it on her lap.

'Can we do our crackers now?' Emma whined.

Sue agreed. Emma brandished a cracker at her and Sue, cheating, held the thin strip of paper inside, and instructed Emma to do so too, to ensure a bang. Sure enough, there was a satisfying crack. Sue noticed Jasmin fold her arms over her bulge in a rather protective gesture.

'Mummy! Look! I've got a fimble!'

'*I've* got a lucky charm!' said Lizzie, with more than a trace of smugness.

'The prawn cocktails!' Sue shouted. 'I completely forget about them! Mark – look – put the turkey on the sideboard. I made starters for us all. Lizzie and Emma, you like prawn cocktail, don't you?'

Lizzie licked her lips obscenely.

'Sue,' said Jasmin. 'I shan't have any.'

'Are you sure?'

'Yes. Very sure. I've been advised not to eat prawns.'

'By your doctor?'

'Not her. But seafood isn't safe.'

'Oh,' Sue said.

'Have some bubbly instead,' Mark said to her, proffering a bottle of Veuve du Vernay.

'I don't drink any more,' said Jasmin.

'Some Perrier water?' he suggested.

'Yes, please,' said Jasmin.

The prawn cocktail was nice, Sue thought, and the mayonnaise was rich and creamy. But her pleasure in it was diminished by Jasmin, who bit slowly at a finger of brown bread and butter and sipped at her Perrier. Still, she thought, there was the Christmas dinner to come. She would eat that. The children, she was glad to notice, enjoyed the prawn cocktail.

'So, how many weeks to go, Jasmin?' asked Mark, his purple paper hat rather askew.

'Seven,' she said. 'It isn't very long, I know.'

'Enjoy yourself while you can,' he said. 'And stock up on sleep.' He took another spoonful of his prawn cocktail. 'Who's going to be with you at the birth, and afterwards?' He looked at Jasmin and saw her grateful glance at Sue. Sue spoke next.

'I've got some holiday due. I thought if I took it around the time of Jasmin's baby . . .'

'Good idea,' he said. 'But what about your mother?'

He saw Sue lift a finger to her lips and knew he had stumbled on some woman's secret. 'Fine,' he said, and carried on eating.

'Mummy, I'm still hungry!' demanded Lizzie.

'Good,' Sue said, 'because dinner isn't over yet!' She stood to collect the dirty plates, and Mark rose to help her. He rescued the turkey from the sideboard and continued to carve while Sue went in and out of the dining room, fetching bowls of vegetables and plates and potato salad.

'Potato salad – yummy scrummy!' Lizzie announced.

'Pass me your plate, Jasmin,' Mark instructed her, 'and I'll give you some turkey. White meat or brown?'

'Has it cooked right through, Sue?' Jasmin asked.

'More or less. You can never be sure with these big birds.'

'None for me, thank you, Mark,' Jasmin said.

Mark looked at her quizzically.

'Salmonella,' she said, rubbing her bulge with a circular movement of the palm of her hand.

'What's salmonella?' asked Lizzie. 'Can I have some?'

Sue thought back to when she was pregnant with Lizzie. She ate turkey, she was sure. But she would respect Jasmin's whims; she was their guest, and alone too.

'Have some vegetables now,' Sue said, 'and then later you can have some delicious Brie I've bought with some biscuits.'

'No thank you,' Jasmin said. 'I don't eat soft cheese.'

Jasmin realized she was pulling at her fingers, something she only did when she was feeling tense. That would never do. She must think of the baby. The tension would upset the baby's digestion, would impede her healthy growth. Relax, she ordered herself, relax. It was wrong of Sue, she thought with an uncharacteristic rush of resentment, not to check the turkey was properly cooked and not to think about the risks of seafood. She did not want to hurt Sue's feelings, but really!

'Carrots, Jasmin?'

'A few, thank you. No, that's enough. No, I don't like Brussels.'

'I don't want venchtables too!' Emma announced. 'I only want a little bit of turkey and lots and lots of stuffing.'

It crossed Sue's mind that Jasmin was setting the girls a bad example. But, no, she was their guest, she reminded herself again.

'No roast potatoes, I'm afraid, Jasmin. I forgot to put the turkey in the large baking tray. I've made a potato salad instead – with home-made mayonnaise!' Sue lifted the bowl and took a spoon to scoop some out for Jasmin.

'Mayonnaise with raw eggs?' inquired Jasmin.

'Yes,' Sue said.

'I shan't have any, thank you.'

Mark glanced swiftly at Sue and it was a relief to her to exchange glances with him. Within a few minutes, the dinner commenced. On Jasmin's plate were a few carrots and a spoonful of bread sauce. She cut and ate the carrots slowly, aware of the children's chatter providing a background to her own internal monologue. It was important to eat, she knew. But she could not eat the food that Sue had provided. And she had got that wonderful surprise for Sue, and Sue didn't deserve it! The resulting tension she could feel as a physical force, knotting her stomach, cramping her toes and her fingers. Anger at Sue bubbled up. Anger, Grant had told her, distressed the foetus. Anger, tension and conflict must be avoided at all cost. And she must eat a healthy diet. But no soft cheese, raw eggs, unwashed salad, raw meat, anything of which there was the least doubt.

For heaven's sake, thought Sue, why wasn't Jasmin eating? Was it personal? Was it something she had said? Sue found it impossible to enjoy her own dinner. For once, her own children were eating. The one Christmas when the children actually decide to eat most of their Christmas dinner, she has to invite a guest who doesn't eat hers. Sue looked at her own plate – gravy-soaked Brussels, slivers of carrots, a mountain of potato salad. No wonder Jasmin wasn't eating any. It all looked revolting. She put down her knife and fork. She didn't want any more. If only Jasmin would eat.

'Jasmin?' she asked her. 'Would you like some pudding instead?'

225

'Christmas pudding?' Jasmin said, her face brightening.

'No,' Sue said. 'No, I forgot to tell you. We don't have Christmas pudding. None of us likes it and so I haven't made any for years. I do my own chocolate mousse.'

'I can't eat chocolate mousse,' Jasmin said.

'Not chocolate mousse?'

'Raw eggs,' said Jasmin.

'Jasmin! You must eat something! You and your baby will starve!' Sue raised her voice and she regretted it instantly.

'How can I eat what you've given me? Do you expect me to risk my baby's life?' Jasmin shouted back. 'And now look what you've made me do! I'm angry! Look! Oh, God! I'm sorry, baby – Alison – I'm not angry at you. But –' Jasmin looked around her wildly. The children had stopped eating, their mouths open in astonishment. Mark's incomprehension paralysed him. 'I'm sorry,' Jasmin said, 'I've got to go!' She pushed back her chair and stumbled out of the room. Sue rose immediately and, before Jasmin could reach the front door, she laid a hand on her shoulder.

'I think we need to talk, Jasmin,' she said.

'Leave me alone.'

'No,' Sue said, 'Come upstairs. Mark!' she shouted. 'Finish your dinner and see to the girls. We'll be down soon.'

'Come in here,' Sue said, opening the door of her bedroom. She scanned it quickly. It wasn't too bad. The bed was made, at least, and Mark's clothes were hanging over chairs rather than on the floor. Crumpled wrapping paper littered the carpet, but that didn't matter either. Sue took a pile of towels off the chair and insisted that Jasmin sat there. She sat by her on the corner of the bed.

'Jasmin, why aren't you eating?'

Jasmin would not meet Sue's eyes. 'None of the food you

226

gave me was suitable. What if I caught listeria? Or worse? I can't take that risk, can I?'

'Jasmin. When I first met you, I saw you smoking cannabis, for heaven's sake!'

'Yes, but that was before –' Jasmin stopped.

'Before?'

'Before I joined FAM,' Jasmin said. 'They've given me a folder all about nutrition – food to avoid, and the vitamins and minerals I need. Sue, how can you even imply it's not important? We're talking about my baby's life! Are you suggesting I should eat to please you and kill my baby?'

'Jasmin, calm down!'

'And look at me now! I'm shouting! And do you realize that my poor little baby probably has her little hands over her ears and is wondering what she's done to deserve this? How she feels is entirely dependent on me. Surely you can see that? I have a responsibility to remain calm and assured. I've been practising this daily. Now look what a mess I'm making!'

Sue left the bed and knelt by Jasmin, taking her hands and stroking them. 'You're not making a mess. Your baby's fine. You can be in a bad mood when you're pregnant. Every woman is from time to time, you know.'

'But don't you see? That's where mothers go wrong. Can you imagine what it must be like to be a foetus, Sue? In your little dark world. And every movement of your mother's, every sound and every change in her mood affect you, and you're at the mercy of this person who is your whole universe and there you are, understanding nothing. What a terrifying way to start life! I have such a great responsibility. I never realized this properly before – before I started FAM. How can I possibly do less than my best for this baby? How can any woman do less than her best?'

'Is this what you've been learning at your group?'

'Yes. Except it's common sense too.'

227

'Jasmin, isn't this all rather extreme?'

'I wasn't the only person there. I wasn't the only person who found what he said convincing.'

'*He* said? The group is run by a man?'

'And his wife,' Jasmin said proudly. 'She's important too. Don't sound so cynical!'

There was a hysterical edge to Jasmin's voice. Sue knew she was listening to stored thoughts; thoughts that had been nurtured, re-examined and solidified in the isolation of Jasmin's empty house. She knew she had to tread carefully.

'I think every mother wants to do her best. Both when she's a mother-to-be and afterwards. But circumstances get in the way. We're not perfect – no one's perfect – and in a way, Jasmin, it's as well to prepare a child for the imperfections in life too. If your baby knows you're feeling upset now – which I doubt very much – it's a good preparation for when you're upset when she's born, when she won't sleep or put her toys away. Jasmin, you really don't have to be perfect.'

'Yes, you do. You must try to be perfect. It's immoral not to. Are you suggesting I try to be imperfect?'

'Well, yes!'

'Like you, you mean?' Jasmin lifted her chin as she spoke. She knew she had to prove to herself that Grant was right and Sue was wrong.

'What do you mean, like me?'

'Well, you try deliberately to be imperfect. I've watched you.' Jasmin's voice gathered force now. 'You're a coward, Sue. You won't try. You won't try to be perfect because you're scared you'll fail. Even in little things. You see Lizzie and Emma arguing and you say to me, *I* can't stop them, so you don't and they carry on arguing and you feel a failure. And you're bored and trapped by your life and you

228

won't do a thing about it. Will you? You're prepared to settle for second best all round. Well, I'm not. That's where we're different.'

Now there was a palpable silence. Sue felt winded. The pain she felt was physical. Jasmin thought she was a coward – thought she had settled for second best. She was kneeling on the floor, only seeing in front of her the discarded wrapping paper, with Santas and reindeer and Santas and reindeer. Repeated. And repeated. So that was what Jasmin thought of her.

'Oh, Sue, I'm sorry! I don't know why I said all that.' Jasmin was on the floor with her, her arms round Sue. Sue was stunned still. 'I'm so sorry. I think . . . I think I was trying to get my revenge. I don't mean any of it. I was hitting back and that was wrong. I'm so sorry. Please, please forgive me! You're not second best – you're my best friend. Look, can I give you your Christmas present now? Please!'

Sue looked up at the face next to hers. There was real contrition in it and once again Jasmin seemed so young to Sue. But the seismic waves of her comments still rocked Sue. She was a coward. She had settled for second best. She had let things happen to her. She had only ever reacted to life, never acted. She could see all this now.

'Yes, I will give you your present, Sue. Except it's not a present you can give. But I've arranged for you to do something exciting. You know I told you about my friend Isabel, who works in that pirate radio station? It's no longer a pirate. They've got a licence to broadcast legitimately and I've arranged for you to spend an afternoon in the new studio, and Isabel's going to try you out for a project she's working on. A mid-morning music and chat show aimed at women. I've told her ever so much about you, and how funny and interesting you are. It's in two weeks. That's your Christmas present.'

'I can't do that!' Sue said.

'Coward!' Jasmin said teasingly.

Once again Sue was surprised by Jasmin's presumption. She had assumed that Sue wanted to do this – to be auditioned for the radio! It was a ridiculous idea. She wasn't a coward; she was just utterly realistic. What could she say to her?

They sat on the floor still. Sue ran her hands through her hair. 'It's wonderful for you to arrange this. But I don't know . . . I'm just a librarian. What can I find to say?'

'Say whatever's in your head. Don't you ever daydream? Don't you ever make up conversations?'

'Yes,' Sue said.

'There we are then.'

Sue laughed. It was a way of expressing her panic. But there were two weeks to go. She would find a way of getting out of it. She would explain to Jasmin when both of them were feeling less hysterical. Then she remembered. 'Jasmin. I have a present for you too.' Sue scrambled to her feet. On Mark's desk was a small box wrapped in gold foil. She handed it to Jasmin.

'I'm afraid it's not as original as your present to me.'

'There you go,' said Jasmin, with mock severity. 'Putting yourself down again. This really must stop, Sue!' She removed the gold foil from the box. Inside was a bottle of perfume. Eternity. Jasmin looked at it, fingered it.

'Thank you,' she said in a small voice.

'Is that all right?' Sue asked her.

'Yes, yes,' she said quickly. 'But I can't wear it yet.'

'Why?'

'Smell is important too, you know. As a means of recognition. New mothers mustn't wear perfume or use talcum powder in case the baby doesn't recognize them. That's what Grant . . . that's what I've read.'

'So you won't wear any perfume, or express any of your emotions, or eat the food you like, because you're going to be a mother?'

Something that had been hard and knotted and rigid in Jasmin was crumbling. Sue's pointed questions were like little knives piercing that internalized picture of Grant as guru. It was an exquisite relief to her. But she remained silent. She let Sue continue.

'I don't know what you've been learning in that group. Motherhood's important, but don't turn it into a religion. When you do that, you just end up feeling guilty all the time, because you'll think you're never good enough.' Sue knew dimly she was addressing herself too. 'Being a mother isn't about sacrifice, Jasmin. It's not even about duty. It's about love. And you can't plan to be the perfect mother. It's trial and error in the end. Promise me you'll leave that group. Now please open that box. I want to see if the perfume suits your skin type.'

Obediently, a smile playing around her lips, Jasmin undid the packaging. She took off the stopper and dabbed some scent on her wrists.

'I like it,' she said. 'And Sue, I'm starving. I could murder a turkey sandwich!'

Joyce Carpenter shook her glass gently and the ice made a satisfying clink against the edge. She contemplated the thin slice of lemon and the small bubbles of the tonic playing around it. She recrossed her legs, repositioning her foot on the alabaster floor. Her husband sat at an angle to her, a turkey sandwich on a plate on his lap. She shook her glass again, then took a small sip of her gin and tonic. The mirrors along one wall reflected her action and revealed a tall, erect, grey-haired woman, elegant, poised, with an aristocratic lift to her chin. She placed her drink on the glass table in front of her. There was silence in the room, except for the wail of the muezzin from a nearby mosque.

'I don't believe her, George,' Joyce Carpenter said.

'She said they had no telephone.' He coughed apologetically once he had spoken.

As she thought, Joyce ran the tip of her tongue along her upper lip. 'We haven't seen her since September, George. She didn't look well then. She has never missed a Christmas with us. Never. But apparently Juliet's parents are contemplating separation and Juliet had begged Jasmin to stay with her. This Christmas was their last attempt at a reconciliation. When I met Juliet's parents, I thought they seemed very happy together. But if it were true,' she mused, 'it's good of Jasmin, isn't it?'

'She's a loyal friend,' George said.

'I miss her,' Joyce said.

There was another silence. I have coped, thought Joyce Carpenter, I have coped. I have done my duty. She glanced at her husband – meek, silent, utterly distasteful to her. But now, she thought, I want to go home to my daughter. Jasmin, she knew, was hers. She had made sure of that. They were as close as sisters. What else could she do? She had to have a companion.

'In many ways, George, we no longer need the Rectory in Boltham. We have no ties there. And if Jasmin does get a first and stays on for her Ph.D., it might be nice to buy a house in Oxford, or nearby. So much more convenient. Pleasant for you when you retire.'

George nodded.

Joyce Carpenter's eyes were deep-set; her glasses hung by a gold chain around her neck. She spoke with exquisite clarity; all thoughts, all sentences, completely rounded. There was deliberation in her every word, every gesture. She took her drink again and sipped it thoughtfully.

232

'The Rectory is empty now,' she said. 'When the holiday is over, I shall telephone the agent and see if she can arrange to put the house on the market. She always knew there was that possibility. Then I think I shall visit Jasmin in Oxford. Yes, I shall. It will be a surprise. I shall take a taxi from Heathrow. Then, while I am there, I can look for a house. Jasmin shall help me.'

George nodded again.

'The weather here is dreadful,' Joyce said with loathing. She stood and drew open the thick velvet curtains that hid their view of the Bosporus. But all she could see was the grey of the thick snow that covered the streets, and darkness where the Bosporus lay silently. She knew her intention was to leave. She would not spend another winter here. And the Turks were undisciplined, and Istanbul untidy and polluted. She would return to England and be with Jasmin. That was her Christmas present to herself.

Yes. She would stay with Jasmin through her finals. She recalled her daughter to her mind, her demure, self-contained presence. Her perfection. So much like her; nothing of George, nothing. She missed her badly, but it would not be long now. Not long at all. Not at all.

CHAPTER FIFTEEN

'I think,' said Cheryl, as she pushed open the Infants' school door, 'they're bound to have noticed the improvement.'

'I'm sure you're right,' Arthur said, as he looked to his left and noticed with surprise how low the pegs were, and saw the little cages for the small black pumps, and smelt that evocative aroma of old crayons and dust and damp.

'She can sing along to the two times table song now,' Cheryl continued. 'And I think she knows what she's doing when she adds up. It's the second classroom on the left. That's Mrs Williams's room.'

Arthur knew that Cheryl was talkative because she was nervous. It was an unfortunate coincidence, he felt, having Jenny's parents' evening the night before her Boltham Grammar School entrance examination. Not that it would affect Jenny. Jenny seemed supremely calm about it all, and when they put it to her that she was going to spend a morning in her cousin Francine's school and then be taken out for lunch, she seemed quite content. No, it was Cheryl who was nervous. She had picked at her dinner that night and had winced with pain several times during the evening. She suffered from a nervous stomach, he knew. Still, just suppose . . . Just suppose Mrs Williams did say that Jenny had improved. What a boost that would be.

He stood by Cheryl as she examined the paintings on the wall, looking for Jenny's. Last night, he remembered, Jenny had thrown a tantrum, which was unusual for her. Her disposition was essentially placid. She took after him, he

234

thought. But she would not practise the maths problems that Cheryl had set down in front of her. First she had kicked the table, until Cheryl had told her to stop. Then she had repeated that she didn't want to do them, and Cheryl had been very patient and explained that she had to do them, that the practice would help her. But he could hear that sharp note in Cheryl's voice. Then Jenny had shouted out silly answers to Cheryl's questioning and when Cheryl – perhaps she was a bit harsh – when Cheryl had told her she was a silly, naughty girl and it wasn't surprising she was so low in her class, Jenny had begun to cry – her face had crumpled and there was distress in her eyes. Then Cheryl had cried too. He was hard put to it to soothe both of them, but he did. It was his role.

Cheryl had been inconsolable all night and he had talked to her in the early hours of the morning, sitting up in bed, saying Jenny was tired, and she was too, and all parents lose their tempers occasionally. But now, looking at the paintings of mummies, Arthur saw Jenny's attempt and he regarded it with real pleasure. Yes, it really did look like Cheryl. There was her hair, and that anxious, pleading expression. How had Jenny caught that? Arthur was impressed.

'It's good, isn't it?' Cheryl said. 'But do you see my point, Arthur. If she can draw like that, why is her handwriting so scrappy? It's really as if she hasn't motivated herself.'

'Mrs Williams is free now,' he said. 'We might as well go in.'

Cheryl took his arm. Mrs Williams caught their eye and beckoned them to her desk, which she had pushed to one wall, out of hearing of the other parents, who milled around the classroom, picking up exercise books and exchanging gossip. Cheryl and Arthur took a seat each. Cheryl folded her hands in her lap, like a good girl. Arthur found that he sat back, slightly intimidated by Mrs Williams.

Perhaps it was because he knew she was a teacher and she wore that air of kindly authority that always made him feel clumsy and insignificant. Or was it that she had knowledge of his daughter and that this knowledge was so vitally important? It must be that, for Cheryl was a teacher too and yet he sensed that she felt as awkward as he did.

'Jenny's parents,' Mrs Williams said, and Cheryl knew, knew from the sympathy in her voice, that it was not going to be good. She stiffened. She watched Mrs Williams pick up a report that she and Arthur were not allowed to see.

'This is what I have written about Jenny,' she said, in measured, neutral tones. 'English. Jenny can spell simple words but has difficulty in completing most tasks without assistance. Her reading is slowly improving but occasionally shows lack of comprehension. She enjoys storytime but cannot concentrate for long periods. Mathematics. Jenny has difficulty in learning new skills and still cannot tell the time —'

'Yes, she can,' said Cheryl.

'Still cannot tell the time and cope with simple money sums. Her tables work is improving. She needs to practise her basic skills —'

'No, I'm sorry, Mrs Williams. I do practise with Jenny. I practise every night. As you know, she's taking the Boltham Grammar entrance exam tomorrow.'

The way that Mrs Williams shook her head slowly from side to side was tinged with disdain, Cheryl thought. No wonder Jenny had made slow progress at school, with such an unpleasant, cold, insensitive, mean-spirited teacher, who could find no words of encouragement, or of hope.

'By all means let her try, Mrs Davidson. But I don't think Jenny shows much academic potential.'

'She's only six,' Arthur cut in. 'She's just a slow starter.'

236

Mrs Williams looked with infinite pity at him and said nothing.

'Look,' he said, desperate to score a point, 'Winston Churchill never passed an exam in his life. He didn't do too badly.'

'When she copies from the board, Mr Davidson, her letters are often back to front and words are missed out.'

Arthur felt stupid. Faced with the overpowering authority of the Infants' school teacher, he felt as if he was blundering idiotically. There was something so inalienably right about everything she said. But she was so damning about Jenny. If this was true . . .

'I think she works better at home,' Cheryl said. 'I think she's more relaxed in a home setting.'

Behind Mrs Williams's glasses, Arthur thought he saw a malicious enjoyment. This woman felt it was right that his daughter, who had experienced difficulties at school, should be labelled 'hopeless'. She refused to give any encouragement. He was angry. But what could he say?

'Do you think she has a chance tomorrow, Mrs Williams?' Cheryl asked.

'No,' she said decisively.

'But if we try her again at eleven, she might have improved,' faltered Arthur.

Mrs Williams was silent again, that same wry smile playing at her lips.

Arthur was angry. How could Jenny do her best work with that dragon of a woman criticizing her every attempt. There's always hope, he thought, and Jenny might surprise them all.

'Her art is very good,' he said assertively.

'It is,' Mrs Williams agreed.

'But why?' Cheryl asked. 'Why isn't she doing well?'

'I really don't know,' the teacher said. 'She needs to learn

237

to concentrate and to stop making silly mistakes. I'll read you the rest of her report . . .'

But Cheryl did not listen. This could not be true; none of it could be true. She had done all that work with Jenny and the report was just the same as last year's. Didn't that woman *like* Jenny? That was the first feeling she had – that for some reason Mrs Williams didn't like Jenny – and it was something she could not begin to understand. Worse was the feeling that she had done something wrong. If Jenny wasn't getting on at school as well as she should, then surely it was her fault – there was something special she had omitted to do that other mothers do. Or it was genetic. She wasn't clever and so Jenny wasn't clever.

She thanked Mrs Williams automatically, rose from the chair and left the classroom with Arthur, not pausing to look at Jenny's books, or the other displays of work. If what Mrs Williams said was true, then Jenny might not pass. There in front of her was a gaping abyss down which she could not look. She followed Arthur out to the car. He unlocked the passenger seat and she got in. Then she turned to him.

'What do you think?' she said. Her voice was tinged with panic.

What could he say? If the report was true, then Jenny was wasting her time tomorrow. But that thought was submerged by a tidal wave of passionate loyalty towards Jenny and towards his wife.

'I think she doesn't know Jenny at all. I think it's her who's failed to get Jenny interested. She'll surprise them yet!' The engine growled and he released the clutch.

'Yes! I think that! That's exactly what I think. It's because it's such a bad school. When she gets to Boltham, there'll be a change. And she did say she was making some progress. She's such a harsh woman. Sue was saying that

238

Emma hated her when Emma was in her class. She terrorizes the children, you know. She's very unpopular. The children are frightened of her.'

'I was terrified myself,' Arthur said, and chuckled.

'She reminded me,' Cheryl said, 'of my teacher, when I was little.'

A fleeting memory of Mrs Stringer passed through Cheryl's consciousness. 'You're such a silly girl, Cheryl. For heaven's sake, can't you try to stop crying? It's your fault for not concentrating when I explained it! The rest of the class know how to take away!' She was a stern, grey-haired woman who liked only the clever little boys and girls. It was important to be clever.

'No wonder Jenny's learned nothing,' Arthur said with decision.

'Do you think she will pass the exam, Arthur?' Cheryl asked.

'It depends,' he said, 'how she is on the day. On a good day . . .'

'Yes, on a good day . . .'

It was not a good day. The rain poured relentlessly down in Heaton Close, bouncing off the pavement in sharp, wet needles. The morning was only slightly brighter than the night which had preceded it. Cheryl saw all this as she lifted the curtain in her bedroom, very gently, so as not to disturb Arthur. She felt light-headed and dizzy, and knew this was due to lack of sleep. The knowledge that she had to be on time at Boltham Grammar had prevented her sleeping, had jerked her into full consciousness at two and four and six o'clock. Now, however, it was morning. At least, she reflected, Jenny had slept well.

She entered Jenny's bedroom. Jenny was clutching the duvet in her sleep, her cheeks puffy, her fair hair wisping

239

over her face. Cheryl's heart contracted with love. Something in her sleeping pose reminded Cheryl of the baby Jenny slumbering in her carrycot. She bent over her and placed a butterfly kiss on her cheek. Jenny did not stir. Cheryl moved a lock of hair from her cheek and she then saw Jenny's eyes flicker. She watched as Jenny moved languidly and smiled, drunk with sleep, at her mother.

'It's an important day today,' Cheryl said.

As she spoke, a familiar, sharp pain stabbed her stomach.

'Back in a moment, darling,' she said.

It did not seem long before Jenny was seated in state at the breakfast bar, in front of a bowl of Ready-Brek and toast.

'No, I'm not nervous. No, really I'm fine now. I've taken two Panadol and that will help with the headache.'

'Good, Cheryl,' Arthur said to her, and placed his arm affectionately round her shoulder. 'Now promise you'll ring to say she's arrived, and ring again as soon as she's out.'

'Yes, of course.'

'Now remember, breathe deeply, and keep busy.'

'I know,' Cheryl nodded.

'What's wrong, Mummy?'

'Oh, nothing!' Cheryl said breezily. 'Now you eat all of your breakfast, like a good girl.'

The rain drummed down ceaselessly, but Cheryl had taken the precaution of putting the big golfing umbrella in the car, which was lucky, as all the parking spaces by the school were full. The six-plus examination was held simultaneously with the senior school entrance examination. She had to leave the car at quite a distance. Cheryl emerged from the car first and put up the umbrella. Jenny, clutching a plastic bag with pens and pencils, got out after her and sheltered under the striped fabric. They scurried along to the main entrance of the school, avoiding puddles, Jenny laughing with pleasure at the haste and clumsiness.

Mothers, fathers and daughters were walking up to the door and Cheryl joined them, glad she seemed to be punctual. Three of the sixth-form girls were at the door and Jenny's name was checked off against a list.

'The Prep's down here,' one said. 'You can collect her again at eleven o'clock.'

'Collect her? Can't I come in?'

'No. Sorry. We don't let parents in.'

'But . . .' Cheryl held tightly on to Jenny's hand.

An older woman, evidently a member of staff, whom Cheryl did not recognize, came up and explained.

'I'm very sorry, but the girls are right. We don't have room for all the parents who would like to stay. But she'll be fine, won't you?' said the teacher to Jenny. Jenny had her head bowed in pleased shyness. The sixth-former who had spoken earlier took Jenny by the hand and Cheryl watched her being led away down a wide corridor, in the direction of the Junior Department. Her disappearance was a physical wrench.

Well, that was it. At least, Cheryl thought, something tightening at her throat, Jenny hadn't cried. Cheryl's eyes pricked. She struggled to put up the umbrella and made her way back to the car. Her face was wet. She put the dripping umbrella in the boot and quickly got into the car. Two hours to wait.

Two whole hours. She had assumed that she would be able to wait in the school; she had imagined watching Jenny doing the tests. She had not bargained for being sent away for two hours. She knew she could go home – there was time – but to do so seemed disloyal. Where could she go? She was too agitated to shop. A coffee. She would go and buy herself a coffee. She would find somewhere nice in the centre of Boltham and pass the time having a coffee. She started up the engine of the car.

She started by writing her name. JeNy DavidSon. It looked nicer with the big letters in the middle. And she only wanted to put one 'N' in her name for a change. It looked more grown up. The teacher said to begin, so she looked at the sums. Adding ones. She could do adding ones. She would do them very, very quickly and the nice lady with the black curly hair would be very pleased with her. It was nice doing all the sums quickly. The lady with the black curly hair had given her a big hug. It was a nice room and it was all full of posters.

The posters were of northern Italy – clearly the owners of the coffee shop had a liking for the place – and so as Cheryl sipped her cappuccino, dampening her lips with the warm froth, she looked at a view of the roofs of Florence, and rich, green hills. The café itself was tiny. The owners had tried to squeeze in as many tables and chairs as they possibly could and the only free table was at the back. Cheryl was hemmed in by other, older women drinking tea, and damp coats and shoes and umbrellas made the café even more claustrophobic. She could smell rain everywhere.

She could see the rain. She could see the lines of the rain outside the classroom window and it was nice to watch the rain. If she had wellingtons she could splash in the puddles. She wished she was splashing in the puddles. She drew a boot. That was good. That was a good boot. She drew another boot. She was good at drawing boots. The nice lady with the black curly hair who gave her a hug would like the boots. The sums were silly sums anyway. She didn't understand how to do sums with words in.

★

She didn't understand why she was feeling so distressed. Jenny stood a very good chance. Mrs Williams's pessimism was typical of her ungenerous attitude. It was impossible for the Boltham entrance examination to be *that* difficult. Heavens, it was only for six-year-olds! Jenny would be fine. Her hand trembled as she perused the plastic folder containing the menu. Perhaps if she ate, she would not feel so light-headed. She scanned the menu card.

It was hard. It was a hard story. She didn't understand it. It had a magic finger. She looked at her finger and wondered if it could be magic. If she wiggled it, it would be magic. She looked at the other little girls. There was a girl with long hair like a princess. There was another girl wearing a bright, red dress. She looked up and saw the nice lady again. The lady smiled at her. She smiled at the lady.

Then she looked in her purse for the change and handed it to the woman behind the counter. It was time to drive back to Boltham. Besides, she was eager to leave the claustrophobic café. Well, she reflected, as she walked out into the wet street, when she got back to the school it would all be over. She would no longer have to give Jenny those awful nightly lessons and force her to do sums, to read aloud, to learn spellings. That was good. They could have a normal life again. She hadn't taken Jenny swimming for weeks. But it was worth it, a stern voice inside said. Nothing is more important than a good education. There was nothing as good as being clever. Cheryl remembered, as she walked along, her own infant days again. She was bottom of the class once and Mrs Stringer had read out her position. It was meant to make her try harder, but the other children had teased her about it. It was true, she wasn't very bright. She knew it. She didn't want Jenny to go through that humiliation. It was an insistent, relentless pressure that told Cheryl she had to make her daughter clever; Arthur's mother only intensified it. Altogether, she had no choice.

'You can choose anything to write a story about, Jenny. You don't have to pick one of these titles. You can write about your family.'

The nice kind lady said that. She had a pretty smile. Jenny began to write. 'One day ther was I litl girl caLLed JeNy and MuMMy and Dady and they livd in I house.' Then she decided to draw the house. There were the walls and windows and door. Here is me. Here is Daddy. Here is Mummy and Mummy is worried. Then Jenny remembered that Mummy was worried because she had to try hard at this school. 'I no my to times tabel,' she wrote. Then the nice lady told her to stop writing.

Cheryl stood just inside the main entrance, her eyes fixed in the distance from where she expected Jenny to emerge. She remembered the school building well. It was an intimidating building and Cheryl almost smelt her old inadequacy. She was only the art teacher. She never dared join in staffroom conversations. Unexpectedly, now, she felt as if she wanted to escape. She didn't want to have to come here again every day, even with Jenny. What was she thinking? She was tired, that was all. She wanted nothing more than to be able to come here every day, with Jenny as a Boltham Grammar School Prep girl. Didn't she?

Soon, some small children – other candidates, no doubt – came escorted towards the main entrance. In the rear, she saw Jenny, holding the hand of the teacher, who bent down and let Jenny give her a little kiss. Then Jenny saw her and ran up eagerly.

'Well?' Cheryl asked.

'I'm hungry,' Jenny said.

'Did you answer all the questions?'

'Yes. Easy peasy lemon squeezy!'

Cheryl's heart sang. She had found it easy! 'Did you do your best?'

'Yes. The teacher was nice. Have you got somefink to eat?'

Jenny had got on with the teacher! That had to be a good sign. She was happy too. Now, even a small child would feel miserable if she was unable to complete work. It had been a success. It was all worthwhile. She would allow herself to hope. She squeezed Jenny's hand tightly.

Sue's firm conviction, as she walked along Victoria Street to Radio Northside's premises, was that the whole thing must be a mistake. She could not understand why Jasmin's friend would even agree to see her. She was no one. No one, that is, who had anything to do with the world of radio or television. She had a superstitious dread that she would arrive, give her name and the receptionist would look blankly at her and say that no such name was listed and that it would all be a great mistake.

Here were the offices. Yes, Sue was haunted by the feeling that she shouldn't be there. The reception area of Radio Northside was glass-fronted and looked almost like any office reception area. A girl sat behind a desk, attending to a switchboard. But there were no stairs visible, just a corridor to the left of the reception desk. The entrance lobby itself was bare. Sue knew, as Jasmin had told her, that Radio Northside was presently only broadcasting the occasional test transmission while settling into these new studios. The furniture seemed light and modern. Sue saw all this from outside. She would not dare to go in.

What added to her feeling of unreality was that she had

not told anyone what she was doing. Chris and Betty and Glenys thought she had taken the afternoon off to catch up with the housework. That was such an amusing idea it made her smile even now. Only Jasmin and Mark knew, which was just as well, for the whole idea was preposterous really. She was only doing it for Jasmin. She had intended to call it all off, but when she had suggested it, Jasmin had looked so disappointed.

Yes, it was for Jasmin. It gave Jasmin something to think about apart from her impending delivery date. Since severing her links with FAM, Jasmin had been slightly more relaxed. Yet she was haunted now by the possibilities of what might go wrong. On more than one occasion Jasmin had repeated that she knew nothing of Tom's family; what if there was hereditary illness? This was an obsession for Jasmin and it wore Sue down. It was a relief for both of them when Sue spoke instead about *her* coming ordeal. In fact she realized that were it not for the positive effects this audition had on Jasmin, she would have cancelled it. For it was impossible that she would have anything interesting to say. Still she had not gone in.

Suddenly summoning something akin to courage, Sue decided that if the receptionist had not been given her name, she would go straight back home, and that would, in its way, be some sort of relief. She pushed open the glass door and entered.

In the background was the voice of a male D.J., a fruity, northern voice, brimming with assurance. Sue did not listen to what was being said, but made her way to the receptionist.

'I've an appointment to see Isabel Clayton,' she said.

Her suspicions had been correct. The receptionist looked bemused. No appointment had been made for her at all. Sue swallowed hard. The receptionist consulted a book.

246

'Sue Turner, is it?'

'Yes,' came a small voice.

'Can you take a seat, please.'

Sue did so. She lowered herself on to a small striped settee and looked around the lobby. There was nothing to see. She became super-aware of herself and wondered what the receptionist made of her. Did she look like someone who was used to the radio? Probably not. She looked, she imagined, like a dressed-up librarian. On the coffee table in front of her were some leaflets advertising local cinema presentations and concerts. But Sue did not pick one up. She watched the corridor, waiting for Isabel Clayton to appear. Jasmin's friend.

No one emerged from the corridor. Perhaps Isabel had forgotten. Sue was certain now she should have stayed in the library. She coughed a little, to clear her throat, which was tightening. She would wait only fifteen minutes and then go.

Now someone did emerge from the corridor. A short, untidy girl, with shaggy, unruly hair and a large sweater that reached her knees, almost covering her black leggings. Sue watched her go and speak to the receptionist. Then she turned and smiled at Sue.

'Are you Sue Turner?' she asked, in an unusually low, husky voice. 'I'm Isabel Clayton. Hi!'

Sue stood up, and was embarrassed to discover that she was at least nine inches taller than this girl. She felt as if it was her fault. She also felt far too smart. She had worn her grey suit and white blouse, with silver earrings. She had remodelled her face along the lines of her recent transformation. Isabel looked as if she had spent the morning lounging about at home. Her sweater had slipped off one shoulder, revealing a T-shirt below. Her face was open, pleased and communicative.

247

'Thanks so much for coming this afternoon. It was an ace idea of Jasmin's. Did she explain? Radio Northside is going to be half talk, half music, with half female presenters too. For our morning programme we want to go for the zoo radio format – we thought of having two or three co-presenters – and I've been keen on finding a woman who's fresh to radio. I've been trying people out. So when Jasmin contacted me, it was certainly a coincidence. Anyway, come to the studio!'

She led Sue off. Sue felt her shoulders hunch. It was her instinctive reaction when she felt too tall for a situation. She followed this Isabel down a short corridor, round a corner, through a door and into a room with no windows. Here was a man seated at a console with a bewildering array of switches and dials. There was another woman too, seated near him, in front of a computer screen, and she smiled at Sue, but said nothing. Through a glass panel she could see another man, alone, speaking into a large microphone, absorbed in his own conversation. He was in shadow. So this was radio, she thought. She had expected something far more glamorous.

Isabel offered to take her coat, but Sue removed it and hung it on a coatstand by the door. She was glad to have something normal to do, such as taking off her coat. Isabel was speaking to the other woman and Sue stood nervously, desperately trying to take it all in: the console, the man in glasses who was probably some sort of technician, the plastic cups that had once held coffee, the studio itself where the man talked to himself, or rather addressed that black cylindrical microphone, exchanging confidences with it. Sue was offered a seat, a swivel chair, and she perched on it, aware that with the slightest movement she would sway from side to side. She no longer worried what Isabel thought of her; it was a matter of surviving from one minute to the next.

'Alex, this is Sue Turner. She knows my friend Jasmin. Do you remember I told you about Jasmin?'

'Oh, yes,' said the other woman, sober-looking, plain, with a ponytail scraping all of her hair back from her face. 'Your friend who's having a baby.'

'Yes,' Isabel said. 'It was such a shock to all of us. And a surprise, too, that she wanted to go through with it all. When is she due?' Isabel looked at Sue for the answer.

'Four weeks,' Sue said.

She felt easier now they were to sit here in this back room and talk about Jasmin. It occurred to her too that Isabel would know Jasmin well; would know rather more about her life at Oxford than she did. She was keen to ask her certain things. For example, how –

'Malcolm should be finished in a minute or two,' Isabel said. 'We'll go straight in and have a play about.' Sue watched her pick up a folder and take out a photocopied sheet of paper. 'Take a look at that,' she instructed her. 'You can have a go at reading it on the air.'

Sue read the paper in front of her. It was part of a news broadcast. It was something to do with the stock market. She read the words to herself. They did not make sense. She read them again. It was possible to guess the intonation she should use by the sentence structure, much as she used to do in school, when she was reading Shakespeare aloud and didn't understand a word. Isabel was now bending over the console, talking to the technician. The words on Sue's page swam before her eyes. Then she noticed the radio presenter in the studio rise and leave. The seat by the table with the microphone lay empty.

'Right! Let's go,' Isabel announced. Sue followed her, out of one door, which Isabel shut carefully, into a tiny anteroom and then through another door into the studio itself. It was a plain, utterly bare room, containing one square table and large microphones. Sue took the seat the previous speaker had occupied; it was still warm. She held the paper up to read it.

'No,' Isabel said. 'Put it down. You might rustle it if you hold it.'

Feeling awkward, Sue placed the paper on the table. She sat very, very still, waiting for instructions. Isabel sat a little way from her.

'First we want to check the sound levels,' Isabel said. 'Just say something into the mike.'

Sue's mind was completely blank. She could think of nothing to say at all.

'Hello,' she said, and wondered why her voice sounded so high and squeaky.

'No, we'll need more than that. Read from your sheet. Would you like the cans?'

Sue was mystified. The only cans she could think of were cans of beans, of spaghetti hoops, of tomato soup. But Isabel brought over a pair of black earphones and Sue put them on. They slipped uncomfortably down her head, pressing against her face. She began to read.

'Consumer goods' suppliers suffered some sharp losses as price cuts by branded products –'

'Fine. That's fine.' Sue watched Isabel wave at the technician. 'Now we'll do it for real. It's just to get the feel of your voice. See that light on your right? When it shines green, you can begin.'

Sue's shoulders ached from tension. Now she knew what the small, enclosed studio reminded her of – it was an operating theatre. The green light shone.

'Consumer goods' suppliers suffered some sharp losses –'

'Good, but you're not reading to an audience. Keep it intimate.'

'Consumer goods' suppliers suffered some sharp losses –'

'Good. A bit louder.'

250

'Consumer goods' suppliers suffered some sharp losses as price cuts by branded products' manufacturers . . .'

The voice Sue could hear echoing around her earphones was not hers. It was a nervous, strangulated sound magnified many times. The news bulletin was like a raging river she must swim across and could not pause, for if she did, she would be swept away.

'OK!' announced Isabel. 'Would you like to hear that?' She gestured to the technician again and within a few moments Sue's voice came yet again to torment her, this time through into the studio, and now it sounded like someone completely alien to her – like a newsreader on the verge of a nervous breakdown. She poured herself some water from the jug on the table as her throat was dry.

'Right, Sue, that was great. Now, what I'm actually working on right now are voices and personalities for a mid-morning chat show, and so now we'll try something more informal. Have a go at interviewing me. Let's think of a general topic. Something mildly controversial. I know. I'll pretend to be a child-care expert and you interview me about the wisdom of smacking children as a disciplinary measure. Come in on the green light.'

Sue immediately felt guilty. Of all the subjects she could have chosen, this was the most sensitive. For just that morning, Lizzie and Emma had conducted an explosive argument, ending in blows and insults, and although Sue had restrained herself then, it was when she had spotted Emma deliberately pinching Lizzie's leg under the table that she delivered a short, sharp smack to Emma's arm. Of course, it only resulted in a renewal of hostilities and accusations, and Sue feeling as if it was all her fault. And now she had to interview the young girl, who clearly knew nothing about children, on smacking. The light turned green.

Sue experienced an exquisite moment of total paralysis, in which she realized she knew nothing about conducting interviews. Then she plunged in.

'Do you agree with smacking children?'

'No,' said Isabel.

Another eternity of silence.

'Why don't you –' she cleared her throat – 'agree with smacking children?'

'Oh, it teaches them that violence is acceptable, as they see their parents using it.'

If she's right, thought Sue, their constant arguments *are* my fault. She felt threatened. Her mind was about to seize up again.

'Are there any occasions when you would advise smacking a child?'

'No.'

You can certainly tell she's not had children, Sue thought. We start with the best intentions and then something snaps. It's something we all do and none of us can justify. Now, if mothers had time and sufficient support, perhaps things would be different. But these child-care experts prescribe a code of ideal behaviour to us and then sit back and fail us because we can't put it into practice.

'I'm sorry,' Sue said. 'I can't think of anything else to ask.'

Isabel gestured to the technician again. 'That's fine,' she said. 'It's hard simply to interview without any research and preparation. It's better, when you're interviewing, not to ask questions that elicit only the answer "yes" or "no". OK.'

Sue knew she had failed utterly. Humiliation pricked at her skin. She desperately wished she was somewhere else – anywhere else. Isabel excused herself and went to consult with the woman called Alex and the technician. Sue was left alone. She realized that she had not relaxed one bit; she was still sitting straight, her mouth next to the microphone, her hands clasped tightly in her lap. She should have never presumed to come here. She should have never listened to Jasmin. Isabel came back in.

'Time for coffee,' she said brightly, not choosing to acknowledge Sue's disastrous debut. 'Alex is bringing it, and I'm glad, because that gives us a chance to talk about Jasmin. Do you know, I haven't seen her since she came back to Boltham! We've spoken on the phone, but I've been working all hours and I've been without a car. How is she?'

'Physically, she's very well. She's having a very healthy pregnancy. But I don't think it's been easy for her, having the baby alone, so to speak. I worry that she spends too much time alone in the house. I suppose you know her parents are in Turkey.'

'Yes, she explained to me that they can't come over. I find that so hard to believe. When we were at St Luke's, Jasmin's mother was always writing and telephoning. It was a bit of a joke among the rest of us.'

'Then Jasmin didn't tell you the rest of it. You know, she hasn't even let her mother know she's pregnant.'

'Really? Is that because she's scared?'

'No, that's the funny thing. The only thing that scares Jasmin right now is that her baby won't be all right. I think she hasn't told her mother because she simply wants to have the baby all to herself. She doesn't want her mother to take it over. She seems to feel that her mother would.'

Isabel was about to reply, but the studio door opened and Alex came in with a tray of three coffees. Isabel apologized for the quality of the coffee and Alex sat on the table, to talk to them.

'We're talking about Jasmin,' Isabel explained.

'I've told her that she must let her mother know,' Sue

continued, eager to go on, 'but I feel I can only put pressure on her; I can't force her to tell. I'm sure she'll feel she wants her mother when the baby is born. I do wish someone was living with her now.'

'Ah!' said Alex. 'But that's what most pregnant women do – stay at home alone. My sister has a baby and she spent the last six weeks of the pregnancy at home, on her maternity leave.'

'So did I,' Sue said. 'It was dreadful. When I was pregnant at work there were other women around to talk to and to reassure me. Once I was imprisoned in the house – and because I was a working woman, I didn't know many of my neighbours – there was no one to talk to. If I felt anxious about something, I had hours and hours to brood. I realized why the Victorians referred to pregnancy and labour as confinement; I felt like I was under house arrest. Just when I most needed company, I was isolated. For Jasmin, it's worse. She's cut herself off from all of her previous life and I think she just sees herself as a glorified womb now. That's why I think she's been a little neurotic lately.'

'Perhaps I ought to visit her,' Isabel mused.

'You knew her well at college, didn't you? Do you feel she'll be able to cope with the baby?'

'I can't tell. She was a hard-working student, but enjoyed her social life too. It was an escape for her.'

'One thing she hasn't chosen to speak to me about is the boy who got her pregnant in the first place. He was called Tom, wasn't he? Do you know anything about their relationship?'

'He was just another in a long line of boyfriends. Boys liked Jasmin. Especially once she got her hair cut. That was one of her first acts of rebellion.'

'That's interesting. What made her decide to –'

254

The studio door opened again. The receptionist put her head round and mentioned that the station boss wanted to speak to Isabel. She jumped up and Alex was left to escort Sue out of the recording area.

Sue consulted her watch. Although she had enjoyed their last conversation, she was anxious to be gone and bury the whole experience. She explained to Alex that she had to collect her children – thank God for children; they provided an excuse for everything! So she made her farewells to Alex, asked her to convey her thanks to Isabel, although she was conscious of being faintly rude, and scurried through the reception area and out into the street.

Isabel put down the receiver and left her office to return to the studio. Alex was waiting for her; both were exultant.

'Jasmin was absolutely right!' Isabel exclaimed. 'She's a natural. Did you manage to record all of that, Jim?'

The man at the console nodded.

'Did you hear what she was saying about female isolation?'

'Yes!' Alex said. 'And the way she was interviewing you about Jasmin . . .'

Joyce Carpenter stood at a check-in desk at Ataturk airport, two suitcases by her side. She shrank a little from the other passengers – there were a French family chattering excitedly, two Australian students travelling the world with backpacks and rolled sleeping-bags, and three smart Turkish businessmen. She did not like the way that air travel brought you into close contact with such a variety of people. But as she edged forward in the queue she knew that every minute brought her nearer to Jasmin.

Ataturk airport was not like Heathrow. It was small and dark; outside young Turks clamoured to help you with your luggage, at a price. The surrounding countryside, if you

255

could call it that, was bleak and polluted, with half-built apartments where headscarved women hung out shabby washing. She was glad, so glad, to be leaving it all behind. For Jasmin did not know this, and George did not know this, but she was not coming back. George himself had fifteen months left on his contract. She intended to spend those fifteen months in a north Oxford flat to be near Jasmin. *Her* daughter. She handed the clerk her documents and nodded briefly to the young Australian who lifted her suitcases on to the rollers.

She made her way to the departure lounge. She was impatient for the plane to leave and anticipated eagerly that walk through the short tunnel that led magically from the departure lounge on to the plane itself. She would be seated at the front. She would brace herself for the lift-off. Then she would arrive at Heathrow and, ignoring the expense, she would take a taxi to Oxford and book into the Randolph. She would wait until the morning before surprising Jasmin. The smile that played around her lips was severe, and the small Pakistani girl who had dropped a toy at her feet looked up at her and was instantly subdued.

CHAPTER SIXTEEN

Sue rapped sharply on Jasmin's kitchen door. Since the kitchen light was on, she expected that Jasmin would not be far away. There was no reply. She rapped again, more loudly. Still no reply. Jasmin was certainly in, no doubt of that. Sue knocked for the third time and became aware of how cold the evening was. It was possible, Sue thought, that the door would be unlocked and so she tried to turn the handle. To her pleasure, it gave, and she stepped into the kitchen.

There were signs of habitation. A copy of the *Independent* lay on the kitchen table, together with an empty cup of tea. A chair was pushed to one side. Now, Sue knew that if Jasmin had gone out, the cup and saucer would have been washed and left to dry and the chair would have been pushed squarely under the table. So Jasmin was somewhere in the house. Ought she to shout to her? Sue was about to, but then thought that she might be sleeping and she would not wish to disturb her.

So she walked into the dining room, which was empty, and through to the lounge. No one was there either. There was no sound anywhere in the house. She ascended the stairs.

'Jasmin?' she said softly. No reply. Sue glanced into the bathroom, but it was empty. Here was Jasmin's bedroom. 'Jasmin?' she said again, and pushed open the door.

Jasmin was lying on her back on her bed, like a sacrificial victim, like an Indian widow awaiting immolation. That she was not sleeping was apparent by the stiffness of her pose. Gradually she eased herself up to speak to Sue.

'I'm practising relaxation,' she said. 'For in between contractions.' Awkwardly, Jasmin rose completely and invited Sue downstairs. Jasmin was getting big. From the back she still retained her slim figure, Sue thought, as she followed her downstairs, but from the front she was splendidly rounded. On reaching the lounge Jasmin let herself down on to the settee and Sue sat on the armchair facing her.

'Is everything OK?' Sue asked. She was not keen to recount the humiliations of this afternoon. She would tell Jasmin later, and laugh about it, but now she preferred to ask Jasmin about her antenatal appointment at the hospital.

'Yes. The baby's a good size, they said.'

'That's good.'

'So I've been practising this evening,' said Jasmin. 'My deep-breathing is very good now, and I can squat for one minute without pain, and I've done my active birth exercises twice today, and concentrated on my pelvic area, like Sylvie said. Then I've been relaxing. I'm hopeless at that. I can't seem to clear my mind. I just keep thinking – oh, God!' And Jasmin burst into tears.

Sue was quick to comfort her, stroking her hands and fetching tissues. 'Come on now,' she said. 'Tell me what it is.'

Jasmin snorted as she sniffed, and still trembled from her sobs. 'At the hospital,' she murmured. 'It was the things they said.'

'But I thought you liked your midwife?'

'Yes, yes. Not the midwife. No. The other women.'

'What other women?'

Jasmin played with the damp tissue in her hand. Haltingly, she began to talk to Sue.

'Well, there was a delay this afternoon, some emergency delivery, I think. And I was sitting with some other women waiting for appointments. And one of them – she had two

258

little boys in the crèche, and I thought she sounded quite intelligent – she was telling me about her first labour. She said it lasted thirty-six hours. She said she didn't know why midwives call contractions "contractions" – she said pains were more appropriate – and she was in agony. She said that she never slept for the whole of the time she was in labour. And she was sick a lot too. And she said if men had the babies the human race would soon be extinct. She was in the third stage of labour for ninety minutes and they had to use forceps and it ruined the shape of her baby's head. Then she tore so badly that in order to sew her up they had to reconstruct her whole vagina!'

'Some labour!' said Sue.

'Yes,' replied Jasmin. 'Then the other woman at our table told me about her labour. She said she was induced. She had her legs in stirrups and they broke her waters and gave her an oxytocin drip and turned it up every half-hour. So the contractions became more and more frequent. No pain relief worked. The gas and air had no effect, the TENS machine was useless, even the pethidine just sent her into a light sleep and every so often she jerked out of it with a massive contraction. And then her contractions came continuously and she begged for a Caesarean but they wouldn't give her one. She said she thought she was dying. They had to give her oxygen and glucose and everything, and fitted a scalp electrode to her baby's head because the foetal-heart monitor broke.'

'Oh, Jasmin!'

'And then the last woman joined in. She said they were lucky. She had a good labour, she said, but when her baby was born they wouldn't let her see him. She thought he was dreadfully deformed. Can you imagine, Sue? It was because the baby had a harelip. She said they can operate when he's a bit older. But then I began to think of all the things that could go wrong, and I can't be sure, can I, that my baby will be normal? What would I do? I've been trying to relax upstairs, but every time I lie down I think, what if Alison isn't normal? How would I cope? And what about the pain? And I know you think Grant and his FAM were just freaks, but at least they said you could have a pain-free labour if you breathe properly and relax and squat or use the birthing pool.' Jasmin was breathless. 'So I've decided I want to adapt the model birth plan he gave me – whatever you say!'

She handed Sue a sheet of paper. On it, in Jasmin's regular handwriting, was the birth plan. Sue read it.

I want the atmosphere in the delivery suite to be calm and soothing, and wish to keep the lighting low, and someone to play a Chopin nocturne. I wish to remain active and mobile during labour and not to deliver on my back. My baby and I wish to avoid continuous electronic monitoring. I wish to avoid artificial pain relief as far as possible and to use breathing and relaxation instead. I want to be able to talk to my baby while she is being delivered and to be left alone after her birth so I can get to know her.

Sue put the sheet of paper down.

'Have I ever told you the story of Emma's delivery?'

'No,' said Jasmin.

'Like you, I was keen on natural childbirth and practised the proper relaxation techniques and learned about active birth. In our NCT class, we were taught to count backwards in between contractions to stop us becoming too aware of the pain. I decided to recite "The Owl and the Pussycat" instead. Mark came to a few classes and learned how to rub my back, and we'd planned a lovely romantic birth. I was open-minded about pain relief.

'When I started at home with a low backache, I knew that was the beginning. So we drove off to the hospital – it was early evening. I was doing very well. When I got there,

260

I was given an internal and the midwife said I was hardly dilated and, since they were busy, they put us in a guest room. I walked around and Mark did a crossword. It was all an anticlimax. There's so much waiting around, Jasmin! That's the worst part. Then I thought the contractions were getting stronger, but when the midwife examined me, she said there still wasn't much doing. She told Mark to go home and get some sleep and come back in the morning. He did.

'I took two Paracetamol for the backache and stepped into the bed. That was when my waters broke. So I walked over to the nurses' station to tell them and they sent a relief midwife back with me. Then the contractions came fast and furious. Right, I thought. Time for relaxation. Then I began to laugh. I'd never felt less like relaxing in my life. But as I'd been taught, I got on all fours on the bed and breathed properly, and in between contractions I recited. "The owl and the pussycat went to sea in a beautiful pea-green boat . . ." Then suddenly I saw myself in my nightie, on all fours on a hospital bed, reciting a nursery rhyme, and this was it – this was the transcendental experience of childbirth. So I began to laugh. When the midwife came in again I was almost fully dilated and, like a giggling school-girl, I was trying not to laugh when the doctor came rushing in to deliver me. A few pushes and that was it. There was Emma, and I was exhausted with laughter.'

'Didn't you have any pethidine?'

'I asked for it, but it was too late.'

'Does it hurt, Sue?'

'Yes. But it's a healthy pain. It's impossible to describe.'

'I wish you could describe it.'

'You feel as if your body had a mind of its own. The pain comes in waves, but then it recedes and you know it will recede. It's the most physical thing I've ever experienced. I'm glad I did.'

261

'You did well, not to have any pain relief.'

'Rot! There isn't such a thing as doing well at childbirth. It's not a test. It happens to you. You cope as best you can. I was lucky because I started laughing.'

'Will my baby be all right, Sue?'

Sue knew how much Jasmin wanted her to give an unequivocal 'yes'. It was every expectant mother's fear. It had been her fear. She was reminded of Lizzie's recent question, while watching some soap when a character was being killed off with leukaemia: will I get it? Sue told her it was very, very unlikely.

'I think your baby will almost certainly be all right.'

'Almost . . .'

'Jasmin! I'm not God! How should I know? Not only do I not have psychic powers but I can't even perform on the radio!'

'Sue! I'd completely forgotten. You've spent the afternoon with Isabel. How did you get on? I bet she loved you!'

Sue smiled wryly. 'I was far too nervous,' she said. 'I could hardly read aloud, and when she gave me an opportunity to interview her, I fluffed it. Never mind. I thought about it afterwards and realized a career in radio would hardly have suited me. There are the children. I couldn't give any new career my full commitment.'

Jasmin, feeling her baby twist and turn, placed her hands on her stomach. 'Why?' she asked.

'The children must come first.'

'But Lizzie is ten and Emma is eight. You can pay some attention to you now. A woman's life isn't over when she becomes a mother. Even I'm going to go back and finish my degree.'

Sue shook her head slowly and sadly. 'You're young,' she said. 'It's different for you.'

'You're young too.'

'Jasmin, stop it. We've been through this before.'

'You're hiding behind your children.'

'Look, I wasn't any good today. That's final. I'm quite happy with my life. I shouldn't need to make any changes. Now, what about your birth plan?'

'Don't you think it's good?'

'I think it's an excellent work of fiction.'

'But surely I'm entitled to say what I want to happen?'

'What do you want to happen?'

Jasmin thought. Once again she saw in her mind the delivery suite that Mary Whelan had shown her. In four weeks or less she would be there and she would be giving birth. There she was. Jasmin, Mary Whelan and –

'Sue. Will you be with me?'

Sue thought. It would be difficult to explain at work, but she could build up some hours on her flexitime.

'Yes,' she said.

Jasmin's face brightened. She realized that if Sue was there, nothing could go wrong. It was an irrational notion, but none the less powerful for that.

'Yes! I want you there, and I do want to walk around and not lie on that bed.'

'Fine. We'll perform a two-step!'

'Shall I practise a nursery rhyme too?'

'If you like.'

'No. Chaucer! I shall recite some Chaucer. Sue, you bring in the complete works and you can read to me. Can you read medieval English?'

'Used to be able to.'

'Great! You can read to me, and we'll walk about, and you can make me laugh.'

'Make you laugh?'

'Yes. You said that you were lucky because you were able to laugh. Do something funny to make me laugh. And talk to me and keep me distracted. You can be with me when Alison is delivered. And you can help me make up my mind if things don't go according to plan.'

It was a huge responsibility, Sue knew. For a moment she hesitated. She would ask Jasmin if she could speak to her midwife and discuss this. But, if it helped Jasmin . . .

'I'll be there,' she said.

It was ten-thirty when Joyce Carpenter arrived at St Luke's. She stepped out of the taxi and looked with pleasure at the main entrance of the college. St Luke's had started its existence as a women's college and thus was a Victorian building, but it lacked none of Oxford's sense of its own importance. It was over two years since she had seen the college. She remembered bringing Jasmin here the day she had taken up residence in the Main Building; she also remembered accompanying Jasmin to her interview. She was horrified by the fact she was the only mother present; women these days took the responsibilities of motherhood so casually. She entered the college and allowed three students to move aside to let her in.

Jasmin was no longer living in that shared house in Walton Street. Joyce was glad of that. The facilities had been so basic. Now, for her final year, she was back in college – Jasmin had written with her new room number; she was in the New Building. It was Joyce's intention to go there first, to knock on her door, to see Jasmin's face change from surprise to delight and to tell her that she was home for good.

So she made her way through the Main Building, past the college library and the Junior Common Room, past the students' pigeon-holes and into the portico that led to New Building. She looked for staircase five. Here it was. She ascended just one flight of stairs to reach room three. Now she stopped and spent one moment in an ecstasy of anticipation. In the silence, she could hear the sounds of someone moving about. It was her one fear that Jasmin would be at a lecture, or in the Bodleian. But she was in. Joyce rapped sharply at the door.

She heard the catch unlocked and the door was opened. Facing her was a tall bearded youth in a Megadeath T-shirt and pyjama bottoms. He looked as surprised as she did.

'This is Jasmin Carpenter's room,' Joyce said icily.

'No, it's not,' the youth said, in flat Midland tones. 'It's mine.'

'Staircase five, room three,' Joyce said.

'My room,' he said.

'Do you know my daughter, Jasmin Carpenter?' she asked.

'No, sorry,' he said. 'She's not on this staircase.'

Joyce tried to see all she could of his room. He seemed to be the sole occupant, apart from some sports gear lying on the bed, a jumble of books and a ghetto blaster. She was utterly mystified. With a faint apology, she let him close the door and stood outside for a while to recollect herself. She was positive this was the number Jasmin had given her. Neither of them was ever inaccurate. She descended the staircase and checked an early letter of Jasmin's that she carried in her handbag. Staircase five, room three.

Perhaps, she thought, as she made her way back to the Main Building, intent on seeing the Bursar, there had been a recent room change. That would explain it. But in that case, why had that boy not heard of Jasmin? She reached the Bursar's office and knocked. Shortly the door was opened by a young woman who offered Joyce her assistance.

'I'm looking for my daughter, Jasmin Carpenter,' she said. 'I've been to her room only to discover someone else is living there. Whereabouts in college is she?'

'I'm just the secretary,' the young woman explained. 'I'm new here. The Bursar's at a meeting. I can look on the college list, though.'

Joyce waited with growing impatience as the secretary examined the list of rooms and students. Is the girl illiterate, Joyce thought? She is taking ages.

'I'm sorry,' the secretary said. 'She's not in college and I can't find her on our list of students living out. Are you sure she's at this college?'

'Excuse me!' Joyce said, livid. 'Are you suggesting I don't know the college of my own daughter? This is preposterous. Is there someone more senior I can speak to?'

The secretary was quaking visibly. 'Does she have a moral tutor?' she suggested.

'Yes, Dr Cooper. Can you tell me where I can find her?'

'Now Dr Cooper's in college this morning. I think I saw her on her way to the Senior Common Room.'

'Where is the Senior Common Room?'

'If you carry on down the corridor . . .'

Joyce left the Bursar's office and walked briskly to the Senior Common Room. The door was shut. She rapped on it with tremendous force and it was opened by a raven-haired woman in a tweed skirt and black jumper. Her expression was vague and she seemed unperturbed by Joyce's controlled anger.

'Dr Cooper?' she said. 'Yes, she's having coffee. Who shall I say wishes to see her?'

'Joyce Carpenter. Jasmin's mother.'

Joyce waited. She could distinguish the sounds of conversation in the Senior Common Room. Then a barrel of a woman emerged, in ill-fitting clothes, with badly cut short hair. Her protuberant eyes made her look rather stupid. This was evidently the cleaner. Joyce stood aside to let her past. But she remained obstinately in the doorway.

266

'Mrs Carpenter?' she said. 'I'm Grainne Cooper.'

'May I speak to you?' Joyce asked.

'Come to my office,' Dr Cooper said. She waddled off down the corridor and Joyce followed her. She opened a door and ushered Joyce in. It was a tiny office. Apart from a large desk stacked with books, there were only two dilapidated easy chairs by a window overlooking the college gardens. Dr Cooper indicated that Joyce should take a seat.

Dr Cooper beamed at her. 'I'm so glad you've come,' she said. 'I have something for Jasmin.' Joyce watched her reach over and open the bottom drawer in her desk. She removed a crumpled brown paper bag with evident pride. She handed it to Joyce. Joyce opened it. It was some sort of knitting. She took out a tiny matinée jacket in a sickening shade of yellow, with several dropped stitches, and two large bootees.

'For Jasmin?' she said wonderingly.

'Yes. I have so enjoyed making them. I had to learn to knit from a booklet, you know. I have been inspired by the attempt. I began to realize why it was that so many Victorian novelists use some form of knitting or embroidery as images of entanglement in their fiction. George Eliot, for example –'

'Why have you knitted this jacket and bootees for my daughter?'

'They're not for Jasmin,' Dr Cooper remarked equably. 'They're for her baby.'

'Her baby?'

Joyce felt as if she had walked into some surreal drama. Jasmin was not in her room and now was thought to be having a baby. Nothing seemed real any more. Surely there was some simple explanation for the whole thing. Perhaps there were two Jasmin Carpenters.

'Yes. Jasmin writes to tell me she expects the baby to be

born next month. She has asked me to be the baby's Godmother.' Dr Cooper's face glowed with pleasure.

'Dr Cooper,' Joyce said. 'You have made a mistake. My daughter is not having a baby. She is here in your college completing the final year of her English degree.'

Grainne Cooper considered the woman in front of her. Her firmness of purpose was admirable. She reminded her rather of the Principal. But was she entirely sane?

'There must be some misunderstanding, Mrs Carpenter. I have written to you to explain the arrangements made so that Jasmin can have her baby at home in Boltham and I have received a typewritten letter from yourself confirming this.'

'I've received no such letter from you.'

Dr Cooper fingered her mole and cleared her throat. Either Jasmin was not pregnant and she had constructed a tissue of lies to have a year off her studies, which – no, that was impossible. Or she had omitted to tell her mother and had forged her mother's reply. Years of studying English literature had given Dr Cooper an insight into human behaviour. She knew for a certainty that Jasmin had lied to her mother. Looking at Mrs Carpenter now, she felt she could almost imagine why.

She spoke to Mrs Carpenter as if she was explaining an obscure Middle English text to a particularly obtuse student.

'Jasmin saw me in September,' she said. 'She was pregnant then. She knows the father, but wants nothing to do with him. She told me you supported her decision to have the baby at home. She stayed with an old school friend, but then returned home, and I believed until now that you were planning to join her. Clearly she has some reason for not wanting you to know about all this. But please don't worry about her welfare. She tells me she has been befriended by a neighbour who has given her excellent support.'

268

'How dare you withhold all of this from me! You are completely irresponsible. I demand to see the Principal.'

Dr Cooper blanched momentarily at the thought of the Principal. Then she realized that the Principal was in this as deeply as she was.

'None of this is true!' Joyce spoke slowly, giving the force of her words the power to change reality. 'You are teasing me.'

'Shall I take you to see the Principal?'

'What have you done to my daughter?' Joyce shouted. 'There was nothing wrong with her before she came here. I shall complain, you know.'

This is rather like a Jacobean tragedy, Dr Cooper thought, and the idea calmed her. Mother discovers daughter is with child; mother grows mad; then corpses strew the stage. Thank God, thought Grainne Cooper, that I don't have a daughter. She lifted the receiver of her telephone to dial the Principal's office.

Cheryl was tremblingly aware of his closeness to her. As she saw him approach, she tensed in an exquisite agony. He was coming now, now, but he passed her door, and walked up to Sue's front door, depositing some letters there. The anticlimax was both a relief and a disappointment. Surely Jenny would hear soon; it was almost half-term and the Head of the Preparatory Department at Boltham Grammar School had promised to announce the results by then.

Throughout each day, Cheryl was intensely aware of the impending result. With a superstitious awe inherited from her own mother, she would not imagine the situation if Jenny got her place, for that would be tempting fate; neither could she bear to imagine what would happen if Jenny did not get a place. During those weeks the earrings she made took the shape of flashes of lightning; she knew it was symbolic.

Arthur's mother was less worried. Cheryl realized ruefully that the older woman had more faith in Jenny than she did. Arthur's mother would talk charmingly of when both Jenny and Francine were at Boltham Grammar, and how Jenny was becoming a true Davidson. There were brains on the Davidson side, she said. She had told Jenny that when she got her place she would take her out to buy her uniform. Cheryl got over her pang of jealousy by reminding herself that Arthur's mother rarely had any pleasure; she usually only went as far as the local shops, and it would be a treat for her to take Jenny shopping.

Cheryl had spoken to Jenny herself. She had asked her if she had liked Boltham Grammar and Jenny had said that she liked the nice lady. Cheryl had since deduced that this lady was in fact the Head of the Preparatory Department, a Mrs Reid. Cheryl believed that she had been an ordinary classroom teacher there when she taught at Boltham, but she had had little to do with the Prep. When Cheryl and Arthur had asked Jenny if she would like to leave Heaton Primary, Jenny had said 'no', but then, they consoled themselves, that was natural. Jenny did not know that the results were pending; she lived entirely for the moment. Cheryl reflected that maybe this was half the trouble.

As she walked down Heaton Close, having dropped Jenny off at school and collected the dry-cleaning, she knew there was a chance that later post would have arrived. So that now familiar tension gathered in her as she approached her own front door.

She unlocked it. There *were* letters on the mat. All of Cheryl's senses met and concentrated on the letters. The top one was the gas bill. She picked up the letters. The next was a circular from Greenpeace. The next was a handwritten letter to her. The final letter had the Boltham Grammar School crest on it.

Cheryl's heart thudded against her chest. It prevented her hearing anything. The hall was shadowy, as the dull February morning did not provide much light. Cheryl held the envelope for a moment. This was it. There was no doubt that this letter contained the results. Cheryl's stomach went into spasm again.

The envelope would not tear. It would not. Impatiently she ripped it. She took out the letter. It was a brief letter, and certain words and phrases scarred Cheryl's vision. 'We are very sorry' . . . 'has not reached the required standard' . . . 'competition has been very fierce'. Her hand shook. It was a duplicated letter, personalized only by the handwritten 'Dear Mr and Mrs Davidson'. Cheryl took the letter into the kitchen and sat down to read it again.

She felt as if someone had slapped her round the face. She felt as she had done when she was small and she had tripped, and the floor had hit her, and she was angry with the floor. She and Jenny had been tested and found wanting. It was utterly, utterly humiliating. With that came the knowledge that she would have to share this news. Arthur would understand and would feel as she did. Arthur's mother . . . She would not think of Arthur's mother. And Jenny. She would have to let Jenny know that she did not pass the exam. Now the tears came to her eyes. No, she could not tell Jenny that. She would pretend that Mummy did not like the school; that Mummy and Daddy had changed their minds. At all events, she must protect Jenny. Now she allowed herself the luxury of tears.

The crying helped. Glad she was alone, to indulge in her tears, Cheryl switched on the kettle to make a hot drink. She felt drained, empty of all emotion. She spooned the coffee into her mug automatically. She repeated the new

271

reality to herself. Jenny has failed the Boltham Grammar School entrance examination. She would stay at Heaton Primary. It was all over. All of it.

The phone rang. Cheryl jumped and listened while it rang. Then she went back into the hall to answer it. It was Arthur's mother.

'Hello, Cheryl. How are you?'

'All right.'

'Good. There are one or two things I need from the shops and, since you're coming up this afternoon, I wondered if you might fetch them for me. I need some sugar and some cooking apples. Now, I want you to have a good look at them and –'

'Grandma. I've just this minute had a letter from Boltham Grammar School. Jenny hasn't got in.'

A silence. Quite a long one. For a moment Cheryl thought that she should not have told her over the phone; perhaps she had had one of her turns. But Arthur's mother's voice came through clearly.

'What were her marks?'

'I don't know. The letter didn't say.'

'I think you ought to find out. If she's only just failed, perhaps we could get her on a waiting list, especially if you mention Francine. I'd find out if I were you, Cheryl. You want to do your best by her, don't you? You used to work at the school. Ask to speak to the Head.'

'No, Grandma. I can't do that.' It was an honest reply. Cheryl's desire now was to walk away from the whole situation. But Arthur's mother was bearing down upon her with her implacable will.

'All you need do is telephone the school and ask to discuss Jenny's results. There might even have been a mistake. These things do happen, you know. No. Visit the school. Drive down there now. You can't give up like this.

You can come to visit me afterwards. It doesn't matter about the sugar and the apples; you can get those later on.'

What Grandma said was true, Cheryl thought, as she put on her coat. What if there had been an error? Or if Jenny had only just failed, it might be worth trying again. It was likely, too that, because of her connection with the school, someone would speak to her. She locked the door and went to the car.

The secretaries in the school office were delighted to see Cheryl. They took off their dictaphones and eagerly asked after her and whether she was visiting. Embarrassed, she explained that she wanted to speak to Mrs Reid and told them about Jenny. They looked sympathetic. For, reflected Cheryl, they probably knew Jenny's results. She stood in the outer office as one of the secretaries dialled Mrs Reid's office. There was a brief conversation.

'Mrs Reid will see you,' the secretary explained. 'You know where her office is.'

Cheryl walked through the school, feeling desperately out of place. She knew she shouldn't be here; she knew, when she left seven years ago, that she should never have returned. But here was Mrs Reid's office. As she got there, the door was opened and a tall, dark-haired lady, with kind eyes and a welcoming smile, beckoned her in.

She did remember Mrs Reid's face. In fact, she had hardly aged. She took a seat by her desk.

'I remember you now!' Mrs Reid declared. 'You were the art teacher. Wasn't it you who helped the girls to make those wonderful tapestries for the school centenary?'

'Yes,' said Cheryl.

'We loved your work here in the Prep. The Head was so upset when you left. You used to put up such excellent displays. Are you working for yourself now?'

273

'I make jewellery,' Cheryl said. 'And I'm hoping to start painting.'

'You're so lucky,' she said. 'Imagine having a creative talent. Now, how can I help you?'

Cheryl explained. Explained that Jenny Davidson was her daughter, and that she had heard this morning how Jenny had failed, and that her mother-in-law had suggested she should find out just how badly Jenny had done.

'Was she the curly-headed child who gave me a little kiss before she left?'

'Yes, probably.'

'She's a lovely little girl, Cheryl. I have the papers here. Let's have a look.'

Cheryl watched Mrs Reid sort through a box and extract a set of examination papers. She watched Mrs Reid look through them, and her face changed from curiosity to concern.

'Ah, yes,' she said.

She took the papers out and showed them to Cheryl. There was Jenny's handwriting. Heavens! The girl had not even spelt her name correctly! Cheryl leafed through them. Nearly all the sums were marked wrong. Then at the bottom of one page was a line of wellington boots. Cheryl and Mrs Reid laughed at them.

'They're good boots,' Cheryl said.

'Aren't they?' said Mrs Reid. 'And look, she's drawn a puddle too, and that's a rainbow. She's rather artistic.'

Cheryl looked at the English paper. All the comprehension answers were blank. Her story comprised two sentences and a lovely drawing of a house with a family.

'You know, I think Jenny's caught your resemblance,' Mrs Reid said.

There was no need for her to say any more. Cheryl knew it all. Jenny had failed spectacularly. Tears pricked at her eyes again. Mrs Reid laid her hand on Cheryl's arm.

274

'Never mind,' she said. 'She's only six. She's a sweet, affectionate little girl and I'm sure she has your artistic streak.'

'I wanted her to have more than that,' Cheryl said. 'I didn't want her to be like me.'

'Whyever not?' Mrs Reid looked astonished. 'I used to envy you so much when you taught here. I even took up watercolours, you know, and the evening-class teacher advised me to leave!'

Cheryl laughed. She liked Mrs Reid.

'I would have loved a little girl like Jenny,' she continued. 'But I've got two strapping lads. You're lucky.' Mrs Reid paused. 'I think it's a great pity for the girls who come here and struggle all the time, and, despite all we can do, they feel failures. It's not good. Jenny is very confident now.'

'More confident than I was.'

'She'll surprise you, I feel.' Mrs Reid beamed at Cheryl. Cheryl felt her heart lift. They spoke some more, discussing mutual friends. Then, when a school bell rang, Cheryl got up to go.

She left the school swiftly and knew she was feeling better, without understanding properly why. She got in the car and began the drive home.

It was astonishing to realize that people at Boltham Grammar School looked up to her. To her! She would take her oils out of the garage. She would let Jenny paint. Mrs Reid actually envied her; it felt so strange to have the approval of a teacher. Cheryl's soul basked in the warmth of Mrs Reid's admiration. Jenny could paint too. In fact, Jenny was quite like her. Mrs Reid saw it. She wasn't a Davidson at all. Of course, she had Arthur's gentleness and affection, but nothing, absolutely nothing of his mother. Thank God! And now she was not going to Boltham, there would be no money changing hands. She had not thought of that. But it felt good. She was free of Arthur's mother. There would be no more pushing Jenny. No more worry and hard work and trying to measure up to expectations.

Cheryl realized that, despite everything, she was happy. Jenny had failed, and she was happy! It was then that she decided she had to celebrate. And who better to celebrate with than Jenny?

The car passed Heaton Primary. Acting on the same impulse, Cheryl pulled up on the zig zag yellow lines outside the school. She left the car and entered the school. There was the Head. She explained to him that she had forgotten to send a note about a dental appointment of Jenny's and she had to take her now, and he gave his permission. She entered Mrs Williams's classroom with assurance. The children were bent over some work and Cheryl explained quite haughtily to Mrs Williams that Jenny had the Head's permission to leave school. Jenny, delighted, went obediently with her mother.

Cheryl strapped her up in the back of the car and they drove off. Once round the corner, Cheryl stopped the car.

'I thought I'd give you a surprise today, Jenny. I'm not going to visit Grandma and I'm going to ring to tell her so in a minute. I thought instead we'd be naughty and take the rest of the day off school.' Jenny's face widened with delight. 'Now *you* tell me. What would you like to do?'

CHAPTER SEVENTEEN

This morning Joyce Carpenter was well enough to take a light breakfast. She ordered some orange juice and tried to eat some of a triangular slice of toast from the toast rack. She ate because she knew she needed the strength, not through appetite. It had been an unspeakable migraine; it was brought on, she knew, by the shock. The staff at the Randolph had been most understanding and had offered the services of a doctor. She had declined; she had all the medication she needed. She had lost three days. It was an effort to swallow the toast. Last night, however, she had been able to make the arrangements she needed. She had contacted a reputable car-rental firm and was leaving the hotel this morning. It seemed sensible, she decided, to drive straight to Boltham.

Coming down to the restaurant to eat breakfast helped to restore her sense of normality. She could hear the husky morning voices of businessmen and the clatter of plates coming from the kitchen. The waitresses soothed her with their deft, deferential movements. If the faint aroma of bacon became any worse, she decided, she would leave. She would leave, in any case, by nine o'clock. It was a long drive to Boltham and she would have to concentrate quite consciously on driving on the left.

Her suitcases were by her side as she stood at the reception desk to pay her bill. She caught her reflection in a mirror; she saw her dark-ringed eyes and knew that her hair badly needed attention. She looked all of her age. Joyce turned from the spectre in the mirror and signed the chit of paper and explained to the porter where her hired car was parked.

And now she was behind the wheel, and now driving through Oxford, with slow deliberation, practising handling the car, glad to have time to get the feel of it before arriving at the motorway. Once she was on the motorway, she thought, she would listen to Radio Four.

In fact, she didn't. The motorway was busy and, to keep out of the way of the lorries that rumbled and heaved past each other in the two inside lanes, she kept to the outside lane at a steady eighty. She checked her rear mirror. Nothing there. How dare she deceive me! A red car coming up quickly. She moved back into the middle lane to allow him to overtake. She deceived me. Then back behind the red Sierra. She knew in the summer and she didn't tell me. Birmingham crowded in on her, a tumble of houses and factories and junctions. She was not able to travel any faster than seventy. She deceived me.

Then, as the M1 led into the M6 and Joyce joined the rush of traffic to the north-west, the other, more painful thought recurred. I have failed. She got back into the fast lane. I have failed. She didn't understand how she could have failed. She had done nothing wrong. She had been the perfect mother and so, despite everything else, Jasmin should have been a shining reflection of the best of her. But this thing had happened. The fencing by the side of the motorway ceased now and the M6 was a ribbon of road that climbed into the distance, towards the north.

She knew she ought to rest and pulled in at the next service station. She deceived me. The lobby of the service station was crowded with travelling families – women in tight trousers over spreading waistlines, loud, raucous toddlers skittering about the entrance – fruit machines flashing and a line of chattering elderly ladies with permed white

278

hair queuing by the Ladies. Joyce's soul revolted. She glanced in the restaurant and knew that the strong artificial light would hurt her eyes. From the shop she bought some fruit juice and took it back to her car.

Her vision now was entirely adjusted to driving. Without conscious thought, she noticed the position and speed of other traffic and moved accordingly and automatically. She deceived me. I have failed. The speedometer informed her she was doing over ninety miles an hour; she slowed. In front of her, signs pointed to the M62. She was almost home, if Boltham could be described as such. In front of her, all was a mist. She had not thought what she was going to say to Jasmin, or what she was going to do. She only knew that she must find her; yes, she must find her, and then . . . and then . . .

She moved into the inside lane to join the M62. I have failed. The M62 was still familiar to her, that long stretch of empty fields outside Warrington, then the conurbation of Greater Manchester, the intricate pattern of junctions, the dominating church spire – she was nearly there. Her head throbbed. Please God, she prayed, not again.

It was a relief to be able to slow down and pause at traffic lights on the slow crawl up to Boltham. She noticed a McDonald's that was not there before. There was a new office block too. Everything else was the same. She wondered what possessed Jasmin to come back here. Boltham was such an aggressively ordinary place. She could have stayed in Oxford – but no. It was better, much better, that she came back here. For that much, Joyce was grateful.

Boltham town centre. She joined the queue of traffic edging through the main street, past the Central Library. Now out to the north, along the Boltham Road, and into Heaton. Down the track leading to the Rectory – and there it was. Utterly unchanged. She parked in the carport, turned off the engine and rubbed her forehead vigorously to disperse the tension. She glanced in the rear-view mirror. She looked appalling. But what did that matter now? She left the car and was about to search her handbag for the keys. She realized then that she did not have them. All keys were left with the agent. Presumably her deceitful daughter had obtained the keys; she would have to knock to gain entry. It was humiliating, the whole affair was humiliating.

She rapped at the kitchen door. No reply. There was no light on, but then, it was mid-afternoon. Joyce walked round the side of the house and went to the front door. She rang the bell. It clanged relentlessly as she pressed it once, and twice, and three times. Nothing. Was Jasmin here after all? Worried, she returned to the back of the house and peered through the kitchen window. She could see the kitchen table, but it was bare. The chairs were tucked tidily under it. She returned to the front and looked into the dining room. She could see nothing that would indicate habitation. She stalked her way to the lounge window. There was the piano and there was some music by it. That was a sign! Unless, of course, the previous tenants had left it there.

Unable to rest, she returned to the kitchen. She peered in at the window again. What if Jasmin had left it slightly open and she was able to lift it and get inside? It was her house, after all. She tried to get purchase with her hands. In her intense concentration, she did not hear the footsteps crunching along the path.

Sue had made a list. That, in itself, was a start. She looked at it. Ring S. and L. But they would not be in until the evening. Clean bathroom. That was her least favourite job. She would have to do that when she was in a much better mood. Shampoo, get watch battery fixed, pay telephone

280

bill. That would have to wait a week until Mark's salary came through. Answer reunion letter.

Sue rubbed the back of her neck. She really ought to get that letter off to Michelle to decline. It was only three weeks now. She could go, she thought, and announce proudly, I am married, I have two children, I'm a librarian now. Her friends would be barristers, fashion designers, headmistresses, no doubt. Still, she thought, I have nothing of which to be ashamed. She thought of her recent failed attempts at change and blushed, the memory of the débâcle at Radio Northside still fresh in her mind.

Jasmin's right, she thought, rocking back on her chair at the dining-room table. I am a coward. But that's something that it's far too late to change. She would not go to the reunion. The letter alone had upset her; the reunion itself would be more distressing. Later, she would write an apologetic letter.

Sue looked at her list again. She did not feel like doing any of it. She knew she would idle away this half-day. She gathered her resolve and took herself upstairs, where the ironing was waiting, and turned on the radio. She straightened a leg of Lizzie's jeans and ran the iron over it.

'And this afternoon on Radio Northside we're playing some grooves from the grave. Are you a geriatric raver? Do you remember this?' The nursery-rhyme rhythm of a sixties pop tune pounded from the bedside radio.

Sue was surprised. She thought that the radio station was not due to broadcast regularly until March, but then she realized that she had tuned into a test transmission. The D.J. was embarrassingly bad. She wondered if it was the man who had been in the studio before her. Heavens, she could do better than this garbage.

Suddenly there was a flash at the plug socket. Sue jumped. The iron cooled. Everything in the house seemed to be breaking right now. They needed a new cistern in the toilet and the guttering was blocked. She felt guilty. She knew she should be able to fix the plug, but she had habitually left these things to Mark. It wasn't, she told an imaginary audience, because she was a woman, but because she just didn't understand these things.

Defeated, she went downstairs. That was when the idea of calling in at Jasmin's occurred to her. It was an attractive proposition. Jasmin had lunched at Vicki's, she knew, but would almost certainly be home by now. Lizzie and Emma were playing with friends this afternoon. There was time.

So she took her keys and coat, locked her door and walked briskly down the path leading to the Rectory. She had promised Jasmin that they would practise back massage and now was a good opportunity. If Jasmin was in, Sue knew, she would be in the kitchen. So she made her way round to the back of the house. That was when she saw the woman trying to break into the house.

A moment of pure terror. She had interrupted a housebreaker. What ought she to do? Run and fetch the police? Make a citizen's arrest? Her heart pounded. The woman had not seen her. She was a well-dressed woman in a tight grey skirt and three-quarter-length coat. That was her car in the carport: a BMW. Sue realized that this was no housebreaker. Was something wrong? Was this a doctor trying to gain access because Jasmin was ill?

'Excuse me,' Sue said, rather loudly. 'Who are you?'

The woman jumped visibly. She turned, and Sue was frozen by her icy question.

'Who, may I ask, are you?'

'I'm Jasmin's neighbour. This is Jasmin Carpenter's house.'

'This is my house.'

It was then that Sue understood. This was Jasmin's mother. It was the same woman she had seen in the photograph. Besides, there was a startling resemblance to Jasmin. Except this woman's face was hard and Jasmin's face still had that uncertainty and freshness of youth. Sue also knew that this moment was bound to happen. There was going to be a lot of explaining to do. She was glad, in a way, that she had met Jasmin's mother first; doing so might help Jasmin.

'Where is my daughter?'

The question suggested that Sue had her held captive.

'She's visiting her friend Vicki. She'll be home any time. I thought she would be home now, which is why I was calling. Would you like to wait for her in my house?'

'I don't know you,' Joyce stated, implying that she had no desire to prolong the acquaintance.

'I'm Sue Turner. I am . . . I've been looking after Jasmin. She's –' Sue stopped in her tracks. She did not know how much Jasmin's mother knew.

'So you are the neighbour who has colluded in hiding my daughter and her condition from me. Dr Cooper told me about you.'

Sue was filled with disbelief. 'I'm sorry,' she said, instantly regretting the phrase. 'I am Jasmin's friend. I have not been hiding her. I know it might seem like that to you, but there's much more to it. Will you let me explain?'

Joyce looked at the woman in front of her. Untidy, ordinary, like Boltham itself. She wondered how well she knew Jasmin. In thinking that, another thought occurred: it was the dangerous thought; the thought that must at all costs not be allowed space. But when she thought of this woman's friendship with Jasmin, and that she had been in this house, and that, if Jasmin was taking some form of revenge, she might know, she was filled with a generalized loathing that she directed at Sue.

'You can explain nothing to me. Jasmin is my daughter. You can go now.'

Sue stood there mulishly.

'She is my daughter. Your services are no longer required.'

Sue felt she was being dismissed like a menial. And Jasmin had said her mother was the perfect mother. She had said that she had never put a foot wrong, and that she would not be distressed at Jasmin's pregnancy so much as wanting to take it over. But Jasmin was clearly wrong. This woman was a monster. It was then it occurred to her that the best and only thing she could do was to warn Jasmin. She might still be with Vicki. There was still time.

'I shall go,' Sue said. She walked away, her head held high, and then, out of sight of Jasmin's mother, ran, as fast as she could, back to her house and, breathless, looked in her address book and dialled Vicki Merchant's number. It rang and rang and rang. Then the receiver was lifted. Sue prayed it was not an answering machine.

The reassuring noise of a squalling toddler told Sue it was Vicki herself.

'Vicki. It's me, Sue. I must speak to Jasmin.'

'Be quiet, Sebastian! Sorry, Sue. She's gone. John's driving her back. She left five minutes ago.'

'I'm too late!'

'Too late for what?'

'It's Jasmin's mother. She's waiting outside the house.'

'Oh, God!'

'Can we do anything?'

'Shut up, Sebastian! No. She'll be home any minute. Was she expecting her?'

Sue replied in the negative, spoke a little longer, then put the phone down. There was nothing she could do to prevent the meeting. What would the shock do to Jasmin? Ought she to demand to be there? No. Jasmin's mother was right. Jasmin was her daughter.

★

John leaned over and opened the car door for Jasmin, patting her stomach as he did so. 'Not long to go,' he said with pleasure.

Jasmin smiled to herself. It amused her that everyone she knew treated her bulge as if it was public property, patting it and staring at it, when really Alison was *her* baby. John passed her the embroidered bag at her feet and Jasmin proceeded down the drive that led to the Rectory. It was a relief to straighten her back. She felt the weight of the baby now and enjoyed the dreaming inwardness of this final stage of her pregnancy. Now, more than ever, only the baby mattered. Last night she had dreamt she was a whale and the booming, singing noises were her baby. Her bag hit against her legs and she thought, when she got home, she would doze for a while.

There was a car in the carport. At first, that was just a simple fact. A car in the carport. Slowly she realized she must have a visitor. The car was unfamiliar to her. There was someone standing by her kitchen door. She recognized her outline immediately. At last, Jasmin thought dreamily. I'm glad she's here.

'Hello, Mum,' she said.

It was the obscenity of Jasmin's new shape that shocked Joyce. How dare she ruin her body like that? Even her face was rounded, and her eyes – her eyes had lost that sharp, intelligent, questioning expression and now were distant, vacant. How was she to gain control again?

'I've got the keys,' Jasmin said. 'Come in and have some tea. I have some Earl Grey and I'll make a pot.'

Jasmin unlocked the door and switched on the light. She removed her coat and hung it over the back of the chair. She checked there was sufficient water in the kettle and pressed a button to turn it on. She stretched up to get the teapot. Her mother's silence made her increasingly nervous.

Of course, Jasmin thought, her mother was bound to be shocked; she knew she must allow her an emotional response, just as she was allowed to be upset, if an exam was hard or she fell over – for a while. She placed two teacups in saucers and then sat at the table, to wait. Her mother still stood by the door and had not removed her jacket.

'I'm sorry,' Jasmin said.

'*You're* sorry?'

'Well, no, not exactly. I want this baby and I am quite happy. I can go back to St Luke's next year and Dr Cooper will arrange a place in the university crèche. The baby is due next week!' said Jasmin, with pride.

'I was at St Luke's a few days ago.'

'Did they explain to you?'

'As best they could. Jasmin, how could you do this to me?'

Now Jasmin was silent. She bowed her head. It was bound to come.

'I don't understand!' Joyce shrieked. 'After everything you had, all those advantages, all my undivided attention, everything I did for you . . . No other child had what you had – I gave up my career for you – and look at you!'

'I'm sorry.'

'Have you thought about me? Have you thought about your father? You are an unmarried mother. I still don't quite believe it. What did I do wrong? We discussed all of this, this sex thing. You knew all this at fifteen. How could you make such a mistake?'

'It wasn't a mistake.'

Now Joyce was silent.

'At the time, when I realized I was pregnant, I thought it was a mistake, but soon I knew I wanted this baby. I'm happy, Mum – really I am. You taught me I could have everything I wanted and it's true. But recently I understood

286

something else too. I have missed you. I've been so used to your companionship, and even though I had Alison to have something of my own that didn't belong to you – my rebellion,' Jasmin added in explanation, 'now I can see that I missed your company when I was away from you. I'm used to having someone close to me. Now Alison will be close to me. But it's not only that. I admire you as well. You were the perfect mother. I think I want to be like you too! I want to have a daughter and make as good a job of her as you have of me! I know you're upset I didn't tell you earlier, but I needed to think it all out and do things the way I wanted to do them. And I am doing. I'm excellent at deep-breathing and squatting, and I've been reading up on child care, and I've written my birth plan, and I've made a wonderful new friend – I'd like you to meet Sue. Look, the kettle's boiled!'

Joyce watched her daughter rise and attend to the kettle. From the back she still looked like Jasmin. Just for that moment Joyce had an impulse to accept this pregnancy, to sit down with Jasmin, share the pot of tea and discuss converting the guest bedroom to a nursery. But, no. For Jasmin had to know, had to understand fully, what she had done. And if she did, it would be Joyce's best hope of gaining control. There was one way, she knew, that would bind them indissolubly together. But she hesitated still.

'Come and sit down,' Jasmin said. 'I have some biscuits too. They're home-made. Do you remember my old art teacher, Mrs Davidson? She lives near us and brought me these.' Jasmin took a tin from the dresser.

'So everyone at Boltham Grammar School knows too?'

'No. Only Vicki Merchant, who I stayed with. Do you remember Vicki Moss? She's married now.'

'I always told you she was a bad influence. She was cheap, even then!'

'Don't be so old-fashioned, Mum.'

'So morality is old-fashioned? Clearly you think so.'

'It was different for you,' Jasmin said, knowing her argument was lame.

'It was no different for me.' Joyce sat down now, opposite Jasmin. Yes, it was important she should know. But she would be kind.

'You said, Jasmin, that you wanted this baby because you realized you wanted to be like me. Well, you have succeeded. You have succeeded more completely than you could ever have imagined. You are *my* daughter, Jasmin. Just my daughter. George is not your father – not your biological father. I had an affair with an Oxford lecturer; it seemed daring and exciting at the time. Luckily, by the time I realized I was pregnant, I had already met George.

'It was different for me in one respect, however. I knew I had to get married. I got George to marry me and he always believed that you were his. You weren't. There was no need for me to feel guilty, because I decided that my mistake would stop there. I did everything I could to be the perfect mother and to make us the perfect family. No one would ever guess that we were any less. I did my duty. Now look what you've done!'

'So Dad isn't my father?'

It was a relief for Joyce to say all this. 'No. Your father taught classics at Oxford. For all I know, he's there still. He didn't want to have much to do with me afterwards. I despised myself and him for the whole débâcle. Then I buried it all.' And you, Jasmin, like a tracker dog, like a bloodhound, have come scrabbling and dug it all up, Joyce thought.

'Are you joking? Are you saying this to teach me how it feels? I'm very shocked, Mum. Is that good enough? Can you stop pretending now?'

'It's true, Jasmin.'

288

The hazy picture Jasmin had of her father, the man in the armchair with *The Times*, faded and dissolved. In its place, nothing. In its place, the notion that her baby had neither a father nor a grandfather. And the fairy-tale castle of her childhood, her devoted mother, her easy-going father, their conscious pride in each other, all a façade. Jasmin pressed her hands against the sides of her womb. How could she know her own mother so little? Who was she? The colour drained from her face. For a moment she thought she was going to faint. She was drowning; she wished Sue was with her.

'Jasmin!' There was alarm in her mother's voice. 'Jasmin! Everything will be fine. I had to tell you. You needed to know. It was for your own good. Everything I have done was for your good.' Joyce was filled with regret, for she saw she had hurt her daughter, who was now her only reason for existence. 'Look. I'm with you now. I've come back. Jasmin! I'm not angry. Don't look like that!'

She has deceived me, Jasmin thought. She stared at her mother's haunted eyes and wild hair and grey skin.

'Everything's fine now, Jasmin. We'll look after your baby together. Tell me when you're due. Where are you having the baby? If you like, we can pay for a private consultant. I'll convert the guest bedroom to a nursery. Once the baby is born, we can go shopping. You don't have to do a thing now; you rest. I'll make dinner. You've forgotten to pour the tea; I'll do it.'

Jasmin watched her mother attend to the tea things. She felt dizzy; she was floating. She could not absorb it all. What had been solid land was now a wide, wide sea; there was land, there was refuge, where Sue was, or in Oxford, but now she was drowning.

No. She would not drown. Jasmin shook her head to dispel her growing nausea. She would just take things as they came. One step at a time. She would drink her tea. She would try one of Mrs Davidson's biscuits. She would let her mother make dinner.

With relief, Joyce saw Jasmin sip at the tea. She was glad she had told her. No one was better qualified to take over now than she was. Everything would be fine. She would stay with Jasmin now, forever. She would return to Oxford with her to care for the baby. Joyce's spirits rose. They would find a house. She would separate from George. Jasmin could still complete her degree, of course. Little stigma should attach itself to her. In that way, things were certainly different in the nineties. Now she must take up the reins again.

'When are you due?'

'In eight days.'

'I'm not surprised. You're big, and you're carrying the baby low. Now where are you having it?'

'At Boltham General.'

Joyce pulled a face. 'I suppose that will have to do. I'm sure you've prepared yourself for the labour, but you mustn't worry. I shall be there with you.'

Jasmin looked up sharply. She said nothing.

'What have you bought for the baby?'

'I have some dresses and Babygros. Sue took me out last week and we bought a little crib. It's in my room.'

'You'll need a great deal more than that. There really is no reason why I shouldn't go out tomorrow, while I've got the car, and get a few things. We must think about the pram, of course, and a baby bath, and lots of clothes. Do you know, your tutor at St Luke's gave me the most appalling matinée jacket and bootees she had knitted herself, but don't worry – they found their way to the nearest waste-paper bin.'

Jasmin felt that loss as a physical pain. Dr Cooper had

290

learned to knit and it was all for her. And her mother had discarded the gift!

'Now, I hope you've been eating properly. Labour is not called "labour" for nothing. It's hard work. You have a week to prepare. If you have some fresh ingredients in the fridge, I'll make us a small meal this evening and, as I said, we can shop tomorrow. I shall keep the car for a few more days and then I think I'll buy myself a runabout, as we'll need it. Do you know, Jasmin, I feel better already!'

Seeing the cups were empty, Joyce rose to wash them, instructing Jasmin to stay seated and put her feet up. She continued to chatter, her words weaving the normality she craved.

'Now, you said you'd written a birth plan. I *am* interested. I think birth plans are an excellent idea; they give a mother control. What have you stipulated?'

'I want an active birth and I'll try to have as little pain relief as possible. And Sue will be with me.'

'No, she won't,' said Joyce gently. 'I will.' Jasmin was silent. 'I think it's preposterous to have a stranger at such an intimate occasion. Really a midwife is bad enough. Now, Jasmin, have you prepared a name?'

'No,' said Jasmin.

'You must have an early night and, when I've unpacked, I shall think. Choosing names is a delight. I really shan't object tremendously if you want to use my name. I'm sure it will be a girl, Jasmin. Ellen has two girls, just as Ellen and I were two girls. There aren't boys in the family. Your great-grandmother's name was Constance.'

Deep in Jasmin's womb, Alison squirmed. Once again, Jasmin wondered what it must be like for her in there, dark, wet, confined. What did she see? Did she see colours with eyes tightly shut? Was she rocked as Jasmin walked? Did she hear the rushing of blood? Did she feel as if she must escape? Did she will her birth to happen? If it was me, thought Jasmin, I would want to escape.

Jasmin lay in bed, hardly breathing. As she had expected, there were soft footsteps in the hall. Her bedroom door was opened, just as it always had been for years and years. Her mother stood there.

'Are you comfortable?'

'Yes,' Jasmin said.

'Sleep well, darling,' she said.

'To you too.'

The door was closed softly. Jasmin was alone. She knew instinctively that her decision just to exist for the moment, not to think or reflect yet, was absolutely right. She would concentrate only on the next step. She must let Sue know what had happened. Eventually she would tell her all of it and Sue would help her accept it all. For now, she must simply tell Sue that her mother had arrived and that she didn't want her at the labour. So she sat up and reached under her bed for the telephone extension.

It was pushed too far back for her to reach without getting out of bed, so she flung back the duvet and left her bed. She knelt on the floor to retrieve her telephone set. It wasn't there. She sat by the side of her bed and stretched her arm under as far as it would go. Nothing. Then she felt the telephone socket. It was empty. The enormity of this act struck her immediately. Her mother had taken it. She was to have no unauthorized contact.

A calm voice told her that there was nothing she could do tonight. It was half-past ten and rain pattered incessantly against her windowpane. At all costs she must protect her baby. Again she felt slightly sick. You must sleep, she told herself. What could she do to make herself sleep? She would read. Her eyes scanned the titles of the books on her bookshelf. The small brown book was Langland's *Piers Plowman*. He was to be her set poet next year, with Chaucer. She was not in the mood for Chaucer right now. She took her Langland and settled in bed.

The soporific rhythm washed over her.

> In a somer seson whan soft was the sonne,
> I shope me in shroudes as I a shepe were,
> In habite as an heremite unholy of workes . . .

Unholy of workes. She thought of her mother. She would not think of her mother.

> Ac on a May mornynge on Malverne hulles,
> Me byfel a ferly of fairy, me thoughte;

She read on. Her eyes felt heavy. Langland always had this effect on her. A faire felde ful of folke . . . merchants and beggars and pilgrims and friars and pardoners, and Jasmin wondered why there were no mothers. Because in the end, that's what it was all about. Having babies. And it didn't matter if you were a pardoner or a friar or a king or a cardinal or an insurance salesman or a deputy manager or a company executive. Jasmin's vision was a field full of mothers. Then the image blurred, and she thought she would shut her eyes, just for a while, and sleep shrouded her.

When she woke, it was still dark. But the darkness had a thin quality; Jasmin knew it was the darkness that preceded dawn. She stretched to pick up her watch from the bedside table. It was five minutes to six. She had to go the toilet; there was a pain in her stomach. Some sort of spasm. It subsided. She woke completely now. She did not know who her own father was. Her mother was back. Her mother had taken the telephone extension from her room. It was not a stomach ache; it was more like backache, the sort of backache she had during a heavy period, except it retreated and she wondered whether she had imagined it. She decided to lie there in bed and wait and see. A light wind ruffled the branches outside her window. Her body was still.

She did need to go to the loo. She rose and softly, so as not to wake her mother – she noticed her bedroom door was tightly shut – she padded to the bathroom. Yes, there was a touch of backache. She did not turn on the light in the bathroom. When she had finished and wiped herself, still hazy with sleep, she felt something unusual. Awkwardly, the Andrex still in her hand, she fumbled to find the light. There, on the paper, was a clot of pink-streaked mucus. She had read about this. It was her show; her labour had begun.

Jasmin stood there. It has begun, she thought. She was suddenly wide awake. She was filled with fear, or with excitement, or both. She flushed her show away and washed her hands in just a trickle of water. The important thing, she thought, was not to wake her mother.

Could she dress and present herself at Sue's? Was there time? Perhaps not. Her mother was an early riser. So, taking a sudden decision, Jasmin stepped softly across the landing again and crept down the stairs, listening all the time. No sound. She picked up the telephone and dialled Sue's number. She flinched at the harsh ringing; she prayed her mother would not hear.

It was Mark who answered, his voice thick with sleep.

'It's Jasmin. I must speak to Sue!' Now she spoke, she could hear her own voice was hysterical.

She heard muffled sounds from Sue's bedroom. The receiver was passed over.

'Jasmin. Are you all right?'

'No. Yes. I've started, Sue. I've had a show. I've got a sort of backache. But my mother's here and she doesn't want you to be there. But you must be there. Stop her, please stop her. I think I'd better go to the hospital. Can you come round?'

Jasmin froze as she sensed her mother's presence at the top of the stairs.

'To whom are you speaking, Jasmin?'

Jasmin replaced the receiver. Sue heard a click, then silence.

CHAPTER EIGHTEEN

'Mark. She's started.'

'Started what?'

'With the baby. Now what should I do?'

Sue did not expect an answer from Mark. Her question was almost unanswerable. She sat up in bed and tried to think it all through. If she insisted on being with Jasmin, Jasmin's mother would refuse to let her have access to the delivery room. Could she do that? If she didn't go, if she backed off now that Jasmin's real mother was home – which was the respectable thing to do – she would be breaking faith with Jasmin. That was unthinkable. What was equally unthinkable was a duel of any sort with Jasmin's formidable mother. Her heart thumped against her chest.

'I'll ask Arthur if he can drop Lizzie and Emma off at school. It'll make us both late, but I'll ring in. You can have the car,' Mark said.

So Mark had made her mind up for her after all. She was warm with gratitude. And he was right, she thought, as she stood under the shower and began to wake more fully. It was no crime to go to the hospital. She would speak to Jasmin's midwife and explain the situation. That was important. She had already had a long telephone conversation with Mary Whelan and found her brisk, practical and not without a sense of humour. Yes. She had to go to the hospital.

When she opened the bathroom door a small figure in an Olive Oyl nightdress stood grinning in front of her. Emma always looked proud of herself for waking up. She smiled blearily at Sue and put her arms out for a hug, resting her head against Sue's bare stomach. There was a time, when Emma was younger, that Sue frequently remembered her as a small baby. Now that memory returned in full force. Emma was red and wizened with an enormous nose. Now she was an ebullient, obstinate little girl who still clung.

'Come on,' Sue said. 'I've got to get dressed. I'm going somewhere important this morning.'

Sue woke Lizzie, who blinked a bit and left her bed. Sue dressed rapidly and with a growing sense of excitement. She began to realize that she was looking forward to the birth of this baby as much as she had done when her sister had hers. She really could not wait to get to the hospital. Her energy made her unusually cheerful. She joked with the girls, and explained to them that Jasmin's baby was coming and she was going to spend the day in the hospital to help Jasmin.

'Help take the baby out?'

'No. Jasmin pushes it out and the baby comes out of her bottom.'

Emma giggled. Lizzie said, 'That's so inbarrassing!'

'I think Jasmin will be past caring about her embarrassment,' Sue remarked.

'Can we see the baby?' Lizzie asked.

'In a few days.'

Lizzie continued spooning her Weetabix into her mouth. She watched her mother sip at her coffee and glance at the kitchen clock. She knew her mother was the best mother in the whole world and she would be the best person to help Jasmin's baby come out. Lizzie tried to think to herself why her mother was the best mother. Because she's funny, she thought. And silly. And just nice. She couldn't think of any more reasons. But when she grew up she wouldn't have a baby. She would adopt one, perhaps, and Mummy could

297

look after it and she would have a nice job. That was a good idea.

'I'll go now,' Sue announced. 'I'll keep in touch.' She gave each member of her family a brief kiss and left.

It was a clear, crisp morning, chilly but invigorating. Sue estimated it would take her only fifteen minutes to reach the hospital, as the local traffic would not be heavy. She hoped she was not too late. It was possible, of course, that Jasmin's mother had insisted on being there, or had even insisted on Sue being refused entry as an undesirable. It was no use speculating. Her job was simply to go to the hospital and see Mary Whelan.

Here she was in the hospital car-park. She pulled a ticket from the machine and the barrier lifted to admit her. Being so early, there were quite a few spaces. Sue drove to the part of the car-park nearest the maternity wing of the hospital and left the car there.

She had not been to Boltham General very often. She had had Emma there, of course, and had been there on one occasion since, when she had had some tricky dental work. She was not one of those people who were anxious in hospitals. The bureaucracy of large hospitals and the air of authority of the specialists and consultants annoyed her, but she was intrigued by the way that Boltham General existed as a complete village in the heart of Boltham and lived by its own laws. This was where Jasmin was to have her baby.

She walked along a corridor with windows on either side, which led into the main hospital corridor. She knew where to find the maternity department and moved there purpose-fully, knowing she was outside visiting hours and hoping not to be stopped and questioned. She arrived at the mater-nity block.

No one was around. To her left and to her right were

offices and a little further on was a room where the door was open. Sue coughed loudly. No one came. Then a woman in a dressing-gown over an enormous bulge came padding out of a ward. She looked at Sue curiously.

'Is there a midwife about?'

'Should be,' the woman replied in a strong Boltham accent. She left Sue and went into a dayroom, and Sue heard the sound of a radio being switched on. It was then that a figure emerged from the room on her left: a small woman with ginger hair. She looked inquiringly at Sue.

'Can I speak to Mary Whelan, please?'

'That's me,' the woman said.

'I'm Sue Turner,' Sue said. 'I spoke to you a few weeks ago. I'm Jasmin Carpenter's friend.' She saw Mary Whelan size her up and look satisfied. 'Has she booked in yet?'

'No,' Mary Whelan said. 'But I spoke to her mother half an hour ago. They're on their way.'

'Can we talk?' asked Sue.

Mary Whelan opened the door of her office and invited Sue in. She took a seat by the side of the desk and explained Jasmin's situation. The midwife listened attentively, but her expression gave nothing away.

'And so,' Sue concluded, 'I'm here because Jasmin wanted me to come, but I'm fairly certain her mother, who will bring her, will want me off the premises.'

Mary Whelan picked up a biro and tapped it on her desk. Then she turned it upside-down and tapped it again. The manoeuvre was clearly an aid to thought.

'My job,' she said, 'is to respect the wishes of my mother-to-be. When Jasmin arrives, I shall ask her who she wants present at the labour and I shall support her.'

Sue was glad. Mary Whelan was wise. Like King Solomon, she thought, and was reminded of the two mothers who each claimed the baby. The real mother, she remembered, was the one who would not harm her child, even at the risk of losing him.

'Jasmin's mother doesn't like me,' Sue said. 'I'm worried that my presence alone might inflame the situation. I almost didn't come here. It can't be good for Jasmin if there's a scene. She'll be scared enough as it is.'

'I take your point,' the midwife said. 'It won't be easy for Jasmin to choose between you.'

In her mind's eye Sue saw Jasmin and her mother arriving at the hospital, and Mary Whelan asking her, which, if either, of these two women do you wish to be with you? . . . It was impossible. Jasmin could not be expected to do that. There had to be another solution. Yet she could not leave Jasmin to have this baby alone. Think, Sue, think. She narrowed her eyes in concentration.

When the idea came, it was so stupendous it took her breath away. It was the obvious solution. Sue knew that if she stopped to think about it too carefully, she might not do it, so she had to act now.

'I've got it,' she said to Mary Whelan. 'I'm going now. I don't think it's a good idea for Jasmin's mother to meet me. But I'll ring you soon. Will I be able to contact you?'

'Yes,' the midwife said.

'If Jasmin asks for me, tell her I'll be there,' she said. 'But don't ask me to explain now. I really must dash.' Sue ran breathless down the hospital corridor. This is for Jasmin, she told herself. It's the only way I can keep my promise. I'm doing this for Jasmin!

'I can walk by myself, Mum,' Jasmin said, as they made their way towards the maternity wing.

Joyce held her arm firmly.

'Did you time your contractions in the car?'

300

'About every ten minutes, I think.'

'Good. The midwife will need to know that. I shall tell her. Here we are. Hello!' Joyce shouted.

Mary Whelan emerged again from her office. She smiled at Jasmin.

'The little one's going to be early, then?'

Jasmin nodded and answered with a smile.

'You're a lucky girl,' Mary continued. 'We're quiet this morning. I'm going to take you to a private room where I can see how far on you are and complete a few prepping procedures.'

'I shall come in with her,' Joyce said.

'Would you like your mother with you?' Mary asked mildly.

Jasmin shook her head very faintly.

'I'm sorry, Mrs Carpenter,' Mary began. 'This must be Jasmin's decision.'

'Jasmin! Don't be so foolish. You will need me. You're obviously feeling very emotional now and you'll regret not having me there. You'll regret it bitterly.'

'Sue's coming,' Jasmin said.

'Sue is not coming,' she said. 'I am your mother. You don't have a husband. You'll need someone, won't she, sister?'

Mary Whelan's voice was quite level. 'Jasmin must do whatever she thinks will suit her best. I think it's important not to distress her, don't you?'

'Are you refusing me access to my own child?'

'Jasmin is not a minor.'

'Your obstructive behaviour is entirely unprofessional. I would like to see the consultant obstetrician.'

'He hasn't arrived yet.'

'I shall find the hospital manager. I knew him socially. He will sort out this ridiculous situation. I shall be back, Jasmin. When you change your mind, I'll be here for you.'

Joyce turned her back and walked off into the centre of the hospital.

'Come on, young lady!' Mary Whelan said. 'We have work to do.'

Jasmin sat quietly as the midwife circled her arm with the now familiar black tubing to take her blood pressure.

'It's up a bit,' Mary said, 'but I expect that's due to your emotional state. Will you change your mind?' she asked her, as she removed the tubing. 'Do you want your mother?'

'Sue's coming,' Jasmin said.

'Sue's already been here. She left a message to tell you she'll be with you, but she'll ring me first. I think she felt it was better not to meet your mother.'

'Oh!' said Jasmin. 'That one hurt!'

Jasmin lay on the bed on her back, her feet planted firmly down and her knees apart, as Mary Whelan checked her dilation.

'You're certainly on the way,' she said. 'I make that about four centimetres.'

'What do I do now?' Jasmin asked.

'Not a lot,' Mary said. 'Your contractions will build up slowly, and look – here's a buzzer by your bed. If you find it hard to cope, you can call for me. There isn't really a lot I can do for you now. Later we'll move to the delivery room, but for now, I'm afraid, you'll have to wait.'

'I don't even have a book to read,' Jasmin said.

'I'll fetch you a magazine,' Mary said. She bustled out of the room.

Jasmin left the bed. She was surprised how alert she felt. Every nerve, every muscle, was fully alive. Her contractions were painful when they came, but the movement, this pacing up and down, relieved her. She knew too that it would hurry the baby. The books said so.

Now she was here, alone in this room, everything else

302

seemed to recede. Her mother, thank God, had gone. She would deal with her later. Even the baby seemed distant to her. She, Jasmin, was facing something completely unknown, unfathomable. She realized for the first time that all her preparation had been an absurdity. The clinical descriptions in the book, the lurid accounts of other mothers, none of them matched her experience right now. What she was living through now, no one had ever lived through before. She was the only person ever to have a baby. She was terrified. She paced the room, and from a high window there was a patch of white sky. She was wearing a lacy nightdress her mother had saved from her schooldays. It was singularly inappropriate and her bulge stretched the thin cotton. The baby was quite still now.

Again. Here it was again. A slow ache, starting in the back and travelling everywhere. Jasmin was surprised that it hurt her. She was surprised that her body wanted to hurt itself. She leant on the windowsill and she discovered that taking the weight on her arms helped her. So she stayed there, leaning. She waited for the next contraction, counting. Her back seemed to ache all the time now. She paced the room again. Her bare feet were cold against the linoleum. The room had floral wallpaper, little sprigs of violet. The room was pretending to be a bedroom. Now. It was starting. Back to the windowsill.

Breathe, she told herself. Inhale one, two, three, four – now relax! No. She'd got that wrong. She was to relax between contractions. But it was impossible to relax. She waited anxiously for Mary Whelan. Where was Sue?

Jasmin sat on the bed. She shivered. Her flesh was all goosepimples. Her eyes were strained with fear. If only she could think about something else. Yet the other things she had to think about were worse. Here was another one! That was close. She tried to rub her own back, but felt like a contortionist. Surely she was nearly fully dilated. She wondered about gas and air. Where was Sue? Had her mother stopped her? And what was her mother doing?

Joyce was lost. Signs pointed to the genito-urinary clinic, radiography, neurology, pathology. Where ought she to go? She hated hospitals. It was where people went to die. Had she been with Jasmin at the beginning, she would never have allowed her to come to Boltham General, where the maternity unit was part of the main hospital. God knows what the baby would pick up! She looked once more at the array of signs. Now what should she do?

It seemed so very, very wrong to her that she and Jasmin should be apart at this time. Yet the midwife could not see that. Jasmin was obviously irrational. Hormones, Joyce thought; all those hormones coursing through her body, and the shock too of Joyce's arrival. She was certain she could persuade someone in authority to let her in to be with her daughter.

But could she? Jasmin was twenty-one now. Joyce suddenly felt chilly. She realized that she had no legal rights. At that moment a hospital orderly came into her field of vision, pushing a frail old lady in a wheelchair. Her face was skeletal; there was a drip attached to the chair and from it a tube led into her arm. Joyce flinched at the sight, but looked once more at the woman before she was moved on. Her eyes were expressionless.

Then Joyce knew that the most important thing was not to lose Jasmin. She would not insist on seeing her. She would wait until the baby was born. She would return to the maternity unit and find somewhere to sit. She had no one except Jasmin now. And Jasmin's baby. Her granddaughter. Something hard and clenched in Joyce relaxed fractionally. It might be possible, she thought, to adapt

herself to these new circumstances. She walked back towards Jasmin. Provided that awful neighbour didn't turn
up, she would cope. All was not lost.

Where was Mary Whelan? Jasmin tried to decide whether
she should press the buzzer. She was in pain now and
wondered when it was that she could have gas and air. The
walking did help. How long was this going to go on for? She
was alone in the room with this pain that crept up on her,
and overtook her, and then retreated. Jasmin now began to
wonder whether she should have sent her mother away.

Surely the midwife should be coming back! Jasmin sat on
the bed again and looked at the foetal-heart monitor. She
did not like it when she had to lie on the bed and have those
straps and pads around her. Please, somebody, come in!
Jasmin imagined that her mother had met Sue and turned
her away – for that could be the only explanation for her
absence. It was all going wrong. She winced with pain as
the next contraction came.

At last! The door opened and the midwife came in again,
carrying with her not a magazine, but an old-fashioned
transistor radio.

'I'll try to be with you all I can,' she said, 'but I've
borrowed this from the dayroom. It'll keep you company.'

'Thank you,' said Jasmin, feeling more alone than ever.

'Let me tune it for you,' Mary said.

Jasmin sat on the end of the bed, hearing the set swerve
from station to station, from the loud thumping of Radio
One to the rich South-East accents of Radio Four.

'This is it, I think!' Mary said. Then she went to sit by
Jasmin. 'I've just had a call from your friend Sue,' she said.
'Her instructions were that you were to tune into Radio
Northside. I think I've got the correct wavelength.'

'*We have a guest in the studio this morning,*' a male voice

305

said. 'Sue Turner, a housewife and librarian from Boltham. Good morning, Sue!'

'Good morning,' she said. 'Jasmin! Can you hear me? Isabel said I could use a test transmission to talk to you. Now whatever happens, stay tuned to this station. I expect you're in the first stage of labour now. The worst part is the waiting. But I'm going to try to distract you –'

'Excuse me!' the male voice said. 'Isabel! Hey, Isabel! Stop the transmission! She can't do this! There'll be trouble!'

'Were you playing music?' Sue said sweetly. 'Can I ask for a request? Jasmin, listen. This one's for you. Malcolm, find me "Reach out, I'll be there". Is it the Four Tops?'

'The music's all on the computer. We can't take requests. Isabel! This woman's demented. You can't have this on a test transmission!'

'This is Sue Turner here, talking to Jasmin Carpenter and anyone else who might be having a baby today. Now, later on in the programme there'll be more music, chat and some poetry too! Can you put some music on, Malcolm, please?'

'Who does this silly bitch think she is? Yeah. I hope you like this one.'

'Please can you put it on?'

Silence. And then,

'Oh, Mary! That's the Smurfs' song. He's playing a kids' record. That was to annoy her! She'll get her revenge, you wait. Turn it up,' Jasmin said.

'Thank you, father Abraham,' Sue said. 'I know another sixties song called "Little Children" – Billy J. Kramer and the Dakotas – which I'd like to dedicate to our resident DJ. Jasmin, the trouble is I don't know how to operate the records, so I think we're going to have to abandon the music part of the show. It's a shame, as I'd love to play some old seventies stuff. Did you ever listen to Marc Bolan? Hello to you too, Mary. Thanks for helping to arrange this. Here's Isabel now.'

306

'Hello, Jasmin? It's me, Isabel. We're all with you at Radio Northside. I'm just praying we don't get into trouble for this!'

'Get up on the bed now, Jasmin, and I'll check you again. How are the contractions?'

'They're OK. Mary, she must have gone there especially because she didn't want to fight with my mother. She told me she disgraced herself when she did her audition, but she's great.'

'That's nearly six centimetres! Well done. I think it might be as well to move to the delivery room.'

Still carrying the transistor, Mary Whelan led Jasmin to a room further down the corridor. This was a considerably bigger room, with another high bed and, to Jasmin's surprise, a birthing pool filled with water. Here too was a little glass cot on wheels, with a white crocheted blanket and sheets. That was for her baby, Jasmin realized. There was other equipment too and lights over the bed. Jasmin tensed again. The sense of what was about to happen to her affected her strongly at that moment.

The midwife was reading through Jasmin's birth plan. Then she looked up.

'Do you want to use the birthing pool? I can get someone to assist.'

Jasmin thought for a moment. She had read the most wonderful descriptions of birth under water. Yet, faced with the reality of that plastic pool filled with warm water, she flinched. It seemed an odd thing to do, give birth in the bath. Feeling slightly shamefaced, she suggested she would just deliver on the hospital bed.

'That's fine,' Mary said. 'Let's listen to Sue again.'

'I was looking through the papers in reception, Jasmin, so I thought I'd tell you about the interesting stuff in the news. There's a feature today on this new hairdresser who's all set to

take over where *Vidal Sassoon* left off. But this is what makes me mad. He's a man! I don't understand why it is that nearly all hairdressers are women and yet to reach the top you have to be male.'

'It stands to reason,' said Malcolm, the DJ. 'A male hairdresser makes a woman look sexy – he projects his fantasies on to her. A woman hairdresser won't make her customer any more attractive than she is. Women prefer male hairdressers.'

'So basically what you're saying is that women only have their hair cut to look sexy and women in general are bitterly competitive. You have a rather limited view of women, don't you? What about you, Isabel? What are you looking for in a hairdresser?'

'I think I do want to look sexy, but I can trust a woman to do that for me. I think a woman is more likely to listen to me than a man. Anyway, aren't all male hairdressers gay?'

'Can we have a phone-in on this, Isabel? I'd like to hear what other women think. But there is a political point here. In every profession where the bulk of the workers are women, the people at the top are men. Think of male chefs and head teachers. Whose fault is that? The men for maintaining the status quo or the women for allowing it?'

Jasmin listened, entranced. It was what she had hoped. Sue's enthusiasm and love of argument were evident in the timbre of her voice. She was a compelling presenter. Jasmin hung on her every word. Her contractions came and went. Surely Isabel would recognize that Sue had star quality! Jasmin left her bed to lean on the windowsill, where she was more comfortable. As she walked, there was a strange sensation.

'Mary! Something's happened. I think my waters have broken!'

A warm liquid trickled down Jasmin's leg; she looked and saw a puddle forming on the floor. The midwife got her up on to the bed and felt that Jasmin was almost fully dilated. She explained that she would call for one of the junior doctors.

Jasmin lay on her back on the bed. Another contraction assailed her. This one was quite different from the others. It came with an irresistible force and Jasmin felt almost winded by it. What ought she to do? Her fear returned.

'*We haven't forgotten about you, Jasmin. Now, remember what we said. When the going gets tough, you wanted to try getting on all fours and taking the weight off your back.*'

Jasmin turned on the bed, and found some relief.

'*And remember, nothing lasts for ever!*'

Mary Whelan returned.

'They're getting much stronger now,' Jasmin said.

'Yes,' Mary agreed, rubbing her back.

'Here's another one!'

Pain swept through her. Sue's voice buzzed, a comfortable noise in her head. So Sue had made it. She was on the radio. The pain receded.

'That's about two to three minutes,' Mary said.

Another contraction. Now Jasmin let herself whimper. It was bad. She didn't know it was going to be as bad as this. She would ask for some help.

'*Jasmin, I'm still here. This one's from* Sergeant Pepper – "*With a Little Help from my Friends*" . . .'

Mary gave her the transparent mask and Jasmin inhaled greedily at the gas and air.

'Now wait until the contraction begins!' Mary said.

Jasmin felt slightly fuzzy, but the pain was still coming at regular intervals, and it wasn't as if the gas took the pain away, but it changed her mind's relationship to the pain. That scared her. She wished she hadn't taken any. Surely she was ready to deliver.

'*Radio Northside is the only local radio station to bring you both active birth and real culture,*' said Sue. '*Now we'll begin*

309

at the beginning, with the first English poet, Geoffrey Chaucer. Here is an extract from his longest poem, "Troilus and Criseyde". Jasmin, this is for you too. I promised you some Chaucer. I'm sorry if my Middle English is rusty . . .'

'Oh, God, oh, God!' Jasmin screamed. It was almost unbearable. The pain dragged her along screaming. Then it receded and the midwife turned up the radio.

> *O blisful light, of which the bemes clere*
> *Adorneth al the thridde heven faire!*
> *O sonnes lief, O Joves doughter deere –*

'That's Venus, the Goddess of Love,' Jasmin explained to Mary Whelan. 'That's Jove's daughter. This is from the beginning of Book Three. It's Chaucer's hymn to Love. Oh no, it's coming again. Help. I need some pethidine. Oh, God!'

> *In heven and helle, in erthe and salte see*
> *Is felt thi myght, if that I wel descerne . . .*

The door opened and a doctor entered. She stood and listened for a moment to the radio to orientate herself.

'It's too late for the pethidine, Jasmin,' Mary said. 'I think you're almost ready to push.'

Now, when the next contraction came, the pain was accompanied by a new sensation. To her extreme embarrassment, Jasmin thought she was going to soil the bed. What ought she to do?

'Something . . . something . . .' she muttered. She groaned with the pain.

'It's the baby's head!' said Mary.

Jasmin felt herself being propped up on the pillows on the bed. The doctor – a smiling Indian lady – began to busy herself at the end of the bed.

'When you get your next pain,' Mary said, 'push. Push as hard as you can.'

Now the sensation that passed through Jasmin was different. There was an overwhelming pressure. She had no choice. She had to push. And the feeling subsided.

'Push!' cried Mary.

She pushed.

> *And in this world no lyves creature*
> *Withouten love is worth, or may endure . . .*

Mary Whelan wiped her forehead. Jasmin felt as if she had ceased to exist. She was a vehicle for this unbearable pressure.

'Now push again!'

> *Love, that with an holsom alliaunce*
> *Halt peples joyned . . .*

And Jasmin pushed, and grunted.

'Here's the baby's head. Now, just once more. You're doing fine.'

One more push. She concentrated all her efforts. Yes, something had happened. There was a stir of activity. A cry. Jasmin looked wonderingly as Mary placed a real baby on her stomach – a real baby, with a little face and the blue eyes opened, a creamy substance on its body, tiny reddened limbs. There were its fingers and toes. She put her own finger out to touch it.

'It's a boy!' Mary said.

FINALLY . . .

Sue found the hotel without any difficulty. It was a large, white building on the Harrogate Road and looked as if it was once a coaching inn, then a rambling public house and now had been reinvented as a venue for business lunches and weekend breaks and candlelit dinners. She left her car and walked through the oak doors.

To her right she was aware of a babble of voices. There was a sign pointing to the Hardy Suite. So that was it. Surreptitiously, Sue took a small brush from her handbag and ran it through her hair. She straightened her skirt. Then, with decision, she walked towards the room.

There were a number of women standing and drinking glasses of champagne in small groups. As she entered the door, she was conscious that she had become the focal point of attention.

'It's Sue!' screamed a matronly woman in a bright-red sweater sparkling with glittery sequins. 'Sue. It's me. Michelle!'

Sue looked at her. At first it was impossible to find the schoolgirl in that buxom face with a hint of double chin. Then, as her eyes adjusted, she could see that it really was Michelle. Laughter and pleasure competed in her.

'Do you remember Bev Wilson? Here she is. She's a solicitor now. And this is Maggie Spencer – Maggie's driven up from London.'

Sue was disorientated. These familiar faces pulled powerfully at her memory.

'Sue!' screamed another voice. 'It was never you I heard on the radio?'

It was Sally Mitchell. Sue grinned at her.

'It might have been. I work for Radio Northside now. I'm one of the team on a morning chat show. It's a mix of music and discussion.'

'I knew it was you! I told the others. But I can't say I'm surprised. You were never at a loss for something to say. Do you remember when Miss Burns told you . . .'

Sunlight poured in through the windows. Sue found it impossible to concentrate on any one person. There was so much to absorb. Sally had four children; Maggie was a games teacher; Ros Peters was divorced; Karen Lester had never married and was a matron in a rest home. Yet when they were at school she was the most boy-crazy and pleasure-seeking of all of them. Life was so unpredictable.

Ruth Holden came to speak to her. She was dressed formally in a dark skirt and cream blouse and, with her raven-black hair at shoulder length, looked more distinguished than ever. She was the clever one in the class, and Sue had always envied her. Ruth was impressed to hear of Sue's new career.

'I stayed in academia,' Ruth explained. 'I worked as a research chemist in ICI for a while, but never settled. I went back to university teaching and I'm at St Luke's College, Oxford, now as a Junior Lecturer.'

'St Luke's!' Sue exclaimed. 'Do you know Jasmin Carpenter?'

'Now, the name is familiar. She's not a chemist?'

'No. An English student. She had a baby.'

'Of course! She's one of Grainne's. I remember seeing her mother once. Is she related to you?'

'She's my friend,' Sue said proudly. 'She had a boy, you know. Geoffrey William. She lives very near me.'

'And she's well?'

'She's well.' Sue remembered how hard it was to prevent her calling the baby Troilus. Jasmin had adjusted to the fact that she had a son remarkably swiftly. She was passionately involved with him, as was Sue. They joked that he was their New Man. He was a good baby who slept a lot and guzzled greedily from the breast.

Jasmin's mother had been subdued since the birth. There were important decisions to be made, Sue knew. It was possible, she believed, that they might all live happily together. She did not know.

'Dr Cooper is the baby's Godmother,' Sue added to Ruth.

'Yes, she's told me. This is such a coincidence!'

'She visited Jasmin last week,' Sue said. 'She's agreed to let me interview her on medieval women for the show.'

Ruth smiled. 'She'll enjoy that,' she said.

Sue knew the champagne had gone to her head. She would shortly change to mineral water, as it was a long drive back to Boltham. But was it the champagne that seemed to transform everything? She had experienced that feeling of light-headedness several times in the past few weeks. No. It was better than that. It was her own life that was intoxicating her.

Sue drained her glass and drank to Jasmin.